DOUBLE CARKEET
A Mystery Guild Omnibus

DOUBLE CARKEET

DOUBLE NEGATIVE

FROM AWAY

BY

DAVID CARKEET

MYSTERY GUILD

GARDEN CITY, NEW YORK

DOUBLE NEGATIVE

ISBN 978-1-59029-300-2

FROM AWAY

ISBN 978-1-59029-304-0

ISBN: 978-1-61664-251-8

Manufactured in the United States of America.

DOUBLE NEGATIVE

NOVELS BY DAVID CARKEET

Double Negative

The Greatest Slump of All Time

I Been There Before

The Full Catastrophe

The Error of Our Ways

From Away

FOR YOUNGER READERS

The Silent Treatment

Quiver River

DOUBLE NEGATIVE

DAVID CARKEET

THE OVERLOOK PRESS
NEW YORK

For Barbara

ONE

"JUST WHAT DO YOU DO WITH THESE BABIES, ANYWAY?" Cook paused at the open door of Wach's office when he heard this question, just out of sight of the two men who were talking inside. He smiled as he listened for the reply. This was exactly the kind of question that made his boss rise to his full, contemptible glory.

"I'm certainly not unwilling to answer that question." Cook could imagine the quick, empty smile. "A number of complex variables intersect in any serious attempt to establish a direction of inquiry, a program thrust, a, an, ah, Jeremy, there you are." Cook had stepped forward. It was too painful to go on listening in helpless silence. "I want you to meet the good reporter from New York, who is writing for . . . for . . . ?"

"For nobody in particular. I'm doing this freelance. Philpot."

This last was directed to Cook, and it must have been a name, but how much of one? As with Chinese names, one didn't know right off where to put the "Mr."

"Jeremy Cook," he said, shaking hands with the rather short man.

"Call me Henry."

Cook was glad to have that little question cleared up. Wach said, "Jeremy here knows all there is to know about this place. And about some other things too, right, Jeremy?" He chuckled coldly. "If you'll be so good as to take Mr. Philpot to the nursery, Jeremy, and to the gym, and some of the other units, and introduce him around—let him meet Woeps and Stiph and Milke and the others—and just have a good time, you two, then later we'll all have lunch together." He looked down at his desk and cleared his throat.

Cook looked at him. Wach was best behind that desk, alone, free of human contact. Why did he pretend to be friendly? The place would run just as well, or better, if he gave it up. And why was he giving these directions? Hadn't he already taken up the preceding afternoon preparing him for this visitor, outlining in unnecessary detail the tour that would most favorably impress Philpot? Wach's superfluous instructions made sense, though, in light of Wach Rule Six: appear to be spontaneous except where the appearance of deliberation is called for.

Cook nodded. "Fine, Walter. We'll be back at twelve." He looked at the freelancing Philpot. "Would you like some coffee? I know I would, and Walter here never has any in his office."

"Never touch the stuff," said Wach, almost shouting.

"I'd love some," said Philpot.

"I've got a pot brewing in my office. We can talk there for a while before I show you around."

Wach yelled out something falsely jovial as Cook led Philpot through the small outer office used by Wach's secretary, who was in her accustomed position—filing her nails, a telephone pressed by one shoulder into her hair. She was fairly new to the place. Cook's final opinion of her after two months was that she was too dumb to have a consistent personality.

"Oh, I hate him all right, but for a different reason," she said into the phone as Cook and Philpot passed her desk. Cook swallowed hard. Her comment disturbed him almost as much as the one he had overheard in the elevator that morning. Two young mothers were delivering their children for the day and were talking on the ground floor as they waited for the elevator. When Cook walked up, they fell silent and remained so as the three of them rode up in the elevator. Just as they reached the seventh floor, one whispered: "That's what happens to people when they live alone for too long." All that morning, as he tried to work in his office, images of deviant solitary behavior danced in his head.

"I can't get a handle on that guy," Philpot said, jerking a thumb over his shoulder.

Cook blinked. "Yeah. He's like that. He's not important, though. He just runs the place."

"That's partly right," Cook said to Philpot. He sipped his coffee and put his feet on his desk. "We're concerned with language acquisition in the earliest stages, up to age five. We combine daycare with close observation, audiotaping, videotaping, and some simple experiments. The kids—I think there are about seventy-five now—range from six months to five years in age. They receive the typical care that any child receives in a daycare center. The only difference is that there are seven linguists here lurking in the halls and in the playrooms and beside the changing tables and under the cribs, listening for verb suffixes and glottalization and such things. It's a strange place—none exactly like it in the country. But after you've been here awhile it seems normal enough."

"Why here? Why southern Indiana?"

"It *is* a bit out of the way. The Wabash Institute was originally a center for primate studies. The old buildings are in back of me on the other side of the little river down there, which is called the Baby Wabash, by the way. It feeds into the larger, better-known one." He gestured to the window behind him, which opened out to a road seven stories below and, beyond it, a narrow river, a field, and a few wooden buildings. "Part of what they did was study language acquisition in chimps, using ASL—American Sign Language, used by the deaf—and that grew and became what they mainly did. At the same time, on this side of the river, a sizeable daycare center developed out of a defunct boys' reformatory, serving a variety of folks—Otis Elevator ten miles to the north, Busby Baptist College six miles to the east, and the town of Kinsey just to the south. There was nothing like the number of kids here now, but there were enough to suggest to the primate people—among them Wach, who was second in command—that the daycare part of it could be secondary and the language study part primary, and then the place would be one big lab for research on language acquisition in different species.

"Grant money poured in. This was in the sixties, when the Department of Defense for reasons mysterious to me showed hot interest in linguistics. The reformatory was further remodeled, and the Wabash Institute began to take its present form. Since then the primate center has virtually folded. There are still two or three people over there, but they've got just a few chimps and they confine themselves to studying how red their fannies get and things like that. We've taken over the language area completely." He paused. "It's nice how the movement of language across the river parallels the course of evolution. In fact people here call the wooden footbridge over it Scopes Bridge."

Philpot laughed. "I can use that."

"But you aren't writing anything down."

"No. I don't need to. It'll come back to me tonight in my room. What do *you* do, exactly?"

Cook squirmed slightly in his seat. When he was asked this by neighbors or by townies in Kinsey, the answers he heard himself give were sheepish and apologetic. What could he say? That he was the "resident genius"? That was what his friend Ed had once called him. Cook had his own research, but he liked to help others too. He could see the virtue of imaginative projects and make them better, and he could spy unpromising work well in advance and discourage it at the outset. Every publication coming out of the Institute since he had joined the staff five years earlier had thanked him by name. But it was hard to hang a simple job description on his work. There were slack days and hours when he sat nearly idle, or just read, matched by hectic days of inspired labor. Maybe it was like freelance writing in that respect.

"My job is a bit like freelance writing," he said to Philpot, and as he went on to describe it he realized with one part of his mind that he had just practiced Wach Rule Fourteen, even though the situation didn't call for it: before you manipulate people or lie to them, point out how similar you are to them. He had been around Wach too long. "It varies a lot from day to day. I'm somewhat unfit for specialization, and I say that unboastfully since I consider it a limitation of sorts."

"What are you working on now?"

"Something that doesn't really have my boss's blessing, but I try to keep him ignorant of it. I'm studying what I call 'idiophenomena.' These are linguistic devices that children develop on their own, with no basis in the adult model. They can range from simple utterances with fixed meanings, like a toddler's *buh* for 'I want the toy duck,' to highly original intonation contours."

Philpot frowned and fingered a pen in his shirt pocket as if to withdraw it, but then he just scratched his chin.

"Parents miss a lot of this. They tend to view language acquisition as a straightforward process of gradual accretion highlighted by comical blunders. But a lot more than that goes on. You have to be able to distance yourself from the steady drivel that comes out of children's mouths to find the rules, and that's the main point of the Wabash Institute. What we do is what a good many linguists have done with their own children—observe them and tape them and analyze the result—only we do it better. From what I've heard, it's hard for a person to be both parent and naturalist at the same time. You can ask Ed Woeps about that." Cook nodded to his left. "A colleague with a sixteen-month-old son here at Wabash. I've observed Ed's son, at least linguistically, much more than he has. It was his son, by the way, who actually used *buh* in the way I indicated."

"Do you have any children of your own here?"

"No," said Cook. "I'm not married."

"Can you tell me about the other linguists here?"

"Let's go meet them," said Cook. "Words would not do them justice."

As the two men stood up a strange and loud laugh was easily heard from the office to Cook's right. Because no other sound preceded the laughter, it was as if they were being watched by a silent eavesdropper who found the sight of *Homo sapiens* rising out of a chair hilarious. But Cook knew better. It was only Orffmann. Orffmann liked to laugh, especially when he was alone. Cook would often be working at his desk with his door closed and his mind engaged, when peals of Orffmann's mirth would crash around him. Many a noble, science-advancing thought had thereby been assassinated. Philpot was frowning uneasily at the wall, but Orffmann was one of those that Wach had left off Philpot's visiting list, and Cook figured the less said about him the better.

The same for Aaskhugh, who, standing as he was just outside the door of Cook's office as he and Philpot stepped into the hall, was less avoidable.

"Who's your friend, Jay?" said Aaskhugh, looking at Cook and then at Philpot. Cook performed the introductions, though he was irrationally tempted to lie. Aaskhugh was unique in having this effect on Cook, not a regular liar and in fact normally a very bad one. It was Aaskhugh's attitude toward information that did it. He traded in it. He collected it and dispensed it, without hesitation or discrimination. His fund of knowledge was great, and to keep it that way he asked questions, forever reminding Cook of the unfortunate fact of life that people were out there ready to think about you if you gave them the chance.

Over the years Cook had developed two evasion tactics. One served most handily when he felt mentally dull, say, after drinking or before his morning coffee: he would ask Aaskhugh a question first. Of course, this brought a great deal of useless information into his brain and made him mentally duller still. The second tactic was more challenging: Cook would raise a general philosophical point, one having no direct connection with his or anyone's life, and he would hold to it with maniacal fervor, always being careful not to let his personality slip through. This ploy guaranteed that, short of resorting to hypnosis, Aaskhugh would never learn anything about Cook beyond what he could squeeze from others, and also that Aaskhugh would never be able to charge Cook publicly with being dull—in the sense of being not talkative, at least.

"How long are you going to be here?" Aaskhugh said to Philpot.

Philpot answered, saying several days, perhaps a week. Where was he staying? Philpot named a motel just outside of Kinsey. Whom was the article for? Philpot explained. What had he written that Aaskhugh might have read? Philpot named some pieces, looking to Cook imploringly.

Cook roused himself and broke in with tactic one. "Adam, perhaps you could tell us what you're doing here. Mr. Philpot might be interested."

By "here" Cook meant the observation window facing into a playroom directly across the hall from Cook's office door. But Aaskhugh looked at Cook as if he had said something very silly indeed. "I'm not doing anything here, Jay."

Cook frowned. "But you were standing right outside my door. Weren't you?"

"No, no, no, Jay. I was passing *by* your door. Passing *by*." Aaskhugh's tone implied that Cook would never understand anything until he mastered his prepositions. "See?" By way of demonstration, he began slowly walking away from Cook and Philpot, looking back over his shoulder with a foolish grin. The curve of the hall finally took him out of their view. Cook turned to Philpot, who stared down the hall in wonder.

"Why does he call you 'Jay'? Isn't your name Jeremy?"

Cook smiled. This was the second thing wrong with Aaskhugh. Or maybe the third. It was hard to keep track. Shunning stale custom, Aaskhugh often ignored the names optimistically given people by their parents in favor of his own inventions. Cook was "Jay" to him. Now and then Ed Woeps was "Daisy" for reasons neither Cook nor Woeps understood. Wach's secretary, Mary—in Cook's mind simply Mary the Secretary—was "Mary, Mary," and Wach's name, which was pronounced like "watch" by its bearer and everyone else at Wabash, occasionally became more Germanic in Aaskhugh's "Wachtmeister." Cook looked forward to the day when he retaliated and rechristened Aaskhugh, perhaps, since the man's first name was Adam, giving him "A" for "Jay," or maybe even "Fucking A."

Cook explained all of this to Philpot as best he could. Then, seeking an antidote to Aaskhugh, he said, "Let me introduce you to Ed," and directed Philpot to Woeps's office next door. Woeps was by far the sanest person on the staff. Though fifteen years his senior, he was the only male friend Cook had. Their having offices next to each other helped, for Cook believed that two people could never become good friends unless they were in daily contact. Of course rollicking Orffmann on the other side proved this was not a sufficient condition.

Woeps was on the phone. Cook heard him say, "Is it bad?" and he suspected his friend was talking to his wife about yet another domestic calamity. Woeps's only serious fault—and it could hardly be called a fault—was his Odyssean attraction for bad luck.

Cook mouthed, "I'll be back." Woeps nodded distractedly and Cook closed the door. "He's busy at the moment," he explained to Philpot, who was still looking wonderingly up the hall.

"I don't understand the shape of this building," said the writer. "And where's the men's bathroom?"

"I'll explain as I show you." He pointed up the hall in the direction Aaskhugh had gone and they began walking. "This building is a circle, in case you didn't notice."

"I'm beginning to."

"It's a seven-story cylinder, actually. It was built for the harder core of the boys in the reformatory. Around the edges of the circle were the cells, expanded and remodeled into offices for us, with the bars removed from the windows. Except in the bathroom, for some reason—you'll see them. Then, working inward to the center of the circle, there is this hall, formerly the catwalk outside the cells. Then there's a central core to our left divided into playrooms, an eating area, a little gymnasium, and so on. The hall goes all the way around it, almost. Wach's office gets in the way. He had it built in such a way that it extends from his window clear to the central core, so the hall ends at each of his walls. We just passed Orffmann's office on the right. You'll meet him later, of course. Here's Miss Pristam's office. She's out of town. Stairs and elevator." He gestured to the right. "There's another wing there, on a tangent with our building, but it's not used now. Neither are the lower floors of the building, except for part of the floor immediately below, where Sally Good's office is. She's the head teacher who runs the daycare side of things. I'll take you down there later. And here is Arthur Stiph's office."

"Whose?"

"Sorry. I'm used to lowering my voice around him. Maybe you'll see why." Cook peeked into the half-open door of Stiph's office and saw what he expected. At a desk in the middle of an office cluttered well beyond the limits of tasteful eccentricity sat Arthur Stiph.

Stiph was asleep. He was often asleep, here in his office, or outside on the shaded lawn gently sloping down to the Baby Wabash, or in a playroom corner, quite oblivious to his crawling, vocalizing, peeing informants. Now, as always, he gave the appearance of being at peace not just with the world, but with all known forces of darkness.

Suddenly Stiph snorted and smacked his lips open and shut, causing his old swivel chair to squeak once before settling back into silence. Reflexively the two men at his door split apart and hid out of sight, like commandos about to pitch grenades.

"That's Arthur Stiph," whispered Cook. "We can catch him another time. The bathrooms are just ahead at the end of the hall. The men's is on the left." He led Philpot away from the door.

"It's eleven in the morning," Philpot whispered. "What's he doing?"

Cook shrugged. "He's old. He works some, but he sleeps too. About as much as a cat. He's fairly new here."

Philpot muttered something and went into the bathroom. As he reached the door Aaskhugh stepped out. He smiled at Philpot as if the bond between them were tighter than that between most mortals, then did the same to Cook. With that same smile on his face he looked in at Stiph as he passed by his office and whispered, loudly enough for Cook to hear but not necessarily for his benefit, "Lazy turd." Cook recoiled. He stepped to the door and looked in at Stiph again. He sat tranquilly, his gray-topped head cocked sharply to one side. He looked almost like a heavy-headed newborn asleep in an infant chair. A small beam of sunlight streaming through a dent in his metal window blinds illuminated his shoulders, where a few leaves—dry, dead leaves—clung to a gray sweater. Cook found the man utterly free of his capacity for censure—something he could say about few other people. He suddenly wished he knew him better. Their contacts had been too brief, too professional. Stiph looked so personable, so approachable—a potential friend, despite the extreme difference in their ages. They could teach each other things.

Cook suddenly heard a scream. It came from the central core—long and high-pitched. He opened the door leading into the core and ran in. A young teacher was stumbling out of the nap room with a baby pressed to her chest. Sally, the head teacher, was with her, trying to get at the baby.

"My God," said the younger woman. The way she said it told Cook she was the one who had screamed.

"But he's all right," said Sally.

"My God," she said again.

"Look. He's all right." Sally pried the baby away from the girl's chest. He squirmed and began to cry. The girl looked at him in amazement.

"I thought—"

"Is everything all right?" asked Cook.

"What's going on here?" asked Wach, approaching from the other direction. "I demand an explanation."

Sally rocked the baby in her arms and looked at Wach. "Just a minute, Walter," she said. "I'm going to put him back down." She opened the door to the nap room. One or two of the other babies inside had been awakened by the noise and were crying. She stepped inside and closed the door behind her.

"I'm sorry, Dr. Wach," said the girl, bringing a hand to her forehead. "I thought . . . it was foolish of me, but I thought it was another crib death."

"Another?" Wach exclaimed. "*Another?* There has never been a death at this Institute during my administration."

"I think she means before, Walter," offered Cook, feeling both compassion for the girl in her awkwardness and shock from those screams. "You know, before you came there was—"

"That doesn't concern me," Wach said loudly, speaking to Cook without looking at him. His eyes remained fixed on the girl. "Just what happened? What's your name?"

"Phyllis, Dr. Wach. I'm sorry. Some of us were talking about crib deaths this morning, so it was on my mind, and the way he was lying there was, well, I felt his chest to see if it was moving, and it wasn't, or I didn't think it was, and I couldn't hear him breathe, and when I picked him up he seemed so limp—"

Sally opened the door from the nap room and stepped into the hall, her index finger to her lips. "Let's step away from the door," she said, herding the group down the hall. "Back to work, everyone," she said to three teachers who had joined the group. Cook saw that Aaskhugh was among them too, his eyebrows dancing with unspoken questions. "Everything's all right," Sally said. "False alarm. Are you okay now, Phyllis?" She put an arm around her as they walked down the hall.

Cook had turned to go in the other direction, back into the main hall, when Wach called out to him.

"Jeremy, I don't want that reporter getting wind of this. If he heard the ruckus, tell him it was a joke or something. Tell him nothing if he didn't. Is that clear?"

"Yes," said Cook. As he opened the door to the main hall he heard Wach speak again:

"You, whatever your name is . . . you come to my office."

Cook closed the door behind him and saw Philpot emerge from the bathroom with a quizzical smile on his face. "I got a little surprise in there," he said to Cook as he joined him. Cook glanced at Stiph, who slept on undisturbed, and began to walk with the writer back up the hall, wondering what he meant. Then he understood. That had to be it. The timing was right, too. Wach must have been responding to the screams, taking a short cut.

"I know," said Cook. "He really ought to knock."

An architectural oddity lay behind Philpot's little surprise. The men's bathroom on this floor was adjacent to Wach's office, and a special small door connected the two. This door was the subject of some controversy at Wabash, for it opened directly into the only toilet stall in the men's bathroom. Despite repeated hints and requests, and even despite a parliamentarily proper motion made by Cook at a recent meeting and instantly seconded by Woeps but then ruled out of order, Wach chose not to knock. Usually he withdrew with apologies. Sometimes he passed boldly through, taking a short cut to the stairs or elevator. One of Cook's revenge fantasies featured the entire staff storming the stall when it was occupied by Wach. Beyond this the fantasy became obscure; it was the initial image that was appealing.

Woeps was hurrying down the hall toward them, pulling a sweater over his head without bothering to remove his glasses. The crew neck of the sweater caught the frame and threw his glasses to the floor at Cook's feet. Cook picked them up, relieved for his friend's sake to see that they were undamaged. He handed them to Woeps and gestured to Philpot.

"Ed, this is—"

"I can't talk, Jeremy. Amy's fallen down and bumped her head hard. I'm meeting Helen at the hospital."

"Is it serious?"

"Going for X rays." He opened the door to the stairwell and was gone.

"That's the one you like?" asked Philpot.

"Yes," said Cook without thinking. Then he saw the implication. It struck him as remarkable that Philpot could have sensed his dislike of the others so easily. "It's sad. His daughter Amy has a muscular problem of some sort."

"And his son, the one who stays here during the day?"

"Wally? He's fine. A healthy kid." He gestured to his right. "Shall we go into the central core? We could see some kids and meet some of the teachers."

They backtracked a few steps and entered through the north door, the one Cook had used when he heard the screams. (Two other doors, one at the east and one at the south, opened into the core from the hall. A fourth door connected Wach's office directly with the core; like the bathroom door, this one was always locked from the inside, public access to Wach from the hall being limited to the route through Mary the Secretary's office.) The door to the nap room was closed and all was quiet. Farther along they paused at an open door.

"This is the playroom for the toddlers," explained Cook. "Nine to twenty-four months."

They looked down upon a frenzy of antisocial activity. Each child was playing with a toy, or his hands, or a piece of dust, as if alone on the moon. Cook greeted Jane, one of the teachers, and introduced her to Philpot, noticing in her eyes the glazed look he often saw at Wabash—the result of long hours spent in baby care. The same thing happened to him when observing. He missed a great deal of data for that reason, no doubt.

"A lotta kids," said Philpot, looking down at the dozen or so children on the floor.

Cook thought he detected a note of distaste. Could Philpot, like Wach, be a kid hater?

"Makes me miss my own," Philpot added.

"How many do you have?" asked Jane.

"Two. Eleven months—a boy—and a girl of three. I'm missing her birthday tomorrow." Philpot sighed. "Couldn't be helped."

Cook suppressed an impulse to put a consoling arm around Philpot's shoulders. There was that much pathos and regret in his voice. Jane, the teacher, looked as if she felt the same way, but then the teachers were a generally sentimental lot. Cook watched another on the floor playing patty-cake with a responsive, rotund lad. She was new as of two days ago. Paula, her name was. Very nice looking. A graduate student at U.C.L.A. and here just for the summer. Very handy, that. It was awkward when they stayed after things with him fizzled out. He watched her reach up with both hands and smooth her long hair away from her forehead. He would have to meet her soon. Why didn't Wach do the right thing and introduce people around when they came instead of letting them drift? If he ran things he would do it that way. Paula sat with her back to the two men, deeply engaged in her game.

One of the children began crying and Jane excused herself and hurried to her. Cook stepped back into the hall with Philpot, and at the same time two boys from the four-year-old group came running down the hall, giggling loudly.

"Shhh," said Cook, pointing up the hall to the nap room. "You kids are supposed to be in the gym." The youngest, easily intimidated, turned to go, but the other pointed into the playroom.

"I wanna show Bobby the baby in there that says 'buck-a-buck.'" The boys giggled again. "All she says is 'buck-a-buck.' What's the matter with her? Is she *stu*pid?"

"She's just young. Go on, now."

"Who's *that*?" the same one said, pointing to Philpot as if he had antlers and a light bulb for a nose.

Cook sighed. "He's a policeman and a fireman and a cowboy and he'll be in the gym in a few minutes to tell you how to be one, so get going."

The boys looked at Cook as if they knew he was a fraud, but since he was a fraud with authority, they obeyed.

"Up ahead," said Cook, continuing the tour, "is the staff lounge. Next to it is an eating area for the kids. We call it McDonald's just to make them happy, though the older ones, like those two, know it's a lie." Cook led him through this room to the other playrooms, and the story-time and crafts rooms. In the last of these, Emory Milke, a large, bearded colleague of Cook's, an excellent linguist and a formidable sexual rival, was setting up a video tape recorder and consulting with a technician.

Cook approved of Milke but didn't like him much. The women at Wabash were always talking about how charming he was. Cook had tried to pin this down on a number of occasions, but all he ever got was some nonsense about his voice and the way he looked at you. But Cook, if pressed, would have admitted there was something commanding about Milke's eyes, surrounded as they were by shaggy black hair atop his head and all over his face. And he was smart, the bastard. It was, in other words, harder to dislike Milke than others—the inquisitive Aaskhugh, say, or orffing Orffmann—but Cook worked hard at it. Milke's name helped, and so Cook thought about it a good deal. It had a slippery quality. For half of the Wabash community it was homonymous with the white liquid; for the other half it was disyllabic, like the cognate adjective. Cook deplored this public confusion and removed himself from it by never referring to the man in conversation. This meant that properly introducing Milke to Philpot was going to be tricky. But as it turned out he was saved from compromising his principles on this point.

"Goddammit, man, no wonder it's not working," Milke shouted at the technician. All conversation in the room stopped, and most of the children looked up from their finger painting expectantly.

The technician mumbled something by way of explanation.

"What do you mean 'no more batteries'? For Christ's sake."

The technician mumbled again.

"That tightwad prick!" shouted Milke. He moved toward Cook and Philpot at the door, as if bent on searching them roughly for hidden batteries in their pockets. They parted and Milke brushed by them. Cook thought he smelled liquor in the air, but it might have been deodorant or cologne. Milke disappeared through the east door into the encircling hall on his way to Wach's office, which was no more than twelve feet from where Cook and Philpot stood if only access through the west door were allowed. Cook turned and looked at it. The thin metal blinds over the window, always closed, were open at one of the slats at eye level, and this popped closed just as Cook's gaze reached it. Wach would not be surprised by his visitor.

As Cook and Philpot passed through McDonald's—Philpot having expressed a desire to return to Cook's office in pursuit of linguistic questions, to which Cook had eagerly consented—Cook reflected on the number of interesting sentences he had overheard so far that day. He was so absorbed with his thoughts that it took him a moment to notice that the new girl, Paula, was standing with Jane at the coffeepot. Their backs were to the room. Cook and Philpot were going to pass by quite close to them. Cook's first "hello" to her, which he hoped would be deep-voiced, as he knew Milke's would be (or had been already?), was well beyond the planning stages when he heard her utter a sentence. The sentence consisted of an arrangement of American English vowels and consonants that could have been random, generated by one of six million monkeys at six million typewriters. Yes, it could have been random, but it probably was not.

"This fellow Cook is supposed to be a complete asshole."

Philpot, leading the way, turned and gave Cook a mournful, mouth-open look of sympathy, while Cook stared straight ahead into the middle distance, where there was nothing but air. With an uncomfortable half-smile fixed on his face, he gave the appearance, but only the appearance, of amused self-confidence.

TWO

COOK'S HALF-SMILE REMAINED FIXED IN PLACE AS HE walked with Philpot back to his office, asked him to take a seat, and said he would return shortly. He hoped his face suggested inner tranquility—first to Philpot, then to Orffmann, who looked up frowningly through his open door as Cook passed by, perhaps wondering why his neighbor, if he was truly amused at some private joke, was not laughing outright after his own fashion. After checking to be sure he was alone, Cook walked up to the bathroom mirror, relaxed his face, and watched himself turn into an aphasic middle line-backer.

"Gnnarnghrackagh goddammit grack oh jesus ghorki," he yelled. He kicked the large metal trash can and sent it rolling into a corner. It made such a violent noise that fear of discovery suddenly calmed him, or at least stopped him from making more noise. He leaned forward on the sink, bringing his face close to the mirror, and looked into his eyes. Yes, it was easy to imagine. Someone had been showing her around, pointing out the rooms and toys and things, telling her about the people she was meeting and the people she would soon meet, among them one Jeremy Cook, who, by the way, was a real asshole. No—*complete* asshole. Or the original utterance could have been "a real asshole," incorrectly remembered by Paula as "a complete asshole." Or maybe the original was just "somewhat of an asshole," or "a slight asshole," or "not too much of an asshole," or even "not an asshole like the other people here." No, that was going too far. In fact, there was no dodging it at all. In someone's mind he was a complete (or real, total, consummate, etc.) asshole, and this person talked about it, so in other people's minds he was *supposed to be* a complete (or real, etc.) asshole.

"Supposed to be." The classic mark of a secondhand report.

Wasn't there some American Indian language that made a distinction in its verb forms between knowledge acquired firsthand and knowledge acquired secondhand? Hopi? Navaho? Well, English had an equivalent device, Cook now realized. It was less integral to English structure, but it still told you how things stood: "supposed to be."

But was it really "supposed to *be*"? Hadn't he read somewhere that in some languages *be* and *have* were the same verb? And didn't English *have* replace the perfect auxiliary *be* in the nineteenth century, when "He is arrived" became "He has arrived"? Could he have misheard what she said, or could she have missaid it? "This fellow Cook is supposed to *have* a complete asshole." No. This couldn't save him either. He was upset. His reasoning was all wrong.

"Supposed to be." She didn't necessarily believe it. She had only heard it. From someone. Not from Jane, with whom she had been talking at the coffeepot—one doesn't give information back to one's source. That left the entire adult speaking population of Wabash. A lot of people. Seven linguists, an administrator, a secretary, fifteen or so teachers, an audio-visual man, and some janitors. Mary the Secretary didn't seem to like him much, and she would be likely to speak with newcomers to Wabash and poison them against Cook. Or maybe that horse-faced teacher, Dorothy Plough. She always seemed a bit standoffish. Yes, there were lots of possibilities. Not just at Wabash, either. Paula was from U.C.L.A. In the course of his career had Cook offended some teacher there in an article or review, who had then conveyed these tidings to Paula as a kind of travel tip? If so, or even if not, it was going to be a tough search.

That it was Paula in particular who had been told this nonsense bothered him some, but not greatly. To be sure, there was now a certain obstacle to overcome in his maneuvers, but that was minor. It could even be seen as an advantage, something that made him mysterious. Wasn't it true that people who were initially threatening, on proving to be just moderately pleasant, appeared to be about the most pleasant people on earth? And after Paula met him she would always be looking beyond his winning charm to that essential asshole fundament, until one day she would decide that he had been unjustly vilified. She would reject her source. And reveal it then too? Ah! *That* was the investigative line to pursue. But he would have to move cautiously. Cautiously in that respect, but with lusty dispatch in the other.

He turned on the tap and splashed cold water on his face. As he dried his hands he became aware of loud but unintelligible voices coming from the other side of the wall. Wach and Milke discussing the budget. The thought of this made him smile, but he felt it as a mean, low smile. Did being called a complete asshole make you enjoy such things? He would have to watch himself.

Philpot was not in his office. Cook went into the gym in search of him, assuming he had gone exploring on his own. Jane, the teacher who had been with Paula, walked over to him, and he was suddenly self-conscious. Had she risen to his defense, insisting that he was a complete sweetie? Had she hesitated and withheld comment? Had she said with a sneer, "There's no *supposed to be* about it"? Not knowing, he felt he could not talk to her. He turned away.

"Dr. Cook?" she called out. He turned around and faced her. "Dr. Wach wants to see you. Mary was asking for you."

Cook thanked her in a way that he thought was incompatible with being a complete asshole and left the gym. That's right, Wach, he thought as he walked down the hall. Don't look for people yourself. Send someone after them, and then make sure they come to you.

Mary the Secretary looked up from her desk, where she had been unbending a paper clip. "He's expecting you," she said as if she were important.

Wach stood up from his desk when Cook entered. He circled around the desk and closed the door behind Cook. He pointed to a chair facing his desk. Cook had sat in it many times before. He knew that it was permanently positioned just far enough away from Wach's to make conversation uncomfortable. He sat down, wondering why he had been summoned. Wach never gave one verbal preliminaries to suggest the tone of a visit.

"Where did you leave the reporter?" Wach asked.

"I don't know," said Cook. "I mean in my office, but he's not there now."

"Where is he?"

"I don't know. I was looking for him."

Wach looked at Cook with the impatience of a father whose children had all been unwelcome accidents. "Jeremy, we can't have that man just wandering around here all alone."

Cook shifted in his seat. "I didn't intend for him to, Walter. Anyway, I see no harm in it."

Wach waved his hand back and forth in front of him, as if to bat aside each word as it reached him. "I'm taking you off this case, Jeremy."

Had he really said that? And seriously? "What do you mean?"

Wach pursed his lips a moment and studied Cook. "I don't want you showing Philpot around anymore. Besides, we've got a grant deadline Friday and I need someone to work on it. Ed was going over the draft but he had to leave for the day. I need someone to take over."

Three questions struck Cook simultaneously. The first—why couldn't Wach take over Woeps's job—was unaskable. Wach would see the question as a challenge. The second could be asked, but the answer would probably be maddening.

"Who wrote the draft?"

"Clyde."

It was. Orffmann's general worthlessness extended to, included, and was symbolized by, his prose style. The third question was dangerous, but Cook had to ask it.

"You said 'besides,' Walter. What other reason do you have for taking charge of Philpot?"

Wach's frown approached a scowl. One of his rules, to which Cook had not yet assigned a number because it hadn't yet become fully articulated in his mind, was that between administrators and underlings overt hostilities should never be verbalized.

"Let's just say I think I can do a good job," Wach said.

" 'Let's just say'?" asked Cook. "Instead of what?"

"Well you *have* made a bit of a mess of it, haven't you?" Wach spoke quickly now, his words escaping uncensored. "You let me stumble upon him in the bathroom—rather awkward for both of us, I must say—and then you let him see Emory blow up and stalk out of the playroom. What kind of place must he think this is? And now you don't even know where he is."

Cook laughed. It was either that or leap over the desk and twist the fool's ears off.

"It's more serious than you think, Jeremy. This reporter might well place his article in a magazine with national circulation, and there we are, open to inspection by everyone."

"But there's nothing to hide here, Walter. If you just let him have a good look around, I don't see—"

"You don't understand these things at all, Jeremy. Now you had better get to work on that proposal. I want it on my desk with your revisions at eight tomorrow morning. It's in Ed's office. You can get Mary to open it for you."

"And thanks for pitching in like this, Jeremy. Good of you, especially since it will mean quite a long day and all." Cook supplied these words silently as he stood up, and he found them heartening. When he opened the door he saw Philpot sitting in Mary's office. He gave Cook a friendly smile.

"Dr. Wach will see you now," Mary said dully.

Cook expressed sincere regrets to Philpot that he would not be able to be with him the rest of the day (perhaps even the rest of his visit to Wabash, he thought). Philpot suggested they get together for a drink later that night. Cook wondered if Wach would approve, then hated himself for wondering it and agreed, saying he would call Philpot at his motel when he finished his work.

"It may be quite late, though. Eleven or twelve?"

"No problem," said Philpot. "Have a nice day. And don't let these things get you down."

Cook asked Mary for the master key, and, contrary to policy, she gave it to him instead of walking with him to Woeps's office, unlocking it for him, observing him, and then locking it again. This was fine with Cook. Disobedience on this small point, though motivated by pure laziness, meant that Mary might be counted on when the revolution came.

And what about good old Philpot? "These things." There was the complete asshole business, but since he used the plural he must have sensed other things, like maybe Wach calling him on the carpet. He was sharp, and this meant that Wach couldn't possibly hide anything from him and would only get himself into trouble if he tried.

Whistling and stepping jauntily now, Cook took the draft of the proposal to his office and returned the master key to Mary. On his way back to his office he decided to get away for a few hours to clear his mind. One nice thing, perhaps the only one, about Wach's administration of Wabash was the complete freedom of schedule he allowed the linguists. Wach too had once been committed to the life of the mind, and he knew that professional thinkers did their best thinking when they felt like thinking. Cook would go home, eat, have a beer, and return with a fresh sense of purpose, as if working on the proposal were entirely his own idea.

He took his coat from his office and locked the door. On his way to the elevator he spied an awake Arthur Stiph in one of the playrooms. He paused at the observation window. Stiph was leaning against a wall studying two children playing on the floor with an orange tennis ball. Stiph's sport coat was draped over his shoulders without his arms being in the sleeves. The kids must have just done something funny, because Stiph was gently laughing and his eyes were sparkling as he stood there, armless, against the wall.

Cook moved on, thinking that seeing this had been the nicest thing that had happened to him all day.

* * *

Cook's house was in the country. In some circles this would be a mark of prestige, but in Kinsey County it was a normal thing. Unless one wanted to live elbow-to-elbow with the twanging Kinseyans in town, one lived in the country. His was a two-story wooden frame house set well back from a little-used country road, with five acres of unruly meadow and oaks in the back. Here he slept, worked, entertained guests—usually one at a time—and ate Grunt Meals.

Cook's philosophy toward eating was starkly realistic. Hunger was a pain that interfered with important things like doing linguistics. Food ended that pain. Food allowed you to get on with it. The most popular item on his menu was the Grunt Meal. This consisted of a single dish, casserole-style, with ground beef as the central ingredient; the dish was enhanced, or at least made bigger, by rice or noodles, with tomatoes or chili or condensed soup added to give the illusion of savoriness. For Cook's purposes, the outstanding virtue of a Grunt Meal was not that it made him grunt (though there must have been some connection or he wouldn't have given it such a name), but rather that it ensured that he would not want to eat right away again. If ever.

When he arrived home, Cook dialed Woeps's number to inquire about Amy, but there was no answer. He considered phoning the hospital but decided it would be too hard to get through to Woeps. He went into the kitchen and prepared a Grunt Meal, or rather he reheated the remnants of two previous Grunt Meals, and he dug into the dish with speed, if not relish. When sizzling hot on the plate, Grunt Meals were merely sustaining, neither good nor bad. When warmish or cold they were an offense to God's Green Earth. The two beers he took with the meal made it a little easier. After grunting a bit he poured himself a cup of coffee, put on a pullover sweater, and shuffled out into his backyard, where a moderately maintained lawn gradually shaded into the riotous meadow in the distance. He pulled up a lawn chair and slumped down in it, setting his coffee mug on the brick patio. He leaned back in the chair, put his hands behind his head, and closed his eyes. The wind picked up slightly and blew his hair across his forehead. He wondered if it was going to rain.

When he woke, it was after three o'clock. He jumped from the chair and hurried into the house. Knowing what he knew about grants and Orffmann, there was a good deal of work ahead of him. He drove the six miles back to the Institute. He parked his car, a dull corpse-white Plymouth Valiant, beside a Kinsey County Road Department truck, and wondered vaguely what it was doing there. Then he spied two orange-helmeted engineers, or people of some kind, walking around the far side of the building. He was pleased to see Aaskhugh leaving. One potential distraction from work would be gone for the day.

Outside the elevator he bumped into Sally, who informed him that Phyllis, the screaming teacher, had been fired by Wach. Although he had hardly known the girl, Cook found himself immoderately angered by this news. He swore under his breath.

Sally nodded. "I know," she said grimly. She then asked him if he had met Philpot. He said yes without offering details of his ignominious demotion.

"Walter brought him downstairs to my office," she said. "He seems very nice. I just hope he doesn't get a bad impression of the place."

"Why do you say that?"

"Well, Walter is sticking to him like flypaper. It's obviously making the guy uncomfortable."

Cook smiled. He asked her if she had been watching any of the children he was studying.

"Just Wally Woeps."

"Hear any *m-bwee* from him?"

"No. Just some *fffff* and *n-duh*. I think you're right about the distinction."

"Really? What were the contexts?"

She explained. Cook took mental notes, which he planned to make physical as soon as he was in his office.

"Did you go home and forget something?" she asked.

"No. Pressing work," he said obscurely. "I'm going to be here until the wee hours, I'm afraid." He began to move to the elevator but immediately bumped into someone who proved to be Arthur Stiph, just stepping out on his way home. "Sorry, Arthur," said Cook. He had bumped him quite hard.

"No problem, Jeremy," said Stiph, smiling somewhat sadly and brushing his gray hair back with one hand. "The wee hours, eh?" he said. "Busy boy." He clapped Cook on the shoulder and moved on.

"I'll think of you when I'm on my second martini, Jeremy," said Sally as she waved goodbye. This was a joke in that (a) Sally was a notorious teetotaler at Wabash, and (b) she had once dumbfounded Cook by asking him if he ever worried because he drank so much. Cook waved back and jumped into the elevator just before the doors closed.

The heavy traffic period at Wabash was beginning. Between three-thirty and six every afternoon, the Institute was in a transitional phase. Parents came one after another for their children, hoping to find them still intact after yet another day of linguistic scrutiny. In Kinsey County there was persistent uneasiness about Wabash, and for this reason a tiny fraction of Wach's abundant paranoia was justified. People felt uncomfortable about the disciplined eavesdropping their children were daily subjected to. This discomfort was rarely verbalized, but from many chats with neighbors and other townspeople about his work, Cook knew it was widespread. Luckily the low cost of Wabash daycare was sufficient enticement to keep the data coming in.

The bustle outside Cook's door in the late-afternoon hours never bothered him. He worked well either with steady noise or total silence. It was only intermittent noise, like Orffmann's disembodied laughter, that annoyed him. So he worked well until six, when Wabash closed and the building emptied, and he continued to labor happily in the following silence. He added Sally's information to his file on Wally Woeps and thought about it a bit. Then he went to work on the proposal. Oh, how he hated grant proposals. The hollow promises; the vaunting celebration of past success; the self-advertising emphasis on *importance* and *significance*; the absence of understatement; the omnipresence of exaggeration; the servile allegiance to tradition, formula, and established procedure; the utter predictability of every other sentence; the implicit greed of the genre—these were truly horrible things, and they were at their worst when penned by Orffmann. But Cook worked hard and productively into the evening hours, his brain continually nourished by what he knew was the protein-carbohydrate mixture that constituted the beauty of the Grunt Meal.

At eight o'clock he paused and went down the hall to the bathroom to clean his coffee pot and fill it with water. Back in his office, the perking sound was cheering. He took off his sweater and opened a window slightly. It was cloudy outside, quite dark, and the air was thick with moisture, giving a hint of the humid summer that was just beginning. He gazed for a moment at his books lined along the wall of his office, and then he resumed work. By now he had actually begun to believe in Orffmann's proposal, and he wrote and revised effortlessly.

When he was finished, he slammed his pen down with relief, leaned back in his chair, stretched his arms, and groaned loudly. He rubbed the bridge of his nose under his glasses, sighing with the contentment of the honest toiler. He looked at his watch: eleven-fifteen. He looked up the number of Philpot's motel and dialed it, looking forward to a nightcap or two with the writer. It would be fun talking with him about Wach.

But Philpot wasn't in his room. Nor was he in the bar, according to the clerk at the desk. Cook left his number with a message for Philpot to call when he returned. Leaning back in his chair, he let his mind wander. He thought about Woeps and kicked himself for not remembering to call him again to find out if Amy was all right. She probably was (Woeps tended to be overly fearful about small accidents), and it was too late to call. Married people with kids, he knew, went to bed at unbelievable hours like ten or eleven. Then he thought a bit about the new girl, Paula, her long hair and soft features, and hoped she wouldn't flee in terror when he presented himself. And if she did? Well, there was that young mother he had seen and greeted last week, who, judging from her smile, must have been divorced. Woeps had seen her too and had shared Cook's enthusiasm for the way she looked, though in his case, because he was married, it was necessarily academic. Perhaps that was why Woeps always whistled mournful tunes.

Someone was skidding. Loudly. Brakes had been slammed on hard, and it was a long skid. Cook froze at his desk in anticipation of a crash, but none came. It was suddenly peaceful outside, quiet again, as if nothing had happened. All he heard was the rustle of a paper on his desk from the gentle breeze blowing in the window, and after he placed his hand on the paper there was only the slight stirring of the trees outside.

The skid had been quite near. He stood up, raised the window all the way and leaned out. The road was seven stories below him, running from a small rise to his right down a hill to his left, some fifty yards or so from the building. It was a small road, used much less often than the main road on the other side of the building. He could see its outline in the dark, but down to the left it was obscured from view by the adjoining wing jutting out on a tangent with his own building. The skidding sound seemed to have come from behind the wing, not from the part of the road directly below him. He listened and heard only the soft wind blowing listlessly, struggling against the air heavy with moisture.

He called out, "Everything all right?"

There was a long pause and only silence. He listened, waiting. His voice had seemed weak and puny in the night air, but anyone down there beyond the wing of the building would have heard him.

"Are you all right?"

A long silence. Nothing. The hopeless sound of his own voice caused a sorrow to well up in his chest. He pulled his head in and sat down, rubbing his forehead and trying to shake the feeling. He sat still for a while, silent, hoping to hear something to let him know what had happened.

After a while he began to clean up his desk, gathering the pages of the grant proposal and arranging them in proper order. He evened the edges and set the papers neatly on his desk. Again he paused and listened.

A car door slammed. An engine started. Then the hasty squeal of tires. Cook jumped to his feet and looked out the window. Nothing. He ran out of his office and down the hall to the flight of stairs that led to the other wing of the building, the corner of which had blocked his view. He raced down the seven flights of stairs to the ground floor, taking the steps two and three at a time, and he ran along another hall until he reached the exit at the far end. He opened the door and looked up and down the road.

He walked down a sloping stretch of grass that separated the road from the building and saw nothing at all. Perhaps the whole thing had been a fancy of his bleared, linguistics-riddled mind. Then he saw it—a long skid mark, barely visible in the dark, running a distance of thirty or forty feet. But no glass, no metal, no sign of a crash. He walked up and down the length of the skid mark, examining the road closely, and both shoulders of the road as well. He stood for a moment between the skid marks, thinking.

He shrugged. The driver had seen something and slammed on his brakes. A dog, maybe. Or a cat. The wind came up and chilled him. He rubbed his bare arms, wishing he had brought his sweater down with him from the office, and walked slowly back up the hill toward the building. The darkness seemed to move with him. He fumbled with the door for some time before remembering that his key worked only in the main entrance on the opposite side of the building. He shivered, thought a moment, then turned and began to walk to the parking lot. He was done with his work, and there was no need to return to his office. It seemed important that he leave now, that he get away from the building. He ran the last hundred feet to his car.

But instead of leaving by the exit he normally used, he drove from the parking lot up onto the little road and stopped just short of the skid marks, his motor running and lights on. With an odd sense of urgency prodding him, he again examined the road and shoulders. They were skid marks—not a great deal could be said about them beyond that. As he stood in the middle of the road with his arms folded he became aware of the night sounds. He heard crickets on all sides of him, stretching out in every direction, as if he were standing at the very center of their population. And, far up the hill, he thought he heard an owl scream.

He rubbed his bare arms and hurried back to his car. A dog, a cat, a squirrel. Like Phyllis's screaming, a false alarm. A simple thing. He drove on up the road. When he cleared the wing of the building that jutted out he looked up and saw a lighted office on the seventh floor. It took him a moment to recognize it as his own. He slowed the car down, then stopped. He could see his bookshelves and a picture on a wall. On another wall was a calendar. As he stared up at the window he almost felt as if he hadn't really left his office, as if he were still up there working alone. And yet at the same time he was here, outside in his car, watching from afar—allowed by some freak of nature the rare and horrible privilege of spying on himself.

He had never felt quite so mortal.

THREE

"MARY, I OVERSLEPT. THERE'S A GRANT PROPOSAL ON MY desk that Walter wanted to see at eight this morning. Can you go get it and take it to him? Tell him I'll be there as soon as I can. Can you do that for me?" Cook ran his hand through his knotted hair and groaned softly. His voice was raw and his eyes were thick with the night's crust.

"Sure, Dr. Cook," said Mary the Secretary. "I'll go right down there and get it. Dr. Wach is in, and it's almost nine o'clock now, but he hasn't said anything about a proposal." She paused, then added, with a smile probably playing at her red lips, "Rough night?"

Cook imagined a Prussian boot surprising her secretarial fanny.

"Yes, Mary. Now if you could, it's quite important—"

"All right, Dr. Cook. I'm on my way. And I'll tell Dr. Wach that you're on yours." She giggled. "How do you like the linguistics of that?"

Cook laughed, hung up, and cursed. He dressed, combed his hair, decided to forgo a shave, and hurried out to his car. It was a day dark with clouds, and the air was so heavy with suspended moisture that he felt he could possibly drown if he breathed too heavily. He drove to Wabash, catching more amber lights than green ones, hoping that Wach was in a good mood.

Outside the elevator on the seventh floor he ran into Woeps. His friend seemed even more stooped than normal, and his face carried a sad, bewildered look.

"Jeremy," he said, his face brightening when he saw Cook, without, however, becoming any more cheerful. "Thank God you're here." He whipped his head back and forth, a motion Cook had never seen him perform before. "Jeremy, we found Arthur Stiph in your office this morning."

Cook hesitated, then burst into laughter. "Asleep? Do you mean he—"

"No," Woeps said impatiently. "He's dead. He's dead and in your office."

Cook reached out to lean against the wall, but it was too far away, so he walked two steps backward and leaned against it. Stiph was old and old people died. This was to be expected. But not in his office. Not in his office.

"What . . . I . . . what did he die of?"

Woeps reached out with both hands and held Cook by the shoulders. "Take it easy, Jeremy." He released his grip on him, slowly. "I don't know," he said. "Mary just found him this morning when she opened your office. Screamed like hell."

"But what's he doing *in there*?"

"I don't know. I just don't know."

"I mean . . . did he just wander in there to die?"

"I don't know. I don't understand it. It's all very sad."

"Christ," said Cook under his breath. "I left my door wide open last night. That's how he got in. He must have been walking around and seen the light on and the door open, and he must have just wandered right in. There was this skidding sound outside, so I ran out without closing the door behind me. I was afraid someone got hurt—" His knees felt weak again and he reached for the wall. "Oh Jesus. Jesus."

"What is it?"

Cook didn't answer. He hurried down the hall and forced his way through the throng of people outside his office, all hovering at the threshold as if it were a holy place.

Arthur Stiph sat calmly at Cook's desk. Cook took a few steps forward and stopped, eyeing the body suspiciously, as if fearful that it might suddenly do something indelicate. It was stretched out awkwardly on Cook's chair, straight and rigid, looking as out of place as a solitary mannequin on a Ferris wheel. And yet Stiph, though he was barely balanced on a chair about to slip away from him, reminded Cook of himself in his own favorite office sleeping position: eyes closed, legs extended, neck gouged by the sharp back of the chair (which in turn beneficially retarded blood flow to the brain), the curve of the buttocks against the edge of the seat the only means of support. So there was a naturalness to Stiph's position. But something else about him took away from this.

He had no hair.

The man's shaggy gray crop was missing, and this fact made Cook look even more closely at the body to make certain that it did actually belong to Stiph. But there was no mistaking that form. There he was, poised at last in the achievement of what perhaps had been a secret goal all along.

Cook moved forward, barely hearing the murmur of the people in the crowd at his back, none of whom had yet chosen to join him inside the office. He looked on the floor for Stiph's wig, guessing that Stiph had worn one and had somehow lost it in the course of his journey into the other world. He found nothing. He examined the head and saw patchy spots of stubble here and there and tender streaks of redness, as if the corpse had managed to shave itself. Cook backed off a step. Here indeed, he thought, was a man who followed the beat of a different drummer. He shaves his head, wanders into a strange office, and then gives up the ghost. Perhaps. But there was the skid, the skid, the sadness of that sound in the heavy night air.

"Excuse me, sir, but I want you out of here."

Cook spun around. Just inside the door stood a freckled, fat-faced man, overweight and puffing very loudly.

"Sorry," said Cook. "Are you—"

The man heaved his torso forward at the waist to pull a wallet from his rear pocket. He flashed some sort of credentials by Cook's face in a swift, sweeping motion.

"Lieutenant Leaf," the man explained as he stuffed his wallet back into his pocket. "We got a call. Do you know this man? Is he a friend of yours?"

Cook looked at Stiph's pallid face. "His name is Arthur Stiph. He's a linguist. I don't really know him. I mean not well." He looked at the Lieutenant, who returned his look with a quizzical stare. "My name's Jeremy Cook and this is my office," he quickly added.

"Ah," said Leaf. "Do you know anything about this?"

"No. I just got here. I overslept this morning and I—"

"You don't know how he got here or how he died?"

"No. I just—"

"Okay," said Leaf. "I'd like to sniff around in here. Alone. I would like you to stay close by for a while. Not in here, but close. I'll be wanting to talk to you some more, Mr. . . . Mr. Crook, is it? Har, har, har." The man actually did laugh "har, har, har," and Cook found it mildly disturbing.

"It's Cook."

"All right, Mr. Cook. Thank you." Leaf moved toward Stiph's rigid figure and leaned over the body, bringing his face right up to Stiph's peaceful countenance, and Cook backed out of his office, watching the two of them—the one thin and gaunt and dead, the other roundish and bustling. It was then that Cook realized, in some sense for the very first time, that Arthur Stiph had died. His eyes suddenly welled up with tears and his throat constricted. He forced his way through the crowd in the hall, past a blur of inquisitive and concerned faces, until he finally broke free at the edge of the crowd and found Woeps waiting for him.

"What's going on, Jeremy?"

Cook sighed. "Some detective is in there looking at him. Let's take a walk, Ed. Get away from this." They walked down the hall to the elevator and talked as they rode down to the ground floor and walked out the front door to the grass in front of the building. Cook trod lightly, remembering that it was one of Arthur's favorite napping places. They sat down on a small bench that faced the river. Woeps summarized the events of the morning for Cook. He explained how he had been working at his desk when he heard through his half-open door what he naturally thought was Cook entering his office next door. But instead of hearing the soft groan that so often accompanied Cook's entry into his den of labor, he heard a scream that sent his pen scribbling reflexively across the page. In the hall he found Mary shaking at Cook's door. He reached out to calm her and a spastically swinging elbow caught him on the chin, causing him to bite his tongue painfully. (He showed Cook the welt; it was a large one.) Then he, too, saw Stiph. He examined the body and groped for a pulse—feeling stupid, he said, as he looked for signs of life from a wrist already rigid from death. Then he steered Mary down the hall to a couch in the staff lounge and called the police.

"You noticed his head?" asked Cook.

"Yes." Woeps stared straight ahead for a moment. "It made his whole body look funny. Surprised-like." He turned to Cook. "You were saying something about last night, Jeremy. What happened?"

Cook sighed. "Yes. Last night." He explained what he had heard and what he had done, recreating the events of the night before in some detail—for his own benefit as much as for Woeps's.

"So I left the door wide open and the light on." He paused. "Which suggests . . . well . . . a couple of possibilities, I guess."

"One of them," said Woeps, "is that Arthur was taking a late-night walk and saw the light up there and decided to explore. Or take a nap."

"After shaving his head," added Cook.

"Yes. There is that."

"What I think," said Cook, "is that some sonofabitch ran into him and killed him and thought it would be a neat idea to plant the body in my office."

"After shaving his head," Woeps pointed out.

"Yeah. There is that, isn't there?"

"And that part really bothers me, Jeremy. It suggests a certain craziness, a sickness." Woeps shook his head.

"He was so harmless, so benign," said Cook. "He never said a bad word about anybody. The teachers really loved him. One of the girls in the crowd up there was crying loudly—I mean really sobbing. I heard it while I was in the office looking at him."

"Yes. I heard it too."

The two men sat for a while and stared at the muddy river below them. The spring rains had caused it to rise, and it rushed by noisily. Cook rose to his feet and sighed. "We'd better get back up there. That detective wanted to talk to me."

"Was he the fat, freckled one?"

"Yeah. A weird duck."

Another such approached the two men as they walked back to the front entrance to the building. It was Aaskhugh, apparently just arriving for work. He looked dapper in a seersucker suit and whistled as he walked, as if he were celebrating something.

"Hello, Jay. Hello, Daisy. Hello to the two of you. What's brewing?"

Woeps turned to Cook, giving him the floor. After all, it was in Cook's office that the body had been found. Besides, Woeps didn't talk to Aaskhugh much. Cook's eyes gleamed hard as he framed a response.

"Personally, Adam, I think a storm is brewing. The air has been awfully thick the last few days. Have you ever wondered at the inaccuracy of weather reports in the Midwest? Do you know why they're like that?" Cook noticed Woeps staring at him from the side, his brow creased with wonder at this irrelevance.

"No, Jeremy," said Aaskhugh, faltering a bit, his eyes beginning to dart back and forth.

"Neither do I, Adam. Neither do I. Besides, Arthur Stiph was found dead in my office this morning. Freshly tonsured, too."

Aaskhugh registered surprise, to be sure, but probably less at the fact of Stiph's death than at the fact that Cook, after years of fruitless interrogation, was finally bringing forth news of some substance. He inquired into the matter, showing a true zealot's concern for detail, and, if any were to be found, parties that could conceivably be held responsible. Aaskhugh's inquiries normally went in this direction anyway, so the questions tripped easily from his tongue.

Woeps nudged Cook. "Here comes the ambulance crew, Jeremy." Cook watched two white-coated men roll a stretcher up the sidewalk and through the doors. Accompanying the men were three more policemen.

"I wonder what the autopsy will show," Cook mumbled to no one besides himself.

Aaskhugh heard it. "Do you have reason to believe it will show anything unusual?"

Cook said no and made sure that his tone implied unequivocally that he was hiding something.

"I'd like to see those skid marks, Jeremy," said Woeps with an indiscretion that made Cook want to yell at him.

"What skid marks?" asked Aaskhugh, forever Johnny-on-the-spot.

"The brown skid marks on the inside of your underwear," Cook wanted very much to say. "I'll explain it to you later, Adam," he said, lying for the first time that day.

The threesome walked to the building. As they waited for the elevator, Aaskhugh rocked silently back and forth on his heels, clucking his tongue. He finally spoke.

"Stiph was an odd case. Worked hard before coming here, then tapered off. I found his work in the year or so he was here to be no more than ordinary, though I never said so, at least not to him. But these things have to be said now."

Do they? thought Cook.

"Slept a lot, didn't he?" Aaskhugh continued. "I never could make much sense of that. Shame he had to go though. But perhaps it's for the best."

They stepped into the elevator. Cook wanted to say something, but he was stumped by Aaskhugh's idiocy. Woeps, too, remained silent as the elevator rose, while Aaskhugh continued to rock back and forth on his heels, musing.

"I think I'll just run down and take a little peek," Aaskhugh said as he stepped out of the elevator on the seventh floor and bustled down the hall.

"What an ass!" said Woeps, hissing. "What an utter ass he is."

"I've been telling you that for years, Ed. That was some thumbnail biography, wasn't it? Come on. Let's go get some coffee."

They opened the door into the central core and walked down the hallway. The eating area was crowded with linguists, teachers, and a few parents. Milke and Orffmann were talking to a young mother who appeared to be quite upset. By some quirk, Paula was again standing at the coffeepot and talking, this time to Wach. Cook noticed a redness in her eyes and a puffy look about her. Then he saw the same look on the faces of many of the teachers. Paula turned away from Wach and moved toward Cook and Woeps and then past them into the hall without looking at them. Wach beckoned to Cook, who wondered deeply what his boss was going to say.

"This is a sad day for Wabash," said Wach. Although this was a bit funereal and too public for Cook's taste, it at least suggested that some blood coursed through the man's body. He hadn't, after all, begun by asking Cook why he had been late with the grant proposal. "Wabash will miss Arthur Stiph. We will all miss him." He looked around the immediate area for support. "Do you know anything about this, Jeremy?"

"No." On saying this Cook realized he did know something, so he told Wach what he had told Woeps.

"But you didn't see anything?" asked Wach.

"No."

"Pity." Wach cleared his throat. "I had better get back out to the hall. I want to get the police out of here as soon as possible. This is all very awkward for Wabash, besides being tragic. Very awkward."

As Wach hurried away Cook spied a supine figure on a couch in the corner. It was Mary the Secretary, recovering from her encounter with the Grim Reaper. Cook hesitated a moment, then walked over to the couch to console her.

"How are you doing, Mary?" he asked.

She was lying on her back with one arm raised, sheltering her eyes. At the sound of Cook's voice she pulled her arm away and her eyes popped open. The one action seemed to follow from the other. She reminded Cook of a toy doll that would do interesting things if you moved her limbs just right.

"You!" she said loudly, startling him. She raised her head. "You knew he was in there. You sent me there just to torture me. You *knew* it."

"Don't be silly, Mary," Cook protested gently. "I had no idea—"

"You knew it, you cocksucker!" she screamed, causing all conversations in the room to terminate in mid-syllable. Heads turned. "You cocksucker! You're nothing but a big cocksucker, Dr. Cook!" She gave the word careful articulation, as if she were not used to pronouncing it regularly.

Cook allowed himself to be tugged away by Woeps, thankful indeed that his friend was doing it so that he could get away from this crazed banshee. He smiled awkwardly at the faces that blurred by. At the same time he became aware of crying from the playrooms. The infants and children were crying much more than usual, as if sensing and giving voice to the grief in the building. He heard the voices of the teachers vainly trying to calm them. He began to feel responsible for it all. It was almost as if Mary's accusations were justified. He shook his head at the thought. It was crazy.

The stretcher bearing the draped body of Arthur Stiph rolled past, wheeled by two clean-shaven young men who gave off no odor whatsoever.

"Let's go to my office, Jeremy," said Woeps. "It'll be quiet there." On the way, they were stopped by a uniformed policeman, who finally let them pass after Woeps explained they were going to his office, not to Cook's. Cook glanced into it as they passed by and saw several men in there, among them Lieutenant Leaf, who appeared to be in the act of smelling his fingers.

Leaf spied Cook and called out, "Dr. Cook? I would like to have those few words with you now."

Cook stopped and backed up two steps.

"Where can we talk?" asked Leaf, approaching him and wiping his hands on a handkerchief.

"You can use my office," volunteered Woeps. "It's right next door."

"Ah," said Leaf with a large smile as he turned his attention to Woeps. "That's very handy. Have you been in your office already today, sir?"

"Yes. There's nothing unusual about it. No bodies."

"No bodies, har, har, har. So you were in your office before the deceased was found this morning?"

"Before and during. I heard the secretary scream and I ran out and saw him sitting there at Jeremy's desk. I checked his pulse and called the police."

"Ah. Yes. I'll be wanting to talk to you a little later, Mr. . . . "

"Woeps. Ed Woeps."

"Mr. Woeps. Or should it be *Dr.* Woeps? I can never—"

"It doesn't matter."

Leaf frowned at this. "Very well. The secretary, too. I'll be wanting to talk to her."

"You can find me in the lounge. The secretary should be there, too." Woeps unlocked his door for the two men. He turned to Cook. "I'll see you later, Jeremy. Sit down and take it easy." Cook nodded.

Lieutenant Leaf gestured for Cook to enter the office. He complied, a little nervous, and sat down in Woeps's chair. The desk was littered with medical insurance papers. Leaf leaned against the door, his arms folded across his large torso. He looked at Cook.

"So. Let's begin at the beginning."

* * *

Some time later a weary Cook led the detective down the hall past milling policemen, linguists, teachers, and one escaped toddler who shouldn't have been out in the hall. One of the teachers scooped the child into her arms and took him back into the gym. Cook preceded Leaf down the same stairs he had descended so quickly the night before, then along the hall leading to the back entrance of the building, which opened out onto the road. They were going to look at the skid marks, which Leaf had enthusiastically seized on during Cook's narrative, without, however, indicating to Cook exactly why they interested him so much.

Cook opened the back entrance for Leaf, trying to be obliging in all ways. Leaf grunted his thanks. A strong smell of tar greeted the two men. Cook heard a loud burp from the road, where several county road workers were sprawled on the grass eating lunch. Out of a small trailer-like machine at the edge of the road a thin wisp of black smoke was rising, fouling the air. The road lay in shambles. Jackhammers—Cook suddenly remembered having heard them as he bent over Stiph's body, as he and Woeps sat and talked farther up the road around the corner of the building, and as Leaf interrogated him in Woeps's office.

Leaf turned to Cook after surveying the scene below them. "This is the road?" he asked.

Cook nodded.

"The skid marks were on the part of the road that has been torn up?"

Cook nodded again, biting his lip.

"The skid marks now sit in those two dump trucks over there? They're nothing but little crumbs of asphalt now?"

"I'm afraid so, Lieutenant."

"Mr. Cook," said the detective, raising his hands in front of him, outstretched, palms upward, presenting the scene below them for Cook's consideration, "Mr. Cook, this is a sonofabitch."

Cook looked at Leaf. "Lieutenant, you believe what I told you, don't you?"

Leaf laughed—a brief, impatient chuckle this time, far from his accustomed belly laugh. "Mr. Cook, spare me your selfish fears. I believe everything until I run into things that force me to change my beliefs. That hasn't happened yet." He stared at the workers below them, then stuffed his hands in his pockets and kicked at a pebble on the sidewalk. "I hate coincidences," he said bitterly.

"If ever there was one, this is it," offered Cook.

"And you oversleeping is another," Leaf said quickly.

Cook frowned. "I suppose it is. But not unrelated. In a way I overslept because of the skidding, as I explained earlier."

"Which you coincidentally overheard because you coincidentally were working late in your office, your coincidental window being coincidentally open. Just how often do you work that late at night in your office?"

"Once or twice a month," Cook answered truthfully.

"I'm glad I'm not a statistician," said Leaf. "If I were I'd lock you up on sheer improbability."

Umbrage, said Cook to himself, trying to focus his thoughts. Take umbrage. You have the right. "Now just a minute, Lieutenant," he said with some warmth. "You are in no position legally to make that sort of threat."

"Cook," said Leaf, his bulk suddenly looming larger, "don't disappoint me. I spend far too much time as it is dealing with the mental dregs of Kinsey County, which has plenty, let me tell you. There are more crazy Hoosiers out there than you would ever think possible. Now you are probably an intelligent man. I definitely am. Let's meet each other on that basis and save the butter for our potatoes. I'm a policeman who wants to find out who killed that guy up there. If you didn't do it you can help me find out who did. Whatever happens, don't pretend to be stupid and normal and don't for Christ's sake pull rank on me as a civilian. I'll honor that by not being stupid and normal and by not pulling rank on you as the law. Do I make myself clear?"

Cook hesitated an instant. "Perfectly, Lieutenant. I appreciate your . . . your—"

"Good," Leaf said crisply.

Cook cleared his throat. "You think someone killed him then?"

Leaf smiled. "My preliminary examination showed that the man received a blow to the back of his head so severe that it could have been self-inflicted only if he (a) dropped from a great height and landed only on his head, or (b) ran backward into a brick wall at a speed of say twenty miles per hour."

"Both being rather unlikely, given his presence in my office," said Cook, wanting to contribute.

"Right," said Leaf, smiling slightly. "Right."

"Lieutenant, if someone did kill Stiph, and if he killed him out here by running over him, why wasn't the body mangled? And why was his head shaved?"

"I don't know," Leaf said thoughtfully, "but here's a first approximation. When people . . ." He paused and looked closely at Cook. "What are you smiling at?"

Cook raised a hand, half in self-defense, half in apology. "Sorry.

That's a favorite phrase in linguistic research, when a linguist is formulating a rough hypothesis: 'a first approximation.' "

"Well," said Leaf, appearing more pleased than Cook would have expected, "as I was saying, when people are hit by a car, the major injury is usually sustained as a result of a secondary blow—landing on a pavement, against a tree, against another car. Very often—and this answers your question about his hair, or at least it attempts to answer it—very often the body flies up, the center of gravity being above the bumper in an adult body of normal—"

"Excuse me, Lieutenant," Cook heard from the building in back of them.

Leaf turned to the door. A uniformed policeman held it open for him. "The woman upstairs, Lieutenant, the one who found the body . . . she's giving us a little trouble. Says she wants to go home, and that whoever is supposed to be asking her questions had better do it soon. That's what she said. Stolewicz is trying to calm her down, but she slapped him, and—"

"I'll be right up," said Leaf. He let out a soft string of curse words, then turned to Cook. "Can you stop by my office later this afternoon? About four? It's in the basement of City Hall. I'd like to get a more detailed account of what happened last night—times, skid marks, all that. Try to think of anything else that might help." He headed for the door.

"Suspects, too?" Cook called after him.

Leaf looked back at him. "Hell yes, suspects," he said gruffly. "I want to catch this guy and skewer him."

Cook remained outside for some time, leaning against the building and gazing down at the road now barren of clues. He wondered how much, exactly, a trained eye could have determined from the skid marks. He filed the question away for his next talk with Leaf. Suspects. The body in the office. Key to the office? No, it was unlocked, the door open. Key to the building? Yes. It was always locked at that hour. He realized with dismay that the killer could well be among the other linguists on the staff. None of the teachers had keys to the building, nor did Mary the Secretary. Cook, Woeps, Wach, Aaskhugh, Milke, Orffmann, and Miss Pristam. She was out of town—had been for a month and would be for another two. And unless he was insane, he, Cook, was not a suspect.

Woeps. Wach. Aaskhugh. Milke. Orffmann. That would make day-to-day life somewhat awkward.

He looked down at the road below. One of the workers had stolen an orange from the lunch box of another worker, and a group of them were throwing it around, playing keep-away. The wind came up and the sky blackened. The workers gathered their things together and scrambled for cover, and the heavy rain that had threatened for so long finally made good on the threat. Cook stood close to the building, sheltered, and watched the rain come down.

FOUR

"HELLO?"

"Hello," Cook said into the phone in a voice very different from his normal one. What he aimed for was the crackerjack, fast-talking, wide-lapeled wiseacre who was the newspaper reporter in every American film made in the thirties and forties. High-pitched, like Dan Duryea, with a bit of the owl-faced guy from *Citizen Kane* thrown in. Being a sensitive phonetician, this and other imitations came easily to him. "Is this Miss Dorothy Plough?"

"Yes, it is."

"Philpot here, Dorothy. Henry Philpot." Cook read from a prepared text so that he could concentrate on being sufficiently bumptious. "Haven't got you out of bed, have I?"

"No, not at all. I just finished breakfast. What did you say your—"

"Philpot's the name, writing's the game. I'm doing a little magazine piece on a cozy place down the road known locally as Baby Heaven but a.k.a. the Wabash Institute. Perhaps you've seen me roaming and combing the halls."

"Oh, yes, I've heard of you. In fact—"

"Did we meet?" Cook asked nervously, feeling himself slip out of character as he departed from his text. "I've met so many of you lovely girls I can hardly keep you all straight."

"No, we haven't met. But—"

"Good. Or what I mean is, it's good to be talking to you, Dorothy." He bit his lip and pressed on quickly. "The reason I'm calling is that I like to make a practice of getting in touch with the nuts-and-bolts people in an organization and bellying up to them and feeling them up and down to get a real sense of a place, you know what I mean?"

"Yes," she said uncertainly. "I think so."

"I do it telephonically," he said. "The telephone is the investigative reporter's chief tool of the trade, you know. Somebody said that once, good old what's-his-name. Ha! I'd like some of your impressions of Wabash—the work, the kids, the people there. Straight from the shoulder. The straight dope from the Pope. For example, what do you have to say about this fellow Cook?"

"Dr. Cook?"

"Yes. This fellow Cook." He heard a pause and a sigh. He strained every muscle as he listened. His eyes were popped open at their widest.

"I'm not sure . . ."

"Yes?"

"I'm not sure what you want me to say. What do I think of him?"

"Yes. That."

"Apart from wanting to go to bed with him?" She laughed, boldly.

By way of response Cook coughed and gagged in confusion.

"Seriously, though, he's wonderful. He's just a wonderful man. Friendly, energetic, devoted to his work. He makes that place go. And he never pulls rank on anybody, the way some of the others do. Everyone I know at Wabash is really fond of him."

Fond? Fond?

"Now Dr. Orffmann is a different kettle of fish." As she went on to fry this particular fish, Cook scowled in disappointment. He wanted to get this business out of the way, and here was Dorothy Plough, a prime suspect on the basis of a sneer he thought he had seen from her once, letting him down and in fact talking like someone who would never call him even a marginal asshole.

". . . and Dr. Milke, despite his considerable charm, is a bit overbearing at times . . ."

Cook hardly listened. He didn't care about these people. He had one question he wanted answered. But he couldn't very well call up all fifteen or so teachers at Wabash and run through this Philpot routine with them. And his original plan of getting the information out of Paula seemed ill-conceived too. In fact it was a sudden loss of faith in that plan over breakfast that had prompted this call. Paula probably wouldn't even speak to him, at least not civilly. And she was so good-looking. Buxom, too, as they used to say. Why did they stop saying that? He clenched his fist angrily.

". . . and Dr. Aaskhugh is just a *total* twit . . ."

It was hopeless. He was doomed to wander the halls of Wabash in ridiculous ignorance, a "Complete Asshole" sign taped to his back. With some impatience he interrupted her and said he had an urgent call to make. Fearing he had been a bit abrupt, he added a word of thanks.

"Before you go," she said hurriedly, "I wanted to tell you that Dr. Wach has been asking for you. You haven't been to Wabash for a couple days, have you?"

It took Cook a moment to realize Wach had been looking for Philpot, not himself. "Well, no. Actually, I've been pretty busy here at the . . . at the motel."

She laughed. "Must be some kind of motel."

Cook chuckled nervously. How could he know where Philpot was? He was tired of being asked that question. "Tell him that I'll be in later today. After the Stiph funeral. And thanks again for your help. It really put some things in perspective for me."

"Anytime, Phil."

As he hung up he wondered if Philpot actually was going to the funeral. He hoped this call didn't create any trouble for him. He felt a twinge of guilt about it. The hypothetical baboon he had impersonated had nothing to do with the mild-mannered Philpot. He glanced at his watch and went into the bedroom, and after rummaging around in the dark recesses of his closet he finally found a plain black suit, severely out of both fashion and season. He was surprised that he owned such a thing, and, upon trying it on, that it still fit him.

Arthur Stiph would be pleased. The elderly linguist was scheduled to be laid to rest in one hour, and Cook had decided, after prolonged internal debate, that yes, it would be proper for him to attend the funeral. It had taken him some time to quash the arguments he could raise against his going. After all, he hadn't been very close to Stiph, and he always thought it in bad taste for tangential people to intrude on intimate ceremonies. Also, his name had become connected with Stiph's death in a most uncomfortable way. Since Wednesday morning he had been interviewed more times than he could remember. In each instance he had offered a thorough, businesslike narrative of the events of Tuesday night and carefully declined to speculate when prodded to do so—or to "extrapolate," as he was asked to do by one skinny reporter. But no matter how professionally Cook had spoken, the body had definitely been found sitting at his desk. He became something of a suspect in the public eye, or "a figure linked to the crime," or something. Whatever it was, he didn't like it.

Despite these arguments, Cook had decided to go to the funeral. There were some good arguments for it, of course. It had been two days since Stiph's body was found, and Cook hadn't left the house in all that time. He had called in sick and stayed home, working a bit in his study and puttering around the house. Wabash seemed like a good place to be away from for a few days. Especially his office and desk and chair. It made sense to return to worldly activity via Stiph's funeral. There was a nice unity and completeness to that approach. Besides, he genuinely wanted to have a silent last word with Arthur, and this was sufficient reason for going.

His little holiday at home had been healthy and constructive. He hadn't drunk too much, for example. Also, he had mowed the lawn, painted the back porch railing, and started his small annual garden. But he made a point of not washing his car. It would have been difficult to respond politely to some passer-by's joking query as to whether he had gotten all the blood off. Such a query certainly was possible. The skid marks, brief though their existence was, were public knowledge. Stiph had been run over. This was Leaf's opinion, as Cook had learned in the course of his Wednesday afternoon reunion with the detective, and it was the medical examiner's opinion, as Cook had learned, wincing with every utterance of his own name, from the Wednesday night news. That afternoon Leaf was able to finish making the point he had started to make earlier in the day, namely that the normal human body, having a center of gravity at roughly waist level, upon being struck by the bumper of a car is often thrown into the air in a snapping fashion, causing the head to resound fatally against some portion of the hood near the windshield, if not against the windshield itself. Stiph presumably had struck some car with his head, and Leaf had declared to Cook, "Show me a car with a dent in the hood and you've shown me the weapon." (It was no coincidence that the detective accompanied Cook out to the parking lot near the police station for a casual look at his old Valiant. Leaf found nothing incriminating, but he did say that the car was a rather dull one for a distinguished scholar like Cook to be driving.)

Stiph's head had been shaved, Leaf surmised, so there would be no traces of paint clinging to his hair that might lead an assiduous investigator (such as himself, he added) to the killing vehicle. "We're dealing with a clever fellow," Leaf said to him. "He's taken care of the whole boiling." Cook, amazed at the way Leaf repeatedly taxed his decoding skills, interpreted this to mean that the killer had allowed for all conceivable contingencies. There were, however, traces of the car on Stiph's person that had been overlooked by the driver: a hint of chrome on his pants leg and a bit of windshield wiper rubber embedded in his left ear. Not a great deal, but something.

There was also a trace of the killer in Cook's office—again nothing great, but something. It was a small puddle on the floor made up of bourbon and vanilla ice cream. This fact, stonily reported without elaboration on the Thursday night news, must have baffled all of Kinsey's population with the exception of Cook and the police, for Lieutenant Leaf had briefed Cook on just this point the preceding afternoon. Without mincing any words.

"We figure the guy puked in your office," he announced. "From overexertion, from anxiety, from nausea at hauling a corpse around . . . it's hard to say." When Cook asked if this was an important lead, Leaf shrugged. "Ice cream's ice cream," he said. "Fuck me if I can make anything out of it." Cook nodded uncomfortably at this, not sure of the semantic thrust of the imperative apodosis.

Leaf concluded with a final point, just as Cook was leaving the police station: the building at Wabash had been broken into. Cook smiled warmly at the news, for while it confounded the case, it cleared—or held promise of clearing—his colleagues. There was no point in breaking into a building you had a key to. But Cook's heart sank when Leaf went on to say that he felt "uneasy about the nature of the break-in"—a broken basement window—that something "wasn't quite right" about it, that he had a "funny feeling" about it, and that he just didn't feel "right." These remarks remained obscure and unelaborated, so Cook left the Lieutenant's office with ineffably "funny" feelings about just about everything in the whole case—the whole boiling, in other words.

Cook leaned toward the mirror and straightened his tie. Not a bad dark suit, he thought. Not a very good one either. Warm, too, and it was going to be a hot day. He looked in his closet at some more stylish alternatives. More stylish, to be sure, but all of them inappropriate for a funeral. He closed the closet door. With this suit he would be properly bland and unnoticeable, just part of the background.

He looked at his watch. "Damn!" It had obviously stopped some time ago. He gathered his keys and wallet, ran out to his car, and drove off. The cemetery was on the other side of town. When he reached Kinsey he weaved from lane to lane and swore at the red lights until they turned green. He hoped his tardiness wouldn't be conspicuous. Somehow it seemed in terribly bad taste to be late for a funeral.

He stopped his car at the cemetery gate and looked in. A narrow road ran through the gate and then climbed for a short distance before dropping down into the area where the headstones stretched out. This little hill prevented Cook from seeing any sign of a funeral below, but the cars parked along the narrow road and then spilling out of the gate along the main road in both directions attested to a sizeable crowd down there at Stiph's grave. He backed his car down the main road and parked it at the tail end of the line of cars. Then he trotted back to the gate and up over the little knoll.

A large crowd was gathered at one of the gravesites several hundred feet below him. Cook walked down the gentle slope, recognizing first Woeps's prematurely stooped figure, then, as he came nearer, Orffmann's large neck, Milke's beard and pipe, Wach's plumb-line posture, Paula's long hair, and other people's attributes. A few heads turned as he approached—a solitary figure dressed in black slowly working his way down the green hillside. Then it seemed that a few more gazes settled on him. He moved on resolutely, cursing his luck. That portion of the group that hadn't yet noticed Cook—all those with their backs completely to him—suddenly looked up. En masse they swung their stares in his direction. What had attracted their attention was the mournful sound of taps being played by a bugler perched some distance in back of him at the top of the hill. The naturally curious eyes that rose solemnly from the grave in search of the bugler landed easily on Cook and remained fixed there.

Cook continued on after glancing over his shoulder to locate the bugler and then recommend him to perdition. Then he slowed down. Should he be walking? Shouldn't he stop? Yes. He should stop for the playing of taps. That was why they were all looking at him. He stopped and folded his hands in front of him. A few eyes left him, but not enough. He stood rooted in embarrassment alone on the side of the hill while the clear notes sounded in the air. As the melancholy tune came to an end, the eyes slowly left Cook and returned to Stiph's grave. Cook moved forward again, quickly, and as he arrived at the edge of the crowd he heard someone say "Amen," and a small sigh arose from the crowd. There began a general milling about. Cook sighed, wanting to share at least that much with the crowd. Amid soft murmurs, people began to walk back up the hill. Cook nudged his way through the crowd, fighting against the general flow, trying to get closer to the coffin sitting aboveground beside the open grave. He noticed uneasily that there was a spirited festiveness of color in the dresses and suits on all sides of him—a sharp contrast to his own lugubrious, blackish hue. Didn't people wear black to funerals anymore? He felt stupidly uninformed.

Someone was tugging at his sleeve. For an instant he thought it might be some kind of usher demanding to see his ticket. But, thankfully, it was Woeps. His face carried a look of worry and dread—just the kind of face that was right for a funeral, except that it was more or less his permanent face.

"What happened, Jeremy?"

Cook looked at him and shrugged. "I was late," he said.

"I know you were late, but . . ." Woeps smiled sadly. "Sorry. I see what you're saying. You're saying—"

"I'm saying," Cook whispered hotly to him, "that I was late, and if the killer hadn't stuck the body in my office and if the funeral director hadn't put that stupid trumpeter up on the hill, no one would give a sweet goddamn about it."

Woeps frowned. "Look, Jeremy, don't take it out—"

"Oh I'm not mad at you, Ed," he said. He took his glasses off and rubbed the bridge of his nose. "Jesus, what a rotten time I've been having."

Woeps reached out and squeezed his arm near the shoulder. "You shouldn't let this get to you, Jeremy. None of it's your fault. Come on, I'll buy you a cup of coffee or something."

Cook shook his head. "I'd like to stay here a minute or two, Ed. I didn't come here just to be stared at." He looked at the coffin. Woeps followed his eyes.

"All right, Jeremy. I'll wait for you up by my car."

"Don't wait, Ed." Cook turned to him. "I'll see you back at work." His friend hesitated a moment, then nodded and moved off with the last of the crowd. Cook watched the clusters of people moving up the hillside before he turned back to the gravesite. The coffin lying beside the open grave looked thick, dark, and expensive. Cook began to stare at it, for that's what people were supposed to do at funerals. It was a privilege the living had over the dead. He began to feel better. It was right for him to be alone with Stiph now.

But he was not quite alone. A solitary figure stood directly on the other side of the coffin, an old woman in black. The widow? Not likely, thought Cook. People didn't leave widows alone like that at funerals. A sister? An old, secret lover? She was looking at Cook. Then she was speaking to him.

"Why are you still here?" she called out across the coffin. She hadn't stressed *you*, so she hadn't singled Cook out and questioned, in particular, *his* being there. Her voice was the voice of an old woman, but it was as clear as the notes of the bugle that had sounded just minutes before.

Cook shrugged and put his hands in his pockets. "I was late," he said across the coffin.

She began to move toward him, circling in a wide arc around the coffin. "I noticed," she said. "Who are you?"

"My name's Jeremy Cook. I work at the Wabash Institute."

She cocked her head a bit to one side, coming still closer, moving slowly. When she reached him she turned and faced the coffin and said, "Yes, he mentioned you from time to time."

Cook swallowed. "Arthur?" he asked. "Your husband?"

"Yes," she said. "He died in your office."

"He was found dead in my office, yes."

"Ah." She smiled. "Precision. Arthur was that way, too, Mr. Cook. I hope his *being found dead* in your office hasn't inconvenienced you awfully . . . hasn't been overly embarrassing for you." Cook at first took this as haughty and self-pitying, but a glance at the woman's face told him she was genuinely concerned for his position. She seemed to appreciate the way in which he had, in a sense, been compromised.

"It *has* been a little awkward," he said. He noticed that she was not a beautiful woman. Nor was it possible to see traces of an earlier beauty made dim by time. She was merely old and small. Her hair was unkempt and her black dress frayed and wrinkled.

"My condolences," she said, smiling weakly.

Again Cook was suspicious of her meaning, but again she appeared to be serious. "The same here," he said, gesturing offhandedly toward the coffin. They stood together in silence for a moment. The air was very still. In the distance, over the hill, Cook could faintly hear the slamming of doors and the starting of cars as the mourners drove off.

"What was your husband like, Mrs. Stiph?" Cook asked. "I can't say that I knew him very well as a person."

She stared straight ahead at the coffin, thinking. He tried again.

"Mrs. Stiph, I was wondering what your husband was like." Maybe, he hoped, she liked her questions to be in subordinate clauses.

She stood motionless a while longer before responding. "Mr. Cook, when I walked over here to stand with you I did not do so in the hopes you would ask me questions such as that one." She continued to look straight ahead. Cook waited, not finding it easy. He studied her face. She let him do this, in fact seemed to invite it. She seemed resolved and angry more than anything else. Was she angry because she was alone? Why was there no one to stand by her side at this moment in her life? No one but Cook. Perhaps that was why she was talking with him. Or rather, not talking with him, which was the case right now. But then her eyes changed, taking on a focus that they had lacked.

"Mr. Cook . . . Jeremy—may I call you Jeremy? Yes, I may," she said quickly. "Jeremy, if you were lying in that box instead of my husband, and if I were here at your funeral talking to some friend of yours, let's say that friend you were speaking with just a moment ago, and if I asked him, 'Sir, what was your friend like? What was this fellow Cook like?' what would he say? What would you want him to say?"

She had spoken without once turning to him. She stopped speaking, but her eyes remained brightly focused. She was waiting for an answer. Cook wished she hadn't stopped, at least with that question, for he knew that question well. But he spoke up, trying very hard.

"I would want my friend to say something about me. Something significant."

She stood very still. Then she nodded. "Significant."

"Yes. A story about me. Stories are best. Better than mere words."

"Yes."

Cook sighed a small sigh of relief, feeling stupidly proud of her approval.

"And could he, Jeremy? Could he tell such a story?"

"My friend? The one you just saw?"

"Yes. That one." She looked straight at the coffin, as if she were communicating as much with Arthur as with Jeremy. Her face was determined.

"I don't know," he said softly.

"You don't know. And can you say what story you would want him to tell?"

Cook reached up and rubbed the bridge of his nose under his glasses. "I would have to think about that for a while," he said.

"You would have to think about that for a while," she repeated. "Would you consider it presumptuous of your friend to *try* to—"

"No," he said quickly. "I would definitely want him to try."

She nodded. "I'm afraid I don't have a story to tell you, Jeremy. But I have a story, a written story, to pass on to you. Arthur wrote it when he was an undergraduate at Yale. It tells about a rather . . . unusual and dear man who seeks out certain kinds of people and arranges meetings with them, and then . . . well, I'll let you read it." She paused and tilted her head back and looked at him closely. "I'm giving it to you because it will tell you something important about Arthur and so answer your question, which I take very seriously. This will probably be the last time anyone ever asks me about him. But I'm giving you the story also because it will help you know why he died, or at least why he was where he was when that car struck him. That night, Tuesday night, when he left the house, he said to me, 'Adelle, I'm going out. I've got a backfriend to meet.' "

"A 'backfriend'?"

"Yes. Evidently he had a late-night appointment with someone at Wabash. That was the way he liked to do it."

"But what's a 'backfriend'?"

She smiled. "I'll let Arthur explain it to you. You'll see." She faced the coffin. "Things bothered Arthur, Jeremy. He fought them. He fought hard. I tried to help him where I could." She took a few steps forward, removed a glove from one hand, and reached out and ran a long, bare finger along the top edge of the coffin. Her finger moved slowly, as if she were feeling the wood for imperfections. She turned and looked at Cook. "He had some good years left. He was healthy." She blinked.

For a moment she did not move. Then with an archaic touch of grace, she reached a hand out to Cook. He stepped forward and took it in his own. Together they began the long walk up the grassy hill. Neither of them spoke. Cook was conscious only of isolated sounds in the air—a solitary cardinal high in a tree, in search of a mate, perhaps, a car door slamming somewhere out of sight over the hill as the last of the mourners drove off, a clanking sound from the graveyard toolshed some distance off to the side.

At the top of the hill there were two cars, one just inside the gate, a Volkswagen—Mrs. Stiph's car, apparently—and Cook's Valiant sitting alone far down the main road. Cook walked her to her car. He opened the door for her and she slowly got in.

"Thank you, Jeremy," she said, looking up at him as she reached in her purse for her keys. "I don't need you anymore. You might, though, every now and then, think of an old couple—a couple who were happy for many years." She then said, rather firmly, "I'm glad you turned out the way you are. Good-bye." She waved to him, almost as if he were a great distance away instead of leaning down to the window right beside her.

She drove off. Cook watched the car move down the road and around a turn, and he continued to look long after it had disappeared from view. Then a metallic clank behind him attracted his attention. Curious, he walked back up to the top of the knoll overlooking the graves. In the distance below, two diggers were walking toward Stiph's grave. One of them lazily dragged his shovel behind him, and here and there it banged against a headstone. Cook took one last look at the coffin before turning away.

Not your run-of-the-mill widow, he said to himself as he walked through the cemetery gate. But then Stiph might not have been your run-of-the-mill husband. What about the story she had mentioned? Should he call her about it when he got home? Whom had Stiph planned to meet? Would the story tell him? How could it, if, as she said, he had written it years ago?

He kicked at the gravel along the edge of the road as he walked to his car.

FIVE

NEAR THE WINDSHIELD ON THE DRIVER'S SIDE HE BENT over to look at it, more curious than upset. There was nothing to indicate what might have caused it. No rocks lying in the area, no young ruffians, no vandalizing squirrels scampering about with oversized acorns. As he frowned and stared at the dent, his scalp suddenly chilled, for some passing quirk of his imagination revealed the contours of Arthur Stiph's head in the depression. But that was impossible. Cook hadn't killed him. Someone else had. Several days ago—Tuesday night. This was Friday.

So where had the dent come from? Had Stiph, seeing the way Cook was carrying on with his widow, reached out from the grave with a bony fist and smashed Cook's car in jealous anger?

No, thought Cook with mounting awareness. There was another explanation—one more conformable to earthly laws.

"Damn!" he said loudly. "What a rotten sonofabitch he must be." He felt the dent, then quickly withdrew his hand. He clenched his fists, feeling more keenly than ever the injustice of what was happening to him. To *him*. Forget about Stiph—he was dead and gone and there was no changing that. But why couldn't he go on with his own life? "What a rotten sonofabitch!" he said again. He examined the rest of the car's exterior and found, to his surprise but not to his great surprise, a tiny piece of fabric, jagged at the edges, hooked on a small piece of chrome in the grill.

He quickly resolved to drive directly to the police station and tell Leaf about it. Thank God the detective had already examined his car, thank God for that. He put the piece of wool into his shirt pocket, choosing not to leave it in its natural state for fear it might blow away in transit. Then, as he drove toward the main road leading back into town, he tried to chase down the thought that threatened to elude him. Whoever put that dent in his car must have known that there existed the possibility of a dent—that "dentedness" was a relevant concept. Which proved, or at least contributed substantially to the view, that there was, after all, a dent in the vehicle that had done the killing.

The Lieutenant was out, Cook was told by a large, white-faced sergeant who gave the appearance of being an excellent bowler. When was he expected back? Cook asked politely, though he felt this information should have been offered along with the report that Leaf was out. Forty-five minutes, give or take. Could he be reached? No, impossible. Could he be informed upon his return that Jeremy Cook was looking for him? Yes, for what it was worth. Would it be profitable for Cook to return at one o'clock, when the Lieutenant was expected back? Perhaps, but no one was making any promises. Would the tight-lipped sergeant enjoy squatting on a hot poker? Perhaps, but no one was making any promises.

As he stood on the sidewalk outside City Hall, Cook wondered why some people were allowed to exist when others weren't. He sighed and consulted his stomach. He wasn't hungry—a rather grunty breakfast had had a concretizing effect on his lower system—but if he didn't eat soon he would become hungry, probably at an inconvenient time. He began to walk the two blocks that separated the police station from his favorite bar and grill. This was the Circus Maximus, also known by some in the area as the Circus, by others as Max's. As he walked he felt a strange sleepiness settle over him. He wondered what he should eat or drink to make it go away, and it suddenly struck him that his whole life was a stupidly futile struggle to be mentally alert.

Inside Max's he found a quiet booth for himself after a quick survey revealed none of his colleagues in the crowd at the bar or at any of the tables. A darkish Mediterranean waitress he knew and liked and whose wedding band should have blackened long ago from the frequent curses he directed at it asked him how he was and took his order. He drummed his fingers softly on the table as he waited for his meal to arrive, trying to look pleasantly occupied with thought, a pose familiar to him from years of dining out alone. All he really thought about, though, was how funny he must look in his black suit. Now and then his booth shook uncomfortably as a large man sitting with his back to Cook's shifted from one position to another, giving a perfect edge to Cook's discomfort.

In time, the waitress returned with his linguine and chicken livers. She set a bottle of beer before him. He admired the dew of condensation on the neck and label. Then, because he was unhappy, tired, and alone, the bottle slipped from his eager grasp and spilled with a loud crash across the table. He lunged forward and caught it, but fully half of his beer was lying in a foamy puddle on the table and dripping into the seat opposite him.

"Hey, buddy, do you have to jerk around so much?"

Cook whirled around in his seat. Over his shoulder the face he saw was red and hostile, and Cook met it with his own, prepared to do battle. Perhaps a fight was the thing to turn the day around. Then the face swam into a familiar focus, as if through trick photography, and Lieutenant Leaf was suddenly grinning at him across the partition.

"Jeremy!" he exclaimed. "How are you? Here, let me join you." Leaf turned and grabbed his goods from his table and stood up, all the while declaring his pleasure in meeting Cook like this, and all the while addressing Cook by his first name, suggesting an intimacy Cook found surprising but not unwelcome. When the Lieutenant started to sit down across the table Cook spoke up.

"Hold it, Lieutenant. That seat's all wet." Leaf recoiled, then bent his large body over the seat as if he intended to sniff at the beer. After a quick cleaning, he settled down across from Cook with a fresh cup of coffee and a cigarette, remarking that Cook looked as if he were on his way to a funeral. Cook wondered anew at Leaf's personality; it seemed to be a perfect mixture of an overweight Jack Webb and Bertie Wooster. He was happy to have Leaf there with him, not only because he wanted to talk to someone, but because he wanted to talk to Leaf. There was nothing nicer, he thought, than speaking when you really had something to say, when you had the power to affect with mere words the body chemistry of your listener, and Cook now sensed he was in such a position with Leaf. He told him about the dent in his car and the man set down his cup of cof0 from his pocket and Leaf banged himself on the forehead and loudly uttered an oath, if the expression "Peas and carrots!" can indeed be considered an oath. Then he examined the material closely under the table lamp. He appeared unwilling to say much about it until Cook reminded him that by mutual agreement they were partners in the investigation. Leaf smiled, then said that he guessed, as Cook had earlier, that it was an attempted frame, and a sloppy one at that.

"It's a little late in the day for this guy to go around denting up cars," he said. He stubbed out his cigarette and signaled to the waitress to pour him more coffee. Cook ordered another beer. "This material will probably match Stiph's pants," Leaf continued after a short fit of coughing. "The ones he was wearing when he got hit. I'll check it out when I get back to the station."

"You still have his pants?" Cook asked.

"Of course. What do you think, that we'd auction them off like a bicycle or something?" He sipped his coffee and then lit another cigarette. "Do you have any idea who did this, Jeremy?"

"The dent in the car, or the hit and run?"

"One and the same, don't you think?"

Cook frowned. Of course he did. Then why had he asked Leaf which one he was talking about? He felt very confused. He sighed, noting to himself that one symptom of exhaustion was to give your listener the impression that you held beliefs that you didn't hold at all.

"No, Lieutenant," he said. "I haven't gotten anywhere on it. I haven't really been thinking about it."

"Har, har, har," responded Leaf. "You haven't really been thinking about it."

"No, honestly," said Cook. "I've had other things on my mind."

"You've had other things on your mind, har har har."

Cook gave up trying to explain, figuring that if he succeeded in convincing Leaf he was serious he would look all the more like a fool. The waitress brought his beer, and he carefully reached for it and took a large swallow from the bottle.

"Do you have any leads, Lieutenant?" he asked.

Leaf raised two hands in front of him and with curled thumb and index finger made two small circles, one in each hand. These he raised to his eyes, forming a little pair of goggles with them. He peered at Cook through his fingers in a way that strongly suggested he had taken complete leave of his senses. Then he removed the circles from his eyes and held them up for Cook to examine.

"Zero, Jeremy," he said by way of explanation. "Double zeros. Nothing. Nothing."

The two men paid their checks and left the restaurant. Cook said he would walk with Leaf back to the station, since he had left his car there. Leaf nodded and said he would like to have a look at it, it being a slow day and all, "knock on wood," he added, reaching up and with a stupid grin on his face knocking hard on the top of his own head. He lit up another cigarette and puffed, not only at the cigarette but for mere air. Cook was awed by the man's health, a feature about him he hadn't noticed before. In plain terms it stank. His entire face was over-red, he hacked throatily every few minutes, and now and then he would scowl around at nothing in particular, as if he labored under the disadvantage of some great internal pain.

Cook asked the Lieutenant if he had already examined the cars belonging to the other people with keys to his building at Wabash. Leaf said that he had, finding nothing. Cook asked him if he had mentioned the possibility of a dent in the hood to anyone besides himself. Leaf thought a moment and shook his head, and then, as he saw in advance where Cook was trying to take the argument, pointed out that the new dent in Cook's car did not necessarily prove the existence of a dent in the culpable vehicle, for the killer, on seeing his car examined by the police, might well have drawn that inference for himself and exploited that official assumption in an attempted frame. Cook thought about this and silently cursed the world for being so complex. He decided he should start at the beginning.

"Just what do you make of Stiph's death, Lieutenant?" he asked as they hurriedly crossed against a red light.

"I make of it exactly what you make of it and what the handful of other people of above-dull intelligence should make of it," he said.

"Do you figure it was an accident? Is that it?"

Leaf snorted to himself. "Let's just say that if I were going to kill someone and wanted to do a good job of it I wouldn't count on running him over in the middle of the night in a place where I couldn't really expect him to be, slamming on my brakes as I did so. Hold it!" Leaf stopped in his tracks. Cook waited eagerly for him to share the insight that must have just leaped into his head. But Leaf, judging from his gaze, had halted because of something he had seen. Cook followed his eyes. They led to an item in the window of a men's clothing store—a purple shirt with little flowers embroidered on the collar.

"Love that shirt," said Leaf with feeling. He moved ahead slowly, reluctantly. Cook stood in place for a moment, looking at the shirt in disbelief, then at Leaf to be sure he was serious, then back at the shirt. He wondered how a man who admired a shirt like that could possibly solve crimes.

"What do you mean when you say that Stiph could not really have been expected to be where he was, Lieutenant?" asked Cook.

Leaf looked at Cook. "Why don't you take that idiotic coat off? You're sweating like an unbaptized hog." Cook, suddenly aware of just how uncomfortable he was, complied and draped his jacket over one shoulder. "Arthur Stiph," Leaf continued, "took frequent and unpredictable walks late at night. In all directions and at all times. According to his widow he was on one such when he was killed."

Cook turned to him. "You talked with her?"

"Of course," said Leaf in a bored tone.

Cook thought a moment. Hadn't Leaf earlier given him the impression that he had never met her? He shook his head, trying to arrive at a clear thought. To his surprise he succeeded, for he hit upon a discrepancy. Leaf apparently thought Stiph's walk was a mere stroll for fresh air.

"She told me he was going to meet someone, Lieutenant."

"Who?"

"She didn't say. Because *he* didn't say. He just said he was going to meet a . . . a something. A backfriend."

"I know. But what the hell does it mean—that they gave back rubs to each other?"

"I don't know." He looked at Leaf. "So she told you, too."

"Of course."

"But you weren't about to tell me."

"No."

Cook cleared his throat. "We have an agreement. I thought we were going to work together. Pool our resources."

"Yeah. Sorry. Listen, now that you mention it, I couldn't find that word in my dictionary."

" 'Backfriend'?"

"Yeah."

"I'll check mine. As I was saying, I was hoping you would see your way clear to be a little more generous with—"

"There's still a problem, you know, with the view that the guy he met had planned to kill him." Leaf spoke not just as if Cook hadn't been speaking but as if he were not even there.

"There is?" asked Cook, his head whirling.

"You said there was a swerve in the skid marks."

"That's right. A little swerve."

"That suggests to me an attempt to avoid the victim."

"Or the effect of a sudden impact with something?"

"Who knows? A look at the skid marks might have cleared that up, but they're gone, aren't they?"

"Yes. They're gone." The two of them walked on in silence for a while, Cook thoughtful and measured, the Lieutenant bustling and coughing at his side. Finally, Cook spoke again.

"Lieutenant, you don't seem to know any more than I do, and I'm just a linguist. Haven't you learned anything besides 'zero, zero'?"

Leaf's large features suddenly condensed themselves into a pout. He turned to Cook, head bent in mock submission, and looked as if he were going to deliver himself of another verbal enigma. But then he simply slapped himself once on the belly. Then, as if unexpectedly pleased with the sound, he slapped himself once more.

Cook reflected silently on this turn of events. He wondered how soon he would reach a point where Leaf ceased to amuse him.

"Jeremy," the detective finally said, "do you know what the best lead in this case is?"

"Yes," said Cook. "The body in the building. The person who stashed the body has a key."

"But there were signs of forced entry," he said with a rhetorical singsong to his voice, as if he were giving Cook an oral examination.

"About which you felt 'funny,' Lieutenant. You gave me the impression the forced entry was faked."

"Did I?"

"Yes."

"Well, that's because it was."

Cook frowned and wondered where Leaf had learned the art of conversation. "Why do you say that?"

Leaf inhaled deeply, then spoke very quickly. "Because the broken glass was mainly *outside* the building, on the ground, and it wouldn't be there if it had been broken from the outside, and it was done with the wooden end of a hoe that was kept in the basement, and the guy tried to make it look like the body had been dragged through the basement window by sticking a piece of glass in one cuff of the victim's pants, when any moron of a criminal who really didn't have a key would have just entered the basement alone and then opened the door on the first floor to bring Stiph in that way. He overdid it, in other words. Things like that."

Cook thought about this a moment and nodded. "Sounds solid."

"I ain't no dirt eater."

Cook pondered this disclaimer, then pressed on. "This means that the killer wanted to hide the fact that he had a key, which means that he *had* a key, which means that he was one of five people."

"Six."

"What?"

"Six people."

"No. Miss Pristam is out of town."

"Six."

"Mary the Secretary doesn't have a key. And the janitors work days because my boss doesn't trust them with keys."

"Six."

Cook flung his arms out to his sides in exasperation. "What the hell are you talking about?"

"In the eighteenth century a British explorer traveled to Australia and New Zealand. What was his name?"

"Captain Cook."

Leaf grinned at Cook as if he had just walked into the most cunningly set trap in the annals of Indiana detection. "That's right, Cap'n."

Cook suddenly ceased to find the Lieutenant amusing.

"Six is a good number," Leaf continued excitedly, now in a manic phase. "I have six brothers and sisters. I have six cars in my fleet. I like six. It's my favorite number. That there are six suspects in this case has been, for me, the high point of the investigation." He picked at his teeth with a stubby finger.

"All right, Lieutenant. I won't even try to explore my possible guilt with you. I'll leave that to you. Just tell me this. Doesn't anyone have an alibi for Tuesday night? I don't, of course."

"No, you don't, to put it gently. Being at the scene of the crime at the moment of its commission is not normally considered an alibi, har, har. As for the others, only one of them has an alibi, but his wife is the only corroboration and she's a liar."

"How do you know?"

"Parakeets in the living room. People who own parakeets are liars."

Cook laughed. "You're not serious."

"Yes I am. When you're on the force awhile you learn things."

"I take it then that you've talked to all the suspects?"

"Yes."

"Did you learn anything interesting?"

"Yes."

"What did you learn?"

Leaf paused. "I've learned that your language factory or baby farm or whatever it is contains some choice grade-A dicks, let me tell you."

Cook laughed. "You don't have to tell me."

"They're suspicious and creepy . . . nervous-laughter types. Queer-baits all, and cockchafers. Dicks."

"Well, Ed Woeps is a friend of mine. I wouldn't have guessed you would feel that way about him."

"Then you would have gone fish."

"But he—"

"Dicks dicks dicks dicks dicks."

Sensing that this left little room for debate, Cook said, "Is any one of the suspects more of a suspect than the others?"

"No," Leaf said unconvincingly.

"Do you own any parakeets?"

Leaf stopped in his tracks and laughed raucously, uncontrollably. Cook did not enjoy seeing it, for he realized with a shock that this might have been the first genuine thing Leaf had done all afternoon. But even then he could not be sure.

"Let's go look at your car," said Leaf, his face even redder than normal and somewhat wet around the lips. They crossed the parking lot next to the police station. Cook pointed out his Valiant.

"Not bad," said Leaf as he sprawled across the hood. "Not bad. A human head could have made that mark for all I can tell."

"What is the penalty for this sort of thing, Lieutenant? The killing, I mean. Assuming it was accidental. Manslaughter, I guess."

"How would you define 'manslaughter,' Jeremy?" asked Leaf as he heaved himself up on one fender and sat there. Cook watched his car sag severely to one side under the weight.

He sighed. "Lieutenant, do you have to turn everything into a question?"

"Sorry. You needn't be so touchy." Leaf swung his legs back and forth, scissors-like. "Most people think that manslaughter is just accidental killing. But in this state—in most, I guess—there are two kinds, voluntary and involuntary. If I called you a linguistic dick and you suddenly turned on me and stuck two fingers through my eyeholes into my brain, thereby killing me, you could be found guilty of voluntary manslaughter. It's a kind of murder, actually—in my book, at least—but it's done impulsively. And yet voluntarily. 'In a sudden heat' is how the statute reads." He grinned at Cook for no apparent reason and laughed softly. "But you're probably talking about the other kind. Involuntary manslaughter. That covers accidental deaths committed during the commission of some unlawful act. Like reckless driving. The penalty for that, if recklessness is proved, is two to twenty-one."

Cook raised his eyebrows. "That's pretty serious. For an accident."

Leaf hopped back to his feet and dusted his pants off, as if in silent comment on Cook's maintenance of his car. "Well, the law can't very well let everyone run around rantum scantum." He shrugged. "At any rate you can see why the killer wasn't eager to step forward. Especially since the victim was apparently so likeable and all, at least to hear people talk about him." He paused meaningfully. "But his cover-up seems to have singled you out for some reason."

Cook nodded. "Probably out of simple convenience. My door happened to be open . . . the light was on . . . any idiot could have seen it."

Leaf nodded several times. Then his face took on a doubting look, as if he were debating some private question. When he finally spoke Cook had the feeling that this particular speech had been chosen only after the careful elimination of other quite different speeches.

"Jeremy, I never did tell you what the best lead is in this case. The key to the building is good, very good. But after that it's a question of character. Consider first the accident, again assuming it was an accident.

There are two kinds of people—those who are likely to have such an accident and those who are not. That narrows the field already. Then, if you do have such an accident, there are two things to do and two kinds of people to do them. You can hide or you can come forth and seek the mercy of the court. Our man chose to hide, and that narrows the field further. And he chose to hide in a special way. He didn't just run, for example. He was more careful, more deliberate. That's one thing that strikes me about this case. Deliberation after the fact, a sense of, 'Well, what do I do now?' So our man shaves Stiph's head to protect himself, and rounds it off by seating the body at your desk. That took a very special kind of person. And the busted window in the basement. Then put against those things the fact that the guy puked. Whiskey and ice cream. You see, Jeremy, it's a question of character."

"Yes, but for God's sake what *kind* of character?"

Leaf inhaled sharply and scratched his abundant chin. Then he snapped his fingers. "One thing I forgot to tell you, Jeremy, is that Arthur Stiph's wristwatch was on backward."

Cook looked at Leaf and wondered if the fat man was trying to drive him mad.

"Backward?"

"When we found him in your office his wristwatch was on his left wrist, where I suppose he normally wore it, but it faced outward, as if he was always showing other people what time it was. His wife said he never wore it that way. I mean, it would be pretty dumb, wouldn't it? He was a conventional wristwatch wearer." He looked at Cook's watch. "Like you and me, Jeremy." He gave Cook a pleasantly surprised look, as if he had just learned they shared birthdays.

"That's interesting, Lieutenant, but what do we do with it? It's like the goddamn ice cream and whiskey and—"

"Lieutenant! Lieutenant!" The bowling sergeant was suddenly shouting from the back door of the police station. "Sizzle, Lieutenant!" he shouted. "Sizzle!"

Cook did not wonder who Sizzle was, or what "sizzle" meant, because he remembered Leaf using and then explaining the term in an earlier conversation. "Sizzle" was a peculiarly Kinseyan police ejaculation, no doubt coined by Leaf, used in response to exciting developments—things above the ticket-writing routine.

Leaf looked up across the parking lot at the sergeant. "What is it, John?" He spoke softly and patiently, as if the man were his son.

"We've got a shooting. An apparent suicide."

Cook's gaze moved to the ground and his mind became instantly clear with the vision of an old woman waving to him from a short distance away.

The sergeant went on without mercy. "Some old lady, Lieutenant," he called out as Leaf began to hurry to the door. "In a big house near the Baby Wabash. Blew her head off in the living room. A neighbor called in . . ."

Leaf did not allow Cook to accompany him to the scene of the suicide. Nor did he suggest that Cook follow after him, and when Cook suggested this himself, Leaf, rushing to his car with the sergeant, declared the idea "out of the question." Cook thought this a fresh betrayal of their earlier agreement to treat each other as equals (an agreement he had not yet drawn any striking benefit from or for that matter ever fully understood), but he said nothing. He drove home, hesitated at the phone, then went into the bedroom and began to undress to take a shower. But he stopped before removing his pants, and, shirtless and shoeless, returned to the phone, wanting to know the worst rather than merely suspect it.

He looked up the number and then dialed the home of Arthur Stiph. The voice of the sergeant at the other end confirmed it instantly. Mr. and Mrs. Stiph were together once again. Leaf came on the phone and with telling phrases such as "not a pretty sight" gave Cook a vivid idea of the scene in the Stiph living room. Apparently a neighbor was just about to ring the doorbell to see if she could be of any help when Mrs. Stiph pulled the trigger. The neighbor opened the door in time to see her topple forward from the couch across the coffee table.

The rest of Cook's afternoon was rather lacking in focus. He called Ed Woeps to relieve himself of a portion of his burden of news and sorrow, but his friend was out tending to a thumb he had managed to break or sprain while rough-housing with his daughter. So Cook told Woeps's wife the news, but he didn't feel any better when he hung up. He sat by the phone for several minutes trying to think of other friends he could call. Then, inspired in an altogether different direction, he dialed Aaskhugh's number, scratching his bare chest with a certain anticipation. There was no answer. This filled him with an even greater sense of purpose and he called Orffmann's office. When the big-headed, big-throated laugher answered, Cook pressed the phone hotly to his mouth, shoved his chest out, tilted his upper body back, and let out the loudest, foulest, hyena-like bray he could muster. Orffmann did not respond immediately, and Cook hung up the phone.

Then he went into the kitchen, opened a bottle of bourbon, sat down on the couch in the living room, and, with a dirty glass fetched angrily from the kitchen sink, began to drink.

Arthur Stiph and his wife were playing in an old bell tower, childish grins on their old faces. They were pulling two long bell ropes in rapid succession. Mrs. Stiph's rope produced a high-pitched, buglelike *ding,* Arthur's a lower, sleepier *dong,* and they appeared to be having great fun. This vision faded and Cook awoke to hear a final chime of his doorbell, followed by the sound of his screen door banging to a close. Then he heard footsteps on his gravel driveway moving away from the house.

He rolled and lurched into a sitting position. The only light in the room came from a small table lamp beside the couch. It was completely dark outside. He rubbed his hands through his hair, feeling simultaneously drunk and hung over. This feeling was colored by the incurable exhaustion resulting from long, unnecessary sleep. There was a sickening dryness in his mouth, and his bare back itched from its punishing exposure to the rough surface of the couch. He scratched and moaned as he rose to his feet, softly cursing the Creator for having rested on the seventh day instead of patching up all the cruel mistakes He had made on the first six. By the time he had groped his way to the front door, the bell ringer was gone and a police car was pulling away from the house. He opened the door to run out, but a sudden rebellion in his abdomen slowed him to a stop and he stood and watched the car pull onto the road and disappear from view.

At his feet inside the screen door lay a large manila envelope. He gingerly bent down for it, squatting in order to keep his head upright. As he took it into the living room he faintly remembered a tapping sound near his ear occurring with, or just before, the ringing of the doorbell. Lieutenant Leaf, or whoever it was, must have been tapping at his window right over the couch. Cook winced—his sprawling body must have presented quite a sight. And the empty bottle of bourbon was on the coffee table, its label conveniently turned toward the front window. Excellent!

Under the light of the table lamp he read on the outside of the envelope, in a feminine scribble that appeared ugly from mere habit and not from any particular haste or nervousness, "For Jeremy Cook." The envelope had been sealed but the seal was broken. He nodded, recognizing Lieutenant Leaf's brute force approach. Inside were six sheets of paper—Xeroxed pages from some magazine evidently not proud enough of itself to give its title across the top or bottom of the pages. The first of the sheets did contain a title, however: "The Backside of Mankind." The author was Merlin Flexible. In spite of his condition, Cook deciphered the pseudonym instantly. He hoped the rest of it was as easy. A little note attached to the first page read, "Here's that little piece I mentioned, Jeremy. Adelle Stiph."

Cook's stomach churned as he began to read the story, sensing that doing so would plunge him just a little bit deeper into Arthur Stiph's life and death, but he knew that not reading it was impossible. The first few sentences were lost on him because he kept wondering how soon after penning her note Adelle Stiph had shot herself, and what those minutes must have been like for her. But as he read further he soon began to feel that Arthur was speaking to him directly, and his thoughts were far from her.

The story did not and could not contain the name of Stiph's killer. But it narrowed the field of possible names along an entirely new dimension. The story told of an aging professor of philosophy, a Yale graduate teaching in a small New England college, who after devoting fifty years of thought to problems of good and evil concluded that the only real evil that existed in this world was the peculiar by-product of interpersonal loathing: evil was what we imagined we saw in those we hated anyway. There was really no other kind. Having decided that this view raised certain questions not amenable to armchair solution, the hero of the story resolved to grapple with the issue in bodily form, like Jacob wrestling with the angel. That is, he cultivated close personal relationships with people he hated. And, as could be expected from a product of a school with a rich tradition of secret societies, the hero established a club made up exclusively of mated enemies, individuals who in the outside world detested each other to the limits of human capacity. These paired enemies met on a weekly basis "to explore creatively with each other the various hues and shades of personal repulsion." Reconciliation was not a goal. Indeed, it was assumed to be impossible, and from that assumption, curiously enough, the club members drew strength. While mated couples sometimes met with other couples and even claimed to benefit from the experience, the important unit was the couple itself, each member of which was to work at getting in touch with the unique chemistry of antipathy. Club members learned firsthand about loathsomeness and disgust; they learned about the hostile views held by others about them—the range of objections that could be raised against them as people. The chief goal of the club was knowledge—understanding of the mechanics of the hate-spawned dyad. There, the author assured his readers, if we too followed this course, we would find "mysteries of emotion unapproached by literary classics devoted to the sublimest love."

The story went on to show how the Backside Club grew and grew, and it ended with a message about the ultimate, though disguised, unity of all mankind. Plot there was none. The author's chief concern was the constitution (and Constitution, for one was drawn up) of the club, not the adventures of the club members.

A key word in the story was "backfriend"—the word which, according to his wife, Arthur had used that fateful night. In the world of "The Backside of Mankind" this word denoted an enemy-turned-mate. This established a clear direction of inquiry for Cook. Because Stiph still used the word with his wife, the concept must have been a real one for him—even though he had written the story decades ago. In some sense the Backside Club must have still been alive. Stiph had a mate, a backfriend. Now, whoever he was, he had said nothing about planning to meet Stiph—not to Cook and probably not to Lieutenant Leaf either (despite his bizarre behavior about almost everything, Leaf probably wouldn't keep something like this from Cook). Why hadn't Stiph's backfriend said anything about the meeting?

"Because he was the one who killed him," Cook said aloud to himself. Having said it, he could now sit back and examine it. On increasingly sober reflection it appeared to be the likeliest answer to the question.

SIX

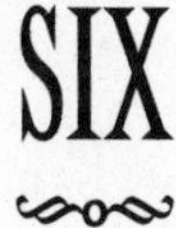

COOK AWOKE WITH THE BIRDS MONDAY MORNING. HE ATE a typically heavy and repugnant breakfast and drove to work, arriving at six-thirty, one half hour before the first teachers and children would appear. His floor was silent and peaceful. He passed his office and walked to the end of the hall to check his mailbox. Among those pleasures in life whose peak is in the preliminary steps, Cook ranked fetching his mail right near sex with a complete stranger. This trip yielded some envelopes containing some promise, but nothing that couldn't wait until he had started his morning coffee perking. As he walked back down the hall he remarked to himself that Wach had not left a note of any kind in his mailbox about the grant proposal. This meant that he found it first-rate. Cook knew this as certainly as if Wach had crawled to him on his knees in sobbing gratitude and told him so.

He entered his office for the first time since Wednesday, when Arthur Stiph had occupied it. He stepped inside gingerly, as if he had been forewarned of some undefined practical joke about to take place, and immediately noticed that his typewriter was gone. This had happened once before, and it had turned up in Orffmann's office; the moron had borrowed it without permission or explanation. Perhaps he had done it again. He would have to wait until Mary the Secretary came in with her master key to the offices. Or could the body-stasher have stolen it? But why? His tape recorder and radio were still there. He couldn't remember if the typewriter had been in its place Wednesday or not. Stiph's larger presence had dominated the scene. He shrugged. He would just have to wait.

He went through his mail. It was a typical mixture of niceness (in particular, a brief note from the editor of *The Kartoffel Quarterly* indicating that his "Reply to Hornswith: In Defense of 'Parsimonious Parsing,'" in which he defended an article by Ed Woeps against reckless criticism by some mean flunky named Hornswith, would be published in the "Open Forum" section of the next issue, with Cook's name withheld, as he had requested), nastiness (a journal number containing two articles by two people he knew from national meetings and didn't like at all), and boredom (everything else). He turned his attention to his present brainchild, idiophenomena. He cleared his desk and took five manila file folders out of his top drawer. In these were daily notes, most taken by himself but some by the teachers, on the linguistic behavior of five carefully selected informants at Wabash, age nine months to two years. The notes showed the progress of their humdrum, stop-and-go acquisition of English, but, more importantly for Cook, they showed the stages in their acquisition of a private language doomed to quick extinction. Thus far his most interesting subject had been Ed Woeps's son, Wally, age one year, four months. Cook's notes showed that Wally's vocabulary presently consisted of a number of conventional items, recorded in broad phonetic transcription:

[ma(ma) . . .]	"mama"
[dada]	"daddy"
[bø] (rising)	"toy bird (used in bathtub)"
[tu]	"shoe"
[m:]	"more"
[lalala(la) . . .]	"music"

But Wally also said some unconventional things with fixed meanings. Cook's notes showed this second list:

[ga::] (falling)	"that's amusing"
[f:]	"look at that (and say something about it)"
[ndə] (+pointing)	"look at that!"
[əpa] (+palm up)	"give me that"
[mbwi:]	—

The last one puzzled Cook. Wally had been observed using it perhaps two dozen times, but the contexts did not lead to a definite meaning. Several of the utterances seemed to involve nearby people, as if he were pointing at them or calling to them, but Cook did not know what meaning he was expressing. Of course, this disyllabic *m-bwee* could have been mere babbling. (That possibility always complicated things. Why didn't babbling just stop when acquisition of meaning began, the way crawling stopped when serious walking began? Why?)

He studied the files on the four other children and compared them with one another. There were no similarities in the pairing of sounds with meanings, although there were the expected sounds and meanings for this age group. The meanings fell into the categories of requests (or commands) and social expressions. There were no clear statements of immediately unobservable fact ("Uranus is a planet"), prediction ("I'll bet you're going to give me carrots for lunch"), or fantasy ("Let's pretend I'm a duck"). He studied the data, but he couldn't get much more out of it than that. He would have to be patient. Longitudinal studies demanded it.

"Do you have a stapler?"

Cook looked up and saw that it was Paula standing at his open door. He felt momentarily inarticulate, dumb in the oldest sense. Even Wally Woeps's *m-bwee* was beyond him at the moment.

"A stapler?" she asked again, perhaps beginning to think bad thoughts about him.

"Yes!" he shouted ebulliently. He clapped his hands together once with enthusiasm and instantly felt like a chucklehead. He began to rummage through a top drawer, his mind racing but empty.

"There's one on your desk. Doesn't it work?"

"Yes!" he said loudly. "Yes!" He reached for the stapler and handed it to her with authority, as if this had been his plan all along—as if, in other words, the best route to one's desk top were through a desk drawer. It was easy to imagine her talking to the other teachers. "Not only is he an asshole," she would say, "but he's a dolt, a clodpate, and a muggins besides."

"I don't believe we've met," she said. "My name is Paula Nouvelles."

"I'm Jeremy Cook," he said, noticing that her jeans were as tight as his voice was. "Please call me Jeremy."

She evened the edges of some sheets of paper against his desk top, standing quite close to him, and stapled them together. "What else would I call you?"

He cleared his throat. "*Dr.* Cook. Too many of the teachers do."

"Why don't you ask them not to?"

"I have."

"But not very forcefully, I'll bet."

"No, honestly, I have."

She studied him without self-consciousness, looking down on him in his chair. "I see that you've quickly identified me as a teacher."

"Yes. I mean . . . aren't you? Someone pointed you out the other day and . . ."

"It just seems rather class-conscious of you, doesn't it? Also the call-me-first-name business. It's a brand of disguised elitism, isn't it?" She said these tags declaratively, the way the British do. Cook swallowed hard and wondered if she was going to box his ears.

"I was just trying to be friendly," he said. The tone of this contained some of the hurt he felt—more, in fact, than he wanted her to know about. Hearing himself speak this way instantly roused him. He would not let her say one more thing like that. He was eager for her to speak again just so he could show his strength.

"I'm sorry," she said softly, giving him a nice smile. "Perhaps you were."

Cook was silent.

"I'll drop a hint to the others about it—about what they should call you. Would that help?"

"That would be nice. But being new here, maybe you—"

"It's no problem. I'll see what I can do. Thanks for the use of the stapler." She set it on his desk and was gone before he could think of anything to keep her there, and he didn't want to anyway. His stomach was in knots. Why did things like this happen to him? What was it about his personality that invited other people to assault it? Unless, in her case, it was just prejudice because of the complete asshole business. If so, had he redeemed himself? She hadn't really given him much of a chance. She seemed friendly in the end, though. Unless she was just pretending, mocking him privately. If so, he dreaded her promised hint to the others: "Get this—the asshole wants to be called Jeremy." Maybe not, though. Yes, *quite* friendly. Tight pants, too. Maybe he should go after her now. Ask her about herself. Yes. He hadn't asked her anything about herself. He stood up, intending hot pursuit. Then he sank back into his chair. He would only make things worse. He had to plan ahead and sort things out before he talked to her again. Like Lieutenant Leaf, she had caught him at a mentally slow moment. He had drunk only two cups of coffee this morning and he wasn't really humming yet. Next time he would make sure he was at a mental peak—though the more he tried to understand his mind and body and nurture and prolong his productive mental states, the shorter they seemed to become. Some days he had only three or four good minutes in him.

He heard footsteps coming down the hall and tensed. He located the stapler and gripped it tightly. When he saw that it was only Woeps at the door, he felt as if six months had been added to his life.

"Good morning, Jeremy," Woeps said, a smile adding some vitality to his face. "Keeping busy?"

Cook hadn't talked with Woeps for some time, apart from the few words they exchanged at the funeral, so he felt he had several days' worth of conversation for him. He noticed an Ace bandage wrapped around Woeps's thumb and wrist, and he observed his long-standing practice of not asking what had happened, so as not to embarrass him. He told him of the latest developments in the disaster he called his life—his talk with the widow, her subsequent suicide, the dent in his car, and his talk with Leaf. He omitted his recent chat with Paula.

"Helen mentioned you had called with the news about Arthur's wife, Jeremy. What a shame. I tried to call you back a couple of times later that night. Were you out?"

"Yes." In a sense he was, he thought, as he pictured himself lying like Raskolnikov in disarray on his couch. "Did you know her, Ed?"

Woeps shook his head. "I hardly knew Arthur, for that matter." He paused. "You know, Jeremy, maybe you ought to take a leave of absence and devote yourself full time to the case."

Cook laughed, then realized he wasn't sure what Woeps had meant. "What do you mean?" he asked.

"Just that it seems to be forcing itself on you—seeking you out, almost. I don't see how you can get any work done."

Cook was struck by the irony of this. He had wondered the same thing about Woeps many times. How, in the face of one domestic calamity after another, could Woeps continue to be the moderately productive linguist he was?

"Now that you mention it, Ed, I was going over my notes on Wally. This *m-bwee* is still a mystery."

"What have you got?" Woeps set his briefcase down and walked around Cook's desk to look over his shoulder. Cook pointed to the top of one of the pages.

"See? I've recorded quite a few nonimitative, spontaneous instances of it, but so far—"

"Nonimitative? Wouldn't they always be nonimitative? Who around here is going to say *m-bwee* anyway?"

"Some of the teachers. They think it's cute, and they're mucking up the picture. I've asked them to stop. Now look at the nonverbal contexts. In six of them he's looking at a person, in three of them he's looking at the aquarium, and in one he's looking outside, out the window. The others are obscure. You see, it's not enough. I'm going to spend most of the day with him." He looked up at Woeps. "Did he produce any this weekend, Ed?"

Woeps brought his hand to his face and stroked his chin as he tried to remember. "I recall one. Yesterday. I was giving him a bath. I had just added more water to the tub and he shouted one at me."

"And he looked at you?"

"Yes."

"For a response?"

"I think so."

"And what did you say?"

"I said . . . I don't know, something like 'Yes, *m-bwee.*' "

"What did he do?"

"He kept saying it and looking at me."

"As if you hadn't gotten the message?"

"Maybe."

Cook looked at his notes again. "Damn!" he said. "I haven't been systematic about getting data on the adult response. That's important. Look, Ed." He pointed to one of the examples. "Here I say 'fish' in response to him and he doesn't say *m-bwee* after that. But then here—he pointed to another example—"I don't say anything and he keeps after me with it, as if to say, 'Damn it, Jeremy, *m-bwee* and what do you have to say about it?' "

"I don't know, Jeremy. This stuff is pretty slippery."

"But you don't doubt that it means something to him, do you?" Cook tried to speak without sounding defensive. He had seen that rigid fear of contradiction in others at Wabash when describing work in progress. Milke, the charmboat, was the worst one in this way.

"No, I guess not. But . . . well, with young kids whose grammar is always developing, how can we know the meaning is constant from day to day? You're comparing data stretching over several weeks."

"We can't."

"Or how can we know that we haven't changed the meaning by studying it—say, by means of rewards we are unconscious of?"

"We can't know that, either."

"What does that leave us with?"

"An impure science." Cook shrugged. "I can live with it."

"There isn't even a name for what you're studying."

"Yes there is. I call them 'idiophenomena.' "

Woeps laughed. "Then it's respectable! No question about it!" He smiled. "See you for lunch?"

"Sure, Ed." Whom else could he eat with at this place? It was good of Woeps, who got along with everybody except Aaskhugh and could enjoy lunch with any of them, to reserve his lunch hour on most days for Cook. It was almost as if they had a contract.

Cook heard footsteps and voices and saw Aaskhugh and Milke walk by on the way to their offices. The four linguists all called out "Good morning" at the same time.

"One more thing, Ed," Cook added as Woeps turned to go. "It's about Arthur. Do you know if he had any enemies here?"

Woeps studied the floor and thought a moment. "I doubt it," he said. "But why do you ask? If his death was accidental, how is it relevant?"

Cook gestured for his friend to sit down, and then he introduced him to the world of "The Backside of Mankind." Woeps listened to his summary of the story with frowning wonder.

"And he was coming here to meet one of these guys, these . . ."

"Backfriends. Yes. That's what his wife said."

Woeps was silent a moment. "I can't imagine who it could be. None of us was very close to him, but I think we all more or less liked him, and I guess vice versa."

"Even though the vice versa doesn't follow."

"No, I guess it doesn't," said Woeps as he stood up from his chair. "And that certainly happens sometimes—people being liked without liking in return. Makes things sticky."

Wach's face appeared in Cook's doorway. It was followed by his body. "Jeremy, if you aren't busy I would like to see you in my office."

"Be right there, Walter." Wach nodded and walked on down the hall, evidently just arriving to work. Mary the Secretary, bearing a heavy load of fresh makeup, trotted by about ten steps behind him.

"I'll keep my eyes open and think about it, Jeremy," said Woeps. "That's important evidence."

Cook followed him out the door and closed it behind him. "It's all we've got," he said. He watched Woeps, at the door of his own office, take his keys out of his pocket, drop them, and reach down for them in such a way that he banged his forehead sharply on the doorknob. Cook winced and stepped toward him.

"Are you all right, Ed?"

Woeps smiled with resignation. "Never better," he said as he unlocked his door.

Cook walked down the hall. As he passed Milke's office he glanced in the open door and saw that it was empty. But the smell of his pipe was quite strong. Then he saw Milke standing just inside Aaskhugh's office, chatting with him. All Cook heard as he walked by was "don't see why the sonofabitch doesn't ever" and he assumed with some confidence that Milke was talking about Wach. Milke seemed to prize Wach about as highly as Cook did, the only difference being that Milke talked about it all the time, often with Wach himself. Milke was a generally argumentative sort. How could he also be the charmer he was supposed to be? Maybe he argued just with men and was charming with women. And maybe Stiph was one of the men he argued with.

Cook filed this away as he approached the end of the hall and Mary the Secretary's desk, which he had to pass to reach Wach's office. His last conversation with her had not been entirely pleasant, but he decided not to worry about it. Since she was the one who had behaved like a ninny, the burden was on her to make amends.

"He's expecting you," she said in a transparently forced attempt at her normal dull style. Cook despised her all the more for this. Far better for her to resume the attack or to retreat with apologies than to follow this meaningless middle path. He silently vowed never to speak to her again and passed her desk wordlessly.

Wach was not in his office. Cook was filled with an urge to destroy things. For the first time in his life he understood the roots of vandalism. Where was Wach? What poor devil was he spying on now? What gave him the right to tell people to come to his office and then not be there? He walked around the room in search of things to loathe. He started at Wach's bookshelf and noticed with rising contempt that the spines of the books were all virginally intact. Then his fury momentarily left him and he sat in the chair across from Wach's desk. He realized that if he didn't put himself into a better mood he might say the wrong thing to Wach and do irreparable damage. He sighed and drummed his fingers on the arm of the chair. A toilet flushed and Wach, as if propelled by the noise, flung open his exclusive door to the bathroom and nodded brusquely in Cook's direction. He sat down behind his desk.

"Jeremy, I was at the Stiph funeral Friday." He paused.

Cook looked at him.

"I'm concerned about what is happening."

Cook said nothing. Where was the fool and tyrant going?

"I think we at Wabash have got some retrenching to do." He blinked. "The metaphor is apt. Very apt. *Retrenching*. I want you to give a lecture to the Kinsey Rotary Club."

"*What?*"

"Something light. Something on the bright side, to let the townspeople know that, hey, we're human over here."

"But why?"

"I just told you why. I think we need to reach out to the community a bit more."

"Public relations," Cook said softly, with disgust.

Wach briefly closed his eyes in comment on Cook's naivete.

"You could call it that. I'm concerned about the community perception of the Institute."

"I know you are."

"In these times especially, what with Arthur and all. People out there are talking about us."

"And I'm to be your emissary."

"The Institute's, Jeremy. I would hope you would look at it in that light." His eyes focused sharply on Cook. "Your image could benefit, too."

Cook returned his stare with a blank expression.

"The funeral, Jeremy. The funeral." He looked at Cook. "Damn it, man, do I have to spell it out? You looked like a fool stumbling down that hill."

"I didn't stumble."

"Besides, you're the jack-of-all-trades here. And you're not working on anything at the moment, are you?"

"Of course I am. What do you think?"

"What, then?"

"Idiophenomena."

Wach smiled. "That can wait."

"No, it can't. I've got to observe Ed's son today. And tomorrow. And—"

"*It will have to wait*, Jeremy. We all have to make sacrifices. That's the name of the game. There are a lot of things I would like to do too, but to do this job right . . . I try to do my share, and I would hope that you would want to see things the same way."

Cook wanted to whimper. Why did Wach use "would" like that? Did he speak this press-conference dialect in bed with his wife? Did he go to bed with his wife? Did he go to bed? If he did, did he first address the sheets, commanding them to remain crisp all night?

"I think something on names would have the right flavor."

Cook studied Wach's thin gray Germanic mustache. "Do you mean names of insult?"

"No. I was thinking more along an onomastic line. Proper names. Place names. Nicknames. You know, *nickname* itself is an interesting word. It comes from *ekename,* which—"

"I know."

". . . literally 'also-name,' and the *n* of the preceding article became incorporated into the word."

"I know, Walter."

"Well, good. See? You know a lot about it already. You can whip up something in no time. Or *Hoosier*. There's another one. People here would like to have its etymology explained for them."

"But, Walter, I don't have any interest in this stuff. I don't give a hoot in hell about *Hoosier*."

"I'm surprised, Jeremy. My own opinion is that there is a wealth of data in this area."

"Data, yes. Theory, no. It's a wasteland."

"Be that as it may, it's for the good of Wabash—hey, there's another one. You could talk about our debt to the Indians. I've taken the liberty of scheduling you for their Sunday meeting of next week."

"*What?*"

Wach raised a hand, palm toward Cook. "That's almost two weeks away, Jeremy. If you get to it I think you can produce a real crackerjack piece."

"Why don't you do it, Walter?"

Wach snorted derisively. "Your question indicates just how little you know about my responsibilities. They are all-consuming." He gave Cook a moment to respond. Then he said, "I've scheduled a meeting of the linguists for ten-thirty this morning. What you could call a retrenching meeting. We've lost some children, you know. The population is down by four since the Stiph thing, what with parents taking their children out of the program. Now I want to be able to tell the others that you've agreed to do this lecture." He looked at Cook.

"So tell them."

"Good. One more thing. When did you last see this reporter fellow, Philpot?"

"Him again? I last saw him on Tuesday, in Mary's office, just about five seconds after you forbade my seeing him."

Wach frowned. "You seem to have a chip on your shoulder this morning, Jeremy."

"Yeah. So where's Philpot? Did he go back to New York?"

"We don't know. He hasn't been here since Tuesday."

"Did you call his motel?"

"No."

"It seems like the logical thing to do."

"It's not my job to go running after reporters. If they want to come here, fine, we'll show them around and be totally above-board. We've got nothing to hide. But I am not about to go chasing after them."

"Fine. Don't call the motel. Keep on wondering where he is."

"*Should* I call the motel? Would you if you were me?"

"The conditional is staggeringly impossible for me to entertain,

Walter." Cook stood up from his chair. "Are we done? I've got some *really heavy* research to do on names."

"Perhaps I should call the motel," Wach said to himself as he stood up from his desk and walked Cook to the door.

"Good idea," muttered Cook. He opened the door and found Aaskhugh very close to it on the other side. Mary looked up from her desk expectantly. Her face was very red, as if she had been laughing hard.

"Looks like you've been the victim of a callous prank of some kind, Jay," Aaskhugh said. "I just found this taped to the door of your office." He held up a hand-lettered sign that read, "Cook's Barbershop."

Wach turned to Cook. "See what I mean, Jeremy? See?"

SEVEN

"He's got laryngitis."

Cook grinned. This was incredibly good news. He had noticed, as he sat down with his colleagues in Wach's office, that Clyde Orffmann was absent, and he had just asked Woeps if he knew where he was. Maybe it would fester into a chronic condition. His neighboring laughter wouldn't be too bad then. He would probably sound like a debarked dog.

"By the way, Jeremy," Woeps continued, "I talked with Clyde Friday about his grant proposal. He said you improved it tremendously."

"He did?"

"Yes. He said that after he looked at your revisions he saw a number of problems that you had cleared up. He says he has hopes of it flying now, and he didn't before."

"You mean after he was done with it, he had no faith in it?"

"Not until you got to it, apparently."

Cook grimaced. "I can't imagine how anyone can work with such little confidence."

"I know what you mean. I think he compares himself with you too much. He's quite in awe of you, you know."

"Really?"

"Oh yes. He told me Friday that he values your friendship highly."

Cook frowned. "But he doesn't have it, Ed. He's a—"

Cook had to cut this sentence short because Wach was tapping his pencil rhythmically on the desk to begin the meeting. This struck Cook as foolishly parliamentarian of him, seeing that there were only five people in the room. But his thoughts were chiefly on Orffmann. In addition to astonishing him, Woeps's news had pleased him, which showed that one's contempt of others in no way reduced one's desire for their approval, even though people always pretended that it did. But at the same time there was something sad about it all.

"I have called this meeting, gentlemen, to sound you out on ideas about the future of the Wabash Institute." Wach paused. It was one of those pauses that left the listener wondering if he should speak or not.

"So what's the problem?" Milke said boldly.

"I wouldn't call it a problem, Emory," said Wach. "Not yet, anyway."

"Well, when you would," said Milke, "what would it be that you would be calling a problem?"

Wach said, "If we don't watch out, if we don't maintain a steady watch on this thing, we could all be in pretty big trouble."

"What thing?" asked Milke, his voice rising impatiently.

"The . . . aftermath of Arthur Stiph, Emory. I'm suggesting it's time for a kind of, oh, retrenching. I'm sorry. I assumed you knew what I was talking about."

"I know you did."

"Fine. Fine." Wach surveyed the room, looking pleased that peace had been made. Cook wondered if the meeting was now over. "It is no small decision," Wach continued ponderously, "for a parent to entrust a child's care to an institution. That institution must remain above reproach on all counts. Since Arthur died there has been a lot of talk about Wabash. People are asking questions. Our population is down by four children from a week ago. That is bad news."

"Who's doing the talking, Walter?" asked Cook.

"Oh . . . people, I'm sure. People talk, you know."

"But have you yourself heard any talk?"

"Of course. I receive phone calls daily now from the two Kinsey newspapers and WKIN. They're asking some hard questions, too."

"But what about parents? Have they been after you?"

"Parents not so much. Not so much. That's an important point. I want to reassure the parental community of our love for children and our benevolent nature. Jeremy here, I'm proud to announce, shares my feelings to the extent that he is going to address the Kinsey Rotary Club next week at their Sunday morning Prayer and Pancake Breakfast with a talk titled 'Southern Indiana Names.'" Cook sat impassively and endured his colleagues' quizzical stares. "I'd like some further suggestions from the rest of you."

"I suggest we go on doing what we have been doing," said Milke, "and that we do it better. And that we give a little more attention to our stockroom. We've got nothing but seventy-five-millimeter tape for the rest of the month. It's ridiculous."

Wach looked at Milke and nodded, as if to say he was pleased to get this feedback but would not speak to it right away. He awaited further response.

"I don't see that we can do much," said Woeps, "or that we ought to feel we need to. Of the four children who have left Wabash, aren't two of them the McConklin kids?"

"That's right," said Wach.

"They were going to leave anyway. Their father was recently transferred." He spoke softly, like the man of reason he was. Cook loved it. He turned to Wach. How was he going to handle it?

"Technically you're right, Ed," he said.

"Who are the other two?" asked Aaskhugh.

"Emil Bumpers—" Wach began.

Milke laughed. "We're well rid of him. I for one am tired of hearing the kids complain about him."

"Emil?" asked Aaskhugh. "Why?"

"Because he's always kissing them. Boys and girls alike. He is the most despised child at Wabash."

"Emory's right about that," said Woeps.

"—and Buford Wilson," said Wach.

Milke laughed again and leaned forward and loudly banged his pipe into the very clean ashtray on Wach's desk. "Old forceps-face?" he said. "He never said anything anyway. He's got an MLU of point zero zero."

"Any other suggestions?" asked Wach.

Milke chuckled something to Aaskhugh. Wach reddened.

"I've got a suggestion for you, Emory," he said loudly. His short-cropped gray hair seemed to be standing straight up. "Stop teaching the Simpkins twins artificial words. Their mother was on the phone to me last week again. I've warned you about this."

Milke smiled sheepishly. "But I *have* stopped, Walter. Pretty much, anyway. And as a result we're missing a great opportunity to see how twins pass on pieces of a private language to each other. I haven't done anything unethical."

"Well, just watch your step. Cease and desist, as they say." Wach added this last in a spirit of lightening the tone.

Cook looked at Milke. If he was discovered to be Stiph's backfriend and killer, then a conviction would no doubt remove him from the scene, and Cook would be left to wage war against his boss all alone. Milke was certainly useful in that regard. But in other regards—his charm, his beard, his pipe, his sexual aggressiveness—Cook would not mourn his absence.

"I've got a suggestion," said Cook. "Suppose we try to find out who killed Arthur? Swift justice in this matter would have a salutary effect on our reputation, don't you think?"

"Hear, hear," said Milke.

"How would you suggest we go about it?" said Aaskhugh.

"Aren't the police—" began Wach.

"You will all be interested," said Cook, "to learn that the case is simplified by the fact that one of us probably killed him. Including Clyde in the bunch."

"Emory and I were talking about this on Friday," said Aaskhugh. "We figured the field of suspects was infinitely large."

"You said that, Adam," argued Milke. "I didn't."

Cook shook his head. "Lieutenant Leaf told me that the guy faked the forced entry into the basement." He quickly summarized Leaf's remarks for them. "He had a key to the building and wanted to hide that fact. How many people have keys, Walter?"

Wach cleared his throat. "I'll tell you what I told the police. Each of the staff linguists has a key to the building, and of course I do too. That's all. Unless carelessness somewhere has led to copies being made."

"Any reason to believe that has happened?" asked Cook. "Like a burglary in the past?"

"Not really," said Wach.

"That's an interesting point about Arthur having a key," said Aaskhugh. "If it was in his pocket when he was killed, then the killer could have gotten the key that way. So the field is wide open again."

Cook shook his head. "While the killer could have gotten a key that way, it would mean he was not a regular keyholder, which means that there would be no point in his faking a break-in."

Woeps laughed. "Unless he thought, 'I will now fake a break-in—fake it so sloppily that it will be discovered to be fake and therefore make everyone believe I am a keyholder trying to hide the fact that I am, so they won't know who I really am: some passing Joe who ran into this man and found a key to a nearby building in his pocket.'"

"You lost me," said Aaskhugh.

Cook shook his head again. "Too clever," he said to Woeps. "Few people think that well under normal conditions"—he tried not to look at Aaskhugh—"let alone after accidentally killing someone. And it's unnecessary besides. Merely using the key in the front door would have the same effect as a deliberately clumsy break-in."

"That's true," said Woeps.

A moment of silence passed as the men looked nervously at one another. Cook's eyes locked with Milke's, and for an instant he felt as though the man were trying to look into his soul. Not wanting to be the one to back down, he hardened his stare until Milke frowned and looked away, a hint of an odd smile just showing under his black beard.

Wach broke the silence. "Jeremy, you say you've spoken to Lieutenant Leaf recently?"

"Friday."

"And is he operating under the assumption you just presented to us?"

"He says quite openly that there are six suspects: the five of us and Orffmann."

"Where *is* Clyde, anyway?" said Aaskhugh.

"He's got—"

"I know he's got laryngitis, but that's a stupid thing to stay home for."

"Are you implying fishiness, Adam?" said Woeps.

Aaskhugh smiled his malicious smile—the only one he had. "Well, it's there, isn't it? It's certainly worth talking about."

"You look pretty fishy to me for saying that," said Milke.

"And you to me for that," Cook said to Milke.

Everyone laughed, but to Cook it seemed to echo hollowly off the walls, like the laughter of river pirates in a bare cave.

"I wonder why they haven't been spending more time here then," Wach said, not very loudly and to no one in particular.

"The police?" asked Aaskhugh.

"Yes. If they think one of us did it."

"It's damned awkward, isn't it?" said Milke. "Rubbing elbows daily with a killer. You know, one of us is really an asshole."

Cook suddenly looked from Milke to Wach, then to Aaskhugh and Woeps. "Maybe we ought to have it out—get Clyde in here and all six of us just have it out."

Milke showed his teeth through his beard. "I like that idea. I like it *a lot*."

"Just what are you suggesting, Jeremy?" asked Wach.

"Let's get together and see what happens. Right now I'd like to be able to say a few words to Arthur's hit-and-run killer and be sure he was hearing me."

"And the asshole who did it might slip up and let something out under the pressure," Milke said eagerly.

"Might be interesting," said Aaskhugh. "We could learn a lot about each other."

"It sounds extremely unpleasant to me," said Woeps. "Sorry, Jeremy."

"It's a ridiculous notion," said Wach. "We don't have time for this kind of thing."

Cook said, "We could meet after hours."

"It's uncivilized," said Wach.

"But if you want Arthur's killer to be found out and drummed out—"

Wach fussed with his pencil. "I'm especially surprised to hear this idea from you, Jeremy. You're always the first to complain when I call a meeting."

"This is different."

"He complains about everything," said Milke, smiling at Cook in a friendly way. Cook squirmed in his chair.

Wach shook his head. "You are all free, of course, to do whatever you like. But as Director of the Institute I am not going to sanction this kind of thing on company time. It would look pretty funny if word of such a meeting got out. That could put us in a pretty pickle indeed. We've got enough problems as it is. And I'm afraid I now must tell you about another one." He launched forth another weighty pause, which made Cook all the more eager to ridicule what he was going to say. "This reporter, Henry Philpot, seems to have disappeared. Some of you met him, if I'm not mistaken. I know Jeremy did. He was good enough to show him around Wabash in the morning hours last Tuesday. Did you meet him, Adam?"

"Yes," said Aaskhugh. "A nice fellow, if somewhat unassuming."

"And Ed?"

"No, I saw him, but only briefly."

"Emory?"

"Righto."

"I'm afraid," Wach continued, "that Mr. Philpot hasn't been seen by anyone since Tuesday. That's almost a week now. I of course called his motel. The manager said that Tuesday night was the last he had seen him. And yet he hasn't checked out. So I called his home in New York and talked to his wife this morning. He is not there either. I think I managed to ask her without worrying her. So I have called the police. Don't be surprised if you see them around here later today."

"What do you think happened to him?" asked Woeps.

Wach shook his head. "I can't speak to that, Ed. I really can't."

"There's something odd here," said Aaskhugh. All eyes swung to him. "I know for a fact that this fellow called one of the teachers Thursday or Friday . . . yes, Friday, the day of the funeral, Dorothy Plough. Most of you know her—she's the tall, horse-faced one?"

There were some nods. Cook did not nod. He sat very still.

"She told me he called and asked her some questions about the Institute," Aaskhugh continued. "And she said he called her from the motel."

"He called . . . he called her on Friday?" Wach said, his face puzzled.

"Did he give her any idea why he hasn't been around here?" asked Woeps. "It's strange of him to show up early in the week to interview people and then disappear until Friday, when he made this phone call."

"Yes, it *is* odd," said Aaskhugh. "I don't know if he talked about that or not. We could have her in to tell us." He rose from his seat.

"I don't think she's here today," said Cook.

"Wrong," said Milke. "You and I walked right by her in the hall on our way here, Jeremy."

"My mistake," Cook said equably.

"I'll get her," said Aaskhugh.

While he was gone the other four men sat in silence, with the exception of Woeps, who twice said, "Curious." When Dorothy came into the room with Aaskhugh, Cook tried to hide behind Woeps to discourage any subliminal memories and associations on her part. She spoke nervously, giving a halting description of the phone call that was rich in flashbacks and self-corrections. Cook wondered why she was so afraid. Was it Aaskhugh? No. She had called him a twit. Wach was the one to blame. Under his rule the sense of hierarchy at Wabash bred this kind of fear. Although he felt sorry for Dorothy, Cook was pleased to see that by the time she finished speaking everyone was quite weary of the subject, and only a few token questions were asked.

Wach thanked her, dismissed her, and said that it was "certainly something to think about" and that he would pass it on to the police when he saw them. He appeared to be on the verge of ending the meeting when Woeps spoke.

"There's one more issue I would like to bring up."

"Go ahead, Ed," said Wach.

"I don't like to see a man's work die with him, especially when there are others around who could bring it to a publishable state. I wonder if there's anything we could do along that line. Was Arthur still working on the acquisition of value terms?"

"I don't think so," said Wach. "I think he had set that aside. And, to be honest and frank and totally open about it, I was getting pretty curious about just what he was up to, and was about to question him about it, when—"

"He was looking at linguistic devices associated with esteem," said Milke. "How does a four-year-old talk to someone he likes as compared with the way he talks to someone he doesn't like? How does acquisition of the adult tools for disguising feelings proceed? Are kids really more honest than adults? Questions like that."

"How far along was he?" asked Woeps.

"Not far," said Milke. "He told me he was particularly interested in following up on the work of Ruhig—you know, at the Deutsches Forschungsinstitut für Kindersprache und Entwicklungspsychologie in Munich. Ruhig maintains that kids up to about age two have an instinctive sense of *quality* in people. They gravitate toward good people and shun bad people. Then sometime after their second birthday this innate moral sense gets corrupted by socialization. Arthur evidently believed this and wanted to explore the role of language in this deterioration. But, as I said, he was just beginning."

"Do you think it would be worthwhile to look at his notes?" asked Woeps.

"It sounds pretty screwy to me," said Aaskhugh. "Especially this Rousseauist twaddle. I wouldn't waste my time on it. But then I always found much of Arthur's work suspect."

"Nice of you to say that," Woeps said with a sudden bitterness that surprised Cook. Woeps looked at Aaskhugh as if he were something he had just spit out of his mouth.

"I have more respect for this kind of thing than Adam," said Milke, "but my time is pretty much taken up with my negation project. How about you, Ed?"

Woeps shifted in his seat. "Well . . . I wasn't really thinking of myself for the job. I have several months' work ahead of me on this dialect competition thing, and—"

"It looks as though everybody wants to do his own work," said Wach, laughing mirthlessly. "That's healthy. Very healthy. And these projects have been approved by all of us, whereas Arthur's has not. What Emory has just described is news to me." In the silence that followed, Cook began to feel oppressed by meaningful glances. He was the only one left.

"Jeremy?" said Woeps.

Cook sighed. "I'll look into it. Ill try to work it in."

Wach began to bluster. "But not at the expense—"

"Not to worry, Walter," Cook said with the heartiness of a team man. "*Hoosier* remains top drawer."

Wach smiled uncertainly, surveyed the group for further remarks, and adjourned the meeting. Lieutenant Leaf was talking to Mary the Secretary when Cook and the others stepped out of Wach's office. He turned and watched the linguists file past, smiling and greeting each by name.

". . . and Dr. Aaskhugh and Dr. Woeps and Dr. Cook." He winked at Cook as he addressed him and turned to Wach, who stood in the doorway of his office. "And the good Dr. Wach," he said, stepping toward him. Cook watched the bustling detective pump Wach's hand and guide him back into his office before slamming the door.

Cook and Woeps ate lunch at Max's and discussed onomastics, idiophenomena, centralized dipthongs, and manslaughter. Woeps remarked that their colleagues were still ignorant of the Backside Club and guessed, correctly, that Cook had not shared Stiph's story with them in the hope that someone would declare himself to be an enemy of Stiph's and thereby implicate himself in Stiph's death. Then Woeps apologized again for not being able to support Cook's proposal for a soul-baring meeting of the suspects, saying that he found it "unorthodox and threatening." He said he feared people might say things they would later regret. Cook agreed that the idea was somewhat strange, and said that it had somehow just popped into his head.

As they paid their checks, Woeps asked what expectations Cook was bringing to his talk at the Kinsey Rotary Club, and Cook said, "Fear, nausea, and self-disgust." When Woeps asked if he could help, Cook said no, that it was hopeless, and, as if cued by these words, Paula entered the front door of Max's and stood very erect and surveyed the crowd. Cook, standing nearby at the cash register, studied her closely. Thus it was very easy for him to see Emory Milke enter right behind her and place a gentle, charmingly guiding hand against what was probably a nice part of her back and steer her to a corner table. Milke moved as if he owned the building—not only owned it, but had designed and built it and might level it tomorrow for the fun of it. As they walked he leaned forward and whispered something into Paula's ear. She threw her head back and laughed quietly. Cook saw all of this and felt as if he were watching a bad movie.

"Ah," said Woeps, his eyes following her. "A Cook target."

Cook sighed and nodded and moved to the door. He didn't want Milke to know he had seen him with her.

"It's good that I see you in pain like this now and then, Jeremy. It keeps me from envying you your bachelorhood too much. She's new, isn't she?"

"Yeah. From U.C.L.A. She's doing a doctorate in linguistics." They stepped outside into the parking lot and blinked in the bright sunlight.

"You'll get your chance. Emory can't be too thick with her. She just got here."

"He's quick off the mark."

"So are you."

"Not with her." In fact, before the race someone had stolen his starting blocks, blindfolded him, pointed him in the wrong direction, and tied his shoelaces together. But he wasn't going to give life to that tale by passing it on to his friend.

Back at Wabash, Cook remained faithful to his vow of never speaking to Mary the Secretary again by sneaking her master key out of her desk when she was away from it. As he did this he felt like a man whose life was becoming disturbingly complex. He went to Orffmann's office and found only Orffmann's small portable typewriter and not his own old, large, rackety Royal. He went from office to office, first knocking on the doors of those he knew were occupied, but he failed to find it. He even checked Stiph's office and Sally Good's on the floor below. One more thing to report to Wach, he thought with annoyance. He stealthily returned the key to Mary's desk and missed by seconds being seen in the process by Aaskhugh.

He went to his office and began to leaf through his books in an unimpassioned search for material for his name lecture. He learned that *Hoosier* came either from the question "Who's 'ere?" asked by the typical gruff, inhospitable bumpkin who settled Indiana, or from the question the same gruff bumpkin asked when, upon walking into a bar where other gruff bumpkins had recently been butting heads and gouging eyes, he looked at a certain piece of detached flesh on the grimy floor and said, "Whose ear?" Hence *Hoosier*. *Quod erat demonstrandum.*

Was this the kind of thing Wach wanted him to talk about? How could he research this crap and lecture on it without his blood actually slowing down to a dead stop? Besides, he already knew what a Hoosier was. In his personal lexicon the entry read, "*Hoosier,* n., etymology obscure and boring: a dumb white man with a fat white wife who eats greens, attaches his muffler to his car with a coat hanger, and leaves refrigerators in his yard for children to suffocate in."

He leaned back in his seat and put his feet up on his desk. He began to think about the morning meeting of the linguists. He had come away with nothing. Or rather, he had come away with a disrespect for all claims based on inference. It was easy to think, for example, that anyone who resisted his suggestion for a man-to-man, head-butting, eye-gouging meeting did so out of fear that he would expose himself as the killer he was; on the other hand, someone who endorsed the meeting could just as easily be thought suspect—perhaps he was performing a simple-minded reversal (Aaskhugh would do something like that and think it clever) or, being a Stiphian backfriend, perhaps he enjoyed this sort of thing and wanted to take it up with a new group, what with the other half of his repugnant dyad being dead and all. The entire meeting had been full of similar double-sided mirrors. He needed more data. He needed to *listen*. The guilty one knew who he was. He knew what he had done. As a linguist, Cook was aware that every day in almost every sentence people regularly (though often inadvertently) informed their audiences of what they knew. He would have to wait.

He looked at his books. He should do more work on names. He drummed his fingers on the desk, sighed, and then took Wally Woeps's file out of his top drawer. He set up a tape on the tape recorder beside his desk and prepared to listen to it as he followed his notes.

Hoosier will always be with us, he said to himself. *M-bwee* will not.

EIGHT

THEY FOUND HENRY PHILPOT'S BODY IN THE BABY Wabash, fifty feet downstream from Scopes Bridge. They found Cook's typewriter too. It had been tied to Philpot's body, presumably for weight, but the ropes had worked loose and slipped down to his ankles. As a result, while the typewriter remained on the sandy bottom of the Baby Wabash, Philpot's gas-filled torso rose upward, and his head bobbed up and down at the surface of the water like an anchored buoy. Martha Simpkins, mother of the twins under Milke's scrutiny and forbidden tutelage, arrived early Thursday afternoon to pick up her children, and she chanced to spend a few minutes strolling on the bridge, whose prospect was generally quite pleasant. It was she who first saw Philpot's head.

Cook had left work early that day, dined at home in his usual fashion, and returned to Wabash around six o'clock to take up, for the first time in earnest, the necessary preparation for his lecture on names, which a morning memo from Wach indicated was now to be titled "Highways and Byways of Southern Indiana Names." When he drove up he counted six police cars and one television van in the parking lot. Two policemen stood on the bank of the river and several more were walking in and out of the building. His first thought was for the children, though he would not have been able to specify the nature of his fear. Then he thought of Woeps and hoped he was all right. He learned the truth from a reporter outside the building who did not seem to know or care who he was. The reporter told him that Philpot had been pulled from the river and taken away about an hour earlier.

Cook turned from the building and walked slowly out onto the bridge. He leaned on the railing. The two policemen on the bank looked up at him for a moment and then ignored him. One of them swept an arm out over the water, pointing up and down the river. After a few minutes they left. The crowd of policemen and reporters outside the front entrance thinned out as well. Cook heard the slamming of car doors and the starting of engines as he looked at the water.

He remembered Philpot standing at the playroom door, looking at the children and expressing his regret that he would be missing his daughter's birthday. The image of his young widow in New York trying to explain his death to that girl, whom Cook had never met and never would, now gave him an odd feeling that he finally identified as sorrow mixed with shame for his own life. He took off his glasses and rubbed his eyes with the heels of his palms. He watched the gray, silent water, which held no secrets now but was simply there, dark and oppressive. The light was fading. He stood up from the bench and was about to turn to go when he heard a footstep on the bridge. Startled, he turned quickly to see who it was. Lieutenant Leaf approached him, his hands in his pockets. Behind him, a policeman waited in an unmarked car at the side of the road.

Leaf walked right up to Cook and said without greeting, "I'm getting sick of this. Sick of it."

Cook didn't want to talk to Leaf. He wanted to go home. "Excuse me, Lieutenant. I—"

"Goddamnit," said Leaf. "I'm sick of it."

Cook looked closely at him and saw that he was livid. He actually looked as though he might fall back at any moment clutching his chest in pain.

"Accidents, okay. Cover-up, okay. Suicides, okay. But this." He pointed out to the water. "Jesus *fuck*. What a world."

"I feel the same way," Cook said softly.

"I'll *bet* you do," said Leaf with bitter sarcasm. "You goddamn intellectuals." He glared at Cook. "A family man comes in from the outside and you kill him. Then you just go on with your rooty-toot nonsense, you sonofabitches." He turned and left Cook standing on the bridge, puzzled but without the energy or desire to try to understand what he had meant.

Leaf was his normal self the next time Cook saw him. He paid Cook an unexpected, unannounced visit at his home. It was late Friday afternoon, the day after their meeting on the bridge. Cook had found it impossible to work at Wabash. Police, press, parents—all were there, strident, frightened, outraged. He had escaped for lunch with Woeps and returned with hopes that it would be quieter. It was not. Again the children seemed upset by the commotion, and the older ones were even less civilized than usual. One boy known to Cook only as Dicky and once characterized by Woeps as being "all boy" smashed a toy wooden mallet against a young girl's mouth and made her cry and bleed. Her mother, there to investigate things for herself to decide whether or not to remove her daughter from Wabash, made her decision very easily after that. Panicked, Wach summarily and publicly fired the teacher responsible—somewhat unfairly, everyone thought, seeing that Dicky's blow lacked forewarning. This noise, and more like it, and the reporters knocking on his door to ask him about his typewriter, had driven him away.

He was mowing the lawn when the police car pulled up, driven by the bowler who doubled as Leaf's chauffeur. Cook looked up and then continued to mow the lawn when he saw who it was. Leaf walked up and stood right in the path of the machine, forcing him to stop. He pointed to it.

"*Noisy!*" he yelled.

Cook understood this as a request and turned it off. Leaf pointed to himself.

"Foolish," he said.

Cook looked at him blankly. Leaf pointed to the left side of his chest.

"Contrite," he said. He pointed to his head. "Bowed."

"Lieutenant," Cook said impatiently, "do you have something to say to me? I've got things to do, and if you're going to talk in adjectives all afternoon you're going to waste my time."

Leaf looked disappointed, as if Cook were denying him an interesting linguistic challenge. "One more, then. Sorry. I'm sorry. Is that an adjective? I lost my head. I was angry. I don't like murder."

"All right. Tell me what you think." Cook gestured to his front porch. The two men began walking. Cook was very glad he had said this before Leaf had said it to him. He wasn't going to let the fat man befuddle his brain this time. He sat down on the porch swing, afraid it might not support Leaf, and pointed to a chair for him. "Sit down."

"I like swings. Scoot over."

Cook held his ground. "No. I was here first. Sit there." He pointed to the chair again. Leaf obeyed.

"What do you know about this Philpot?" asked Leaf.

"No. You tell me first. How long had he been dead when he was discovered? The news reports have been unclear on that point."

Leaf hesitated a moment, then spoke forthrightly. "Maybe a week or more."

"So he could have been killed the same night as Arthur."

"And probably was. And by the same man. Your typewriter is the link."

"What was the cause of death?"

"Choking."

"You mean drowning?"

"No. Strangling. He was throttled. Dead before he hit the water."

Cook did not produce another question right away.

"Evidently the guy we're after threw him down and just choked him with his bare hands," Leaf continued. "He had a busy night of it."

"That would take a lot of strength," said Cook.

"Or motivation."

"In this case . . ."

Leaf shrugged. "Fear of discovery. Philpot must have been a witness."

Cook nodded. He had already gotten this far on his own. "Who was the last to see him?"

"That depends on you. You're the last of the Wabash Six that I have to question on that point. When did you last see him?"

"About noon on Tuesday of last week."

"And what—"

"So who does that make the last to see him?" interrupted Cook.

"Your boss. He dropped him off at his motel about five o'clock."

"So between that time and the time of the accident he met up with one of us."

"Yes. Who?"

"It's hard to say. He could have arranged to meet any of us. In fact he had an appointment with me for a drink late that night."

"You didn't tell me that."

"I haven't had the chance. My point is that he could just as easily have arranged to have dinner or a drink with Emory Milke, or Adam Aaskhugh, or anybody."

". . . who then could have offered to drive him to your office to meet you. Did Philpot know you would be there?"

"Yes. I told him." Cook thought a moment. "That's good. We now have a reason for his being there."

"You know, he would still be alive if you hadn't made that date with him," Leaf said accusingly.

Cook laughed. He was getting a handle on Leaf. He wouldn't ever be bamboozled by him again. "It was pretty reckless of me, Lieutenant. Do I have time to pack before you take me in?"

Leaf said nothing.

"Another thing, Lieutenant. Did that material on my car bumper match the pants?"

"Pants?" Leaf said wonderingly. "Pants?"

"Stiph's pants. You know . . . the piece of wool I found after—"

"Oh. That. Yes, they match. They match, all right. Listen, it's hot and I'm a hot cowboy. What do you have for a working man with a king-size thirst?" He looked around on all sides of him, as if in hopes of finding a spare root beer nearby.

"Lemonade?" asked Cook.

"How about a milkshake?" said Leaf.

Cook frowned. "Well—"

"Don't you have the fixings?"

"The what?"

"The fixings. Ice cream, for example."

"You really want a milkshake?" Cook stood up.

"Do you like ice cream?

"Yes," said Cook, feeling monumentally bored by the question.

"Gimme a bourbon and branch water."

Cook hesitated. "Seriously?" he asked, wondering what new joke or mystery he was walking into.

"Of course."

"What about your man in the car?" Cook looked across the lawn.

"Nah," said Leaf. "Fuck 'im."

As Cook prepared Leaf's drink in the kitchen he resolved to get the upper hand again. Leaf had dominated with the milkshake business. It had put Cook in a weak, domestic position. He knew now how to retaliate, though. Leaf didn't have the answer to one question he knew of—he couldn't. He took a beer out of the refrigerator for himself and returned to the porch, where he found Leaf sitting on the porch swing and smoking a cigarette. Cook handed him his drink and leaned against the porch railing, facing him. Leaf brought the glass to his mouth, sniffed it, and then set it beside him on the swing.

"Lieutenant," said Cook, his breath somewhat short with anticipation, "what do you make of the fact that someone posing as Philpot called one of the teachers on Friday?"

"It puzzles me."

Cook waited for Leaf to elaborate. When he didn't, he said, "Doesn't it rather complicate the case?"

"No." He looked at Cook. "I figure it was just some petty wienie who works there trying to find out what other people think of him." He swung back and forth on the swing, inhaled from his cigarette, and blew smoke up at the porch ceiling—the picture of contentment.

Cook tried to look blank-faced. "So . . . the guy posing as Philpot on the phone isn't necessarily the one who killed him."

"That's right." Leaf continued to swing, his small shoes clicking the porch rhythmically on the backswing. "And yet the profile is the same."

"What do you mean?"

"Fear of judgment. You know, it's a sad thing about this guy. There's a fair chance he wouldn't have been charged with anything. At night that road there is as dark as the inside of a cow, and Stiph was wearing a dark coat. Hell, I could have run over him under those circumstances. Of course the puke in your office suggests the driver was drunk, or had been drinking, but even so, there are ways of hiding that. He definitely overdid it. Or maybe he hadn't been drinking at all before the accident. Maybe he didn't start until afterward, to cheer himself up sort of. Either way, he should have come forth and trusted the judgment of society. Instead he bolts. Digs himself in deeper, even. He won't stop at anything now. You might be next." He began to whistle softly as he swung.

"Me?"

"Sure. In the public eye you are the number-one suspect, so you're showing the greatest desire to find the real killer, right?"

There was no denying it, even though his progress had been nil. "Right."

"If you get too close—*kapowie*!" He smacked his fist against his palm and the force jarred his glass loose from his seat, where it had been swinging, untouched, beside him. The glass bounced on the wooden floor, but it did not break. "They're dropping like flies," said Leaf.

Cook looked at the puddle on the porch floor and said mechanically, "Can I get you another?"

"I think not, Jeremy," said Leaf as he stood up. "I've got to shuffle off to Kokomo."

"Don't you have any other questions for me?"

"Well, one, if you insist. What did you think of that story by Stiph?"

" 'The Backside of Mankind'? I don't know—I haven't thought about it much."

"Har, har, har, you haven't thought about it much."

"No, really. I haven't."

"No, really, you haven't, har, har, har."

Apparently Leaf was prepared to go on doing this the rest of the afternoon. "I thought it was all right, I guess. It was cute."

"It was cute, har, har, har."

"Damn it, it *was*." He paused and looked ahead to where he was going. How did one defend the assertion that a short story was cute? Was that what he now had to do?

"As I understand it—and I'm just a loveable cop, now—he says that evil is just . . . what we imagine about people we don't like. Right?"

"I think so. Something like that. It's an interesting notion, don't you think?"

Leaf grinned at him. It was a grin slow in developing, but it grew quite large. "How much crap do you think it would take to sink a ship, a large ship? Call it the *H.M.S. Philpot.* How much?"

"Quite a bit, I guess," said Cook, beginning to visualize it.

Leaf shook his head and stepped down from the porch. "Arthur Stiph's story could do it all by itself."

Cook sighed and rubbed his hands through his hair. His desk was littered with notes, scraps of paper, and half-open books and journals. He now knew, for what it was worth, that *John, Johann, Jan, Ian, Hans, Hansel, Giovanni, Jean, Juan, Ivan, Vanya, Evan, Sean,* and *Jones* were all ultimately one and the same name; that *Elmer* once was a common greeting name for strangers; that Shakespeare's name was spelled eighty-three different ways in his lifetime; that Lombards were long beards; that Englishmen were crooked fishhooks; and that the folk in Arkansas had turned a certain river named *Purgatoire* into the *Picket Wire*, while American stevedores christened the Norwegian steamer *Björnstjerne Björnson* with the name *Bejesus Be-johnson.* And he finally knew why some people say *uh* for the final vowel of names like *Missouri* and *Cincinnati*, while others say *ee.* This last issue had a special importance to him because he had been asked this very question dozens of times, almost as many times as he had been asked what linguistics was—at parties, at picnics, in bed, at airports, and once, disturbingly, in the restroom of Max's bar. Now, after all these years, he would have an answer.

He took off his glasses and rubbed his eyes. He leaned back in his chair, stretched, and groaned. It was Sunday afternoon, and occasional mysterious squeaks and bangs from elsewhere on the seventh floor told him that he was not the only linguist putting in odd hours. The only incongruity was the contrasting silence from Orffmann's office. Orffmann, like the dormitory roommate you can't stand, was always in. Until recently, at least. His absence worried Cook in that it set up a positive expectation that it might continue, which he knew must someday be crushed. Orffmann's laughter reminded him of carved pumpkins. It suggested a parade of laughing, militaristic pumpkins hell-bent on overthrowing the world. He wondered idly if Orffmann could have been the one to tell Paula he was a complete asshole. It certainly was possible. But Orffmann seemed almost too incompetent, incapable even of slander. And there was that report from Ed that Orffmann considered himself Cook's friend, he just now remembered. No. It was probably Mary the Secretary. Since they were enemies already, he appreciated the economy in thinking she was the one. As guide to new teachers, she had *opportunity*, as a speaker of English (though not a good one), she had *means*, and as someone who probably heard him snicker when he once walked by her desk and saw her empty-headedly playing ticktacktoe with herself, she had *motivation*.

He heard a definitely feminine cough and giggle from the hall. Had Miss Pristam returned to Wabash earlier than expected? If so, he would have to greet her warmly and perpetuate her notion that he was "a nice young man." There it was again. He perked up and leaned forward in his chair, ears straining. It was a giggle. By God . . .

He stood up, opened his door, and stepped out into the hall. To his left, beyond Woeps's office, the door to Milke's office stood open, and out of it came bearded laughter and then Paula Nouvelles, walking toward him, but she called back over her shoulder, "I'll work down here then." She was carrying several books. Cook spun on his heel and went down the hall to his right, hoping he looked like a man on his way to the bathroom. Paula was behind him, following him on her way to wherever she was going. Cook suddenly realized this was foolish and turned to (1) wait for her, (2) greet her, (3) talk to her, and (4) seduce her. None of these, not even the first, was realized. As soon as he turned she too turned—into the central core and out of sight. But not, he noticed, without throwing him a wave and a smile.

He gazed blankly down the empty hall. He turned around. Ahead of him was the bathroom door, perhaps fifty feet away. If he lowered his head and ran full speed into it, the impact might kill him. Of the suicidal options facing him, this was probably the quickest. Had he left junior high school yet? Had he? Then why did this kind of thing make him feel that he hadn't? People said that being single made you feel forever young. Yes, thought Cook, if what they meant was that it made you feel forever foolish.

He stalked back to his office. He was Jeremy Cook, one of the best-known psycholinguists in the country. He gathered up his notes and books on names and dumped them into an unruly pile in one corner. Like Leaf, that stuff fogged up his brain. He took out his notes and tape transcripts, along with a blank yellow legal tablet to help him think.

Thirty minutes later he was as happy, nearly, as he would have been if all four of those things had happened. He dialed Ed Woeps's number. Woeps's wife answered and seemed interested in chatting, but Cook somewhat impolitely urged her to put her husband on the phone.

"Hi, Jeremy," he said. "Any gossip?"

"Not today, Ed. But I think I've figured out Wally's *m-bwee.*"

"Really? Just a second."

Cook heard him asking his wife to take something off his hands. There was some discussion. The something turned out to be Wally, who for some reason remained on Woeps's hands. Cook could hear him intermittently in the background.

"Go ahead, Jeremy."

"I've gone over the occurrences I've got, but I'm going to need more to verify it. It looks like it's a comment on moving objects, as if to say, 'Something is moving,' or 'Locomotion is going on.' All of my notes show him looking at people or animals walking, or fish swimming—"

"Or water pouring into the bathtub."

"Yes. That's one thing I wanted to ask you. Did he say it about you or about the water?"

"He pointed to the water."

"He did? You didn't mention that."

"I forgot. It's easy to overlook these things. He had two more of them today, Jeremy."

"Good," said Cook, smiling to hear Woeps speak of them as if they were bowel movements. "I'm glad to hear it's still alive. What were they about?"

"One was to our neighbor's cat as she ran by, and the other was at an Indian on TV. I think he was riding a horse at the time."

"Good. Did you take note of the intonation contours?"

"I sure didn't."

"See if you can make sense out of this: I've got distinctly rising contours in his remarks on the four people he said it about—you, me, and two teachers, Sarah and Sally—and on the fish and a wind-up toy that scoots across the floor. But the contour is falling with squirrels and birds. He produced four when I was outside with him one morning last week. All falling—two birds, two squirrels."

"Not much physical similarity, is there?" said Woeps.

"No. It could be that the important thing is that we were outside, so *m-bwee* with a falling intonation might mean 'Locomotion is going on outdoors.' That would be pretty odd, though."

"One thing that strikes me is that he really doesn't like birds or squirrels."

Cook raised his eyebrows. "Really?"

"Yes. He's afraid of them for some reason."

"And he likes you and me and the teachers and fish—"

"Yes. As far as I know."

"Jesus," said Cook, feeling somewhat short of breath. "A window into his personal preferences."

"Maybe. You've got me interested in it now. I'll be more attentive to it."

"Ed, I'm hot to study him. Could I have him for a few hours tonight?"

Woeps hesitated. "Helen's folks are coming up from Louisville, and they'll only be here a—"

"Forget it, then. I'll catch him tomorrow."

Another pause followed. Cook's heart sank. "I'm afraid they're all going for a ride tomorrow, Jeremy. Helen's folks will want the kids along."

"Well, I don't want to press you."

"Tomorrow night would be good. We're going out and we'll have a sitter in for Amy. You could be alone with Wally in his room. He'd like that."

Cook laughed. "And if he doesn't he'll let me know."

"What? Oh . . . yeah, provided you keep moving. What do you think? We'll be out of here about six, and you could keep him up until eight or eight-thirty if you like."

"Fine."

"You know, Jeremy, if his like or dislike is involved, that would explain its relative infrequency. I mean, movement is going on all the time, isn't it? But if *m-bwee* demands the conjunction of movement and strong feeling . . ."

"That's right. But it's pretty unusual. That's why I want more examples." He heard some vocal noises, then a whine.

"I've got to go, Jeremy. He's kicking up a fuss. I'm glad you've made progress. See you tomorrow."

Cook stood up. He walked out the door and down the hall and entered the central core where Paula had vanished. She was in the snack bar near the vending machines, her head buried in a book. She looked up when Cook entered. He rejected a temptation to pretend to be there to get coffee out of one of the machines and boldly approached her.

"What are you reading?"

She showed him the spine of the book without speaking. Rather laconic of her, he thought. In fact, absolutely laconic. Bad sign. But the book—*Presupposition, Reference, and What King of France?*—was a good omen, because this particular work contained two articles by him, one of them perhaps the best thing he had ever written. When he asked her if this was an area of special interest, she explained that she was writing a dissertation on intonation and presupposition.

"You know," she said, "problems like how we can get two readings out of 'It's better than sucking eggs.' With one intonation sucking eggs is no fun at all, and with another there's a presupposition that it's really quite a nice thing to do—hard to beat, in fact."

"Yes," he said. "There are fascinating problems there, especially with stated beliefs, as in 'John thinks that I'm an . . . a drunkard.' Have you thought about sentences like that?"

She set her book down—losing her place, Cook noticed—and leaned back in her chair, looking at him closely.

"Why no, Jeremy, I haven't."

NINE

COOK LOOKED AT WACH, WHO WAS SURVEYING THE GROUP before him. If ever there was a time for the pretty pickle speech this was it. It was Monday morning, and the impact of the discovery of Philpot's body Thursday evening was now quite clear. Fully half of the children normally enrolled at Wabash had been kept home. Wach's phone had been ringing all morning. Philpot's opening question took on more meaning: considering what Wabash did to its own staff and people dropping in to write a few words about them, what did they do with those babies anyway? Or what might they do?

Wach had called a ten o'clock meeting of the linguists to discuss their predicament. They now sat in his office and waited for Milke, who had stepped out to have Mary the Secretary call Orffmann to see where he was. As they waited, Cook turned to Woeps and asked for and received permission to bring Wally to Wabash that night, since he had decided to tape as well as observe him. Cook arranged to pick Wally up at six. Milke stepped inside in the middle of this and waited (rather politely, thought Cook) until they were finished talking to give the news about Orffmann. But before he could speak, Aaskhugh, whose back was to the door, asked Wach about the enrollment at Wabash.

Like a government economic forecaster, Wach said, "The outlook is not bright." He cleared his throat and glanced down at some papers on his desk. "We have fifty-five percent absentees today. Of those about half are permanent removals—the Simpkins twins are an example. The other half are temporary, judging from what their parents have told me. I believe they have adopted a wait-and-see position." He gestured broadly with his hands at "wait-and-see," as if the expression were newly coined by him and in need of demonstration.

"Is the forty-five percent solid?" asked Cook. "Will they stay here?"

"I think attendance today indicates a sound parental commitment to the Institute," said Wach.

"Until they find something else," said Milke, stepping forward and taking a seat beside Cook. "Or until their neighbors get to them. 'You mean you're still sending your children *there*?' I'm not very optimistic."

"Where's Clyde?" Aaskhugh asked Milke.

"In the hospital. His wife says he has pneumonia. But even more imp—"

"Hah!" said Aaskhugh. "Hah! Pretty fishy."

Woeps laughed. "And if he dies, Adam, does that settle it? Is that as good as a confession?"

"How has Clyde's work been of late, Walter?" Aaskhugh asked, ignoring Woeps and turning to Wach for support.

Wach blinked once. "Normal."

Aaskhugh nodded. "Anyone notice anything unusual about him lately?"

Milke spoke up. "Your line of inquiry amuses me, Adam. I was going to add that Clyde has been officially cleared of all suspicion."

The linguists greeted this news with astonished gasps and undisguised moans of disappointment.

"Evidently," Milke went on, "he had an alibi but was unable, or perhaps reluctant, to produce witnesses in support of it."

"Reluctant?" asked Cook.

Milke smiled. "I was just on the phone to Lieutenant Leaf about it. Clyde's wife suggested I call him. He said some things I didn't quite follow, but I got the impression that our man Clyde was having an affair. Leaf gave me this impression and yet he avoided female pronouns when talking about the alibi. I think he avoided *all* pronouns."

"An affair?" said Woeps. "Clyde? He doesn't seem capable of it."

"It comes as no surprise to me," said Aaskhugh, effortlessly abandoning his old position for a new one. "His wife is a real battle-ax."

"Well, we're moving in on the bastard, aren't we?" Cook said matter-of-factly.

The four men looked at him; then, as they understood what he had meant, at each other. He was about to follow up on this when Wach spoke.

"The purpose of this meeting, gentlemen, is to divert Wabash from its rapidly declining course. I suggest we stick to that for the moment." Cook suppressed a scowl. "I would be pleased to have a little brainstorming from you about how to handle the situation." Wach said this as if their last such session had been a whopping success. Wach Rule

Number Eight: people forget things, so people who run things can safely treat past failures as if they had been stupendous triumphs.

In the pause that followed, Milke stroked his beard, Aaskhugh studied his hands, Woeps rubbed at a dark stain covering most of his right pants leg above the knee, and Cook watched all of them doing these things.

"As you know," Wach said encouragingly, "Jeremy here is jumping into the fray with his lecture on names—"

"Walter, while you're on that I'd like to see the title changed to just 'Names.' I've got to deal with more than southern Indiana if I'm to speak for more than twenty seconds."

"Will do, Jeremy."

Milke laughed. "Do you all expect the Rotary Club to jump to our defense just because Jeremy here gives them a bang-up lecture—which I'm sure you can do, Jeremy, don't get me wrong—on this somewhat silly topic?"

"I see it as one small part of a general community relations outreach program," said Wach.

"What are the other parts?" asked Milke.

"We're piecing it together now," said Wach. "All of us."

Milke laughed softly and muttered, "I hadn't noticed."

After another longish pause Wach said, "I'll get the ball rolling then. What would you think of changing the name of the Institute?" Four frowns greeted this.

"To what?" asked Cook.

"I'm not sure," said Wach. "That's not important. What's important is the change."

"But what's the point?" asked Milke.

"Associations," said Wach. "People in the community now associate the name 'The Wabash Institute' with death. They can't do that if we change the name."

Very gently, Woeps said, "I'm afraid that's a little thin, Walter."

"It's not even like a Band-Aid on cancer," said Milke incredulously. "It's like *blowing* on cancer to make it go away."

"Fine, fine," said Wach. "I won't push it. But think about it. Don't dismiss it out of hand. We can come back to it. Now how about some suggestions from you? If the situation does not improve, and it won't unless we come up with something, some cutbacks are inevitable."

"Of the linguists?" Woeps asked nervously

"Yes," said Wach. "This has been in the works for some time, actually, and this is as good a time as any to tell you about it. Some time ago Adam informed me that the Himmelhoch Foundation is cutting back on its funding in linguistics. He has a well-placed source in Washington, isn't that right, Adam?"

"Right."

"They've been so generous," said Milke. "What—"

"They've decided to channel a lot of money into research on alternative sources of energy, or some such nonsense," said Aaskhugh.

"Is that right?" said Milke, confounded. "Jesus. We don't even know how kids learn irregular verbs."

"I know, Emory," said Aaskhugh. "It is pretty sickening."

"Now this will not affect us until next year," said Wach. "And it's hard to predict exactly what the effect will be. But you can see that the daycare enrollment becomes more crucial, not only as a source of income for us but as a justification for six full-time linguists."

Cook spoke up. "I would like to find out how each of you got along with Arthur." He let this sink in before continuing, which he did just as the others were about to ask him why. "This is step one on the way to finding out who killed him, and thereby clearing our name, or names. If you will allow me."

Cook undertook a lengthy presentation of the goals and purposes of the Backside Club, insofar as he understood them. He had finally decided that lurking and eavesdropping were not going to tell him who Stiph's backfriend was. After all, who besides Aaskhugh was going to voluntarily say anything bad about a generally well-liked dead man? A frontal assault on the question was the best approach.

"So," he concluded, "now that I've said this much, I don't really expect any of you to jump forward with avowals of mutual hatred for Arthur, but if you know of anything he might have said about one of us—"

"But we're all *here*, Jeremy," said Woeps.

"That's right. You'll have to say it in the person's presence. Except for Orffmann, and now that—"

"Arthur's contempt for Clyde is a matter of public record," said Aaskhugh, instantly warming to the subject. "I often heard him ridicule him."

"Fine," said Cook. "That's the spirit. But since Clyde is no longer a suspect we don't have to worry about him. Can you say the same thing about anyone else, Adam?"

"I once heard him say that Emory was a loud sonofabitch and that his beard smelled like a tobacco plantation," said Aaskhugh.

Milke frowned and his hand slowly went to his beard. "I must say—"

"Apart from the one famous comment about Ed, that's all," said Aaskhugh, looking around the room innocently.

"And what was that comment, Adam?" asked Cook.

"Well, Ed once showed him an old Indian-head nickel he carries in his wallet as a good-luck piece—is that right, Ed?" Woeps stared at him without answering. "And then after you were gone, Ed, Arthur turned to the rest of us, and there were quite a few of us there, and he said, 'I wonder when it's going to start working.' " He looked at Cook and smiled toothily. "I thought everyone knew about it."

"Go soak your head, Adam," said Woeps.

Aaskhugh looked genuinely surprised. "Now, Ed. *Really.* I didn't say any of these things. I was just going along with Jay's suggestion."

"You can't shoot the messenger for bringing bad news, Ed," said Milke.

"You can if the messenger grins as he brings it. Which is what you do, isn't it, Adam?" Woeps's voice rose. "You're really nothing but a skinny, grinning gossip."

"Well, I—"

"Look, Ed—"

"Listen, everyone, maybe we'd better—"

"Hold it!" shouted Cook. "Just hold it." He inhaled deeply and blew out. "We've got to stick to Arthur. What's important is who *he* didn't like."

"Precisely," said Wach, who had been closely but silently following these proceedings. "I'm beginning to think you're on the right track, Jeremy. Our desperate situation calls for extreme measures now. How about the rest of you? What can we reconstruct of Arthur's opinion of us? From what Jeremy says, the one of us whom he hated the most was the one who killed him."

"It's not certain, Walter," said Cook, happily surprised to have Wach on his side now.

"But very probable?" asked Wach.

"Yes."

Milke opened his mouth as if to speak.

"Yes, Emory?" said Wach, uncharacteristically excited.

"Well, I feel a bit funny about it."

"Go ahead," said Wach. "You're among friends."

"He called you a mental lightweight, Walter," said Milke.

Wach sat straight up in his chair. "Oh?"

"Yes. This wasn't long ago. He said some other things too. He said you were a typical administrator in that you wouldn't pass gas without first considering the budgetary ramifications; he said that your field was no longer linguistics—it was niggardliness; and he said you were as mean as you were dumb."

"My goodness! I—"

"Jesus, he certainly—"

"Old Arthur didn't pull any—"

"I think our format is screwed up," Cook said loudly. Everyone calmed down and looked at him. "You're all telling the person involved. You should be telling the rest of us. It is evidence against him for the rest of us to consider. We're not interested in personal growth here."

"Hear, hear," said Milke.

"That's exactly right," said Wach.

"Jeremy," said Milke, looking at him, "I once heard Arthur say something about you. Or rather," he said quickly, turning away from Cook to the others, "he said it about *him*." He pointed to Cook.

"What was it, Emory?" asked Aaskhugh.

"He said that Jeremy Cook flaunted his good looks."

"That's all? That doesn't even—"

"Rather mild."

"Doesn't amount to a hill of—"

"Quite a letdown."

After a pause of palpable disappointment, Wach said, "Anything else on Jeremy?" Everyone looked around and shrugged. "That's funny. It looks as though the very method of investigation suggested by Jeremy could have the effect of clearing him of suspicion." He suddenly stopped speaking and looked at Cook, as did the others.

Cook stood up. "I'll be right back," he said. He went to his office, where "The Backside of Mankind" was filed in his "Unfinished" folder, along with notes and fragments of manuscripts in progress. He brought it back for the group's perusal. Doing this gave him time to think about what everyone had said thus far. *Listen,* he reminded himself. *Listen.*

"You can ask Lieutenant Leaf about it too," he said. "Arthur's wife also told him, not just me, about his intention to meet his backfriend that night. It's all true."

"Looks it," said Milke, leafing through the pages of the story. He looked up at Cook.

"No hard feelings," said Cook. "This suspicion is useful. It's what we need more of."

Aaskhugh was studying the first page of the story and shaking his head. "I didn't know Arthur very well," he said reflectively, "but I never would have thought he was crazy."

Wach nodded vigorously. "It is something of a shock. I blame myself for not knowing more about him. I hadn't any idea."

"What are you talking about?" said Cook. "I don't think this is odd at all. Arthur had a creative bent and he wrote a story many years ago. So what?"

Wach said, "But he still has these . . . these . . ."

"Yes," said Cook. "That's true. But I see this as just a natural interest in human relationships. This is the stuff of life, isn't it?"

There were several complaints and demurrals to this. Wach found it all "unhealthy," Aaskhugh said Stiph was "making a religion" out of it without specifying the "it," Woeps said the important thing was friends, not enemies, and Milke found the whole idea "wild and wonderful."

"But how about you, Jeremy?" asked Woeps. "Don't you have any kind words from Arthur about any of us?"

Cook shook his head. "I've got absolutely nothing. That's why I'm doing this, which I'm not enjoying much either, by the way."

"How about you, Walter?" asked Woeps.

Wach sighed dramatically. "It is for no small reason that I have said nothing thus far," he said. "What I have to say is unfortunately damning to one of us. I say 'us' because I see our danger and misfortune as a collective problem. No doubt this is the case because of my tendency—perhaps a mistaken tendency but the mistake is pardonable, I believe—to see the fate of Walter Wach and that of the Wabash Institute as one and the same." He paused. "I heard the late Arthur Stiph say a bad thing about just one of us. He said that he loathed this person more than he had ever loathed anyone else—yes, and that he *feared* him, too, and that he feared what he, Arthur, might do to him. He hated him that much. It's not a pretty story, to be sure, but there it is. I'm speaking of Emory Milke."

This speech seemed more earnest and heartfelt than those that had gone before, and a hush followed.

"Emory?" Cook finally said, turning to him.

Milke was taking it quite well, not showing any of his usual brashness. "I don't know what to say. I'm quite hurt. I always liked Arthur, or thought I did . . . I really can't imagine him saying that." As if to console himself, he took his empty pipe from his shirt pocket and began to fondle it.

"I stand by my story," said Wach.

This was a strange thing to say—or rather, it was said with a strange insistence. If Cook understood Milke correctly, he was not really saying he doubted Wach's report. He was saying only that it was hard for him to reconcile it with his impression of, and affection for, Stiph. Milke looked at Wach for a moment as though he were about to clarify his original point, but then for some reason he chose not to. Perhaps, on reconsideration, he thought he *should* have made the challenge Wach thought he had made.

"Ed?" Cook asked, turning to his friend. "We haven't heard from you yet."

"Before we leave this," said Aaskhugh, "I'd like to ask Walter a bit more about what he just said."

"Fine," said Cook. "Go ahead."

"Did he elaborate on this fear, Walter?"

"He did not."

"Did he fear bodily harm?"

"That I do not know."

"You have nothing to add, Walter?" asked Cook.

"That is correct."

"When did he say it?" asked Milke. "And where? And why?"

"Approximately two weeks ago. In this office. We were discussing relationships among personnel at Wabash. It is part of my job to see that things go smoothly in that way."

"Then he must have said something to you about other people too," suggested Milke.

"He chose only to speak of Emory," said Wach, cutting off visual contact with Milke and sweeping his eyes across the rest of the group. Milke sat tensed for a moment, then sighed.

"Ed?" said Cook, sensing this dialogue was over.

Woeps smiled. "I didn't speak with Arthur all that often, and I heard him say nothing bad about any of us." He raised his index finger skyward, then aimed it at Aaskhugh. "Except Adam. He quoted an old Spanish proverb to me once as Adam walked by us in the hall. It's this: 'He who knows little soon repeats it.' He then added that Adam was a classic rumormonger: empty head, empty life, full mouth."

"Ouch!" someone said.

"Pithy, isn't it?"

"A good, clean shot."

Aaskhugh gave what looked at first like a courageous smile, but then Cook realized he found these remarks genuinely amusing. He was untouched personally. Perhaps it was impossible to insult a gossip by calling him a gossip.

"Ed, you're not just saying this to get back at Adam, are you?"

"I'm happy to get back at him, as you put it, but that's not why I said it. What do you think, that I made it up?"

"No," said Cook, "but personal involvement might lead you to exaggerate a story like this, or overlook similar stories about others of us."

"I wouldn't forget, Jeremy, even if it was about you. As far as I'm concerned, there are no saints in this room. Nary a one."

"Fine," said Cook, feeling suddenly depressed. Considering how strongly he liked Woeps, he would never have said what Woeps just said. Was it as nasty as it seemed?

"Of the abuse we have thus far had recapitulated for us," said Wach, "I would say my report of Arthur's about Emory is the most serious."

"I agree," said Aaskhugh.

"Yes," said Woeps.

"But if he *feared* Emory," said Cook, "I would think he would be reluctant to meet him late at night like that."

"Good point," said Aaskhugh.

"I agree," said Milke. "This is all really quite bewildering. And I can't believe we can't get any more dirt on Jeremy." Cook looked at him. "Arthur's ruthlessness seems so general," Milke continued, "that I would expect even as pleasant and likeable a fellow as Jeremy to be scorched by it."

Cook's head began to spin. For five years he had carefully nurtured his dislike of Milke. He had even invented new principles according to which Milke fell short and made them part of his own life. Now here was the man publicly proclaiming something like affection for him. Did Milke actually like him? Why hadn't he shown it sooner? It put Cook in a devilishly awkward position. The fact that no one else in the room, not even Milke, knew this made no difference. What was he supposed to do now—dwell on what was good in Milke, or some such nonsense? No. Milke remained an asshole. Given a few minutes, Cook could easily have remembered and explained the reasons why.

"I must say, I'm somewhat disillusioned about Arthur," said Woeps. "While some of his observations are on the mark"—he looked at Aaskhugh—"the general tenor of his personality seems quite misanthropic."

"Hardly the kindly old linguist he appeared to be," added Milke.

"Hardly," said Woeps.

"This of course doesn't reduce the nature of the crime," said Cook, and as he said it he realized that it did, even though everyone immediately and unthinkingly agreed with him. "And there's Henry Philpot.

His death changes everything. I can imagine any of us accidentally killing someone and then covering it up in a panic. But now with Philpot it's a different story."

"You're right," said Milke. "A very pleasant man."

"He was all right," said Aaskhugh. "Nothing special."

"I wonder," said Milke, "if anything in Arthur's office could tell us who he was going to meet that night. His calendar, for example."

"Or his notes," said Wach enthusiastically. "He's beginning to sound stranger all the time. He may have kept notes on his meetings with this backfriend fellow."

Cook said, "I'm going to get in his office this afternoon to check through his work in progress—the stuff Emory told us about last time. I'll keep an eye out for anything interesting along those lines."

"Hmmm," said Milke. "Puts you in a rather privileged position, doesn't it?"

"If I find anything you can be sure that I will show it to you," said Cook.

"And destroy it if it implicates you," said Milke.

"We all ought to go through his stuff," said Aaskhugh. "And at the same time."

"That's right," Milke nodded. "The sooner the better."

"Well . . . it's a bit unorthodox." Wach pursed his lips. "And yet Emory and Adam do have a point. As far as Arthur's personal effects go, his wife was here and took them out the day before she, ah . . . so we don't have to worry about, well, what the family would think and all, and if we—" He looked at his watch. "I've got an appointment with Lieutenant Leaf in forty minutes, and it might look funny if he saw us in there prowling around. We would have to make it snappy." He bit his lower lip and then clapped his hands together once, decisively. "Good. Let's do it."

His impulsiveness was contagious. The five men rose from their chairs as one. They stepped out of Wach's office and waited while he obtained the master key from Mary the Secretary, who looked at the group somewhat warily, as if she feared they had been conspiring to pounce on her. The men hurried down the hall to Stiph's office. As they moved, Cook almost felt as if they formed an unwieldy, homicidal circle of some complexity, each man holding a knife at the throat of the one in front, ready to plunge the dagger at the first hint of steel in his own throat.

The blinds were drawn in Stiph's office, and Wach fumbled for the light switch in the darkness while the linguists slowly entered the room. By the time he found it the others were spread all over the office in ready-to-search positions. Wach warned them not to mess things up. Cook began to work through the top drawer of a filing cabinet, leafing through papers from conferences, some correspondence, and offprints of articles.

"Look!" said Aaskhugh from the desk, where he was rifling the papers in a lower drawer. "Some tit magazines." He held up two of them. Milke joined him and took one from him, idly skimming it a few seconds before becoming conscious of the stares of the others and returning it to the drawer. "And here are some pills," said Aaskhugh. " 'Tofranil. Take as directed.' " He looked up. "Anyone know anything about this stuff?"

"Adam, get the hell out of there," Wach yelled from across the room, where he had been looking through a thin black book. "It's obviously irrelevant to what we're doing here."

"You never know," Aaskhugh said somewhat poutishly.

"There's not much here," said Woeps from another filing cabinet, holding up a battered box of Kleenex by way of illustration.

"Nor here," said Milke as he slammed a desk drawer shut.

"Nothing in his appointment book either," said Wach.

"Let me see it, Walter," said Milke. "You can check my work on this side of the desk if you like."

"All right." The two men exchanged places.

"Here are his notes on his work on acquisition of esteem terms," said Cook, lifting a heavy file out of the second drawer of the cabinet. "Some remarks on praise, some more on ridicule . . . here's something on name calling. I'll be taking all of this with me, so the rest of you might want to look through it now too."

Woeps and Aaskhugh drifted over to where he stood. He handed each of them a sheaf of papers. "We'll trade these around," he said. After a few minutes Milke and Wach joined them, and the five men carefully went through the many pages of notes.

"Here's something interesting," said Milke. "I mean just interesting, not important to us. It looks like a table of a sample of the kids here, broken down according to . . . well, it's called 'Love-Hate Chart: Wabash 4-5-Year-Olds.' The initials of about a dozen kids are given along both axes. See, Jeremy?" He showed it to Cook. Next to the names listed vertically was the label "Agent," while above the names listed horizontally was the label "Patient." In the boxes where the names intersected there was an "L," an "H," a blank space, or a dash, the last used where a name intersected itself.

" 'L' for 'Love,' Emory? And 'H' for 'Hate'?" Cook asked.

"I guess so. On the left where it says 'Agent' are the lovers and haters, and across the top are the loved and hated ones."

"It was probably something he was developing as a kind of reference source for his observations," said Cook. "You know, if T. T. said to L. W., 'You're a big boogersnatch,' Stiph could check it against this chart to see if T. T. loved or hated L. W."

"Do you think it was just a two-choice system? And how could he know?"

"Maybe the blanks indicate less strong feelings either way. And he could probably tell by watching the kids, or from reports by the teachers, who know the kids better than we do. Besides, it's fairly easy to tell who likes whom. With kids, at least."

Stiph's phone buzzed. The men turned and looked at it as if it were a voice from the grave. Aaskhugh, who was standing closest to it, picked it up and said cheerily, "Backside Club. May I take your reservation?" Then he giggled. He nodded into the phone a few times. "Okay, Mary," he said. He hung up and turned to Wach. "Lieutenant Leaf is here. Mary sent him on down."

"Oh, shit," said Wach. "Let's get out of here. This looks bad. Put those things away, Adam. Jeremy, you can take those notes with you. I think we've all seen them."

"Bit of a bust," muttered Woeps as he opened the door to the hall.

Lieutenant Leaf was leaning against the wall opposite the door, his arms folded against his chest, and again he named the linguists one by one as they filed out of Stiph's office.

TEN

THAT AFTERNOON COOK REVIEWED HIS NOTES IN PREPARATION for his evening taping session with Wally Woeps. He had gone over them perhaps forty times before, and he now put them away with an onrushing feeling of ennui. It scared him. He hoped he didn't grow tired of idiophenomena before he found and said something interesting about them. He looked at his watch. He had an hour or so before he would go to Max's, eat heavily and drink lightly, then go to Woeps's to pick up Wally. To pass that time he could work on his name lecture, but the tedium attached to that made him want to crawl under his desk and weep. Arthur Stiph's unfinished work was a cheerier prospect.

He took the heavy file from the top of his filing cabinet and began to sift through it. It quickly became clear that most of the material was of a preliminary, exploratory sort. Because Arthur nowhere spelled out what hypotheses he was testing in the area, Cook had only a dim notion of where the notes were going. He came upon the "Love-Hate Chart: Wabash 4-5-Year-Olds" and looked at it, idly trying to match initials with children's names. "D. M." must have been Daniel Masters, a freckled brute of a boy, and he loved no one and hated—his eyes went up the column to where an "H" was entered—"Z. W." That would be Zebra Whipple. This struck Cook as essentially correct, seeing that Daniel had twice tried to smash Zebra's head with a two-by-four (a bit more forceful a demonstration than the almost daily "you're not my friend anymore" he heard in the central core—or, at another level, the kind of thing that Aaskhugh and apparently even Stiph engaged in).

As he propped his feet up on his desk and turned toward the window, the "Love-Hate Chart" became backlit and harder to read because of some writing on the back of it. At first this annoyed Cook.

Then it interested him. He turned the sheet over. On the backside, titled "Love-Hate Chart: Wabash Adult Males," was a grid just like the one he had been studying. But the names were different:

	PATIENT						
AGENT	Aaskhugh	Cook	Milke	Orffmann	Stiph	Wach	Woeps
Aaskhugh	—	L		H			H
Cook	H	—	H	H		H	L
Milke		L	—	H		H	
Orffmann	L	L	L	—		L	L
Stiph					—		
Wach		L	H	H		—	
Woeps	H						—

This interested Cook. Indeed, a personal visit from God—perhaps dropping by to justify bubonic plague or Walter Wach—could not have interested him more. But was this a correct analysis of the Wabash social structure? Cook looked across the row where his own name was entered as "Agent." Yes—it wasn't very pretty, but there you were. He hated them all—all except Stiph, whom he had, well, wondered about but neither hated nor loved. And Woeps? Yes, you could call it love in that he thought about Woeps every day, wondered about his home life a great deal, missed him deeply when he was not at work, worried about him, wanted to help him, and more. Good work, Arthur. Good observation.

Orffmann's profile was striking. As an agent he loved everyone but Stiph, yet as a patient he fared badly in return. Cook thought about this. Orffmann did have a bit of a toadying quality, always expressing indiscriminate awe of everyone. And it was a rare occasion when he was invited to lunch—he generally brown-bagged it alone in his office—and he was rarely spoken of, and if he was, then only dismissively. This meant that there was a fearful asymmetry in Orffmann's life. He was a perfect example of unrequitedness. Cook suddenly found this rather sad. In his memory, Orffmann's solitary laughter now rang hollow, almost pleading.

Cook looked at his own column, blinked with wonder, and looked at it some more. Could this be right? Was he—it made his bowels grumble to think it—loved by Aaskhugh, Milke, Orffmann, and Wach? Why not Woeps? Why was there a blank space where Agent Woeps met Patient Cook? The chart must have been unfinished, or maybe Stiph had made a mistake. He looked for others. Aaskhugh and Woeps—yes, those "H's" seemed to capture the way things stood between them. The same for Milke and Wach. Still, there was something dreadfully wrong about Stiph's perception of Patient Cook.

Stiph's own name was oddly free of emotion, either as giver or receiver. This may have been a gesture of objectivity—perhaps Stiph, as "principal investigator" in this project, felt obliged to make no judgments about himself. And yet there seemed to be a rightness to those blank spaces at his row and column. As an agent he was somewhat aloof in his sleepy way, interacting little with the other linguists, and as a patient he seemed to be the same kind of figure for the others as he was for Cook: a curious object of distant attention and good-natured amusement, but not one of love or hatred. Of course Cook had heard Aaskhugh call Stiph a "lazy turd" some time back, but such words from Aaskhugh's mouth did not signify dislike. Aaskhugh was merely using language in the way he thought it was designed to be used. Even Orffmann, in Stiph's judgment, stopped short of his normal, mindless adoration. It was too bad, though, that the chart was so silent about Stiph. One little "H"—or two, to make it reciprocal—and Cook would know the identity of Stiph's backfriend and killer. He needed something like this, some voice from the outside speaking out and presenting him with a solution to the crimes.

He studied the chart some more and noticed that there were more "H's" than "L's." He wondered if this was true of all groups. Even, say, charitable organizations and churches? He also noticed that while there was reciprocity of hatred (Aaskhugh-Woeps, Milke-Wach), there was none of love. Did this mean there were no true friendships at Wabash? No. Again, Stiph had to be wrong about Woeps. Besides, someone famous once said that a good sign of friendship was two people disliking the same things, and Cook and Woeps both disliked Aaskhugh. Of course Cook and Milke both disliked Wach, and for that matter nearly everyone disliked poor Clyde, all of which proved . . .

Cook stood up and looked out the window and sighed. What did it prove? What was the point of it all? Was there no end to Stiph's perverse idleness? This coldly analytical chart, his general meanness of spirit, his Backside Club—that especially. Cook had thought it was a tantalizing idea at one time. Cute. That was the word he had used in talking about it with Leaf. He looked down from his window to the parking lot, where Clyde Orffmann regularly pulled his weary and disliked bones out of his car and walked to the building where he plied his craft incompetently, and he wondered if Orffmann would find it cute.

When Cook called for Wally, Woeps's wife, Helen, answered the door. As was customary, she leaned forward to be kissed on the mouth by him. He didn't know why she always did this, but because she was nice-looking in a late-forties way, he mildly enjoyed it. Although somewhat high-strung, Helen had to be considered one of the lucky things that had happened to Woeps. And she certainly was nice to Cook. Only recently she had quite embarrassed him by taking him aside and squeezing his arm and telling him how grateful she was for what he did for her husband at work and elsewhere.

Ed was upstairs with Amy, and when Cook was announced he yelled down something about a car seat. Helen led Cook outside and helped him take one of two seats out of their station wagon and put it in his Valiant. As he was doing this, a man and woman who were no doubt Helen's parents wheeled around the corner of the house. Wally leaned forward in his stroller and pointed at Cook as if identifying him as the man who had stolen his Tommee Tippee cup. Helen introduced Cook to her parents. Wally let Cook take him out of the stroller and put him in the car seat. Amid a thunderclap of bye-byes Cook drove off.

Wally was silent all the way to Wabash, simply smiling in the breeze of the car. Outside the building, he decided to look at a dandelion on the grass. Cook indulged him. Wally picked it and held it out for Cook to take, which he did, thanking him. Judging from the number of repetitions of this that ensued, Wally must have found it richly rewarding. Cook finally pitched a handful of mangled dandelions to the ground behind his back and scooped Wally up in his arms. As he unlocked the front door to the building Wally said, "Uhpah," so Cook gave him his keys to play with as they walked in. He let Wally push the elevator button, and as the light came on Wally said, "Gah," to which Cook agreed.

Upstairs he took Wally to his office and set him up on the floor with his keys and some books on semiotics that he had no intention of ever reading. As Wally began his systematic destruction of the books, Cook unlocked the door to the gym directly across the hall. He turned on the lights and glanced inside, happy to see most of the moveable toys that Woeps had specified as objects of his son's pleasure or displeasure. Unfortunately there was only one of the latter that Woeps knew about—a large, geared contraption on wheels, looking something like a huge watch with its backplate removed. When pulled, its parts moved, and it gave off a hideous thunking sound. Cook didn't much like it either. He hid the experimental objects, for he knew that Wally usually said *m-bwee* only once about an object in a given social situation, and he wanted to be sure he knew which object Wally was talking about.

He stepped across the hall and walked Wally into the gym, closing his office door behind him. He checked the tape in his recorder mounted high on one wall and took down a large clipboard with a blank legal tablet attached to it. He went to where Wally was standing and sucking his thumb, and he sat with him awhile to put him at ease. Wally seemed a bit overwhelmed by the emptiness of the room, since he normally saw it only when filled with many competitive peers. The opportunities for uninterrupted play, for sole possession of each and every piece of equipment, seemed to make him suspicious. This didn't bother Cook. He had even expected it and for that reason hadn't set the tape going right off. He would wait. He spied a *Mother Goose* book on a nearby chair and read to Wally to help him relax. Cook hadn't read the rhymes in a long time, and he now marveled at the cruelty of some of them and at the verb forms of others. Wally lost interest just as Cook finished with "Dr. Fell" and walked to the Creative Playthings slide and began to climb on it. He began babbling, but it wasn't until nearly twenty minutes later that Cook, heavy-lidded and yawning, judged that Wally was his normal sociable self and stood up to turn on the tape recorder.

As he walked across the room Wally looked at him and said *m-bwee* with a clearly rising intonation. Cook told Wally he liked him too. He turned on the recorder and waited a few minutes before producing a wind-up scooting bug, one of Wally's favorites. With almost boring predictability Wally greeted its motion with the same approving *m-bwee* he had just given Cook. A few minutes later Cook produced another favorite toy of Wally's, a duck, and without winding it up he set it out on the floor when Wally wasn't looking. When he finally spied it he squealed, smiled, stood up, and walked to it, banged it around, mouthed it, and did many other things to it, but he did not say *m-bwee* to it. When he set it down Cook quickly wound it up and sent it across the floor. Wally's rising *m-bwee* this time made Cook laugh.

Next came the painful part. He took the disgusting mechanical thing that Wally didn't like from behind a tarp near the door and set it in the middle of the room. He took one end of the long pull cord with him across the room and waited there with it while Wally played, his back turned, with a nondescript plastic block that kept causing him to laugh hysterically every few seconds. As Cook sat there, crouched, he felt like some dumb, bad cowboy in a grade-B film waiting to trip some equally dumb, but good, cowboy by yanking the rope as he rode by. Wally's block spent its power to amuse him and he turned around as if to ask, "What now?" Cook began to pull the toy, slowly and steadily. It sent out one of its *thunk* noises and Wally looked at it, eyes wide open. The accompanying *m-bwee* held a level tone for some time and then began to drop, slowly at first, then quickly all the way to the bottom of Wally's register. He ran to Cook, giving the toy wide berth, and raised his arms to be picked up. Cook obliged him, giving the watch toy a kick that sent it back behind the tarp, and he apologized to the boy.

He decided Wally deserved a break. He stood up and carried him to the tape recorder. As he looked at the counter to see how much playing time was left, Wally's hand squeezed the skin on his neck painfully and the boy's body tensed as he said *m-bwee* again. As just before, the intonation was falling. Cook pried Wally's hand away from his neck and turned around to see what he was looking at. One edge of the watch toy protruded from behind the tarp, and Wally was looking in that direction, his eyes darting back and forth nervously in an arc that included the tarp area and both sides of it as well.

Two things baffled Cook. The watch toy was not moving, and Wally had already said *m-bwee* to it, or about it. He turned the recorder off. Then he began to take Wally out into the hall for a walk, but this meant that they must walk right by the tarp, which lay against the wall next to the door, and this was too much for Wally. He whined and squirmed and clawed at Cook's neck, so Cook turned and left the gym by the door going into the hallway in the central core. This appeared to be fine with Wally. Cook set him down and followed him down this narrow hall to the door opening into the main hall near the bathroom. Cook opened it for him and the two of them moved back down the curving hall toward Cook's office at a torturously slow pace. When they finally reached it, to their right was the open door leading back into the gym—the one that Wally had refused to pass through coming in the other direction. Cook watched Wally strut, with boldness or ignorance, into the gym, oblivious to the tarp and watch toy as he passed by them.

Near the door Cook sat down on a bean bag chair and watched Wally play in the middle of the room. He yawned. He leaned back in the chair and stretched his legs out in front of him. He shook his head quickly when he felt himself dropping off to sleep, and then stood up. He would get a few more positive *m-bwee*'s (the negative ones were too cruel) and then go home. He started the tape recorder and joined Wally on the floor, his knees cracking as he bent down. He said a few friendly words to the boy to put him in good humor.

He heard a scraping sound through the open door that he shouldn't have heard. Or was it his imagination? Wally's sudden alertness—he had turned and looked to the door expectantly—confirmed his suspicion and gave him a chill. The sound seemed to have come from his office across the hall, which he had left unlocked with the door closed. He stood up and walked to it. The realization that he was moving stealthily produced a sinking feeling in his stomach. He reached the door of his office and looked back over his shoulder. Wally was watching with great interest. Very gently, Cook tried the doorknob.

It was locked. His keys were on the floor, inside the office, where Wally had been playing with them. The door could not have locked itself. It took little reasoning to conclude that someone was in there. Who? Should he press the issue? If he did, tomorrow would it be Jeremy Cook sitting in that chair, hairless and muscles taut with death? He should call the police for help. But the other offices were no doubt locked, and so the nearest accessible phone was the pay phone on the first floor. He didn't want whoever was on the other side of the door slipping out while he swapped neologisms with Lieutenant Leaf.

Another scraping sound. A rustle of paper. A squeak.

He knocked sharply on the door. "Who's there?" he said authoritatively. Or so he hoped.

There was no reply.

"I know someone's in there. Open the door."

The silence rebuked him for being a fool.

"For Christ's sake—"

A scraping sound again, as of a chair being moved out of the way. Cook listened carefully. Suddenly a soft, pathetic, frightened whimper came from the other side of the door. Cook's mouth dropped open and he winced to hear it. It was unearthly. He heard it grow slightly in volume and suddenly stop. Heavy footsteps moved away from the door, away from Cook, and a masculine groan of some kind was followed instantly by a loud crash of glass. After a few seconds of horrible silence, there was a faint but unmistakable thud from some distance away.

"Jesus. Oh Jesus."

Cook ran for the stairwell and hurried down the seven flights, trying to believe in all of the other possible explanations, although none of these was as vivid in his mind as the one he was trying not to believe. Outside, in the dark, the black shape crumpled in the distance proved to be the heavy wooden swivel chair from his office, its back broken and barely connected to the seat. It was otherwise undamaged, for it had landed on soft grass. It was as if the chair had tried to die from the fall much as a human would have died.

Cook looked up to the window of his office. A dark figure leaning out disappeared inside, and an unfamiliar, high-pitched, derisive cackle rained down on him.

Cook thought of Wally and yelled out in reflexive panic. He sprinted to the door and ran up the stairs. When he reached the top he heard Wally screaming and crying loudly from the gym. He ran down the hall. The boy was alone, unhurt, and very frightened, sitting in the middle of the room where Cook had left him. He lifted him up in his arms and comforted him. Wally's thumb went to his mouth, and in the sudden quiet Cook heard running footsteps from the end of the hall near the stairs, then the banging of the stairwell door. He listened but did not give chase. He eased himself down on the mat covering the floor in the center of the gym and sat cross-legged, holding Wally against his shoulder and rocking back and forth.

"Jeremy, I would think by now you would have learned to lock your office."

Lieutenant Leaf, fat and to all appearances uncomfortable behind the wheel of his patrol car, glanced at Cook as he said this and narrowly missed clipping the bumper of a parked car as he turned the corner too sharply. They were returning to Wabash from Woeps's house, where Leaf had driven Cook and Wally. Cook had had to call someone for transportation, because the intruder had taken his keys and locked his office before escaping. Leaf would want to know about the prowler anyway, so Cook had called him from the pay phone downstairs. His first concern was getting Wally home and in bed. When Leaf and his driver arrived at Wabash, Cook found Leaf amiably willing to drive him and Wally to Wally's home. Without ceremony he ordered his driver to wait outside the door of Cook's office until they returned. It was then, as he walked to Leaf's car, that Cook saw that his own car had been stolen. It was turning into a rough night all around. At Woeps's, Cook changed Wally and put him to bed while Leaf, amused, watched from the door of Wally's room. Cook left a message with the babysitter for Woeps to call him at the office or at home when he came in.

"Believe me, Lieutenant," said Cook as Leaf pulled out onto the highway leading to Wabash, "I'll lock it from now on." He looked at Leaf's transmitter on the dashboard. "Can you use that thing to have someone call my boss? His secretary has a master key and they can get us into my office. No point in breaking the door down."

"Right," said Leaf, reaching for his mike. After he was done with this he turned to Cook again. "So . . . as you come out of the stairwell the bathroom is just down the hall to the right."

"Yes."

"And you went down the hall to the left."

"Yes."

"And you figure he was hiding in the bathroom, waiting for you to go in the other direction so he could slip down the stairs."

"Yes."

"Why didn't you check the bathroom? Afraid?"

"No. Wally was crying and I was worried about him."

"But it would have taken just a second—"

"But the kid was screaming. I didn't know what was happening to him."

"Ah." Leaf thought about this. "It's a lot like the way you automatically assumed the guy had jumped out the window."

Cook frowned. "How's that?"

"Why do you think the boy was crying?" asked Leaf, ignoring Cook's question. "Do you think this guy did anything to him?"

"No. He seemed okay to me. Just upset. Maybe because I left him alone. I feel horrible about that."

"No harm done."

Leaf was driving fast on the country highway. Cook glanced at the speedometer. Just over eighty. He reached for the seat belt at the side of the seat next to the door.

"The belt's busted," said Leaf. "Who do you think it was?"

"It could have been any of us but Woeps, I guess."

"Why not him?"

"He's out with his wife and in-laws."

"I'll check that. Did you call any of the others to see if they were home?"

"When? You mean after I—" He slapped himself on the forehead.

"Yes. Just after it happened, just after the guy got away. If they were home and hadn't had time to get home from Wabash, that would tell us something. You didn't do that, did you?"

"No."

Leaf was silent for a while. Then he said, "This fellow Woeps is a friend of yours, isn't he?"

"That's right."

"And you think what happens tonight clears him?"

"In my mind, yes."

"And it's supposed to in mine?"

Cook looked at him. "Slow down, Lieutenant, damn it. You're driving too fast."

Leaf obediently eased back on the accelerator.

"I don't care what you think," said Cook.

"Is there any reason for me to think you didn't make all this up?"

Cook laughed, in frustration and disbelief. "There's no point to it. That's a pretty good reason."

"Except that it could clear your friend. But it won't. It's easy for a desperate man to get his family to lie for him. I want you to know that I plan to ignore what they have to say."

"Where's my car, then?" said Cook, hating himself for allowing Leaf to bait him.

"You tell me."

"I can't."

"Too bad for you."

Cook decided to stop talking. What was he to do next—stick his tongue out at Leaf?

"So," said Leaf in a fresh new tone, as if the conversation were just now beginning, "why do you think this guy was in your office?" He slowed the car and turned into the road following the river up to the building.

"I don't know," Cook said wearily. "Maybe we'll find out when my boss gets here and lets us in."

But they didn't. Wach arrived, dressed as he always was in a tie and long-sleeved shirt, and then Mary the Secretary arrived with her hair in curlers. After Mary let Wach into her desk, he sent her home. Then he opened Cook's office. Except for the absent chair and the glass fragments on the desk and floor, it was to all appearances in the same condition it had been in when Cook had last seen it. He looked through the drawers of the desk and filing cabinet. Nothing seemed to have been disturbed. Wach watched him with concern, but he was taking it well. That is, he did not order Cook to drive immediately to Indianapolis to give a lecture to the Chamber of Commerce on Kickapoo adverbs. His stance was stoic. This was one more cross for him to bear, and bear it he would. He and Wabash both.

When Cook was done examining his office and had turned to the window, wondering what to do about it, the phone rang.

"That must be Ed," he said to the others. "I wanted to tell him right away." He picked up the phone.

"What's your car doing in my driveway, Jay?" It was, of course, Aaskhugh.

"How long has it been there, Adam?"

"I don't know. I just pulled in and there it was. Keys are in it too. And an infant car seat. I didn't know you had a baby, Jay. What's going on?"

Cook explained, or tried to. He told Aaskhugh he would be over soon to pick it up. He successfully resisted Aaskhugh's efforts to explore the matter further and hung up. He told Leaf and Wach what Aaskhugh had said.

"What a mess," said Leaf. "I'm coming with you, Jeremy. I want to check that car."

"For fingerprints?"

"No. For a bomb."

"Really?"

"Not that I expect to find one, but . . . it's sort of like you and your friend's son. I'd be responsible if anything happened to you. I think we're done here."

The phone rang again. This time it was Woeps. Cook explained what had happened. With Leaf's reminder fresh in his memory, he emphasized that Wally had not been hurt by the experience. Just frightened. Woeps listened without interrupting and told him he would talk to him tomorrow.

In the course of the rest of the week, Cook learned a number of things: (1) that Wach had perversely come up with a still more restrictive title for his ominously approaching lecture on names, (2) that Leaf was somewhat famous, (3) of a miscellaneous nature, that Wach's rules numbered fifteen, with no end in sight; that five—count them, *five*—people did not consider him, Cook, a complete asshole; and that he was going to a party, (4) that Woeps had meant it when he told Cook he would talk to him tomorrow, and (5) what that person was doing in his office.

(1) Wach's title, which greeted Cook in his mailbox the morning after the taping with Wally and all that followed, was "The Lore and Magic of Kinsey County (Indiana) Place Names." Cook quickly informed Wach by memo that the title should be "Names." He wrote this in such a way that it did not clearly call attention to itself as a reminder that Wach had already been so informed; nor did it pose ostentatiously as a first communication of this point, for then Wach, if he remembered Cook's earlier request, would resent being patronized. The memo was no small stylistic achievement.

(2) In the Monday issue of Kinsey's local rag, Cook came across an article praising Lieutenant Leaf for his fine service to the community. The occasion of the article was the twenty-fifth anniversary of Leaf's joining the Kinsey Police Department, feted (as small-town journalists liked to say) the preceding night by Kinsey politicians and policemen in some sort of stag party in the banquet room of a downtown hotel. The article, sandwiched on the front page as if by design between two articles titled "Husband Slays Wife While Children Watch" and "Starving Dog Shot," stated that no "suspicious death" cases and only ninety-three

rape cases had gone unsolved since Leaf had come to the Kinsey police force. Leaf was described as "a real go-getter" by the mayor. "He goes and he gets 'em," the mayor was quoted as saying, producing just the kind of joke that Hoosiers laughed at. Cook was skeptical. When would Leaf go and get Arthur Stiph's and Henry Philpot's killer? And how was he going about it?

Unethically, no doubt, judging from subsequent information in the article. Apparently Leaf had a bad reputation among Kinsey judges for violating search-and-seizure laws, as well as other standards of police procedure. The community clearly sided with Leaf on this question (and this explained the inclusion of this background information in the laudatory write-up of the *fete*), so much so that no incumbent judge was ever re-elected. The mulish persistence of every new judge in interpreting the law exactly as his predecessor had (i.e., correctly) must have truly baffled the Kinsey electorate.

(3a) By memo, Cook requested a new typewriter from Wach. By memo, Wach replied with a polite negative. Cook followed this with a polite reaffirmative. Wach responded with a curt denial and a statement that Mary the Secretary's electric typewriter was to be at his disposal. To an outsider this would have looked, if not generous, at least reasonable. But it wasn't. Mary's typewriter, because it was the only electric on the floor (apart from Wach's), was at *everyone's* disposal and had been for years. Wach had thus offered Cook nothing new at all. His gesture was like an apparent counterexample in linguistics (something that at first looks like a counterexample to a claim, but isn't really); it was an *apparent counteroffer,* a disguised way of saying, "Nah." This was at the heart of Wach Rule Fifteen, which Cook had found could be expressed in two ways: offer underlings the status quo as if it were a bold new idea, or, give people nothing, but act as if you were cutting out little pieces of your heart as you did so.

(3b) Cook was able to learn, in one case by telephonic disguise (Mr. Philip Henrypot, credit investigator), in two others by gentle inquiry, and in a fourth by well-timed, pause-at-the-open-door eavesdropping, that four teachers who seemed to him not to like him *did* like him. He was prompted to make these inquiries by the unsolicited, unsought revelation (via a waitress at Max's who got it from a Kinsey League Basketball teammate of Mary the Secretary's ex-boyfriend) that prior to her discovery of Stiph's body in Cook's office Mary "admired" Cook. Cook figured that while some replacement of the lexicon inevitably occurred in the transmission of oral narratives, there was no way to get from "asshole" to "admire" or back again. His chief suspect cleared, he had reluctantly re-opened the investigation.

(3c) In another Paula-related area, Cook received an invitation to a party of the Wabash staff and some neighbors and friends. The invitation came from Milke, but the party was to be "At the Home of Mr. and Mrs. Frank Nouvelles." Cook knew that Nouvelles was Paula's last name. Beyond that, the possibilities were endless—Frank was her husband and she was the Mrs. and both Cook and Milke had been wasting their time; or Frank and the Mrs. were her parents and had overprotectively moved from somewhere to Kinsey to be with their daughter for the duration of her summer job; or ditto and Paula had grown up here (this was supported by the little linguistic evidence he had gotten from his one decent conversation with her: although Paula did not *poosh* her car when it broke down, she did write with a *pin*); or etc. A casual question in Aaskhugh's direction produced a machine-gun volley of facts, among them confirmation of the Paula-a-native-of-Kinsey theory. Nice to know, but what could he do with it? Did the humbleness of her geographical roots make her less attractive (and therefore less painful) to him? No. More attractive (and painful)? No. At any rate the prospect of the party cheered him. Something to look forward to on Saturday night besides linguistics and beef-rice-tomato remnants.

(4) Early Tuesday morning Woeps visited Cook in his office and asked for a recapitulation of the events of the night before. He said he wanted to be sure he understood everything. He also said Wally seemed to be all right—he had awakened him and examined him meticulously right after talking with Cook on the phone. Also, he had given Wally some ipecac to induce vomiting in case he had been poisoned. Cook wondered why Woeps suspected poison, and, when he asked he was told in somewhat impatient language that it was certainly possible that the man who shaved Arthur Stiph and anchored Henry Philpot with a typewriter was the man who had been in Cook's office, and that to such a man poisoning a baby might seem very natural, desirable even, and—here he began yelling—for that reason it had been unforgivable of Cook to do what he had done. Unforgivable. Hadn't it occurred to Cook, he asked, his face reddening with anger, that the entire event was a scheme to get Wally alone so that something horrible could be done to him? And he had fallen for it like a fool. Didn't he know the importance of care with children? He wasn't quite as perfect as everyone thought he was, was he? Woeps shouted down Cook's attempts to justify himself and forbade him from following him to his office to explain further. His final words as he yanked open the door and almost knocked down two window repairmen standing in the hall with a large pane of glass: "Don't speak to me again until I speak to you."

(5) That same afternoon, after a sad and solitary lunch, Cook

looked again at Stiph's notes on acquisition of esteem terms. As he sat in Stiph's chair, which he had taken out of Stiph's office that morning to replace his own, his backside now rubbing where Stiph's had once rubbed, he had an eerie feeling that he was in some sense becoming Arthur Stiph. When he got to the page with the Love-Hate charts, he was a little surprised to see the chart for the adult males at Wabash facing him. When he had finished studying it the day before, he had considered that side the backside and returned the sheet to the folder with the other side up. He looked at the chart closely. The additions were so cleverly forged that he hardly noticed them. Stiph's row and column had been completely blank before, but each now contained one "H." One was in the box where Agent Stiph met Patient Milke, and the other where Agent Milke met Patient Stiph. Cook studied the sheet closely under the light. The ink was slightly different—good evidence that he, Cook, was not going insane. Not so different that you would normally notice, but different nonetheless.

Someone's thinking had duplicated Cook's to a striking degree. One of the suspects had seen this chart (the sheet had been passed around in Stiph's office when they first discovered its frontside; it would have been easy for one of them, without Cook noticing, to see the backside of it and quickly take in its contents); then he had seen the possibilities it presented; then, figuring Cook's office would be accessible that night (Cook had openly—and stupidly, it now turned out—told Woeps about his plans to tape Wally in the gym that night in front of all the others, and it was common practice for the linguists to leave their office doors unlocked when working in the central core with the children), he had acted, picking Milke. The success of the plan hinged crucially on the hope (someone's hope) that Cook had not seen the chart before its alteration. It was not an unreasonable hope either, for Cook had just barely noticed it. And if he hadn't—that is, if he were discovering it for the first time now—how would he view this evidence?

Seriously, he admitted to himself. Seriously indeed. He could easily imagine himself savoring those "H's" and looking forward to life at Wabash without Milke. The choice of those two boxes had been a clever one. He definitely would have acted on it, even though the thought of taking it to Leaf made him smile. First it would confirm Leaf's view that the suspects were a pack of dicklike jackals, or some such, and Cook would have to put up with a kinky speech on that theme. Then Leaf would wonder aloud if Cook himself could have tampered with the chart, or made the whole thing up for that matter, in order to frame Milke and clear himself. But for all that, even as he gave a show of great scorn, Leaf would take the information seriously too.

The image of that fat man mocking him was so striking that Cook decided not to tell him about the attempted frame. He decided not to tell anybody, not even Woeps, despite the fact that being told would put his mind at ease about Wally, for it was now certain that the boy was incidental to the episode. Besides, Woeps had forbidden speech to him, thereby thrusting Cook into a sociolinguistic dilemma he would have found interesting if it had happened to someone else.

The car at Aaskhugh's was another dimension. The intruder probably did not expect to be discovered, so that part must have been spontaneous. Certainly spreading the old guilt around, wasn't he? Since people don't ordinarily frame themselves, did all of this clear Aaskhugh and Milke? Not if you thought like Leaf. In fact he would hang both of them on evidence like this, if only the judiciary would go along with him. The chair-throwing must have been spontaneous too.

Quite a clever man to know how Cook would react.

He seemed to know a lot about Cook. In fact . . . Another thought struck him and made him smile grimly. Maybe the man figured it didn't matter if Cook had already seen the chart or not. Maybe he thought if it failed one way it would work another way, as a *suggestion*, as if to say, "Hey, Jeremy (or Jay), we can really stick it to Emory with this. Think about it."

It gave him a chill. Personal dislike was one thing. This was something altogether different. Maybe there were people in this world who weren't able to draw this distinction, but Cook wasn't one and he wasn't happy about being taken for one, even by a killer.

ELEVEN

"'YOU CAN'T SEE *SHIT* IN THERE'."

"In that case you're not really talking about shit."

"That's right. Just visibility."

"And the other?"

"No stress on *shit.* Descending intonation to *shit,* then rising. The way you'd say, 'You can't see the Alps from there' if you were a well-traveled snot contradicting someone."

"And with that intonation you *are* talking about shit."

"Right. Or the Alps."

She smiled. "That's really very good. I'll work on it. The trick is to find a general explanatory principle."

"That's the trick all right," said Cook.

Paula studied him a moment. He let her do this and tried to look brilliant and handsome. He also tried very hard to think of something more to say.

"I have really enjoyed talking with you, Jeremy," she finally said.

"Oh? Thanks, but . . . does that mean you're going to leave me now?"

She laughed. "No. In fact, that you would even think that's what I meant confirms what I was beginning to believe about you. Emory will be back with our drinks soon, so I have to speak quickly. Listen carefully. I'm having a little difficulty figuring out exactly what you're interested in when you're with me. This is only the second or third time we've had a chance to talk, so maybe I'm speaking too soon, but it seems that whenever we get together you want to talk about linguistics. That's fine with me, of course, but I can't help thinking something else is going on. Of course linguistics is your life's work, but if you were interested solely in the subject I'd expect that that's all you would talk about with everybody. But I've seen you in the halls and in the playrooms talking with Sally and Ed and the others about just everyday things. Are you trying to appear to be something you are not when you are with me, and if so, why?"

Cook hadn't expected her to stop there and began to panic when she did. He searched for verbal cover. Then he caught himself. This was no time for temporizing, disingenuousness, evasion, or any other of the obsolete weapons in his arsenal—obsolete, at least, in the face of this indomitable wench. He rallied and spoke honestly.

"I want to get to know you," he said, not sure what question he was answering but sure that this explained it all.

"Then you should talk about me. And you."

"But I figured since you're a linguist—"

"That's part of me, but there's more."

"And, to be honest, I wanted to impress you."

"And you have. But why? And why do you want to get to know me?"

"Because you are pretty and you have a nice carriage."

She laughed loudly but good-naturedly. She glanced over Cook's shoulder and said quickly, "Maybe some day I'll give you a ride in it."

Emory Milke suddenly appeared from behind a momentarily speechless Cook, grasping a triangle of two glasses and one bottle between his hands. "A gin and tonic for you, my dear," he said around his pipe as he extended one corner of his triangle to Paula, "and a beer for Jeremy, there you are, and the dealer takes a bourbon, and here's to you, cheers, prosit, and so on." He removed his pipe from his mouth and drank a large swallow. Cook watched a bit of liquid trickle down his beard. Then he looked to Paula to see if she had seen it. Over her glass, her eyes were fixed on Cook. He blushed. She smiled, turned to Milke, and thanked him for getting the drinks.

"No trouble at all, dearest chuck," he said. "The chief inconvenience to me was knowing I was leaving you in, or near, the hands of one Dr. Jeremy Cook of the Wabash Institute. You'll note that I did not dally in the kitchen."

"I noticed even if she didn't," said Cook. On reflection he realized with surprise that he had spoken to Milke without malice, sarcasm, or desire to offend. Perhaps it was the three beers he had had at home before the party that made him so friendly. Or Paula's come-on, if that's what it was.

"Quite a crowd in there," said Milke, looking back to the kitchen.

"The place is going to be packed soon. Awfully good of you to throw open your parents' house like this, Paula. And good of them"—here he laughed—"to be in Yugoslavia." He turned to Cook. "Isn't she something, Jeremy? How she just jumps in with both feet? Three weeks on the job and here she is throwing the biggest party in the history of Wabash. Just look at them. They've been absolutely *starving* for something like this. Does Wach think of giving one? Hell, no, the joyless bastard." He laughed. "For that matter, do I think of giving one? Hell, no. But here comes Paula from the far-out Far West, hot to trot and boogie, and she just breathes life into us, doesn't she?" He looked at her affectionately and shook his head. For a moment Cook feared he was going to say, "Oh you kid!" What he did say was nearly as moronic. "Love that spunk." Mike said this with his teeth fiercely gritted, as if in truth he hated Paula. Actually, though, he was just speaking around his pipe again, clenching it firmly between his jaws.

"Pardon me?" said Cook, wanting to call attention to the sentence.

"I said—"

"Oh, stop it, Emory," said Paula in a friendly way.

"Stop what?" asked Aaskhugh, easing into their circle and conversation. Cook had spied him earlier at the far end of the dining room. Aaskhugh's question filled him with a mad temptation to see if he, with the help of others, could keep the "spunk" line under discussion for the rest of the night.

"Emory here," Cook said, "was praising Paula's spontaneity, Adam, and her *joie de vivre*, and he capped it all by saying—"

"Oh now stop it, all of you," laughed Paula. "I'm glad you could make it, Adam."

Without responding to this friendly welcome Aaskhugh went right to work, asking Paula about her exact connection with this house, the precise whereabouts of her parents, her curriculum vitae thus far, and more. Milke and Cook sipped their drinks. Cook half-listened to Aaskhugh and then reminded himself to listen fully and carefully. He resolved to listen to what everyone said.

Milke suddenly turned to him and asked him how his work was going. He added that he was particularly interested in Cook's progress on Stiph's unfinished work. Cook put all his sensory faculties on full alert and told Milke that the work was very complex because Stiph's notes were hard to decipher—so hard that when he came back to them after being away from them he sometimes had to abandon his earlier interpretations, "almost," he said, "as if the notes, believe it or not, had changed while sitting in my office." He packed as much innuendo and meaningful frowning and eyelash-batting into this last part as he could muster, and Milke did look at him a little oddly, but then Milke went on to say quite calmly that if his own notes were any indication he could appreciate how hard it was for one man to decipher another's. This struck Cook as reasonable and apposite and left him with nothing. Milke then wondered out loud just when things were going to settle down at Wabash and if any of their jobs were really in danger, and Aaskhugh turned away from Paula—apparently he was done using her in his own fashion—and addressed himself to Milke's question. He said that his current information on that point was that unless enrollments went back up soon, Ed Woeps would be fired.

"*What?*" asked Cook. "Who told you that?"

Aaskhugh smiled. "I have my sources."

Cook thought, Wach was as tight-lipped as he was tightassed. Who else would know something like this?

"Mary?" he asked. "Did Mary tell you?"

"No fair, Jay," said Aaskhugh, laughing and relishing his power.

"But why Ed?" asked Milke just an instant before Cook was able to.

"I can give you my own opinion on that," said Aaskhugh. "Now that Arthur is dead Ed is the most disposable of us. Clyde is a close second, but Ed is first. His work is the least pioneering, it is the slowest to reach completion, and it is the last to get published. He's not pulling his weight."

"Bullshit," said Cook.

"Adam's right, Jeremy," said Milke. "About Ed relative to the rest of us, at least. Some of his work has been impressive, but compared with you, for example, he falls short."

"Compared with any of us," said Aaskhugh. "You have to admit that, Jay, even though he's your friend. Let's ask Paula. We can use her as a test." He turned to her. "You're a budding psycholinguist, Paula. Who at Wabash had you heard of before you came here?"

She looked at him coolly a moment. "I don't like your question," she finally said.

"But why not?" asked Aaskhugh.

"It promotes invidious comparisons."

"I know," said Aaskhugh, laughing. "That's the whole point. That's what's so wonderful about questions like that. You'll soon learn, Paula, that the first question intellectuals ask about a college or institute is 'Who's there?' Well, when they ask that about Wabash, I just want to know what the answer is. I would especially like to know what the answer is at a place as prestigious as U.C.L.A."

"Come on, Paula," urged Milke. "I'm kind of curious about this too."

Paula looked at Cook, who said nothing.

"All right," she said, "but I would think you men would have more grown-up things to talk about. I had heard of Jeremy, Emory, and Walter."

"Wach?" asked Milke. "He hasn't done a thing in years."

"I don't know about that. I read something he did some time ago on dichotic listening." She paused. "That's all."

"Just as I thought," said Aaskhugh, though less brashly than before. "But surely you've read my classic work on the syntax of interrogatives."

"I can't say that I have, Adam."

"Well," said Aaskhugh, "if that's what's going on at U.C.L.A. I'll have to think twice about what I think about that place. I sure will." He looked to the floor and clucked his tongue. Paula winked at Cook, making him smile in spite of a certain heaviness in his heart. Aaskhugh just had to be wrong about Woeps. And yet Aaskhugh was seldom wrong. He spied Wach passing through the living room, alone, and he knew from other social gatherings that Wach's departure would be within thirty minutes of his arrival, so he called out to him and waved him over to join their group. He heard Milke mutter some noises of discontent and felt obliged to explain.

"I want to check Adam's story, Emory."

Aaskhugh looked up at him. "That's a bit awkward, Jay. I don't think—"

"You brought it up, Adam. Speech has consequences. You're going to have to learn that."

"What?" he asked, quite puzzled.

Cook turned to see where Wach was. He had responded to Cook's invitation but had been detained by one of the teachers. Cook watched them talk. What, besides business, did people discuss with that man? Was the girl asking him if he had noticed from his newspaper reading that these were hard times for dictators?

"Well, I've argued with Walter at all kinds of social events," said Milke. "Meetings, weddings, funerals . . . I hope I can behave tonight."

"He does bring it out in you, doesn't he?" said Paula.

"Funerals?" asked Cook.

"Yes. After Arthur's funeral," said Milke.

"I remember you mentioning that, Emory," said Aaskhugh.

"*Immediately* after?" asked Cook. His question, supremely pointless to anyone who did not know about the dent in his car, drew puzzled looks.

"Yes," said Milke. "Some rare burst of brotherhood joined me to Walter and we walked back to our cars together. But then our conversation took its normal course."

"What did you argue about?" asked Cook, deliberately asking an irrelevant question.

"Who knows? This and that. The meaning of life. Walter could move a catatonic panda to argument. But why does this interest you so much, Jeremy?"

"I was about to ask the same," said Aaskhugh.

"Did he drive off first, or did you?" asked Cook.

Milke thought. "He did. Why?"

Cook frowned. He saw that Wach was moving toward them again and would save him from having to fabricate an explanation. Milke's story seemed to clear Wach of the crime of dent-making, and by implication it threatened to clear him of the other crimes too. This pleased Cook not a whit. He hoped Milke had made up the story to clear himself. But why would he make up an alibi that cleared other suspects as well?

Wach reached out both hands as he neared the group, and Cook wondered what he was going to do with them. With one he clapped Cook awkwardly on the back, like a man who has vowed to overcome physical disgust with human contact. With the other he reached out to pat Paula on the arm, but he more or less missed her.

"Talking shop, everyone?" he asked. "That's healthy. Very healthy. I don't want to interrupt. Other than to say again, Paula, that it is very good of you to entertain us in your home like this."

"No need to thank me," she said. "I hope to have fun tonight like everyone else." Cook looked at Milke, who appeared pleased to be looked at and gave Cook a salacious grin.

"Adam tells us that Ed might be let go," said Cook. "Is that true, Walter?"

Wach looked from Cook to Aaskhugh, then back to Cook. He deliberated. Finally he said, "I'm afraid so. I spoke with him about it yesterday, so it's all right for the rest of you to know. I wanted to give him a head start in looking for something else. It's a shame, but these decisions have to be made. It's not easy for me, but it's part of the job."

"I think it's just a fraction harder for Ed, though," said Cook.

"You don't have to tell me that, Jeremy," Wach said coldly. "At the same time, I am in the position of knowing that if something isn't done soon Wabash will be in a pretty pickle of a financial crisis. By the way, Jeremy, I can only assume that your lecture is ready."

"Is that all you can do?" asked Cook. "It's ready."

"Bright and early tomorrow" said Wach. "They want you there at eight."

"I know."

"I just wanted to make sure you did."

"What about Ed's work?" asked Cook. "He's right in the middle of it."

"He has all the data he needs. He can take it with him and finish it wherever he goes."

"Provided he lands a job that allows him time to do it," said Cook. "Research positions are hard to come by."

"He could teach," suggested Aaskhugh. "He might be good at that."

"Teaching. Jesus," said Milke. "Death."

"It would be improper for us to discuss this further," said Wach. He did not elaborate, and so a silence fell.

"Can I get you a drink, Walter?" asked Paula.

"No. I don't."

"You don't?"

"No."

"I, on the other hand, *do*," said Milke, "and I'm going to do it some more. Refills, anyone?"

Everyone but Wach said yes. Cook gave Milke his empty beer bottle to discard and thought about Wach's sudden termination of the discussion of Woeps. It had made him feel guilty and Aaskhugh-like for treating his friend as conversational fodder. And yet his sole interest in raising the subject had been to find out the truth, out of concern for Woeps. He wanted to return to it, but he wasn't sure how.

"What do you think of Emory's drinking habit, Paula?" asked Aaskhugh as soon as Milke was out of range.

"How do you mean?"

"Doesn't his consumption exceed that of the average American male?"

"I can't speak for him. You'd better ask him." She spoke calmly, as if Aaskhugh's questions were not value-laden. Or, Cook realized with a surge of joy, as if she had no personal stake in the matter.

"He probably drinks daily," said Aaskhugh to no one in particular.

"Do you consider that excessive, Adam?" asked Cook.

"I'm sure I don't know, Jay."

"From the way you asked I thought you had an opinion."

"I sure don't."

Cook decided to leave him alone for the moment and asked the entire group if Ed was at the party. No one knew. Paula said he had told her the preceding day that he intended to come, but Cook didn't know if that was before or after Wach had given him the bad news about his future. He could have figured it out by asking Paula and Wach more questions, but it wasn't worth it. He looked around the dining room and through the door into the living room but did not see him. He wanted to find him and take him aside and cheer him up or sympathize or do whatever Ed wanted him to do. But his friend had not yet uttered the sentence—any sentence would do—that would lift his ban on Cook's talking to him.

Milke returned, this time with a tray, and he handed drinks around—another bourbon for himself, a beer for Cook, nothing for Wach, and seltzer with lime for Paula and Aaskhugh.

"Adam was asking Paula about your drinking, Emory," said Cook.

"Jay! It wasn't like that at all. What are you trying—"

"It was exactly like that, Adam," said Cook.

"But Emory here is going to think—"

"Relax, Adam," said Milke. "I drink abundantly and daily, Jeremy. How about you?"

"Mmmm, somewhat the same, I'm afraid. At night mainly."

"At all hours for me," said Milke.

"Doesn't it interfere with your work?" asked Cook.

"I guess not. After all, I was one of those Paula had heard of, wasn't I?"

"But maybe you could do even more if you didn't drink."

"Or less. Maybe it helps me."

"How could it?" asked Wach. "It damages the brain—the seat of reason."

"I know, Walter," said Milke, "but it relaxes me, and I'm counting on it to damage just those cells devoted to knowledge of trivial stuff that doesn't affect my work—things like my aunts' birthdays, the Bill of Rights, and so on."

Cook laughed and started to say something friendly, but he caught himself.

"Of course I try not to drink when I'm working at Wabash. That would get in the way."

"I should think so, Emory," said Wach, his jowls shaking in a way that Cook found new and exciting. "I wouldn't want—"

"—people, let's see, from *the community* finding me falling down drunk and buggering some toddler. I know, Walter," said Milke. "Don't pull rank on me here, for Christ's sake."

"I'm glad you are aware of the potential complications," said Wach.

"Unfortunately," said Cook, "drinking can have a chaotic effect on one's memory even if it is confined to after hours." From behind, someone approached and bumped Cook gently on the shoulder blade, but he didn't turn around.

"How's that, Jeremy?" asked Milke.

"It's been my experience," Cook continued, "and I've read of experimental demonstrations of it, that what you forget depends on the state you were in when you first acquired the knowledge and the state you are in when you're trying to remember it. Facts learned when sober are of course best remembered when sober. Sober facts are forgotten in drunkenness, and drunkenly acquired facts are often forgotten in sobriety. None of this is too surprising, really. But this is: knowledge acquired when one is drunk is best remembered in a drunken state. For example, if you take ten people and get them all drunk in the laboratory and teach them a bunch of nonsense words, and then the next day if you divide the group in half and get one half drunk and keep the other half sober, the drunken half will do better on the re-test than the sober half."

"Is that right?" asked Paula.

"People always say the same things over and over at cocktail parties." Cook turned around and found the speaker to be Ed Woeps, who had been standing to his side and just in back of him. Even as he had been speaking Cook had noticed Paula's eyes glancing over his shoulder. Woeps was quite drunk. Cook wondered why he had said what he did. Cook had never given this particular talk before. He hoped Woeps was not so drunk he would embarrass himself.

"What do you mean, Ed?" asked Paula.

"People always say the same things over and over. When they drink. Because they can remember. To say only the things. They have said before. When they were drinking before. State-dependent." He turned and looked at Cook, tilting his head back and raising his eyebrows very high. "Does that make sense, Jeremy?"

Cook sighed with relief. "It sure does, Ed. I think you have nicely placed an accurate observation under the umbrella of a general explanation."

"That's my job," said Woeps.

Cook heard Aaskhugh say something to someone else, and the resulting conversation was loud enough to drown out what he wanted to say to Woeps, so he said it, gripping him by the upper arm: "And I hope it will continue to be, Ed." Woeps nodded slowly several times but looked ahead blankly, and Cook couldn't be sure his meaning had penetrated.

Milke took another request for refills. This time Cook asked for a bourbon on the rocks, to which Milke said, "Now we're cooking with gas." He came back with a tray on which sat a fresh bottle, an ice bucket, and two glasses. He set it on the dining room table and poured drinks for himself and Cook. Wach observed the ceremony coldly—or it seemed so to Cook—and he finally spoke.

"I suppose it hasn't occurred to you that your drinking incriminates you in the death of Arthur."

"How's that?" asked Milke.

"You will recall—I hope you're not that far gone yet, eh, Jeremy?—the vomitus on the floor of Jeremy's office. Whiskey, as I remember."

"Yes," said Aaskhugh enthusiastically. "Bourbon. Which I never touch."

"Oh, horseshit," said Milke.

"Ditto," said Cook. "If it had been me I wouldn't now advertise the fact that I drink bourbon."

"Ditto," said Milke.

"What have *you* been drinking, Ed?" asked Aaskhugh.

Woeps was a little slow to respond. He smiled a dreamy smile, then rocked forward a bit toward Aaskhugh and slurred, "Your blood."

"What?" said Aaskhugh.

"Ed, that's pretty silly," said Cook, laughing. Woeps began to laugh too. Aaskhugh looked at the two of them nervously.

"Along these lines," said Milke, "one could argue, in fact one *will* argue, and I am that one, that because you, Walter, have a master key to the offices, only you could have gotten into Jeremy's office this week to do whatever was done in there.

"Nonsense," said Wach, pressing his narrow lips together in a smile of delight at having caught Milke in a mistake. "First, it is common knowledge that Jeremy left his door unlocked, or have you forgotten?" He looked at the drink in Milke's hand. "Any one of us could have walked in there. Second, I do not have a master key. Mary has the only one. It is kept locked in her desk, to which she has a key, but she lacks a key to her office. One of us must be there for her to have access to the key. Thus no single person, including myself, exclusively controls the master key. The security is impeccable."

"I didn't know it was so well thought out," Milke said sarcastically. "Maybe you're right about the key business, but there must be other incriminating evidence against you. There's got to be. You're such a scoundrel." Milke laughed after saying this, and a stranger to the group would have thought he had spoken lightheartedly.

"I'm afraid there isn't, Emory," said Wach. "On the contrary, the fact that the crime and, in particular, the placing of the body in Jeremy's office call attention to Wabash and cast it into disrepute makes me an unlikely suspect. I would never do anything so damaging to the Institute. You all know of my abiding concern for our reputation in the community."

"Yeah, I heard something about that once," Milke said.

"Rather well prepared with that argument, aren't you, Walter?" said Cook.

"I am of the orientation that one ought always to be prepared," Wach said ponderously. Cook suddenly imagined how horrible it would be to be Wach's son or daughter. The people who would have been his children if he had had any were just as well off not existing.

"What I meant to suggest," Cook went on, "is that only a guilty man would have a defense so well prepared."

Wach did not speak. Cook did not know if he was exercising Wach Rule Four (in dangerous times wise men say nothing), or if he was just "not going to dignify that statement with a response," also a Wach Rule with a number he couldn't remember just now. Preferring drinking and forgetting to abstaining and remembering, he went to the table and poured himself another drink without asking if anyone else wanted one. He sensed it was every man for himself now. When he returned to his place in the circle he noticed that Paula was gone. He spotted her at the foot of the stairs in the living room, just on her way up.

Milke must have noticed Cook looking at her, because he bumped him and said, "Something, eh?" Cook made a face. If the setting had been a gangster movie, and if Milke and he had been discussing their—what was the word? *molls*?—he might have been able to say something. Milke added, "So young. Such a tight body, eh?" He saved Cook the anguish of yet another search for words by suddenly turning to Wach and shouting, "What did you say?"

Wach had been speaking to Aaskhugh and Woeps. He turned to Milke and arched his back. "That you are the primary suspect on my list, Emory."

"Oh? We're even then, because you're front and center on mine. Nothing personal, of course. Or rather, a lot."

"Listen, now—" began Wach, squaring his shoulders.

"Who's first on your list, Jay?" said Aaskhugh.

Cook watched Milke and Wach settle down as he thought about Aaskhugh's question. He gave an honest answer. "Nobody's first. Everyone's in even contention except Ed. He's last. He's not even on the list." He turned and looked at him. Woeps stood rooted in place, staring straight ahead as if he hadn't heard anything. Cook was pleased to see he was not drinking.

"Odd you should say that," said Aaskhugh, "seeing that he's first on my list."

"That's ridiculous," said Cook.

"Arthur's death was an accident, wasn't it?" said Aaskhugh. "That's enough for me."

Aaskhugh, who said bad things about people only in their absence, must have considered that Woeps now was, for all practical purposes, absent. Cook looked at Woeps. He stood there impassively.

"Perhaps. Perhaps not. But Philpot's death was not, Adam," he said, turning back to Aaskhugh. "It was calculated, deliberate, and cruel. Ed is none of those things. He can't speak for himself right now, so I will. You're a shitty judge of character."

"I'm glad you brought up Philpot," said Milke before Aaskhugh could respond. "I can't help wondering if any of us is strong enough to strangle a man."

"Oh, I've seen you wrap yourself around an air conditioner like it was nothing," Aaskhugh said to him. "Jeremy too. He helped me move once. Remember, Jay? We almost lost one out a window, though. It was a fun afternoon. I'm sure either of you could choke a man to death. I doubt that I could, though."

"You shake hands with a strong grip, Adam," said Milke. "I remember. Here." He stepped forward and reached out his right hand. Aaskhugh took it automatically. They clasped hands. "Oh come on," said Milke, and Aaskhugh rose to the challenge. Milke grinned. "Yes, I was right."

"Let me shake your hand, Walter," said Cook. Wach give him a bone-crunching grip, and Cook's own grip tightened reflexively. After a moment they released simultaneously.

"No point in pretending to be weak," Wach said under his breath. "Weakness is never a good quality." He looked at Milke and Aaskhugh. "Anybody else?" he asked, extending his hand like some champion Indian wrestler taking on all comers.

Milke laughed. "Relax, Walter. Mellow out, if possible. I want to know why I'm number one on your list."

"Because of what Arthur said about you, Emory," said Wach as he took a handkerchief out of his pocket and wiped his hands. "That report that was aired at our last meeting was quite compelling in the way it incriminated you. Also because of your temper. A certain passion would be called for in a man for him to strangle another man."

"I agree," said Milke. "And that is the one weakness in my case against you." He spun on his heel and went to the table for another drink. Wach followed him with his eyes. His lips were pressed tightly closed. Then they parted and his words flew out.

"Oh, yes. You *are* the expert on that, aren't you, Emory. Of one kind, anyway. I ought to know. I'm the one who has to hire teachers to replace the ones you use up and drive away." He had to speak loudly, shout almost, so that Milke could hear him at the table several steps away. This made his words sound even angrier than they were. It also brought the attention of all others in the dining room to the circle of five linguists. A few of the bystanders began to drift away, seeking more of a true party atmosphere in the kitchen or living room.

"That's a fine construction to put on the discontent at Wabash," shouted Milke from the table. He hastily finished pouring his drink and rejoined the group. "The fact of the matter is that human nature craves freedom and sociability, and those are two things your administration discourages. You make people feel like they have to sneak laughs and good fellowship when you're not looking. Which goes with what I said about passion, actually. In my view, better for a man to be guilty of a little excess here and there—ask Jeremy about that, he'll back me up—than to be the emotional cripple you are."

"Why you lush, you bearded, stinking prick, you—" Wach clenched his fists.

"I'm gonna slug me a fishwife," Woeps announced matter-of-factly, as if something had just magically released him from some spell. He stepped toward Aaskhugh, who was observing Milke and Wach intently. Cook reacted too slowly to stop him, and Woeps's roundhouse blow caught Aaskhugh by surprise on the side of his head just behind his left eye. He dropped to the floor as if shot, and Woeps dived or fell on him. Cook tried to part them, and then things became confused. At first Milke appeared to be helping him pull Woeps away, but then someone behind Milke wrapped a hand around his face and Milke was suddenly gone. Then he was back, falling on the pile composed, in order, of Aaskhugh, Woeps, and Cook, and Cook found it hard to breathe and began to gasp, when the pile suddenly flew apart and someone had him down and was trying to hit him in the face. It was Woeps. Cook tried to explain to Woeps what he was doing in his drunken fury, and when it occurred to him that Woeps knew perfectly well what he was doing and was prepared to go on doing it, he threw him off with one angry lunge. He rose to his knees and gasped, panting like a dog. He looked around for Woeps. The last thing he remembered was someone in the midst of the fight, through gritted teeth, saying, "I do not like thee, Dr. Fell."

TWELVE

COOK AWOKE WITH A JOLT AND LOOKED AT THE CEILING. It wasn't his, so it followed that it must be someone else's. This small conclusion cost him so much in the way of energy that he would have felt justified in rolling over and sleeping for another twelve hours.

At least he was in bed. Whose? He looked to the side, where a soft breathing was audible. Unless some very powerful being had played a trick on him, he was now in bed with Paula. She lay on her right side and faced him. The sheet was pulled up to her neck, but a bit of bare shoulder suggested possibilities. Those few square inches of bare skin came close to canceling out the heavy weight of misery and turmoil of the past three weeks. But how did he come to be here? What claim did he have, other than proximity, to those few square inches? After a moment of reflection he communed with his parts and easily determined he was naked. He studied Paula's face for a while, then cast his mind back . . . back to his arrival at the house, his chat with her, especially its highly charged climax—that must have some bearing on his present nakedness and location—then Milke and something about spunk. Aaskhugh and . . . yes, hard news about Woeps. Wach confirming it. Woeps joining them at some point. Very drunk. But then so was he. Some bad-ass accusations and fisticuffs. Then waking up in bed.

Something was missing. His last recollection of the party was a clear image of himself on all fours, panting like an over-worked young dog in the desert. That image made his body tense suddenly, and Paula stirred, moaned, sighed, and suddenly opened her brown eyes and looked right at him. For an instant he feared she was going to say, "Get out of my bed, you miserable little turd." Instead, she smiled.

"Feeling all right?" she asked.

"Fine." Except for the headache, sore back, and dry mouth, he thought. "Just a little empty-headed."

She raised herself up on one elbow. Somehow, without her holding on to it, the sheet remained in place over her chest. "Headache, you mean?"

"That, too. What I meant was . . . what happened last night?"

She laughed and stretched. "Starting from when? Your lecture on drink and memory—rather appropriate now, isn't it?—or the brawl, or the police, or the talk afterward, or your final lecture on crime and intonation, or us?"

He fell back on the pillow and gazed at the ceiling. This was serious. "Paula, I don't remember a thing after the fight."

"You're kidding." Her tone told him just how much he had missed.

"No. Can you, er . . ." He rose up on his elbow and looked at her.

"Summarize it?"

"Yes."

She sighed. "Well, you fainted or something . . . do you remember that?"

"Not really. Go ahead."

"You came to right away and we finally settled everybody down. But some idiot had called the police, and they came butting in about five minutes later. They didn't stay long, though one of them sniffed around a lot."

"A fat guy? Imperious? Talks with a funny kind of—"

"That's him. When he saw you he shouted, 'O Captain, my Captain!' "

"Did he talk to me?"

"A little." She stopped and looked at him with concern. "Jeremy, you don't remember a thing, do you? I'm worried. Coupled with your fainting—"

"It's all right," he said, thrilling to hear her say she was worried. Was this what being married was like? Waking to hear a lovely woman tell you she was worried about you? Did it ever grow old? How could it? "It's just the alcohol. And I think I must have hyperventilated during the fight. I'm not used to that kind of thing."

"Oddly enough, you kept drinking after the fight."

He winced and silently swore never to drink to excess again.

"Well, after the police left, you all calmed down and the party sort of broke up. But just as your friends were getting ready to go, saying good night to me and so on, you gave a long and—I'm sorry, Jeremy—

largely incoherent speech about how you were going to solve this crime with intonation. You warned everyone that you were listening to all of them and had been for some time, and then you shouted out some of the sentences you and I had discussed, sort of as examples for everyone to consider, but you didn't explain them very well and everyone was quite confused. Then you contradicted everything you had said before by saying that listening for intonation while people were talking to you was impossible because language had evolved for communication, not analysis, and one couldn't do both, and you, for one, were not going to fly in the face of evolution." She paused. "We were kind of confused by that, too. Your friend Ed collapsed on the floor, he was laughing so hard. Which is odd, considering. In the end your speech went unanswered—it was unanswerable, really—and everyone went home."

"Did I really make a fool of myself?"

"A little. It was cute, though."

"Why did you say it was odd about Ed?"

"Well . . . because of what he's been saying about you lately."

"What has he said?"

"Oh, just a lot of moaning and grousing about what a super hotshot you are and how everything always falls in your lap and how his wife is always talking about you. I think he's jealous, Jeremy. That's all."

"Jealous? Of me? He's got two kids, a nice wife, a decent life . . . *my* life's a wreck."

"He probably doesn't see it that way. You had better talk to him about it. I don't want to speak for him."

"When did you hear him talk like this?"

"Oh . . . twice on Friday and once earlier in the week. I'm surprised it's news to you."

Cook was silent. He felt as though someone had carved out part of his past, a good part filled with happy memories, and thrown it away, leaving nothing in its place.

"Anyway, that's why his laughter was so odd. It was very good-natured. He shook your hand afterward and said, 'Well done, Jeremy.' I think it was good that he saw you being, well, ridiculous." She paused. "And then everyone went home."

"Everyone but me."

"That's right."

"What about Milke?"

"Emory? I sent him home."

"How did he like that?"

"He didn't."

"Did he know I was staying? I mean, I assume I stayed. Here I am."

"I don't know if he knew. It doesn't matter." She spoke as of a dead man.

"I thought you and he . . ." His voice trailed off.

"We were, or did. It was brief."

"I won't ask what happened."

"He's an adorable sexist that I got tired of trying to reform."

"I see," said Cook, instantly feeling like an adorable sexist and wondering what he could do to hide it. "As far as that goes, that is, along related lines, did we—er—"

"We started but we didn't finish." She smiled. "One of us was not able to, ummm, meet his or her obligations."

"Well, I hope he or she does better next time." He fell back on the pillow, laughing. It was really marvelous, and so was she. And here he was, still in bed with her. He could make up for last night right away. He shifted and moved toward her. As he did so, he saw her open her mouth just slightly to meet his, but he also saw over her shoulder a large, framed picture of Arthur Stiph staring somberly at him. He shouted out "Aagh" in a seizure of fear and pointed to the night table. "What's that?" he said. "What's Stiph doing in here?"

Paula glanced at the picture. "He's my grandfather. Jesus, you scared me, Jeremy. What's the idea? This is my parents' bed, and my mother has a picture of her father on the night-stand. I swear—if being with you is always this crazy, I'm beginning to have second—"

"I'm sorry," he said. "It's just . . ." He looked at her. "Your grandfather? Why didn't I know that? Is it a secret?"

"Walter was afraid it would look bad. He said if the staff knew, they would make charges of favoritism, or something like that. He made me promise not to tell anyone when he hired me. Of course when he was killed it was even harder, but I stuck with it. The hardest part has been listening to people speculate about his death. Like last night. And Walter was the one who brought it up in front of me—the only man who knew I was his granddaughter."

"Yes. He's a total prick. I'm sorry, Paula. Sorry about Arthur."

"Don't let Walter know you know."

"I won't. Did you . . . were you close to him?"

"No, not really. Neither were my parents. They didn't even come back from Europe for the funeral."

Cook frowned. "That *is* estrangement, isn't it?"

"Like I said, they weren't close. And my parents hated his wife. He married her about ten years ago. She and Grandpa were impossible in many ways. They drove everyone crazy."

"How?"

She sighed. "They couldn't leave things alone. When a relationship went bad they couldn't let it be. That's why they moved back here, where my parents were. Grandpa was delighted to take the job at Wabash just so he could be near the daughter and son-in-law who didn't particularly care for him. My grandpa was obsessed with relationships. Quite the opposite of my parents, who are always getting involved with the rottenest people in political causes, but they put up with the people for the sake of the cause. Grandpa could never do that. He didn't care about anything except being best friends with the man who came to clean the roots out of the sewer."

"That's why Arthur's widow was all alone at the funeral?"

"Yes. I didn't want to be with her. I said a few words to her earlier, and that was all I could manage. The funeral is a perfect example of Grandpa's obsession. Do you remember that taps were played?"

"Yes." No one better, he thought.

"Grandpa wasn't in the service. Ever. But he wanted taps played just so people at the funeral who had been in the service would think he had been too and like him better for it."

Cook looked again at the picture over Paula's shoulder. Stiph stared back at him, his face unrevealing and enigmatic.

"If you and your parents felt that way about him, why is his picture in here?"

"I normally sleep in the other room—my old bedroom—and that's where they keep this picture, but I didn't want it in there so I brought it in here when I first got here this summer."

"Then why are we in here instead of in there?"

"Because you threw up in that bed last night."

Cook moaned. "Perhaps we should stop talking. What other abominations will I uncover?"

"I think that's all of them."

His stomach growled, and he decided to sit up in the bed. He propped his pillow against the headboard and leaned his back against it. Doing this gave him time to think about Paula's connection with Stiph. He thought of something, wondered if he should bring it up, and then went ahead.

"Emory and I are both suspects in his death, Paula. And yet you're friendly with both of us."

"It's not a problem. I know neither of you did it."

"How?"

"Because of who you are. You're both good people."

"Both of us? Him, too?"

"Sure. You're alike in a lot of ways. Your opinions about people. Your enthusiasm for your work. The way you talk to the kids—you two are exactly alike in your concern for them, your respect for them. It doesn't surprise me that you're friends."

"Emory and me? We're not friends."

"He told me you are. He adores you, Jeremy."

Cook steadied himself. He feared that his system could not stand many more surprises this morning. Was she prepared to spend the day watching him foul her beds and then moving to still higher ground with him?

"Of course there are some differences," she continued. "They have to do with what I was talking to you about last night, while Emory was fetching our drinks. But then you probably don't remember."

"I remember that part."

"What I was going to go on to say was that your back-door approach to me was in a sense unnecessary. Besides being confusing to me, I mean. You really had nothing to fear from a more direct approach, something on the order of 'Let's have lunch sometime.' I would have welcomed that, as would most women. But instead you came at me with John thinking I'm a drunkard and not being able to see shit in there, which is all really a kind of apology for talking to me in the first place, isn't it, as if to say, 'I'm sorry to take up your time but I'll try to make it useful for you.' You know, diffidence is not a good quality. It invites, well, attack from some people, but in me it induces other things, like a desire to leave or a desire to put an end to it so that we can get on with other things. That's why I said what I did last night. Your lack of confidence makes no sense to me. And that's where you and Emory differ. Cut his aggressiveness in half and give half to you and you both would be better off." She paused, but just for a moment. "I suppose part of what I'm talking about falls into the category of flirting. When overdone, it's laughable, but in the normal course of things it definitely has its place. You, Jeremy, don't have a flirting bone in your body." She looked at him sympathetically. "You ought to try it. You would be quite a charmer if you did." For a moment he thought she was going to kiss him. She said, "Does your breath always smell this bad?"

He inhaled and moved away from her. "Someday, Paula, I'm going to record your speech—yours and that Lieutenant's —and then I'm going to study it for a monograph to be titled 'Conversation as Agony.' I assume my breath smells this way because it's morning and I drank incontinently last night. Give me a break."

"Sorry. Let's have some breakfast, then. I'll fix you some eggs and pancakes."

"Aagh! Aagh!" he screamed, groping to see the clock on the nightstand and knocking Stiph's picture to the floor. It was twenty minutes to eight. The Grange Hall, where the Annual Rotary Prayer and Pancake Breakfast was to be held, was not far from his house, and if he dashed like a madman he could go home, change, and get his lecture notes—no, his notes were in his coat pocket, hanging in the hall closet downstairs—but he would have to go home and change anyway, and with luck he could make it to the breakfast by eight, or near eight, or not much after nine. He jumped from the bed and began to search the room frantically.

"Where are my clothes? Where are my clothes?" he asked.

"In the other bedroom. Down the hall to the right. What's going on? What's wrong?"

He shot out the door, feeling naked and dumb as he threw the words "Pancake and Prayer" over his shoulder. He found his clothes at various locations in Paula's bedroom, as if they had been placed by a random computer program. Paula came into the room, naked and yawning, as he buttoned his shirt.

"Jesus," he said, looking at her. "Don't go anywhere today, okay? It's Sunday and you don't have to go out, okay? I'll pick up a paper after this thing is over and be back in a couple hours and we'll make some coffee and hang out all day, okay?"

"Fine," she said through her yawn, nodding. "What thing?"

"I'll explain later. It's too absurd. I won't kiss you goodbye. It would be excruciating. Sorry about the bed and my breath and being shy and not flirting and my drunkenness and the fight . . ." He continued the list as he hurried into the hall, down the stairs to the closet, where he grabbed his coat, and out the front door to his car.

"Nice to have you aboard, Sonny."

Cook shook hands with the wizened old man across the table, which was covered with a long sheet of butcher paper secured by thumbtacks. One of these had popped loose, and Cook had been idly playing with it, rolling it back and forth across his empty plate, as he listened to the men around him, responded to their friendly questions about Wabash and himself, and wondered what he was doing there. From the kitchen at the end of the long warehouselike building the smell of pancakes and eggs and bacon produced activity in his torso best described as an intermittent circular swell beginning down low, rising up to his throat, then dropping back down again. He imagined his stomach to be a tetherball tied to his esophagus and swinging around on a swivel anchored somewhere at the back of his mouth. On all sides of him male voices rang out heartily. He wished for three things: aspirin, solitude, and coolness—like cool sheets, or a quiet electric fan blowing in his face. He felt at an intellectual low and wondered where the coffee was. It was his only hope for renewal.

Part of his misery had to do with the size of the crowd. He had anticipated a small band of twenty or thirty local misfits. As it was, over two hundred men were already seated at the long tables, and more were pouring in the doors as if fleeing radioactive contamination outside. Such a large crowd demanded something more theatrical than his modest observations on onomastics. Surely they weren't all there to learn about names.

"Here we are," said the man to his right, who had been assigned the job of looking out for him. His name was Hawkins and he sold farm equipment somewhere. He was showing Cook a program. "I'm afraid you've been saved until the very end, Dr. Cook. Just before the benediction." He handed it to Cook, who saw for the first time that the title of his talk was announced as "From Putnamville to Witch's Pudding: Humorous Anglo-Saxon Place Names of Southern Kinsey County, Indiana." Had Wach totally taken leave of his senses? What was the meaning of his perverse narrowing of the topic to sheer nothingness? More important, for the moment at least, what was Cook going to do about it? "Witch's Pudding"? "Humorous"? The only facts he had that came close to fitting this title were his stories about *Hoosier,* admittedly corny but bound to please this bunch. They would probably be the high point of the lecture. He would have to come up with a way of getting around that title to justify the rest of his material. Something like "No talk on mumble-mumble would be complete without also considering blather-blather." A lame formula, to be sure, but there was no alternative.

His eyes fell on other items on the agenda. Chief among them was the introduction of, and a speech by, basketball star Bud Bumbman, graduating senior of a nearby state college known for its winning basketball team. Bumbman, a key man this past year in generating plenty of what was known in the area as "Hoosier Hysteria," was probably the most powerful man in the state. Cook was to speak right after him. While Cook preferred his own title and subject to Bumbman's ("Jesus Christ at the Foul Line"), he knew as certainly as a breakfasting kamikaze pilot that a fatal dive was part of his day's destiny.

"I wonder if I could have a cup of coffee," Cook said to Hawkins as he returned the program to him. Hawkins sprang to his feet and was gone in an instant, leading Cook to believe that Rotarians took their charges very seriously indeed. But then as he watched him make inquiries at the door of the kitchen, then shake hands and laugh with some friends and perhaps close a few tractor deals, he realized that Hawkins had only welcomed the opportunity to get away from him. Cook shared his feeling. Earlier the two men had devoted nearly fifteen minutes of conversation to those areas of life that can be discussed naturally by complete strangers of unlike dispositions, and after only a few minutes Cook was surprised to feel his brain actually shrinking in size. But knowing that the feeling was mutual did not make being abandoned by Hawkins any less depressing. If it were not for the memory of where he had awakened and the prospect of returning there, he would have been the saddest Hoosier of them all. He looked to his left for possible companionship and saw only a small, dour man scowling straight ahead. Perhaps he was a key figure in a local Klan chapter.

"Like some o.j.?" asked the old man across the table, the one who had called him "Sonny."

"No, thanks."

"Really good o.j.," he said. He held up a large Thermos, apparently his private supply.

"No. Thanks very much though."

"Might help you relax."

"No. I'll just have some coffee."

"Donkey piss."

"Pardon me?"

"The coffee here tastes like donkey piss."

Cook smiled. "Thanks for the warning."

"Really good o.j.," he said again, adding a Bacchanalian smile.

"No, thanks."

"Suit yourself, Sonny."

"I'm fascinated by etymology."

This last sentence was delivered without prelude by the scowling man to his left. Cook could only assume it was meant for him. He said, "Really?"

"I think it's a wonderful thing."

"Good," said Cook, unnerved. The man's expression had not changed as he said this. In fact he barely opened his mouth when he spoke. His face seemed frozen into a permanently mean, unhappy look, somewhat at odds with what he was saying. It was as if he found etymology wonderful as a torture device.

"I learned just the other day that the word *yoga* is akin to *yoke*, that there is an etymological relation between them going back to the ancient Indo-European tongue. That is an interesting fact when you consider that both are concerned with union in a basic sense."

"Yes. That is interesting," said Cook guardedly.

"Also interesting is the fact that common people often alter foreign words in such a way that they become more familiar. *Woodchuck,* for example, comes from the Cree *otchek,* but *otchek* doesn't look or sound like English, so over time it was transformed into the more palatable *woodchuck,* which looks like a good old native compound. The same thing happened to the Algonquian *musquash* when it became *muskrat,* and the Old French *appentis,* which meant 'something attached to something'—you can see the relation with *append, appendix,* and so on—when it became *penthouse.* The transformation always makes the word appear more native: *house, rat, wood, musk* though ironically *musk* is of probable Sanskrit origin. This transforming process is called 'folk etymology.' "

"That's quite right," said Cook.

"The folk make other mistakes with language. I'm thinking of the area of popular explanations for the origins of words. *Yankee* is a good example. There are many fanciful explanations of that word. *Okay* is another. One hears ridiculous stories about these and other expressions."

"Yes. I've heard some of them."

"Or take *Hoosier.* There are those who would have us believe it comes from *who's there,* or even *whose ear,* with silly stories about the occasion for these utterances, when in fact the word is of Cumberland dialect origin, coming from *hoozer,* meaning 'anything unusually large.' Because the truth is less interesting than that other nonsense, the nonsense is forever perpetuated. I can't abide nonsense, and I speak out publicly against it whenever I have the opportunity."

"I share your feelings deeply," said Cook. He turned to the man across the table, who had been watching their conversation as if it were a television quiz show whose rules he didn't understand. "I'll take some of that o.j. now," he said.

"Glad to oblige." The man poured into Cook's cup about five percent more liquid than it could hold. The excess formed a small puddle on the butcher paper. Cook sipped the mixture, which was good o.j. in the sense that it was only about one-quarter o.j. The man grinned at him from across the table. The Grand Dragon to his left seemed oblivious to them and stared straight ahead, perhaps pondering the true origins of words. In a matter of a minute or so Cook emptied his cup and set it on the table in front of him in an ambiguous location just far enough out so that his new friend could fill it if he chose to. He chose to. As Cook brought it to his lips again he thought of a word of his own: splendid. The juice was cool and splendid, and it made him feel splendid, and his headache was splendidly going away, and even the sour etymologizer at his side was splendid, and so was Lieutenant Leaf, old Uncle Rebus himself, who now approached Cook and greeted him and those around him. He looked at Cook closely and told him he wanted a word with him after his "little talk." Cook asked him why he was there—was it just to see him? No, said Leaf. He was there because he believed in the power of prayer. Cook thought that was splendid too, and he set his cup down and lo! it was filled again. He said he hoped Leaf enjoyed his talk. Leaf answered that that was extremely unlikely. He added that he couldn't understand what Cook did with his life. He said he had four children and they learned to say *dog* for *dog* because a dog was a dog and that was that. Cook thought that was just splendid. Suddenly Leaf was gone and that was splendid too. So were the pancakes Hawkins finally set before him. They were splendidly shitty, with burnt edges and splendid uncooked batter in the middle.

After a prayer, an introduction, a speech, a prayer, and an introduction, Bud Bumbman took the podium. Cook realized he was next, and his cool disregard for that was splendid. His brain was emptying by the minute. He could feel the names leaving, one by one, like guests leaving a party. Names—the first thing to go when one is under the influence. But he had his notes. He felt the inside of his coat pocket for the five-by-seven cards. Yes, there they were. And the old-timer was right; he was relaxed. Like Bud Bumbman, he thought, gazing down the length of the table to the stage. If looking angelic, if looking almost androgynous, if looking as though you were not just born again but born last week—if looking this way meant you were relaxed, Bumbman was relaxed. What was that he said? The Trinity was like *what?* The three-point play? Did he really say that?

At the same time that names were leaving his head in droves, other things were coming in. Images. Words. Phrases. Adam Aaskhugh's face swam before his eyes, his lips pursed for a *wh,* his favorite sentence-initial digraph, and then Woeps was there, laughing, saying "of all the rotten luck" as if speaking about someone else, then Paula was there, her lips pursed much like Aaskhugh's but in her case for a kiss, but that too was unconsummated, obscured by something the baby-faced dribbler on stage had said, and Cook now saw with concern edging into panic that Bumbman was concluding his cruelly brief speech. No more o.j. for him, he decided. He reached into his coat pocket for his note cards, sweeping his eyes over the crowd as he did so. All eyes were on

Bumbman. They were enthralled. The Boy-God could have emptied the floor with an altar call. And Cook was next. From Putnamsomething to Witch's What-was-it? God and onomastics was a *perfect* combination. But why was Leaf, sitting at the head table on one side of Bumbman, not looking at the speaker as the other disciples at the table were? Why was he, in fact, looking directly at Cook? And why did he want to see Cook after the breakfast?

Cook scooted his chair back so that he could set his cards in his lap and skim them unobtrusively. The first one facing him had a large *A* drawn on it. He didn't remember writing that. What could he have intended it to mean? He flipped the card over. The other side was blank. The second card showed an *S*. The next five spelled *S-H-O-L-E,* not an English word, but when it was combined with the first two letters, what resulted was—as the self-made linguist to his left might put it—a good old native compound, one with which Cook was quite familiar. The question of who had effected this substitution, and why, and when, interested him less than the question of what he was now going to do about it. What could he remember? That writers of Old English avoided relative clauses in the middle of sentences. Yes, he could remember that from graduate school, but would it fly in the Kinsey County Grange Hall on this June morning? That Polyphemus was the son of Poseidon. Where had that come from? Undergraduate school? That nine times six was fifty-four. He was going in the wrong direction. He forced his mind back closer to the present, hearing Bumbman ask for questions and gasping with relief to see a hand go up at the next table. Again, visions from the party of the night before tantalized and distracted him. It was no wonder, he realized with dismay. The principle of state-dependent recall doomed him. Because he had been disgustingly sober in all phases of preparation for this lecture, he could not now remember a consonant, vowel, or semivowel of it. The party enslaved his mind.

Again Bumbman asked for questions, and just as it appeared that none were forthcoming, the scowling linguist to his left leaped to his feet and challenged the premises of the Christian faith. Bumbman smiled beatifically and undertook to answer the question with a long locker-room parable. For this reprieve, however short-lived it was to be, Cook wanted to throw the man to the floor and smother him with kisses, and this thought suddenly reminded him of Paula, late at night in her living room—no, upstairs, on a throw rug on the floor of her bedroom—but that was gone and he was still on the floor, this time in the dining room, and so were other people, and some phantom rose up before him and uttered a sentence that immediately reminded him of another sentence, a short one, and he simultaneously hated himself for not having remembered it before and loved himself for remembering it now.

He had to get to Wabash. Nothing else mattered now. He stacked his note cards in order, with the *A* on top, and he handed them to the no-nonsense atheist/linguist/Rotarian to his left, saying, "These are for you." Then he stood up and made for the door, not caring that this august body would remain uninformed about names from Puckey Huddle to Witch's Pussy, not caring that Bumbman was now saying, "Jesus Christ gave one hundred and ten percent on the cross," not caring.

THIRTEEN

THUNK.

"*M-bwee.*" (falling tone)

(running steps; kicking of toy)

"I'm sorry for scaring you, Wally. Let's take a break."

(walking steps)

"*M-bwee.*" (falling tone)

(recorder turned off)

(recorder turned on)

"Okay, Wally. Here we go again."

(pause of fifteen seconds; walking steps;
pause of eighteen seconds; knocking on door)

"Who's there?"

"I know someone's in there. Open the door."

"For Christ's sake—"

(pause of twelve seconds; groan; glass breaking)

"Jesus. Oh Jesus."

(running steps; pause of fifty-eight seconds;
high-pitched laughter; door opening, being locked)

"*M-bwee.*" (falling tone)

(hissing noise; Wally cries; running steps; pause
of one minute, seven seconds; running steps)

"It's all right, Wally. It's all right."

(comforting sounds; tape runs out)

Cook slammed his hand down on the desk with finality. He grabbed himself by the hair and pulled—not in drunkenness, for he was quite sober now—but in triumph and self-reproach. How could he have forgotten the importance of that unexplained *m-bwee*? How could he have forgotten that the tape recorder was running during the entire episode?

As he had played the tape and roughed out a transcript of it, he had reconstructed the events of that Monday night. The thunking watch toy had scared Wally and elicited a negative *m-bwee* from him. He had run to Cook, who kicked the toy aside and apologized to him for using him so callously for the advancement of science. Then Wally evidently saw the intruder going into Cook's office and gave *him* a negative *m-bwee* while Cook fussed with the recorder, his back to the door. Cook now remembered puzzling over that one *m-bwee*, but then he had forgotten about it, his forgetting aided by his natural discomfort in the face of anomalous data. After a short break and walk down the hall they had resumed. Cook heard a noise from his office, walked to the door, knocked on it, and uttered some normal, banal sentences at it. The chair was then thrown through the window, and he—the fool—ran downstairs and outside, only to be insulted with laughter from above. The culprit left his office, locking the door behind him, and received another negative *m-bwee* from Wally, forever observant and consistent in his judgments. Then the intruder, or maybe Wally, produced an odd hissing noise. Then he ran off. Cook returned upstairs to calm the boy, and the tape continued to play for a minute or so until it ran out. The recorder shut off automatically and the tape had sat there untouched for almost a week. Several other machines were mounted on the wall, and if any of his colleagues had done any taping in the gym that week they had simply used one of those.

He leaned back in his chair and wondered if, in the annals of crime, a sixteen-month-old toddler had ever identified a suspect from a lineup. All that remained was for Cook to choreograph it. Perhaps Leaf could help him there. But any man who thought a dog was a dog and that was that might balk at the notion that *m-bwee* means "locomotion is in progress and I like/ don't like that which is doing it." Cook would be better off making the plans by himself. But what to do with the killer once Wally had singled him out? He would just have to figure that out when the time came.

The phone rang. He hesitated, wondered why he was doing that, and then answered it.

"Jeremy, Lieutenant Leaf is looking for you. He says it's urgent." It was Paula.

"Where is he? What does he want?"

"He's on his way to Wabash. I don't know what he wants you for. He had three patrol cars with him. It was like the goddamn Gestapo in here, the way they stomped all through the house. The last of them just left."

"Come out with your hands up." It was Lieutenant Leaf, amplified.

"Excuse me just a second, Paula," Cook said as evenly as possible. He walked to the window and looked out. Five or six rifles or shotguns or bazookas were presently pointing upward, trained on his head. At the other end of them crouched flunkies under Leaf's command. He was to be seen leaning heavily on the roof of his car, using it for protection against any pencils or erasers Cook might be tempted to throw at him, and he was bellowing into a megaphone.

"The building is surrounded," he went on predictably. *"Come out."*

Cook stepped back and tried not to panic. He understood what Leaf was doing because he wanted to do exactly the same thing. Also, his belief in justice and the American way, though presently shaken, remained strong enough to give him confidence. He picked up the phone and told Paula everything was all right. He would be with her later, he said. She began to protest and asked for an explanation of the voice she had heard, but he simply repeated that it was all right and hung up. He locked his office and took the elevator downstairs. He walked boldly out the front door and waved. The policemen were still gazing up at the seventh floor and aiming their guns there.

"Resistance is futile," Leaf droned on.

"Hi, Lieutenant," Cook called out. "Save me any pancakes?"

Leaf turned and stared at him a long moment. Then he lowered the megaphone and put a grin on his face. "Jeremy!" he said. "I didn't know you were here. How very good to see you. We're on maneuvers. We must have given you quite a scare. I thought the building was empty."

Cook pointed to his Valiant, conspicuous in the parking lot. "You think I store it here on weekends and walk home?" he asked.

"Silly goose that I am! Silly goose!" said Leaf, broadening his grin. "I get so caught up in these things, making sure these young bucks don't shoot their toes off, that I sometimes overlook the obvious." He turned to his troops. "Okay, men," he shouted. "Duck squat to the river and wait there for orders." As if motorized, Kinsey's finest dropped to their haunches and waddled across the parking lot and out of sight down the hill. Leaf watched them critically and lit a cigarette. Then he turned to Cook and said, "I must say, Jeremy, I enjoyed your talk this morning much more than I expected to. I thought it was just the right length, har, har, har."

Cook barely heard him. His mind was racing. He hadn't expected Leaf to abandon his plan so quickly. And yet it made sense. Once Leaf had seen it was not working, he had to give up on it immediately. What struck Cook was that if he had been guilty it would have worked. Leaf's large, unyielding presence could have a telling effect. He could use Leaf now, but he would have to be careful.

"Lieutenant, could you muster this kind of force if I produced the killer of Stiph and Philpot for you?"

Leaf frowned deeply. "It wouldn't take this many men to bring in one of you twirpy eggheads, no offense I'm sure."

"I don't need it for that. I mean to scare him into bolting. His running away will be a confession."

"*Hey!* I like that! What a fresh idea. Boy, that's a head you've got on your shoulders, even if it isn't as pasty white and perfectly round as mine. That just may be worth a shot."

"Could we plan it for tomorrow? Here at work?"

"Sure. These young bucks will be out in the country on more maneuvers, but I've got some old uniforms kicking around and I can deputize some of the locals. But how will you know?"

"I'd rather not say. You'll think I'm silly."

"Trust me."

Cook laughed hard at that, and Leaf joined in. Cook sensed it was a rare, human moment for the Lieutenant. "I'll tell you afterward," he said. "But it's solid. It's a linguistic cue."

"A what? Oh. That. I wouldn't want to hear it anyway. That crap bores me."

The two men made plans for the next day. Cook was surprised at Leaf's cooperativeness. It seemed that for the first time since Stiph's death Cook was free of suspicion, or at least as free as anyone could be with Leaf. Free enough, at any rate, to be listened to and taken seriously. And Leaf was desperate. Tactics like his present one must have been part of his last-resort arsenal. But most important of all, Leaf must have been grateful to Cook for participating in the maneuvers pretense. To maintain that pretense Cook did not ask Leaf what he had wanted to see him about, either after the Pancake and Prayer Breakfast or at Paula's. Nice touches, those. Especially the one after the other, with the alerting, terror-promoting phone call from Paula a safe assumption.

"I'll see you tomorrow, then," Leaf said in parting. "I may be able to make a little contribution to your plan. The old hair trick. I'll be by first thing in the morning for samples from all of you, to set it up. We'll talk then." He walked toward the river. Cook looked after him and heard him call out to his men, "Okay, you shitheads. Let's go back to the station and have some Spam."

After the policemen had piled into their cars and driven away, Cook walked out onto the footbridge and thought. Then he returned to his office and listened to the tape once more, just to be sure. As he was locking the tape in a desk drawer, the phone rang. It was Paula, worried about him. He gave her a brief account of his meeting with Leaf and told her he had more to tell her too, but he would save it until he saw her. She said she had some things to pick up at the store for dinner. He looked at his watch and was surprised to see it was almost four o'clock. He hadn't eaten breakfast or lunch, and he had had only three or four hours of sleep the night before. He told her he felt like a nap. She said she would leave the door unlocked and he could let himself in. She closed by saying she was very, very eager to see him again.

Talking with Paula reminded him of what she had said that morning about Woeps. He decided to call him.

"Ed, how are you feeling?" he asked.

"Worse. It will be better soon, though. I hope."

"Can we talk? I've learned something—a couple of things—that make it rather important that I see you."

"Yes. I'm glad you called, Jeremy. I was going to call you later, when my head cleared. It appears that that is not going to happen, so this is as good a time as any. Why don't you come over? I've got an explanation or two to give you, and a peace offering to make. Maybe a bit of the hair of the dog—"

"No! Not that! But I *will* be over, right away."

The phone rang again as soon as he hung up.

"I demand an explanation." It was, of course, Wach.

"You're referring to my lecture, Walter?" asked Cook. Word travels fast, he thought.

"I am."

Cook sighed and decided he should know only half the reason for its nondelivery. "It would have been a bust, Walter. Maybe biblical onomastics would have done it, or basketball onomastics, but I'm not even sure of that. They're all fundamentalists."

"I don't see how the religious orientation of the audience permits you to just walk out on an assignment I have long viewed with some gravity. What were you thinking, man?"

"You don't understand, Walter. I would have bored their pants off. The best thing I ever did for Wabash was to not give that talk. Besides, I've got a little bone to pick with you. The title on that program had nothing to do—"

"Are you complaining about the way I execute my responsibilities?"

"Well, in this instance—"

"I do my job as I see fit."

"I'm sure you do, but—"

"I was elected from the staff to serve, was I not?"

"That's right. Of course nobody else wanted the job, but—"

"And I have delivered, have I not?"

"Well, sure, I mean—"

"If you have reservations about the way things are going, Jeremy, it might be better for you to consider your options elsewhere."

"I don't have options elsewhere, Walter, and I love my work here."

"Ed could stay on if you left. He's got a family and less flexibility. He's a friend of yours and that puts you under a certain obligation to him. You see, Jeremy, I feel I can approach things with a greater sense of fairness than you can. I think my moral sense is keener than yours. That's my opinion."

"Well, you're entitled to it, of course."

"Don't be offended. In my position I try to remain above personal acrimony."

"I'm sure you do, Walter."

"Think about your job. We'll talk about it tomorrow. Meanwhile, I'll make apologies to the good people in the Rotary Club." He hung up.

"So you're suggesting a kind of contract, Ed?" Cook squinted against the sunshine. They were sitting in lawn chairs in Woeps's backyard, watching Wally chase a neighbor's cat and say things to it.

"You could call it that, but I don't think it does justice to the trust we place in each other. And don't look so downcast. We're still friends."

"Why doesn't it feel like it?"

"Because I've popped one of your balloons, I guess. But you've really got to start thinking about these things, Jeremy. You're too isolated. My main point is that you're going to have to start devoting as much energy to your friendships as you do to your . . . your enemyships. Is there a word for that?"

Cook thought about it. "Backfriendships?"

"Good enough," said Woeps.

"Run through it again, Ed. What do you want me to do?"

"First, stop complaining to me about other people. I'm sick of it, and it makes me feel insecure too. Besides, it's hypocritical. You make fun of Emory and Clyde and then you chat with them daily. It's quite cruel, really—saying good and friendly things to them and then bad things about them."

"I don't know how else to get along."

Woeps suddenly jumped to his feet to see what Wally was putting into his mouth. Nothing, apparently, for after examining him he returned to his chair.

"Try liking people," said Woeps as he sat down. "Your objections to them are really quite trivial. Clyde's laughter in his office, for example. I mean really."

"There's more, somehow."

"But that's all you talk about, so whatever else there is it couldn't be too substantial. I really don't care if you like them or not, but I do want you to stop complaining to me about them."

"But I'm not alone in doing this," said Cook, taking the offensive for a change. "You've been saying things about me, haven't you?"

"Yes, I have."

"So what's the difference? You're friendly to me—up until last night, that is—and yet you say bad things behind my backside."

"But I caught myself and resolved to speak man-to-man with you. I didn't keep on doing it the way you do."

"So it's just recently that you've been talking about me?"

"Yes."

"So you didn't call me a complete asshole about three weeks ago?"

"No. Why?"

"I have reason to believe someone did. It's haunting me."

"Ignore it."

"I can't."

"Then look for good things that people have said about you, for the sake of balance."

"Those don't impress me. My own bad thoughts about myself meet them on their way in and annihilate them."

Woeps laughed. "I really don't know how to help you with that, and we're drifting far afield. Speaking of help, I want you to stop trying to help me. You're always looking for ways to improve my life. Don't. I can manage."

"You've never mentioned this before."

"No. But it's a big problem. And here's another one. Stop being so successful. Just stop it. It makes me mad. You don't have to take that one seriously, of course, but I'm serious in saying it. It's something I've wanted to say for a long time, and lately I've learned the importance of speaking my mind. I am resolved to face my problems head-on now, and to stop bowing and suffering. Speaking up to Adam has helped me there. Maybe this kind of approach will turn my luck around." He paused and looked off into the distance, as if in dreamy contemplation. "Anyway, I can sum up all these things under one injunction: forget about perfection. In me, in others, in yourself. Forget about it."

As Cook puzzled over this, Woeps's wife opened the screen door and yelled something to her husband. Woeps jumped to his feet.

"What is it, Ed?"

"Long-distance call. The Director of the Center for Applied Linguistics. Adam knows him and put me on to him. They have an opening. My chances are nil, but I've got to try for it. Can you watch Wally for a moment?"

"Sure."

"Stay for dinner." Woeps hurried toward the house.

"No, I'll go," said Cook. "I've got other plans."

"I'll be there early tomorrow with Wally," Woeps called back over his shoulder. "This thing had better work or we'll all look pretty silly."

"It will," Cook called after him. Then he added, "I'm surprised that nincompoop knows anyone important. Is there anything I can do to help you get the job?"

Woeps frowned over his shoulder and hurried on to the house, shaking his head.

"*M-bwee,*" said Wally, looking at his father.

"I like him too, Wally," said Cook. "But damn the complications of friendship."

Paula was still out when Cook finally got back to her house. He went upstairs and collapsed on the bed. When he awoke it was dark in the room. She was beside him, asleep. He looked at the clock. It was two in the morning. He looked at her a moment and wondered what he should do. He decided to let her sleep. He slipped out of bed and went downstairs, where a nice note told him where the lasagna was and suggested they get together sometime. He found the lasagna in the refrigerator and put it in the oven to reheat it. Then he sat down at the kitchen table and thought about the day ahead of him.

"Adam, this is Jeremy. Could you come down to my office for a moment? In going through Arthur's files more carefully I've come upon transcripts of some sex counseling sessions involving Ed and his wife. Also some notes on Walter's recent psychoanalysis, and something that suggests that Emory, Clyde, and Mary the Secretary have a weekly thing going. Some diagrams too. I don't know how Arthur came by this stuff, and it's not really all that interesting, but I would be honored if you could find time to come down here and go over it with me."

"Jay, I'm on my way," and he was. Cook could hear him opening his office door even as he hung up his own phone. Cook hurried out of his office and looked into the open door of the gym, where Wally Woeps sat with his father, facing the door some twenty feet from it. Woeps gave Cook an "okay" sign, and Cook took up a position in the hall about five feet from the door. He and Woeps, using little-understood principles of body space, had established this as the optimal location to cause an approaching pedestrian from the other side of the door to slow down as he passed Wally's field of vision. Aaskhugh bustled toward him, his fingers twitching. Cook gestured to him to come close, and, being human, Aaskhugh behaved as planned, slowing his walk as he passed the open door and pulling up to a stop in front of Cook just beyond it. Cook raised a finger to his lips and listened. Aaskhugh frowned at him.

"M-bwee," said Wally. The rising tone pronounced Aaskhugh not guilty. Part of Cook was saddened by this. He stepped to the door and looked in.

"I heard it, Ed. Real good."

"He's being very cooperative," said Woeps.

"Jay, what is this?" Aaskhugh whispered to him. "Does Ed know you're going to show me this stuff?"

"There's no stuff, Adam. You have been an unwitting subject in a little experiment on idiophenomena. I just wanted you to walk down here. Thanks for your help. You can go back to your office now. I'll share the results of the study with you when I'm finished." He smiled to hear himself utter this standard palliative to experimental subjects. Nobody ever honored it.

"Jay! This is quite a disappointment. I must say . . ." Aaskhugh went on in this vein, a model of frustration, as he turned and walked back down the hall.

"Ready for the next one?" Cook asked Woeps.

"Ready. Call him."

Cook went to his phone and dialed the intercom. "Emory, there's a young divorcée down here with her tits hanging all over the place who says she's going to name you in a paternity suit. Would you know anything about it?"

"God, Jeremy, tell her I'm out. I'll try to sneak out the back way through Walter's office and the bathroom."

"She knows you're here, Emory. I think maybe you can talk her out of it. It's the best way. Come on down to my office."

Milke moaned a bit. "All right," he finally said. When he appeared in the hall he was biting his thumbnail and looking nervously toward Cook. When he passed the open door, in spite of his beard, aggressiveness, tobacco smell, sexism, etc., he received a positive recommendation from Wally. For some reason, Cook was not surprised. At the same time, he suddenly feared that his reasoning about *m-bwee* was all wrong. What if Wally gave Wach a rising intonation too? Where would he be then?

"Sorry to scare you, Emory, but it's for a good cause," said Cook. Drawing a distinction between Milke and Aaskhugh, he went on to explain to him exactly what they were doing. As he did so, one of the teachers began bringing several children into the gym, and Woeps chased them off, asking for a few more minutes of privacy.

"Incredible, Jeremy," said Milke. "And the prick is the only one left. If you're right about this business it's got to be him."

Cook nodded. "We have to hear the falling intonation from Wally."

"Let's get him down here and ice it, the bastard," said Milke.

"Wait in here out of sight," said Cook, directing him to stand behind the open door. "It's good you're here. We can use one more witness."

Cook went to his office and called Mary the Secretary, with whom Wach insulated himself. When she answered he said, "Walter? Walter?" He knew very well that it was Mary, but pretending to be thinking he was addressing Wach was the only way he could make good his vow never to speak to her again.

"I'll ring him. Is this Dr. Cook?"

"Walter? This is Jeremy."

"I'll *ring* him. Hold your horses."

"Yes?" Wach said in his unfriendly way.

"Walter, this is Jeremy. I've got someone from an outfit called Videohype here in my office, and he's pushing a closed circuit camera system. He says they're having a promotional campaign and he's willing to give us free installation, maintenance, and rent of the equipment for two years. You know—a camera in every playroom, even in every office, if you like, all hooked up to monitors in a convenient central location such as your office. Ideal for staying on top of things. Would you like to come down and meet this guy or should I send him packing?"

Wach tried not to sound too interested. He said, "That's not an unattractive concept, Jeremy. I'll be there presently. Afterward, we can address ourselves to that other matter."

"I look forward to that, Walter."

Cook took up his position beyond the door and waited nervously. Wach finally appeared, stepping toward him like some Prussian parade marshal. He passed the door and Cook again raised a hushing finger to his lips and listened. He heard a giggle and scampering noises, but no *m-bwee.* Wally suddenly appeared at the door and turned and began to walk with his propulsive, precipitate gait down the hall in the opposite direction. Wach, who had been looking at Cook as if about to demand an explanation, turned and saw Wally.

He hissed, and the sound of it made Cook's skin crawl. "That child should not be in the hall," he said. "Where are those teachers?"

Wally halted at the sound of Wach's voice and turned around. Wach took three steps to the door to look into the gym, and Wally watched him move and then said it, with an intonation that went down, down, down. He stood rooted in place. Then, as if he knew more than he could possibly know, he raised a stubby finger at Wach and pointed at him.

"*Ecce homo*," said Cook under his breath.

"What's going on here?" said Wach, looking from Woeps to Cook.

Woeps stepped out into the hall. "All of a sudden he decided to play Chase-the-Baby, Jeremy. Sorry."

"It's okay, Ed. He said it."

"Did he say it?" said Milke, stepping out from behind the gym door.

Wach looked at him, bewildered. "I demand an explanation," he said loudly.

Cook looked at Wach. For five years the sonofabitch had kept him hopping. His relief in knowing that this period of his life was over was nearly as great as that in knowing who killed Stiph and Philpot. He began to whistle "Sweethearts on Parade."

As arranged, Lieutenant Leaf stepped boldly out from the nook near the stairwell with what looked like the Third Army behind him. It was an intimidating show of force. They moved down the hall with plenty of noise, if not precision. Leaf looked at Cook, Woeps, Milke, Wach, and then Aaskhugh, who was coming down the hall inquisitively from the other direction, and then he looked at Cook again. Cook did not stroke an imaginary beard or purse his lips into a *wh.* Instead, he stiffened his back and pointed to his watch. Leaf nodded.

"Dr. Wach," he said loudly. "You are under arrest. The lab shows traces of your hair under Henry Philpot's fingernails." He shrugged and grinned at Wach. "These things happen," he said in a friendly way.

Wach bolted. He blurted out something inarticulate and bumped Woeps to one side as he began to run down the hall toward his office.

"Stop him!" Cook yelled to Aaskhugh, who, his mouth open in wonder, watched Wach give him a stiff-arm to the face that banged his head back against the wall and sent him to his knees. His subsequent groveling on the floor of the hall slowed pursuit. Wach shot into his office. Behind him, Cook led Woeps, Milke, Leaf, and the Kinsey Police Department to the door. Mary the Secretary looked up from her empty desk and began to scream to no purpose. Wach's door was locked, and Cook kicked at it angrily.

"The bathroom!" he shouted. "Some of you stay here." He forced his way through the crowd of confused policemen and began to sprint down the curving hallway, hurdling Aaskhugh's still struggling body on the floor, and clenching his fists as he approached the bathroom. Behind him trailed the others. They packed into the bathroom, only to find the connecting door to Wach's office locked.

"Some of you stay here and watch this door," he shouted. "There's another way out." He led a smaller group back into the hall and into the central core. The door from Wach's office leading into the core was wide open. Cook ran into the gym. Milke had apparently anticipated Wach's escape by that route and had turned into the gym as the others were running to the bathroom. He had struggled with Wach and lost. He lay on his back next to a tipped-over changing table, dazed and moaning. A spilled diaper pail lay next to him, the liquid forming a puddle all around his shaggy head. Paula and another teacher had just discovered him and were trying to help him.

"He got Wally," he was saying over and over. "He got Wally. He got Wally."

Cook cursed and ran to the stairwell with Woeps right behind him. They stopped at the top to listen. Wach was several floors below, running. They ran down after him. Farther upstairs, Leaf and the others followed. By the time Cook and Woeps reached the ground floor and ran out to the parking lot, Wach was nearly to the footbridge. He was carrying Wally like a football under his right arm. Cook and Woeps gave chase. When Wach reached the center of the bridge he raised Wally at arm's length above his head with both hands, one at his feet and one at his neck. He turned and looked back to the parking lot. Wally, no doubt dazed and overwhelmed, was silent.

"Keep him looking this way," said Woeps. He veered off to the right, crouching, hidden from Wach's view by the parked cars. Cook looked at Woeps. He was making for the river, upstream from the bridge. Cook began to walk to the bridge slowly. Behind him, he heard Leaf order his troops to stop.

"Take it easy, Walter," Cook shouted.

Wach glared at him, his eyes wild. Wally began to wriggle above his head, and Wach tightened his grip on the boy's feet and neck. Wally began crying then.

"Don't hurt him," Cook shouted. "There's no point." He watched Wach carefully to see how he reacted. He felt helpless to say the right thing. He glanced to his right. Woeps had just reached the water. Wally began to cry loudly now, and Wach shook him over his head.

"The boy has nothing to do with this," Cook yelled, beginning to panic. He wanted to run out there and throttle him. But Wach could throw Wally into the water or dash him against the floor of the bridge. Wally began to scream now and Wach shook him harder.

"For God's sake, Walter," he shouted.

"Put up that rifle, Hawkins," he heard Leaf say behind him. "Better yet, give it to me."

Woeps was floating to the bridge now. His son's cries grew louder and more frantic. When he reached the bridge he stretched one hand up and just caught the edge of the floor. He struggled against the current to pull himself up. Wally's crying seemed to enrage Wach, and he lowered the boy to his eye level, stood him on the railing of the bridge, and began to choke him with both hands. Cook ran for the bridge then. He saw Woeps lose his grip on the bridge and fall back into the water. The current swept him under the bridge. Cook heard a shot and saw Wach's head snap back. He stopped running and watched. Wally fell into the water, almost landing on his father. Woeps fished for him and caught him, supporting him with both hands as he kicked awkwardly for shore. His son's screaming was a welcome sound now.

"Thank God," Cook heard someone behind him say.

"There he goes," said another, and Cook saw Wach teeter for a long moment on the railing and then splash into the water. He ran to the shore and waded out to help Woeps. Wally clung to his father and kept looking back to the bridge as if fearful of pursuit. He was sobbing hysterically now, gasping for air, and his father tried in vain to soothe him as he carried him to land and held him. Whichever way Woeps held him, Wally spun and looked back to the bridge. Then he saw what he was looking for. Wach's body had caught on a snag, and now it spun free and floated close to the shore. His face rolled up, streaked with watery blood, as he floated slowly past. Cook heard Leaf give an order for someone to go after him.

"*M-bwee,*" said Wally, his intonation going down as he watched the water carry Wach's body downstream and away from him. He became calmer then, and his sobs grew fainter.

FOURTEEN

"I THINK HE PLANNED ON THE LECTURE BEING A DISASTER, Jeremy," said Woeps as he took an armload of books from his shelf and stacked them on a cart. "It would have given him an excuse to fire you."

"But why would he want to fire me?"

"Because he probably saw you as a threat—as the person most likely to crack the case. Turns out he was right, though my boy did his share too, didn't he? And even if by some miracle your lecture didn't bomb, the preparation for it had your attention for a few weeks. He probably wanted to keep your mind occupied."

"So you don't think there was any sincerity in his claim that it might have important p.r. value for Wabash?"

"Not an ounce. He was just looking out for himself."

Cook shook his head. "That bastard. I worked like a dog on that stupid thing."

Woeps emptied one shelf and began on another one. "He had all of us hopping. He told me he wanted a preliminary report on my dialect competition work in two months—an impossible deadline, particularly because it wasn't going anywhere at all. He did the same thing to Emory and Adam, too."

"What thing?" asked Aaskhugh, who had just arrived, or at least now showed himself, at the door of Woeps's office. Woeps smiled thinly and told him what he had just told Cook.

Aaskhugh looked at the empty shelves. "Moving already?" he asked.

"That's right," said Woeps.

"Are you that power-hungry?"

"Nothing of the sort. You don't want the ship of state to drift without a rudder, do you?"

It was like Woeps to compare himself to a rudder rather than, say, a brave helmsman, in referring to his new position as Director of the Wabash Institute, a position to which he had been nearly unanimously elected by the other linguists the day after his predecessor and justice encountered each other for the first time.

"Can I help move this stuff down the hall, Ed?" asked Aaskhugh.

"No, thanks. Jeremy's been helping me and we're nearly finished. Once I'm settled, though, I'll be needing your help. I'll be needing everyone's help."

"Hell, Ed. You can count on me."

"Good." For a microsecond, the two men smiled warmly at each other.

Milke appeared at the door and greeted everyone. "Lovely morning, isn't it? Just lovely. The birds. The trees."

"Emory," said Cook, "it's hotter than hell, and the humidity turned my shirt into a hot washrag before I could finish breakfast." He paused. "And yet . . ."

"Ah," said Milke. "You take my meaning."

"I do. I do."

"Walter's palpable absence almost makes up for a setback in another arena of my life, Jeremy. *Almost*. Do you take my meaning once again? Do you?"

Cook swallowed. "Yes, Emory. I'm awfully sorry—"

Milke reached out and put a hand over Cook's mouth. It was a very gentle touch. "Not a word more, lad. All's fair in love, etc., other fish in the sea, etc., probably better off anyway, etc. You see, I can cope. The three of us must have lunch sometime, though. Maybe I'll manage to spill a bowl of soup on your head, ha, ha. Today, maybe?"

"I'd like that," said Cook, "but hold the soup. I think tomorrow would be better. I'm meeting Clyde for lunch today."

"Orffmann?" said Aaskhugh with disbelief.

"That's right. The poor guy's been in the hospital for two weeks now and no one's been to see him."

Milke nodded and said, "Jeremy's right. It didn't even occur to us to consult him about Ed's election."

"You're welcome to join me," Cook said to him. "You're all welcome."

"I'll try to make it," said Woeps. "We have to talk to him and see if Wednesday nights are okay with him."

"Right," said Milke. "With Walter gone Clyde's essential."

"I'll bring a copy of the story for him," said Cook. He turned to Aaskhugh. "Adam? Lunch with Clyde?"

"If I don't go you'll probably talk about me." Everyone laughed.

"How's Wally, Ed?" said Milke.

"He's fine, Emory." Woeps turned to Cook. "You know, *m-bwee* is dead."

"*What?*"

"He doesn't say it anymore. He's had several opportunities since Monday and he just hasn't said it."

"I'll be damned," said Cook.

"Got room for a fat man?"

They all turned to the door. It was Lieutenant Leaf. Once he stepped inside his question seemed apt, for there was just barely room for him. Everyone negotiated around the boxes and carts to accommodate him.

"The place seems busy this morning," he said. "A lot of cars pulling up with little cherubs in them."

"That's right, Lieutenant," said Woeps. "Enrollment is climbing back up already." He looked at everyone sternly and attempted an imitation of Wach. "I need not remind you of the importance of maintaining this trend or of the dangers of over-optimism." The linguists laughed at this while Leaf watched.

"I always thought it was Walter," said Aaskhugh. "He was a bad one, wasn't he?"

This met with several nods and a hearty "Hear, hear" from Milke.

Leaf laughed. "I'm glad to see you all getting along so famously. It wasn't long ago, you know, that you were pointing fingers every which way." He folded his arms across his chest, index fingers extended, pointing to both sides at once.

Everyone muttered disclaimers and shifted uneasily.

"I bring this up only because I am here to say, with some sadness, that I have reason to believe that Walter Wach had an accomplice." He looked from one linguist to the next, and as he watched their jaws drop and their eyes go to their neighbors with the old suspicion, he guffawed. "Just kidding, har, har, har. Human nature kills me. How about you, Jeremy?

Cook smiled weakly.

Mary the Secretary appeared at the door. "Dr. Woeps? WKIN is on line three. They want to send a team over for an interview."

"Thanks, Mary," said Woeps, reaching for his phone. "Let's look sharp when they get here, men," he said to his colleagues as they began to move toward the door. This time it was hard to tell whether or not he was kidding.

Milke said it for all of them. "Don't turn into a jerk, Ed."

Woeps laughed and pushed a button on his phone. "No chance," he said cockily.

"We'll make sure," Aaskhugh said as he stepped into the hall.

"Oh?" Woeps called after him. "Physician heal thyself, Adam."

"Save it, guys," said Cook. He and Leaf followed Aaskhugh out the door and closed it behind him. Aaskhugh swallowed his rejoinder—he looked as if he had one ready—and began to walk down the hall with Milke. Milke said something to him about a problem that had come up in his work and asked him to come to his office. Watching the two of them talk like this gave Cook a sudden sense that workaday life at Wabash was back to normal. His mind began to drift back to his own unfinished research projects.

"Well, old pal," said Leaf, "I hate to make apologies—who knows, the day after I apologize to someone he may give me a good reason to arrest him or shoot him in the head, and then where am I?—but one is in order here. Until Monday I thought you were the one."

"You mean I was first on your list?"

"You were the *only* one on my list."

"Jesus, Lieutenant. Do I really strike you as the kind of person who could do those things?"

Leaf sighed. "That did give me pause. My only hope was that you were good at hiding your true nature. I should have seen earlier that no one could be that good at it. All along I was thumpin' on the wrong watermelon. So it's time for me to say I'm sorry about the dent."

"The dent?"

"Yes. The dent I made in your car."

"You did that?"

"Yes. After the funeral."

"Why?"

"I wanted to spook you, see how you would react. Anything less than pure outrage at being framed would have sent you to the gallows."

"And my reaction?"

"Pure outrage at being framed."

"And still . . ."

"Still I suspected you. Your calling that girl who works here, pretending to be Philpot, confounded me. It looked like an obvious attempt to confuse the investigation. Come to think of it, just why did—"

"How did you know about that?"

"I put a tap on your phone the day after the killings," he said matter-of-factly.

"Did you get a court order?"

"Nah. Nobody cares about that stuff. The important thing is to catch killers. So, like I said, I'm sorry about the dent."

"That's all you're sorry about?"

"Sure. What else is there?"

"Well, apart from your illegal activities, there's your suspicion of me. I deserve an apology for that."

"I don't see why. There was nothing personal about it. The personal element does not exist in my line of work."

"Why didn't you suspect Wach? *He*'s the type."

Leaf shrugged. "I didn't know him. But you did. Why didn't you suspect him?"

Cook blinked and felt his mind go blank. "I don't know," he said slowly.

Leaf looked down the hall toward the elevator. Cook began walking with him.

"He was quite a case," said Leaf. "Drank like hell. Alone at night. That's what his wife said. She's been really burning our ears about him, as if she's been saving it up for years."

"He pretended not to drink," said Cook.

"Doesn't surprise me," said Leaf. "He pretended a lot of things. I checked his record. He was arrested on a child molesting charge back in 1946. He was a teenager then, and the charge didn't hold up, but from what his wife says . . . well, without being active he was still chronically inclined in that direction. People like that dedicate their lives to hiding things. The watch is a good example. I figured Stiph's watch broke when he was run over, and then—get this—he was afraid people would think of his name, *Wach*, when the watch was discovered broken, so he goes home and gets an old watch from somewhere for Stiph, but then he puts the damn thing on backward. Now isn't that a crazy sonofabitch who does something like that? All he did was call even more attention to the watch, and in spite of that no one thought of his name in connection with it, which shows how far-gone his thinking was in the first place. Did you know he was going to change his name, too?"

"Really?"

"Yes. That's what his wife told us. After you and I had arranged our signals Monday morning I thought about it. While I was cooped up trying to keep my men quiet, I thought of the watch being on backward and its connection with his name. So at that moment, without having any idea how you were going to crack it, I was convinced I had, too. If he hadn't bolted I would have gotten it out of him anyway. Once I'm sure, I can get it out of people."

"I don't doubt that." They reached the elevator and Cook pushed the button for him.

"Considering he was basically a hider of things, these meetings with Stiph are a real puzzle—you know, this childish club. How could such a secretive man open himself up to an enemy? It doesn't make sense. And yet we have to figure that Stiph was on his way to meet Wach that night, since we have to assume that the killer is the man Stiph met. Like you once said to me, why else would this man not step forward and say, 'Yes, I'm the one Arthur Stiph planned to meet'?"

"Unless that person didn't know," said Cook, surprised that he hadn't thought of this before. "Maybe this was their first meeting, and Stiph was going to surprise him with it. It could have been any one of the linguists. It could have been *me.*" Cook laughed at the idea.

"What's so funny about that? Why couldn't it have been you?"

"No, no."

"Why not?"

"I just have the feeling that . . . he liked me."

Leaf snorted. "What's not to like, eh?"

The elevator doors opened and Leaf stepped inside and turned the toggle switch to "Off." It apparently did not concern him that someone on the ground floor might want to ride up.

"I assume I will be compensated for the dent, Lieutenant. Should I get estimates from some body shops?"

Leaf laughed loudly. "Are you kidding? For that piece-of-shit car?" He coughed and reached for a cigarette in his shirt pocket. "Well, keep your nose clean, and don't let your nose hairs grow too long. But don't pull them out, either. That can cause an infection. Bye." He flipped the switch to "On" and stepped back and leaned against the back wall of the elevator. The doors closed on his smiling, round face.

Cook walked to his office. He thought about Leaf's suspicion of him and, more keenly, his own insufficient suspicion of Wach. He saw now that he had reasoned badly, or rather that he had not reasoned at all. Distracted by the other suspects, he had not stopped to ask himself if it followed that being disliked by Jeremy Cook made one capable of murder. Aaskhugh, Milke, Orffmann—it was easy to draw from his lexicon of disparagement in talking about these men, but that did not make them murderers. To think otherwise was to commit the classic Stiphian blunder. It suddenly struck him that the world was made up of two kinds of people—those who believed in good and evil, and those who fussed over friends and enemies. The second type made lousy detectives. Not one of his gang—not even Milke, whose suspicion of Wach was personal—had stopped to ask this question in its pure form: who among us is evil?

He took out the file of Stiph's notes on love and hate. Then he went to Mary's office, first locking his door behind him—no telling but that if he left it unlocked the ghost of Geronimo or Ramses II might wander in—and he asked Mary for the master key to the offices and thanked her when she gave it to him, speaking words right to her. Then he walked down the long hall to Stiph's office and deposited the file in the drawer where he had found it, not caring if posterity produced a temperament more suitable than his own for carrying on Stiph's research.

"But what reminded you to go back to the tape?" Paula held the bottle of wine over his glass and looked at him. He shook his head.

"I've had enough, thanks. It was a *Mother Goose* rhyme. 'I do not like thee, Dr. Fell . . .' "

"I know it:

The reason why, I cannot tell.
Yet this I know, and know full well,
I do not like thee, Dr. Fell.

I like to read it to the four-year-olds. It's one of their favorites."

"Well, somebody said it, or a fragment of it, at the party, during the slugfest," Cook continued. "It lodged somewhere in my bleary brain and then a nice man with some orange juice brought it out again at the Pancake and Prayer Breakfast. I suddenly realized that Wally Woeps, whom most people regard as almost prelinguistic, was capable of making such a declaration, that he had in fact made such a declaration at a crucial moment, and that he was capable of making it again." He reached for a piece of French bread and began to butter it. He planned to use it to shovel the rest of the excellent salad Paula had made onto his fork. No more Grunt Meals for him.

"How does he say it?"

"*M-bwee*," said Cook, giving it a downward tone. "An important sentence, it turned out."

He looked at her a moment and set his fork down. The one nagging mystery in his life could be solved in a matter of seconds. All he had to do was ask her. But he felt a new Cook emerging, one for whom it was distasteful to dwell on such things. So he wouldn't ask her. He picked his fork up. Then he set it down again. Well . . . at least asking about it was now distasteful. That was something, wasn't it?

"There's another one I would like to take up with you, Paula, now that I know you."

"Another sentence?"

"Yes. Let me start by asking you how you first formed your impressions of people at Wabash. Before starting work, I mean. Did anyone brief you?"

"Well, Walter told me a few things about people, but not much. Grandpa told me a lot. He went down the staff of linguists one by one and summed up his views for me. It was quite tedious. Remember, I told you he was consumed by petty likes and dislikes—a trait I've seen evidence of in you, by the way."

"Well I can't help it," he said impatiently. "Especially when people are running around saying bad things about me all the time."

"About you? Are you crazy? If you don't know just how well liked you are, and how highly—"

"Listen to this, then." He described in fanatical detail the scene, time of day, parties present, and general atmosphere of the occasion of her utterance. " 'This fellow Cook is supposed to be a complete asshole.' That's what you said. You bitch." He said this last jokingly, but he was surprised at how much he enjoyed saying it.

She laughed. "I did? I'm sure I don't . . ." She frowned and looked away from him, as if trying to remember. Her eyes danced back and forth, and he couldn't be sure she was taking him seriously. "Oh!" she said enthusiastically. "Yes, I remember. I remember it very well now. We weren't talking about you at all. We were talking about a guy I know at, ah, Max's. Jane, the girl I was talking with, has a friend who works as a cook there, and one day he was telling me what a creep this other guy who cooks there was, and I didn't know if Jane knew that about the other cook, so I said to her, 'This fellow cook—that is, this cooking colleague—is supposed to be—' "

Cook exploded with laughter. He slapped himself on the side of the head and banged his fist on the table. What a relief! He was free!

Paula laughed too, harder and longer than he did. In fact, to his mild surprise she spontaneously burst into laughter several times as the evening wore on, well after they had left that subject and had begun to talk about more important things.

FROM AWAY

NOVELS BY DAVID CARKEET

Double Negative

The Greatest Slump of All Time

I Been There Before

The Full Catastrophe

The Error of Our Ways

From Away

FOR YOUNGER READERS

The Silent Treatment

Quiver River

FROM AWAY

DAVID CARKEET

THE OVERLOOK PRESS
NEW YORK

For Molly

FROM AWAY

ONE

WHERE WAS HIS REAR END GOING? THE HIGHWAY HAD not visibly changed, but the back end of his car was suddenly way off to the side, swinging out there like a big ass in an airplane aisle bumping passengers in the head.

"Big ass!" he shouted. He tried correcting for the skid by steering into it, but the adjustment threw him the other way, and he had to correct for *that*. Back and forth he went. His ass was really sashaying down the aisle now, knocking hats off passengers.

"Hog on ice!" he cried out, but as soon as he named this stage it ended with a complete reversal, and now he faced the drivers following him. He waved, hoping they could see him through the blowing snow, but they did not return the greeting. No matter, because it was time to say goodbye. The car made a slow, graceful sweep forward, so frictionless that he seemed to be in a dream of flying. He wanted to end the dream, but the tires did not respond to the steering wheel. He was like a kid with pretend controls while Daddy did the real driving.

"Toy wheel!" he shouted, and he knew it would come to this: he skidded off the road into the median, sliding into it at a weird diagonal. He tried not to notice that the median sloped.

"Out of my hands!" he yelled, even as his hands furiously worked that toy wheel. The median gulped him. He felt a bump and some confusion about his orientation. Several more jolts turned him into a stuck Jack-in-the-box pounded on the floor by a demented boy.

And then it was over. The car sat upright but tilted to the left side, the door pinned against something. He unbuckled his seat belt and squirmed uphill, but the other front door was sealed shut. Scrambling like a claustrophobic astronaut, he squeezed between the two front seats and lunged at the uphill rear door. It opened so easily that his exit felt commonplace, as if he were stepping out to go shopping.

He looked at his limbs and patted his body in self-examination. He felt terrific. He stretched his arms out and twirled, stopping to face the wind and the light snow that danced through the air and sparked his cheeks. People had stopped their cars on the shoulder and were hurrying to him. Hurrying! To him! He threw out his arms and cried, "Welcome to my crash site!"

But in a way it was disappointing. Denny wanted to chat, and everyone else wanted to talk about what to do with him as if he weren't even there. Get him inside where it's warm, one man said. Another argued for laying him down with his feet propped up. All the while, someone was pressing on his scalp just above his forehead. A woman! He winked at her. She said, "I'm trying to stanch the bleeding. Could you take over? I'm having trouble reaching it." He was sad to lose the contact, but he lifted a hand up and pressed on the bandage, which was actually a thick winter glove.

"My head is bloody, but unbowed," he declared to the crowd. No one had anything to say to that.

Denny felt an arm slip around his waist. "Come along, big boy." The voice and encircling arm belonged to a stooped grandpa, his lips hidden under a tangle of gray beard. He nestled in on the side where Denny's hand reached up to his head wound, and the man's skinny neck jutted forward, rooster-like, below Denny's armpit. He wore a faded orange jumpsuit. "You get him, too, Walt," the man said, and Denny felt an embrace from his other side. The second man was a twin of Grandpa, but a generation younger, his beard black, his jumpsuit brighter orange.

They helped him forward. They were small but strong. *Wiry*. He was safely in the grip of wiry men. He wanted them to take him to their hearth and home. Surely they had a spare room where he could stay. He relaxed, and the three of them almost went down on the snowy hillside.

"You'll have to contribute more than that," Grandpa said.

"Sorry," said Denny.

When they reached the shoulder, Grandpa and the one named Walt eased him into the back seat of a large car on the opposite side of the median from where Denny had lost control. Grandpa told him to take off his shoes and socks—a capital idea since they were caked with snow—and suggested he stretch out on the seat. They had left the engine running, and Denny felt as if he were settling into a deep bath.

Grandpa slid in behind the wheel, grabbed a half-eaten apple sitting on the console, and took a bite out of it. Gusts of wind rocked the car to and fro. Denny could have been in a sleeper, swaying on train rails. He wanted the three of them to stay like this forever.

But he heard a window being lowered. Something from the outside was about to change everything. A Vermont state trooper appeared at Grandpa's window, glanced at Denny, and began to talk quietly with Grandpa. Denny and cops were a bad match. They didn't like him—he could never figure out why. He had already had a little encounter that morning with the police in a burg called Waterbury, and it hadn't gone well. He sat up a bit, but he wasn't able to see the gun on the trooper's hip. What would he have to do to make the trooper draw it? How bad did you have to be, how threatening? It was interesting to think about.

The trooper opened the rear door at Denny's feet and bent down. His round hat was tilted forward so far that he had to cock his head back to see past it. He should have a tiny window in the brim, Denny thought. "How are you doing?" the trooper said.

"Outstanding. How about you?"

"Are you in pain? Anything broken?"

"I'm in the pink." Denny smiled and waggled his bare feet right in front of the trooper. He knew what was next, so he heaved his pelvis up and reached for his ass-smashed wallet in his back pocket. He handed the whole thing to the trooper because he wanted the man to get to know him by going through his cards and photos. The trooper didn't ask him to take out the license, but unfortunately he found it himself right away. He was a smart one. Denny tried to remember the last time anyone had held his wallet —such a personal object. He decided never. It had never happened before.

The trooper examined the license, his eyes going back and forth between the photo and Denny's face. Denny could have told him he was heavier now than when the photo was taken, but it was more interesting to let the trooper puzzle over it. Or maybe the trooper had looked at the birth date and wanted to tell Denny that he looked younger than forty-two. Anything was possible. Socially, the sky was the limit.

The trooper handed the wallet back to Denny. "When you run off the road," he said, "it's not the road's fault."

"Beg pardon?" said Denny.

"How fast would you say you were going?"

"No idea," Denny said. "No idea."

"Some folks here said you were driving at a high rate of speed."

"They're wrong. I saw a deer and I hit the brakes."

"A deer?"

"That's right." Denny looked at Grandpa and Walt. They faced forward as if other things were on their mind, but he knew they were listening.

"I talked to some witnesses," the trooper said.

Denny waited. "And?" He loved to say that.

"No one mentioned a deer."

"Maybe no one else saw it. I happen to have twenty-ten vision."

The trooper pulled away and looked toward Denny's car, as if the deer under discussion might be mingling with the crowd gathered there. He leaned in again. "Pretty windy."

"And?"

"Deer don't like to be out in the wind."

"I guess it was an unusual deer. A real individual."

The trooper nodded as if this might actually be possible. Denny was pleased so far. Sometimes he made things up so that the conversation would be more interesting for him. One regret though: after saying, "A real individual," he should have added, "Like me!"

"You hit the brakes," the trooper said. "Then what?"

Denny described the accident. As he spoke, he realized that this was his first telling of it. There would be many more tellings. Knowing that was like having a freezer full of ice cream.

"Were you talking on a cell phone?"

The interruption confused Denny. He hadn't even reached the part where he was sliding backwards. "No," he said.

"Someone here said you were. He said he saw your mouth moving when you passed him. Talking hands-free, sounds like."

"That seems very doubtful."

"But you were passing someone when you lost control, correct?"

Denny had no idea. "Not correct. Not correct."

"Oh? A lotta folks here said you were. They said you were going wicked fast. One fella said you made a sudden cut from the left lane back into the right lane, and that's when you lost it."

Denny swung an arm out. "When do I meet my accusers?" The sentence had popped into his head, and he loved it. Was it from the Bible? He noticed that Grandpa was leaning slightly to one side so that he could see Denny's face in the rearview mirror. Walt had shifted, too, but probably because Denny had accidentally clipped him in the back of the head when he had swung his arm out.

The trooper looked him up and down. "Were you wearing your seat belt?"

"You're asking me that because of my size, aren't you? Driving while chubby—is that a crime?"

The trooper stood up straight. He turned and looked down the highway in one direction, then in the other. He came back to Denny, this time squatting at the open door instead of leaning in. "EMS is on the way. They'll check you out."

"I've got a plane to catch."

The trooper bounced lightly on his haunches, up and down, as if exercising. Denny could never do that. "I don't think you're going to make that plane."

"Fine. But I want to get going."

The trooper stopped bouncing. "Are you refusing medical treatment?"

Denny liked the sound of that. "Yes. I'm refusing medical treatment. Does that make me an asshole?"

"No, sir." The trooper paused. He paused for quite a while. And then he said, "*That* doesn't make you an asshole."

Denny had to hand it to him. The pause had been good, of professional caliber, really. He looked from the trooper to the men in the front seat. Without moving or making a sound, they were chuckling. The amusement was contained, effectively sealed from view, but there could be no mistake. The Yankees were laughing at him.

TWO

DESPITE HIS HEROIC STAND, DENNY RECEIVED MEDICAL treatment after all. Or at least he received a swabbing of his head and neck with something smelly. He had bled not only from his scalp but also from a cut below his Adam's apple, and his left shoulder was chafed from the shoulder harness. Those were his only injuries. He took advantage of the occasion to ask the paramedics about his persistent anal itch, but they seemed reluctant to engage with the subject. And they called themselves medical professionals!

He signed some papers without reading them and stepped away from the ambulance, flagrantly picking his ass as he left. He looked down at his rental car, tilted and jammed against a tall rock—a blue-green outcrop rising from the snow like a huge axe head. One of the rear wheels was splayed. Several people still gathered around the wreck pointed and talked about it, oblivious to the wind and blowing snow. April in Vermont, Denny thought. They were welcome to it. A flatbed tow truck had parked at the edge of the median, and its driver was hauling a cable down to the car. Now and then the cable stuck, jerking the man back and making him swear.

Denny was wondering what to do next when Walt grabbed his arm and took him back to the car, which Denny now recognized as an old gray Mercedes-Benz. Walt had put Denny's suitcase and laptop in the trunk. He said someone had taken them from the back seat of Denny's car, but they had been unable to open his trunk lid. Was there anything in there? Denny wondered if he should say yes even though there wasn't. He finally said no and crawled back into his original position in the back seat. Everything was just as before, warm and quiet. Grandpa's apple, gnawed to the core, sat on the console.

But the trooper ruined everything again. He opened the door and began to blah-blah about speed on the highway and how lucky Denny was that he didn't hit that rock hard. People often lectured Denny about this and that, and he had a way of looking off in the distance when they did. The trooper described an accident scene he had worked where "another speed demon" was pierced through the chest by a guardrail. Denny said that must have made it hard for him to drive, which got the trooper all agitated, and Grandpa had to walk him away from the car. When Grandpa came back, he gave Denny the ticket that the trooper had written. He actually threw it into the back seat, but Denny knew he was just joking around.

Walt told Denny that he and his father planned to get off the interstate in Montpelier, and they could drop him off at a hotel before they went on to their farm. Denny would need a room since he probably wouldn't get a flight until the next day. A back haul, Denny thought, since he remembered passing the Montpelier exit before he ran off the road. He agreed to everything, though he was frankly surprised not to get that invitation to their home. As Grandpa pulled onto the highway, Denny looked back at his rental car being pulled up to the flatbed. He wondered what would happen to it.

In the warm, silent Mercedes, Denny fought off sleep because the men would probably want to chat. *What brings you to Vermont?* After a few miles, he wondered why it wasn't happening. They just sat there. Then—get this—the two men started talking *to each other*. It was as if Denny wasn't even in the car! They weren't talking so much as arguing. Denny had seen them as companionable kinfolk, but now they were really going at it. Denny joined in the argument, after his own fashion: he hummed along privately whenever one of them spoke, his soft tune riding the contours of their speech.

Across a snowy field, railroad tracks paralleled the freeway. Denny couldn't actually see the tracks, but he knew they were there. Tired of the men's jabber, he closed his eyes and pictured his Hiawatha Streamliner layout. When he got home, he would add to it. First, he would insert a tall sliver of blue-green stone on the side of the road next to the westbound track. He wished he had chipped a piece off the block next to his car and put it in his pocket. Second, he would add these Mercedes-driving backwoodsmen to the layout, probably at the depot. He had a couple of figures in mind that he could beard with a little paint. Grandpa would go up in the switching tower. Denny could see his hand placing him there, could feel it happening already. He would give Walt an outdoors job, far away from Grandpa. He didn't want the two of them filling up his rec room with their arguments.

* * *

Denny woke up slowly. He was lying flat on the back seat with his knees up. He normally didn't nap. Did that mean he had had a concussion? He hoped so. Walt was leaning in through the open car door, his black beard floating directly overhead. Denny gave him a dreamy smile, but Walt just urged him out with a jerk of his head. Denny sat up and stretched. Grandpa was giving him the old rearview-mirror scrutiny. Denny thanked him for the ride.

"You'll want to clean up," Grandpa said.

Denny distractedly agreed and climbed out of the car. The hotel, in imitation of big-city style, sported a portico with fake columns leading from the curb to the front door. Walt led Denny inside to the unoccupied front desk. He set Denny's suitcase and laptop on the floor and called out, "Got a live one for you, Betsy."

Denny heard an "Ooh" from the rear, behind a partition of dark wood that hid everything from view. "Is that Walter? What are you doin' in this neck of the woods?"

"Got to run."

"Hold on now." A chair scraped on a bare floor behind the partition.

"He's all yours." Walt hurried away, leaving Denny to puzzle over his sudden departure. After being friendly, had Walt turned sour on him? It was always hard to tell.

And where was the desk clerk? Denny heard a soft exchange of words between a man and a woman, followed by the sound of a chair scooting again. It sounded domestic, as if they had been having a snack back there. The woman who finally appeared was white-haired, with an expectant face so pale that it looked as if it had been lightly dusted with flour. She swept her eyes around the lobby as she approached the counter, which Denny rapped with authority.

"My name is Dennis Braintree, and I would like a room for the night."

The woman pressed her lips together. Strangely, she took no action. She didn't consult any records or look at the computer screen in front of her. Instead, she seemed to perform some sort of mental computation. When she finally spoke, her voice had a dying fall. "I don't have any rooms."

"What?"

"I have nothing," she said simply.

"Nothing? I'm in the middle of nowhere." Denny waved his arms as if to demonstrate this fact. "Is this a ski lodge or something?"

"The legislature is in session."

Denny frowned. Was this an entirely new topic? "And?"

"The hotel is chock-a-block with legislators. Through Wednesday. You should come back Thursday."

Denny laughed. "My goal is not to spend *some* night in *this* hotel. It's to spend *this* night in *any* hotel."

"You'll find everything else booked up, too."

A silence fell. Complete silence. Denny looked suspiciously up the dark wooden staircase. "There's no evidence of activity."

"The legislators are all across the street. Or in our meeting rooms." Her eyes fluttered behind her glasses, and she seemed to size him up. "Of course . . ." The woman frowned in thought.

"And?" Denny said, even though it didn't quite fit.

"Someone brought a suitcase down just now. It could have been Mort Shuler. Bronia said he might have to get back to Brandon early—on account of Freckles, you know."

The cast of characters had exploded. Was Denny supposed to ask who all these people were?

"I'll give you the cubby in the meantime. You seem tired, almost peevish." The front door opened, and she turned toward it and called out, "Have a good outing?"

The woman entering smiled and said, "Yes, I did, Betsy, thanks," and Betsy told her that someone was waiting in the restaurant for her.

Denny asked Betsy—he was good at catching names and using them—about airport transportation, and she gave him a Vermont Transit bus schedule, along with a warning that the new driver, Charles, wasn't nearly as friendly as the old driver, Seth, who was laid up with a bad back. Denny thanked her for the heads-up and asked for the room key. She said the room was unlocked. "This is Vermont, after all," she said.

The elevator was around a corner and down a hall. On his way there, he passed a squat woman staring fiercely at a pay phone. She wore a dull uniform of faded turquoise—a housekeeper. She turned as Denny approached, looked away from him, then looked back sharply as he passed by. The phone rang in her face. She grabbed it and said something in a strange language. This combination of events made Denny feel like a subject of surveillance in a foreign land. She turned to stare at him even after he had stepped into the elevator. He leaned forward and pushed his belly in to check his fly, and he saw that his shirt was splattered with blood. That certainly explained the stare, but it raised a new question. Why hadn't Betsy shown any reaction? What kind of place was this that took in bloodied guests, no questions asked?

In the elevator, he quoted himself to himself: "My goal is not to spend *some* night in *this* hotel. It's to spend *this* night in *any* hotel." It was a shame that people didn't enjoy his company more. He had so much to offer. Puns, for example. No one could match him in that department. But he hadn't punned out loud in more than three months, ever since Ruth had unloaded on him in the snack room. She said that puns were "topic destroyers." She declared them "essentially antisocial." While she was at it, she complained about how he was always in the way. In his defense, he pointed out that the snack room was small, and she said he was in the way *everywhere*—in the copying room, in the hall, in the deli around the corner. "It's not just your size," she said. "You seem to *know* you're in the way and you *stay* in the way." As if *she* was perfect, slow-talker that she was. Her sentences unfolded so glacially that the only way Denny could make them tolerable was to insert secret words of his own: "I wish [with all my heart] that you [and nobody but you] would scrub [a dub dub] the bowl afterward." That memorable gem had to do with the staff toilet, which she insisted he swab every time he shed a little weight into it. His boss backed her up, so he had no choice but to grab the blue cleaner from under the sink and get down on his knees and scrub like a fiend. Those two really knew how to kill the afterglow of a bowel movement. Ruth always complained about something else, too, but he forgot what. It was hard to keep track.

"*Some* night in *this* hotel," he whispered. "*This* night in *any* hotel." If he could reliably perform at that level, he would never lose an argument. When was his next argument scheduled? The airline, certainly. They would blame him for missing his flight. He would have to use the deer again. He could even say, "It was windy, so I wasn't expecting a deer." Or maybe "Being that it was windy, I wasn't expecting a deer." "Being that" sounded smart. He said the sentence a few times, trying different tones. As the elevator doors opened on the fourth floor, he remembered Ruth's other complaint: he talked to himself.

A stocky, red-cheeked man in a too-tight white dress shirt blocked Denny's exit from the elevator. His face was buried in a sheaf of papers stapled at the top, and he was whipping through the pages. He suddenly realized he was in the way and stepped back to let Denny exit the elevator.

"Mort!" a man called out. The speaker was leaning out a room down the hall. "Dinner? Marge'll be there. She's always fun."

The stocky man laughed. "Fun," he said doubtfully. "I can't anyway. Got to get home." He held the elevator door open with an extended arm, his back to Denny. His other arm, as if for balance, held the sheaf of papers out to the side, blocking Denny's progress down the hall.

"To Brandon," Denny said from behind him.

"That's right!" Mort said, throwing a look at Denny as he hurried into the elevator.

"Because of Freckles."

The elevator doors closed, but Denny was able to hear the muffled shout, "Right again!"

Denny chuckled his way down the hall. What a little world he had landed in. Such a dinky town of Betsys and Morts and Marges, and everyone knowing everything because there was so little to know. It was like a model train town full of little people. You could pick them up and put them anywhere you liked.

He followed Betsy's directions to the cubby: down the hall, a hard right into a rear wing of the building (colder than the main wing; she hadn't mentioned that), and another turn to a dead end at a brown-painted wooden door without numbering or lettering. This, Betsy had said, was the mark of the cubby: it bore no mark.

The door immediately banged into a metal bed frame. He squeezed in with his bags. The single bed completely filled the room except for about eighteen inches at its foot and on both sides. There were no windows, and the only door was the one he had entered. No bathroom, but no surprise there. Betsy had suggested that he use the public restroom off the lobby—"if you like," she had added, as if it were one of many options. The cubby lacked a phone on the nightstand. For the record, it also lacked a nightstand. The only object besides the bed was a small purple vinyl box in the corner with a yellow carrying handle. Denny picked it up and set it on the bed. He twisted the heart-shaped plastic latch and opened it. It was a child's jewelry box, filled with rings, necklaces, and oversized earrings. There were also little plastic containers bearing the label "Polly Pocket." They opened to reveal almost microscopic dollhouse rooms and half-inch-high people. Denny began to lose himself in one of those rooms. He made himself close the box and put it back in its corner.

He patted his coat pockets in search of his cell phone, then remembered it had been sitting on the front passenger seat when he had spun out of control. It was somewhere in the wreck of his rental, wherever that was. He would have to call the airline from the pay phone downstairs, assuming Miss Stare-a-Lot was done with it. Which reminded him: he should change his shirt, even though he didn't really want to. Something about wearing a bloody shirt appealed to him. He thought of the porter in his rec room layout and decided to add a dab of blood to his white shirt. Talk about intrigue! Then he had another thought. Grandpa and Walt ran a maple farm. That's what they had argued about in the car—something about operations. Before installing the two men in his layout, he would dip their heads in maple syrup, and he would refresh them every week or so. The result, for the viewer, would be evocative in just the right measure.

He studied the bus schedule as he rode down the elevator. The pay phone was not in use, and the airline agent proved surprisingly helpful. She expressed official company sympathy over his accident and booked him on a new flight to Chicago, scheduled to leave Burlington late the next morning at a time that corresponded well with the bus schedule. He didn't even have to mention the deer. He called the office, but his boss was out. He left a message saying he would try again.

Around the corner at the front desk, Betsy stood wide-eyed and expectant, as if she had done nothing but wait for his return. He asked her where he could buy a cell phone.

"You'll find a phone store right next to where Gretchen's bakery used to be."

Denny failed to picture this. "Is there still a sign there that says 'Gretchen's Bakery'?"

"My lands, no. The building burned to the ground ages ago."

"What stands in its place?"

"The lot's still empty."

"So you could say"—Denny started to wave his arms but caught himself—"the cell phone store is next to an empty lot?"

"I could, yes, but you just did." She bent down for something under the counter. This allowed Denny to bug his eyes out at her. She rose holding a tall pair of black winter boots, fringed at the top. "Wear these."

"What?"

"What you're wearin' ain't right for what's out there. I can tell. What are they—sneakers?" She looked at his face, as if the sight of his shoes repulsed her.

"Yes, sneakers."

She shook the boots in her hand. "Wear these."

"I'm fine. As long as I stay on the sidewalk—"

"Put 'em on."

Denny sighed, slipped out of his shoes, and eased his feet into the boots. They fit quite nicely. He picked up his sneakers and extended them to Betsy. She reached for them, but a gap of a foot remained between her hands and the shoes. When she failed to close it, he looked into her face and realized with a shock that she could not see. He eased the shoes into her hands and she took them in a natural way. "Bear in mind now," she said as she set them under the counter, "that you'll have to make do with Little Timmy at the phone store. His dad'll be out scoutin' toms. Big Timmy come up empty in deer season—took his rifle out for a walk, you might say—and he's gonna make some tom pay."

As Denny buttoned his overcoat, he looked at Betsy and resisted the urge to ask her what it was like to be blind. He knew it would be wrong. Usually he knew something was wrong when it was too late and he had already spoken, but now he knew it in time to shut up, though he could feel the words banging against the inside of his lips like a crowd trying to crash through a door.

Outside, he headed toward what looked like the business district and kept an eye out for an empty lot. It was late afternoon, and the snow had stopped, but a gray mass of cloud seemed to press down on the town and contain it like a tight lid. Some movement on top of a roof caught his attention. It was a man clearing snow with a scoop, sending it cascading down the side of the three-story building into an alley. All of the buildings on the street had flat roofs. Why did they build them that way? Didn't they know it snowed here? A feature like that could look wrong in a layout even though it was actually right. Denny liked the idea of seeming wrong but being right.

"Nice coat."

It didn't register with Denny that these words were meant for him until the speaker had passed by. The man was going the other way, and by the time Denny turned, his back was already to him, a hand waving as if he knew he was being observed. The comment, though decidedly odd, was right—it *was* a nice coat, a big black wool overcoat that Denny liked to swoop around in. He called it his Secret Agent Man coat.

Denny reached a "T" where the street ended—the hub of town, such as it was. No empty lot was in sight, and he didn't know which way to go. He caught the eye of a pale, thin, bearded young man approaching with long strides. "Phone store?" Denny asked.

The man immediately stopped and walked backwards in the opposite direction, the reversal so abrupt that it made Denny think of a pinball recoiling from a bumper. After a few backward strides, the pale fellow stopped at a narrow pedestrian walkway between two brick buildings and pointed dramatically, like an explorer on a commemorative postage stamp. Denny joined him and peered down the walkway. At its end he glimpsed what seemed to be an empty lot—Gretchen's remains, presumably. Denny thanked the mime and looked closely at his beard. It was a two-tone affair, with a red triangle at the chin set against a blond background.

In the store, a more conventional mortal assisted Denny and sent him on his way with a new cell phone. Denny stopped at a sandwich shop and loaded up for dinner. On his way out, he nearly bumped into a woman about his age. She backed up, held the door for him, and then did a double-take. "That's some coat." She laughed. "Who died?"

Denny hurried on. It was true that his black coat suggested mourning. It was also true that apparently no one else in this town wore a full-length winter overcoat. They all seemed to wrap themselves in fleecy things and parkas and plaid get-ups. Still, he had never had a social experience quite like this one, where strangers felt at liberty to comment on his appearance. Weren't New Englanders supposed to be close-mouthed?

Very near the hotel, a man with two golden retrievers called out something to Denny and hurried to him. The dogs heeled without leashes and stayed close by their owner. Denny kept a sharp eye on them and inched toward the hotel entrance. He could feel his fear mounting. He could see it take physical form, a vapor that wafted from his pores into the dogs' nostrils.

"Man, is this the Florida style?" the dog owner said, eyeing, of course, the coat. "Seems kind of warm for down there. But I'd recognize those pussy boots anywhere."

Florida? thought Denny. Pussy boots? The dogs sniffed the fringe on his boots, and their tails began a gentle wag, bumping lightly into each other.

"They're happy to see you," the man said.

"And I'm happy to see them." Denny hoped the dogs could not detect insincerity. He eased away slowly, slowly, slowly, and then broke into a run the last few steps to the door.

THREE

"HAVE A GOOD OUTING?" BETSY CALLED FROM BEHIND the counter.

Denny saw right away what she was doing. She was pretending to know who had just come in the door. For all she knew, he could have been one of those dogs outside. The thought made him want to bark—and he did, a happy puppy bark.

"Ah, Mr. Braintree. I'll take that as a yes. Here—I have a new key for you." She slapped it on the counter with more noise than she had intended, judging from the guilty little face she made. Denny picked it up. "Mort has checked out," Betsy went on. "You'll be in 408 now. You may move at any time, though the sooner, the better. You see, I just learned my nephew's back in town." She sighed. "He's been gone so long, poor boy. Three years. It makes me happy to think he's home again. Happy and sad, too."

Denny liked it when he knew what he was supposed to say. "Why sad?"

"Because if he's in town, why didn't he come give me a hug?"

Denny knew the next thing to say, too. "Maybe he tried to find you and couldn't."

"Thank you for saying that." She reached out as if to touch him. He hesitated, then brushed his hand near where hers had come to rest atop the counter so that she would know it was there, and she covered it with her own. It gave Denny a strange feeling. "He stays here sometimes," she continued. "When he wants company. When he wants a meal cooked by someone who loves him. That big old farmhouse can be too much for him. He becomes troubled. He likes the cubby—his 'crash pad,' he calls it."

"He's welcome to it," Denny said. "No offense."

"None taken." She released his hand, bent down behind the counter, and came up with his shoes. He took off the boots and made sure when he held them out for her that they made contact with her hands.

She mused aloud as he tied his shoelaces. "It's a good thing Mort left and freed up the cubby. I don't know where I'd have put my Homer otherwise. He rented out the farmhouse to Chip Dougherty. There's Sarah's place, but . . ." Her voice drifted off. Denny felt the burden of names again. The front door opened, and she swung toward it. "Have a good outing?" she called out.

"Yes, Betsy, I did," the woman who had entered said brightly.

The phone rang, and Betsy stabbed a hand out and grabbed it. Denny eased away from the counter, then thought perhaps he should let her know he was leaving, so he cleared his throat when he was a few steps away. Still speaking on the phone, and giving the illusion of unbroken eye contact as she tracked the woman across the lobby, Betsy waved a goodbye to Denny. She was good, no doubt about it.

Back in his cubby, he tried reaching his boss but got the office machine again. He left a message giving his new cell phone number. Then he bid adieu to the little room and its box of trinkets and moved down the hall. It was quite an upgrade: two couches, a small refrigerator, and, over the king bed, a chandelier with candle-like bulbs. French doors led to a small wrought-iron balcony. He opened the drapes over a desk next to the balcony doors. Across the street, beyond a broad sweep of grass, was the golden-domed capitol. A statue atop it seemed to look at Denny. He glanced down and saw a real person actually looking at him. It was Two-Tone, the street mime, sitting on a bus-stop bench across the street. His gaze had fallen on Denny at the window, but now he seemed to be challenging him to a stare-off.

Several minutes later, a knock on the door forced Denny to concede. He opened it to find a slight man in half-glasses and a paisley tie. He gave Denny a fierce look over his glasses, then directed his suspicion to the room number on the door.

"Mort had to go back to Brandon because of Freckles." It gave Denny strange pleasure to say this.

The man pressed his lips together, sighed hard through his nose, and left. As Denny closed the door, his cell phone began to ring and vibrate on top of the desk.

It was his boss. Roscoe was talking before Denny could even say hello. "What were you thinking? We talked about what's been happening with your articles. I told you precisely what *not* to do, and then you did it. 'Alec's trainscape did not invite me in. I tried to enter it, but it wouldn't let me. Neither would Alec.' Denny, do you know how many things are wrong with that?"

"Certainly not the flow. It's got a lovely flow."

"The point of *The Fearless Modeler* is to *en*courage modeling, not *dis*courage it. You don't dump all over a layout that took a guy six years to build. That's the number-one wrong thing. Number two is no one *enters* a layout. You're supposed to look at it. That's what normal people do."

"You know what I meant."

"No, I don't, and you always say that and I'm tired of it. I'm tired of the complaints I get about you, too. Alec called after you were there. He said you sprawled on his board."

"I laid my head down on it. That's all."

Roscoe let out a strange laugh. "It was enough to nearly crush his turntable cabin. That's a three-hundred-dollar turntable."

"I was trying to enter the scene."

"Yeah? Enter *this* scene: I'm sitting in my office on Friday and I get back-to-back phone calls from two different advertisers about last month's issue. That piece wasn't as wacko as this one, but both of these guys pointed out that nothing in your write-ups would make a modeler want to go out and buy materials to upgrade. You talk about minute positional alterations. And now you want to *subtract* elements. This feature you proposed—'Undetailing Your Layout'—are you serious?"

"There's so much clutter, Roscoe. It gets in the way."

"Yeah? Well, right now *you're* getting in the way—of my bottom line! Maybe you should stay home and just *imagine* layouts instead of looking at them. Isn't that your ideal?"

"I'm not comfortable writing reviews designed to move product."

Roscoe was silent for a moment. "That's a surprisingly normal sentence, Denny. Is someone coaching you? Listen, nobody ever asked you to 'move product.' If you just wrote in a sane way about the context, readers would want to improve theirs and buy stuff."

"I do write about context."

"Ha! Your context is . . . it's *biographical*, for God's sake. You wrote that Alec should know the complete history of all of his figures. These are little plastic people, Denny. Did you really ask him how long the switchman had been married? Was there a wedding ring on his tiny finger?"

"Yes, there was. It might have been an imperfection, but it got me thinking."

"Yeah? Well, think about *this*. Is there any other way you can make a living? Because I'm worn out. You wear people out, Denny. And look at the bind you've put me in. I've got a deadline and five empty pages because you've given me nothing to work with. I've put up with a lot. I've dealt with your bias against kitbashing. I've scratched out your terrible jokes. I've endured your nagging for a Rod Stewart profile. And what is it with you and waving? Every layout doesn't have to have some yahoo waving his hand."

Denny had gotten two waves that day, one from the man who said, "Nice coat," the other from Betsy as he had left the counter. "I got two waves today, Roscoe."

After a pause, Roscoe said, "I don't know what to say to that, Denny. I just don't know what to say. Listen, I've been willing to edit your words, but I give up trying to edit you. I'm worried about you, Denny. I like you. Well, that's not exactly true, but I *am* worried. Actually, I'm not all that worried. The point is, you're fired. I've never fired anyone, Denny. Ruth still can't spell, but she's my proofreader and I'm sticking with her. You, though—I can't deal with you anymore."

Roscoe kept talking, but Denny didn't want to listen. As he hung up the phone, he came up with a biography for the wedded switchman, a cute little figure with blond locks below his cap. He could be married to a poor speller named Ruth. She would have a job transcribing medical tapes. The switchman happened to be gifted in spelling, and in the evening he would correct Ruth's mistakes. In gratitude, and because she loved her husband so, one morning she let him sleep late, and she put on his uniform and worked the switches, her cap pulled down over her face. All day the yardman peered out his grimy window and muttered, "Olsen looks different. Must have lost some weight."

The knocking came in the middle of the night—repeated taps that felt like ratchets of a machine hoisting him from sleep. The darkness of the hotel room was complete, and he had to feel his way across the room, padding in his socks from bed to bureau to door. He opened it just a crack to say that Mort was not here, but the knocker—an ample woman moving fast—shoved the door open far enough to allow her to scurry inside. She had been looking up and down the hall as she did this, and now she giggled in the dark.

"Whew!" she said. "Ike's out there somewhere. I *don't like* Ike. I don't like that bitch who was with him either." She giggled again. "Where are you?"

"Right here."

"Whoa." The woman felt for the wall switch and threw a harsh light on Denny, who squinted at her in his boxer shorts. "You're not Mort the Sport. Wrong room?"

Denny was hurrying into his pants. "It's the right room," he said, "but Mort left."

The woman touched her fingertips to her forehead as if struck by a revelation. "I knew that. Ike told me at dinner." Her jaw hung open. She seemed stuck on a thought until a logjam of new ideas broke loose and bumped her forward. "We ate and talked. And drank." She stared across the room at nothing. "And I knew you went home . . . I mean *Mort* went home." Another jam, then another rapid burst: "But by the time we got back to the hotel I forgot and came looking for you. For *Mort.*" She swayed. "I gotta sit."

She hurried to the couch and flopped on it, but then she composed herself. She stretched her arms out along its back and crossed her legs, exposing much of the top one. Her curly brown hair sat roundly on her head like half of a basketball, covering much of her forehead. She sized Denny up. "You're not as cute as Mort."

"My name is Denny. I'm just passing through."

She burst into song like a goosed Ethel Merman. "'*Passing throooooo. Passing throooooo. I saw Abraham and Isaac passing throooooooo . . .*' Sing along, Danny. Don't be a party pooper." She fogged up, then came back. "How come Mort left? Was it that fucking Freckles?"

Denny was buttoning his shirt. "I'm afraid so," he said. Then, for effect, he added, "Again."

"Ain't *that* the truth." The woman snorted.

Denny wished he knew who Freckles was. Mort's son? Wife? Horse?

"It's amazing," the woman went on, suddenly philosophical. "I could change his life. I could change it forever. I have . . . a *proposal* for him." She giggled, then suddenly stopped. Her eyes swept over the room. "How does he rate these digs? Chairman of the Natural Resources and Energy Committee. Big whoop." She stared at the chandelier. "I always wanted to swing on one of those. I gotta pee." She stood up and sauntered by Denny, reaching him just as he finished tucking in his shirt. "You don't have to get all dressed up on my account." She poked him hard in the chest, bathing him in her fruity breath.

"You're Marge!" he said, proud of his discovery. "The one who's fun."

She reeled back a bit. "Mort tell you that? Tellin' tales out of school. Out of *shul.*" She grinned at her joke, then frowned. Denny suddenly knew what she was going to do next: she would shake her head as if to clear it. And she did. He also knew she was going to say something silly as she went on into the bathroom, like "Toodleoo."

"Ciao," she said.

Drunk people were so slow, Denny thought. You could see where they were going way before they knew. Wouldn't it be wonderful, in normal life, to be as far ahead of everyone as you were ahead of drunks? You'd be like God.

"Hey, you've got a Jacuzzi!" she yelled through the closed door. He knew before she did it that she was going to turn on the water. Next she would undress and climb into the tub. He replayed the poke in his chest. He had been looking at *her* chest at the time, which was strange, as if the poke were punishment for looking. She had his body type, and he imagined his round cheeks plunging into her cleavage, his roundness meeting hers. He paced the room, then sat down on the edge of his bed and clasped his hands between his knees.

Question: would she have him?

Answer: she was naked in his Jacuzzi.

A little cry of excitement passed his lips as he rose from the bed. He tiptoed to the bathroom door and knocked, but way too shyly, he knew, to be heard over the roar of the water. He knocked loudly.

"Is that you, Mort?" She laughed. "Can I call you Mort?"

"You bet."

"So what do you want? Hah! As if I didn't know. With these jets here, what makes you think I need you?"

He was too scared to speak.

"Oh, what the hell," she said. "Come on in."

Denny grabbed the knob. "It's locked."

"I guess our union's not meant to be." She laughed and yelled something else.

"I didn't hear you," he said.

She yelled, "Do you have a condom? I'm fresh out."

Denny had many thoughts, but he simply shouted, "No."

She hollered the directions to an all-night drugstore and asked him to get her some cigarettes, too. She named the brand, type, length, and packaging style. Denny hurried to the desk and wrote down the information. He felt that everything hinged on getting this right.

"Back in a flash," he called out. As he put on his shoes, he heard another knock on the door. What if it was this man she had mentioned, this Ike, on the hunt for her?

But it was Betsy. "Is everything satisfactory, Mr. Braintree?"

"Everything's fine."

"I'm so glad. Now, while I'm here, did you happen to hear any shouting or singing? Someone called the front desk. I don't want to say they complained, but they did call."

"Well—" Denny was surprised to find that he couldn't lie to her.

"All the other rooms are occupied by legislators. They work hard and they sleep hard. So I thought the noise might have come from your room." She looked at him. Or rather, she seemed to look at him. "You're running the Jacuzzi."

"That's right."

"But you're not *in* the Jacuzzi."

"I intend to be."

"Mm-hmm." She blinked behind her strangely flat glasses. "How shall I put this?" Her flour-white face was unreadable. She took a deep breath. "Here in Vermont, we have direct democracy, and that takes the form of our annual town meetings." She paused and pulled back. "I'm not talking to a naked man, am I?"

"No, of course not."

"You said you intended to be in the Jacuzzi." She turned her head to one side.

"Yes, but—

"Vermont also has representative democracy at the state level," she continued doggedly, her words going down the hall more than to him. "These citizen legislators work hard—"

"—and they sleep hard. I'll be quiet, I promise."

"Then all is well—except for your bare nakedness."

She was gone before he could muster further denial. He put on his shoes and his Secret Agent Man coat and grabbed his room key and wallet. He began to look for his car keys when he remembered that he had no car. He clutched his hair. All was ruined! He went to the bathroom door and knocked loudly.

"Christ, you still here?" Marge yelled. Denny explained his predicament. She shouted, "You're real good at this, aren't you?" She told him to take her car and gave him directions to it in the back lot. "Keys are in my purse," she hollered. Denny found them. He also saw a pack of cigarettes in there with just one remaining. He compared the information on the pack with what he had written on the slip in his pocket. They matched. He saw it as a good sign that Marge felt she would need more than one cigarette for the night ahead.

"A firecracker!" he said to himself on his way out. "A spitfire! A firecracker! Oh, I already said that."

Fortunately, a back door led to the parking lot, and Denny could avoid passing the front desk, which would certainly have provoked a question about the shortness of his Jacuzzi experience. Marge's car, a cluttered Subaru, smelled of tobacco. Inhaling her spent air, he studied the gearshift knob and practiced shifting—he had never mastered a stick shift. In fits and starts, relying heavily on a whining second gear as neither too high nor too low, he drove down a side street to a two-lane highway and tracked down the all-night drugstore without difficulty. Likewise the condom display, though the options dizzied him. He bought three different packages and figured Marge could help him decide from there. He scanned the cigarette display behind the clerk and dictated the specifications from his notes.

The return drive, with its known destination, opened his mind to invasion by thoughts he had kept at bay since Marge had turned on the Jacuzzi. Would he be able to do this well enough—which was to say, long enough? The last time, just over two years ago, he had been too quick and had tried to hide what had happened, but that didn't work very well. His partner—Ramona was her name—made him root around down there, which didn't work all that well either, and talk about a mess! He remembered thinking it was funny that they called it "eating" and how, at the time, he wished he really was eating instead. He was afraid Ramona was going to yell at him for botching everything, but she just fell asleep, and he was able to sneak out of her room. Hotels were great. So was alcohol.

The time before that—Melanie, her name was—when it was all over and Denny was gasping for breath, she said, "I never thought it could be like this." But when he phoned her for another date, she explained what she had meant: she never thought it could be that bad.

The last woman he had had into his apartment—he couldn't remember her name—had left in a huff before he had made any real progress. But the next morning, he was pleased to see that she had left something of herself behind. He was taking a dump, and when he grabbed the toilet paper roll from the tank behind him, he saw that she had blotted her lips on the outside of it. She must have applied fresh lipstick in the hopes of finding someone else that night. Her lips had left a perfect red oval on the toilet paper, and when he wiped, it was almost like she was giving him a nice kiss down there.

The parking lot was eerily quiet. No wonder—it was after 2:00 A.M. He looked up at the hotel. It was creepy to look at dark windows and know that people slept behind them. Overhead, scudding clouds hid stars, presented them like a ringmaster with a musical *ta-da*, and then hid them again. He dashed from the rear door to the elevator. The way his coat flowed behind him, along with the upcoming guaranteed action, really made him feel like a secret agent. On the fourth floor, he paused outside his room to catch his breath.

When he entered, his first thought was that if they were going to have sex, he would have to remove the chandelier from the bed. His second thought was *What the hell?* Electrical wires dangled from the ceiling where the fixture had hung. Marge wasn't on the bed or in the room or in the bathroom. She had sloppily sloshed out of the tub. The crash of the chandelier might have drawn her. (*Did you make that noise, Mort?* God, more shouting.) Then he remembered: she said she had always wanted to swing from a chandelier. He imagined the inspiration seizing her after her bath. She could have climbed up on the bed, grabbed it, and *boom*. What then? Had the noise prompted another visit from Betsy, this one resulting in Marge's ejection? But would the chandelier have made noise falling on the bed? If Marge hit the floor, *she* might have made the noise. She could have hurt herself. Had she gone off to apply a Band-Aid to an injury? If so, would she return to apply a condom to him, or would he have to coax her back? Where was her room?

A light in a window would tell him. The rear of the hotel had been completely dark, and he could check the front from his balcony. He opened the French doors, stepped out, and swept his eyes across the front of the hotel. All was black, not just at the hotel but as far as he could see down the street and over the rooftops. It was a sleepy, virtuous village, no doubt about it. With a sigh, he went back into the room, still clutching his pathetic bag of goodies from the drugstore. He set it on the dresser and began to clean up. The chandelier, though not heavy, required a wide-arm embrace to work it down from the bed to the floor. Chunks of drywall from the ceiling covered the bed. He gathered up the bedspread by its four corners and considered shaking it out on the balcony, but there were parked cars on the street below, so he funneled the debris into a wastebasket. Then he used a towel to mop up the water Marge had sloshed on the bathroom floor. He brushed his teeth, sighed at himself in the mirror, set his alarm for 6:00 A.M., and went to bed.

He couldn't fall asleep, though. Two new ideas for his Hiawatha Streamliner layout kept him dancing in bed—a blind lady and a puzzle. The puzzle would be a chandelier lying on the floor of a ballroom. He could modify the gym over the police station and change it into a ballroom. He had never been happy with the gym anyway, with all its stupid equipment. He would throw it out and empty the room—except for the chandelier on the floor. That would be interesting. He could see it through the little window, could feel the tension zinging from it. Why had it fallen? How long ago? Why had no one picked it up?

And the blind lady. Where would he put her?

FOUR

THIS TIME IT WAS FOG. IT SLOWED EVERYTHING DOWN—traffic, aircraft, thought. When the Vermont Transit bus pulled into the Montpelier station over an hour late, it seemed to float to Denny out of the mist. It delivered him to the airport two hours late, but the planes weren't going anywhere.

He checked his suitcase and staked out the gate waiting area until he could snag a seat with no armrests. He settled into it, closed his eyes, and stretched his legs out as far as he could, knowing he would soon be bound by the tiny box of his coach seat. He remembered the good old days, when he could use his size as the basis for a first-class upgrade at check-in. That was before the airlines got tough. He stopped trying after one airline agent, on hearing his "I'm large" argument, said with a straight face, "But, sir, you knew you were large when you bought your coach ticket." What a zinger!

"Would Chicago passenger Dennis Braintree come to the counter, please? Dennis Braintree?"

Denny's eyes popped open. This was exactly what they said when his request for an upgrade had been successful. But he hadn't made one. He looked to the gate counter, some distance away past several rows of seated travelers. Was there a problem with his ticket? He hoped so. He liked talking to people behind counters. He scooted forward to get up, but then he spied two men standing at the far end of the counter—two watchful men.

He knew exactly what was going on. There was no way that a busty woman could poke him in the chest and get naked in his Jacuzzi without payment being required. Marge had turned against him, and these two men—cops, obviously—were chasing him. What had she accused him of? He had taken her car, yes, but with her permission. That thought made him feel the outside of his pants pocket. He still had her keys. A blunder on his part, yes, but she wouldn't send the police after him just for her keys.

One of the cops was scanning the crowd like a surveillance camera on slow rotation. As his gaze approached Denny's bank of seats, Denny bent over and fussed with a shoe. A minute later, when he looked back up, the cop's eyes were safely beyond him. The other cop signaled something to the agent, and she leaned into her microphone and repeated her summons for Dennis Braintree.

Denny watched a man step to the counter for reasons of his own. The cops intercepted him, demanded his ID and examined it, then dismissed him and stepped away from the counter, a ridiculous duo now, their cover entirely blown. The size of the man told Denny all he needed to know about the description they were working from. He could see Marge's lips form the word.

He would wait them out even if it meant missing his flight. When they gave up and left, he would catch another plane. But the cops, as if reading his mind, suddenly turned their attention to the seated travelers. They began to stroll through the crowd, one on each side of the main concourse aisle, demanding an ID from every husky male. At a moment when both were occupied, Denny rose and made his way through the rows of seats to the main aisle.

"Would Chicago passenger Dennis Braintree come to the counter, please? Dennis Braintree?"

The words seemed to chase him. Still walking, he glanced back. To his surprise, the cops were together again at the counter, and one of them jabbed a finger toward Denny but without looking at him. Denny pressed on. How to hurry without seeming to hurry? He heard rapid footsteps on the carpet behind him and braced himself for a tackle. But the cop whisked by and didn't stop until he was about twenty steps ahead of Denny, at a spot where the gates within earshot of the agent's announcement funneled into a food court. The cop installed himself there and began scrutinizing passersby, rightly thinking that their man might try to give them the slip.

When Denny slowed, the cop instantly noticed the change in the traffic rhythm. Their eyes locked, and it was all over. The cop's jaw dropped, and he pointed his two index fingers at Denny and shot him with them, pumping them like ack-ack guns. Denny was disheartened, but he was also baffled. The pantomime fell well outside the taking-into-custody protocol.

The cop beckoned with a broad sweep of his arm. What could

Denny do but comply? And as he came closer, the cop stepped forward to meet him, and here came the big arm of the law, wrapping around Denny's neck in a fierce embrace. The cop was short, and he had to reach up to do it. He stepped back, grinned, and said, "How long has it been?"

Words failed our hero.

"Were you in Florida all this time? That's what we heard."

Florida. Denny had heard it mentioned before. He nodded.

"You look different. Is it your hair? Have you lost weight?"

Denny gestured vaguely.

The cop shook his head in wonder. "I'm looking for a bad guy and I find a good guy." With this reminder of his mission, he glanced around, then looked back at Denny. He frowned. "Three years," he said, the frown disappearing. "That's how long it's been. Almost exactly. Hey, you know what to call me?" After an excruciating pause, he said, " 'Detective.' We opened our own little BCI two months ago, just like the big boys. So, when did you get in? I thought nothing was landing."

Denny scrolled through several possible answers. "Last night," he said. "Late. I'm waiting for a friend who's arriving. Or *not* arriving." Denny laughed. It didn't sound like his own laugh.

"Yeah. Two spring snowstorms back to back. Then this fog. We gotta catch up, man. You need a ride home?"

The gears of speech failed to engage.

"Is someone picking you up? Sarah?"

There existed no plan for anyone named Sarah to pick Denny up. "No."

"We'll give you a ride. What about your friend? Where's he coming in from?"

"Hong Kong."

"Wow. Through what city?"

"I don't have that information."

The cop waited for more.

"I think I'll just let him call me when he lands," Denny said.

"That's a plan." The cop gave a decisive hand clap and looked over Denny's shoulder. "I've got a new partner. He's a tiger." Denny turned around. The other detective, having abandoned his crowd survey, stood right behind him. How long had he been there? "Lance, this is an old friend of mine. And a fair backstop at Dog River Field, at least when he's sober. Homer, this is Lance." The second detective was Lance. That meant that he, Denny, was Homer. *Homer*. The first detective told Lance that they would give Homer a ride to Montpelier. Lance wasn't particularly interested. He seemed disappointed that Denny wasn't Denny. He looked at his partner and raised his eyebrows as if to say, "What now?"

"I think he skipped."

"Then he's guilty," Lance said. "It's like a confession. I love it when that happens." His lips curled strangely. "I'll go back and give the agent my number in case the creep still tries to board. We should check the toilet, Nick." He pointed to a nearby men's room.

"I got to go anyway," the first cop said as he eased away. *Nick*, Denny thought. His friend was named *Nick*.

The simultaneous departure of the two men in different directions broke the spell like a hypnotist's finger-snap. And what a spell it had been. With just a few words, Nick had turned Denny into an entirely different person. It was an unreal condition, like being in a bubble with fragile, wobbly walls. But it was thrilling to inhabit it. The bubble of Homer.

He watched Nick's partner, Lance, talk with the airline agent and then slowly walk back, his eyes still roaming over the passengers. Denny reviewed the few crumbs of knowledge he had. Homer. Florida. Sarah. A backstop. What was a backstop? Away three years. *Homer*. Where had he heard that name before? From Betsy? She had thrown so many names at him that it was hard to be sure.

Lance pulled to a stop, looked at Denny indifferently, and scrutinized the people walking by—travelers waiting out the weather and drifting in and out of the food court. Lance wore a tight yellow turtleneck shirt that elongated his neck, and he had a lean, angular, face. The people he stared at squirmed under his gaze.

"Who are you looking for?" Denny asked.

Lance scowled. "A creep." He studied the crowd while Denny tried not to look like a creep. Lance asked for a man's identification without showing any of his own. The man complied. "Move along," Lance said by way of thanks. Then to Denny: "We've got shit for a description. 'Fat.' The whole world's fat."

"How fat?" said Denny.

Lance ignored the question. He studied the flow of people.

"What did he do?" Denny said.

Lance's lips curled. "Creep checks into the Ethan Allen. Hooks up with a local. They drink. They fight."

"They fight?"

"If people drink, they fight. Look at them." Lance jerked his bony chin toward a bar where two or three passengers hunched over noonday drinks. To Denny they seemed more depressed than bellicose.

"So," said Denny, striving for understanding. "They drink. They fight."

Lance took it from there. "They hot-tub. They probably get it on. We're looking for semen. We're always looking for semen. It's our bread and butter. The room gets trashed. The fight goes outside onto the balcony. Over she goes. Creep flees."

The sheer volume and variety of information—old, new, false, true—triggered a nervous laugh from Denny. "She fell off the balcony? How do you know? I mean, did she tell you that?"

"She would if we could talk to her."

"Is she unconscious? She's not dead, is she?"

"Four stories? Concrete sidewalk? What are her chances?"

"But . . ." Denny fought a reeling sensation. "How do you know what happened if she didn't tell you?"

"Reconstruction. I'm really good at it." Lance flashed a twisted, vain smile. "Get this: before he takes off, Creep leaves a note behind on the bed. It says he had a visitor in his room and she did some damage and he feels terrible about it. Says the hotel should bill his credit card for the repairs. Like that was his main offense. Like he didn't throw his *visitor* off the balcony."

"Maybe she went out there alone and fell. Maybe he didn't know it."

Lance shook his head. "Two sets of footprints in the snow on the balcony. Hers and Creep's."

Denny nodded, probably more than he should have. When he had gone out to the balcony to look for a light from Marge's hotel room, was it possible that she was lying on the sidewalk four stories below him? But why would she have gone out to the balcony?

"Who found her?"

"Nobody yet."

Denny frowned. "I don't understand."

"What's not to understand?"

"Where is the woman now?" Flustered, he almost said "Marge."

"We're looking for her."

"You and Nick?"

Lance whistled softly—at Denny's stupidity, apparently. "Me and Nick are looking for a fat creep. Others in the department, patrol officers, are looking for the missing victim. Heads up—here comes a porker." Lance stepped forward and stopped another innocent.

Denny kept seeing Marge on the balcony, then off it, tipping over the railing. She must have stepped out there for air. No—for the opposite of air: for a smoke. Her last cigarette. But what made her fall? Drunkenness?

After Lance had dismissed the man, Denny said, "If you haven't found her body, how do you know she fell?"

"From her shit on the sidewalk."

"Her feces?"

Lance stared at Denny. "Her *shit*. A hair brush and a cigarette lighter."

"Oh. But couldn't she have dropped those things and forgotten about them and not fallen at all?"

Lance shot a quick, derisive snort of air through his nostrils. "Homer, here's some career advice. Don't go into police work." Lance laughed hard at that. He laughed and laughed all by himself. "Obviously, she had her purse with her on the balcony when they fought. I can see her picking it up from the dresser in a huff, saying she was leaving. See, that's reconstruction at its best right there—details that are rooted in a behavioral average. She picks up her purse and says she's leaving, and Creep drags her outside. All sorts of shit must have flown out of it when she fell. Creep hurries down and picks it up, but he doesn't get all of it. Then he picks up the body and dumps it somewhere. Or maybe he's doing unspeakable things to it right now."

Lance seemed to hope for this last possibility, just as his strange hope for a major crime had led him to decide that Marge had been thrown from the balcony. Because some items from her purse were found below? Lance's theory made sense only if someone had removed the body, and that someone would have to be the person who had thrown Marge from the balcony, and that someone would have to be the one who had made the second set of footprints, but that someone was Denny and he hadn't done any of those other things—not the throwing or the removing or the unspeakables.

Denny's explanation, though unflattering to himself, had to be the right one: at some point, Marge had decided that she didn't want to sleep with this portly stranger after all, and she had simply departed, leaving Denny holding his bag of condoms. In the course of her decision-making, she had stepped out on the balcony for a smoke—and to brush her hair after being in the Jacuzzi. She had fumbled the lighter and hairbrush and dropped them from the balcony. It actually could have been that small event, dropping those two things, that had tilted her against spending the night with Denny. His sexual outcomes often pivoted on such small variables.

Lance stopped another man, bigger even than Denny—a two-seat purchaser for sure. As Denny watched the man's flustered reaction, he had a happy thought. Since the cops hadn't spoken with Marge, she couldn't have been the one to describe him as fat. But who had given them that description? Blind Betsy? Did Denny *sound* fat? Who else besides Marge had seen him at the hotel?

Nick came out of the bathroom checking his fly with his fingertips and, apparently not satisfied, bent over for a visual check as well. He said, "I hate John surveillance. Washing and combing. What else am I gonna do? Chat? I had my hopes on one stall. Guy was in there forever. Turns out it was a little kid. Probably exploring his unit."

Lance grunted. The two men cast their eyes over the crowd in the gate area. They seemed reluctant to give up.

Without looking at him, Nick asked Denny where his bags were. Denny had anticipated the question. "They didn't make the connection. The baggage office will send them on to me."

"To Sarah's? Are you staying with her?"

"No." In his file cabinet devoted to Homer, the drawer labeled "Sarah" was empty. He needed to get some information into it. "She doesn't know I'm back."

Nick frowned. He wouldn't pry. Nor would he reveal, unfortunately. And the question of his luggage hung in the air. Denny, worrying that short answers might look suspicious, became expansive:

"They're going to send my bags to the Delta office in Barre and hold them there for me."

Lance had been looking around the waiting area. Now he jerked his head to look at Denny. "Where the hell's '*Bar*'? You mean Barre?" Lance's pronunciation sounded like "Barry." Denny had seen the name of the town on a sign during his condom run. It had reminded him of the barre at the dance studio his mom took him to in the winter, and so of course he had pronounced it that way. He had blundered already.

" 'Bar,' " said Nick, laughing lightly. "The classic flatlander mispronunciation—and the old Homer humor." He clapped Denny on the back and looked at him affectionately.

"I live in South Barre," Lance said, an edge to his voice. He was looking at Denny through narrowed eyelids. "Where's this Delta office you're talking about?"

"I'm not sure," said Denny. "It's new."

Lance grunted and looked away, back to the passengers, as did Nick. No further challenge was offered. In fact, Lance's question hadn't even been a challenge—it was just grumpy surprise at an unknown fact. Denny was Homer—this was a given. Any gap in his knowledge, any oddity of behavior, would be strange, yes, but all by itself it wouldn't make him not-Homer. He needed to remember that.

What was odd, *really* odd, was that Denny had a feeling for Homer. He had a leg up, a sense of who he was. How? All he had was his name, but it was a name he associated with a way of being—a sad way. Because he had been away for so long? Was there sadness in the name itself? *Homer*. It made him think of the word *troubled*.

He saw Betsy's lips form the word, and he had his answer. Homer was her beloved nephew, the cubby dweller. Denny inhaled sharply and dispatched his mind to reinterpret his day at the hotel. Someone must have seen him and thought he was Homer and told Betsy, or told someone else who told Betsy. Betsy would have had no idea that the man reported as Homer was actually Denny the hotel guest. All she knew of Denny was his voice, which was evidently not like Homer's, or at least not enough like it to be confused with Homer's.

If he was going to be Homer, he would have to explain the voice. His hand went to his neck. He stroked it in thought.

Another strange aspect of his day in Montpelier now suddenly made sense to him—the excessive familiarity of the townspeople. *Nice coat. Who died? Pussy boots.* And the dogs in front of the hotel! Did the dogs think he was Homer? Denny let out a strange laugh.

Lance threw him a look. So did Nick, but Nick's was friendly. "Good to be home?" said Nick.

Denny gave his friend a happy puppy bark.

FIVE

"SO. THREE YEARS IN FLORIDA. WHATCHA BEEN UP TO?"

Nick's question, cheerfully tossed his way as the three men neared the main terminal exit, sent Denny scurrying into the men's room. Nick called out that he and Lance were parked in the taxi stand, and Denny waved to signal understanding. Homer would know where it was.

Fifteen minutes of hard work in a toilet stall produced a record-breaking bowel movement and, more to the point, a Florida script subject to modification on the fly. By Denny's reckoning, the foggy drive back to Montpelier could take up to two hours. A person could make a lot of mistakes in two hours.

He spotted the taxi curb as soon as he stepped out of the terminal and crossed over to it. A short siren whoop helped him find the unmarked car. Nick was grinning behind the wheel, a cell phone pressed to one ear. Lance, dependably stoic, stared straight ahead.

"No, no, no," Nick said into the phone as Denny settled into the back seat. "We move Earl to first. He never blocked the plate to my satisfaction anyway. Homer—hell, he plants himself there. He's a rock. He's a damn Sphinx. Remember the Thrush Tavern game? Harris is *still* unconscious. . . . Wait, he just got in the car. I'll put him on."

Denny almost took the cell phone that Nick extended over the seat to him, but instead he leaned forward to speak into it, hoping the awkwardness would make for a short exchange. Nick accommodated him by adjusting his grip on the phone.

"And you are?" Denny said into the unknown.

"Hey, big guy."

"Hey yourself."

"This is too much."

"You got that right."

"So what's up?"

"Not much. You?"

"Same ol'. Good to hear your voice."

"Back at ya'."

A silence fell. It felt richer in content than anything that had been said so far.

Denny said, "So when's the first game?"

Nick laughed and repossessed the phone. "What'd I tell you? Ain't he a gamer?"

Lance jerked to attention and pointed straight ahead through the windshield. "Check it out," he said to Nick.

"Gotta go, buddy." Nick flipped the phone shut. The man Lance had indicated stood beyond the line of taxis in the shuttle bus zone, a briefcase on the sidewalk at his side. His arms were folded across his broad chest and he rocked back and forth on his feet as he waited. "That guy?" Nick said.

"He's got the body and the coat both." Lance charged out of the car with such force that two cabbies huddling nearby, smoking cigarettes, startled and jumped aside. He bee-lined for the man, a burly fellow wearing a long dark overcoat like the one Denny owned—and had luckily packed in his checked suitcase. The coat must have figured in the description of him. Lance demanded and examined the man's ID, and then his shoulders seemed to slump. The two men fell into a sort of chat, concluding with a handshake that suggested a happy conclusion—an impression immediately undone by the scowl on Lance's face when he returned to the car.

Nick watched him climb in. "No good?"

"Fuck it."

"What did you talk about?"

"Just go," Lance said, pointing forward.

Nick shifted into gear. "Who was it?"

Lance hesitated. "The lieutenant governor."

Nick peered at the man. "So it is." He chuckled. "Not much of an entourage. The governor gets a trooper for a chauffeur. I guess the l.g. gets shit."

"Let's go," said Lance.

Nick pulled away from the curb. He gave the lieutenant governor a little siren whoop as they passed, producing a smile and a wave from the big man. Denny waved, too. Lance stared straight ahead.

Denny celebrated his success so far—although "far" was a stretch since they had just left the curb—by opening the one-pound bag of M&M peanuts he had bought between his stop at the bathroom and his exit from the terminal. The rustle of the bag made Lance turn around to assess the scene. Nick glanced over in time to see Denny offer Lance a handful and to see his distinctly judgmental headshake.

"Lance isn't exactly a foodie," Nick said. "Give us a typical day's menu, will you, Lance?"

Denny expected nothing, or at most a grunt, but Lance complied. "In the morning, tomato juice for long-range prostate prophylaxis, grapefruit, and tea. No lunch. I never understood lunch—who needs it? Dinner is some lean beef with onions, a few peas."

Nick laughed. "A cornucopia!"

"If I have a salad, vinegar and oil only. Light on the oil."

"Never a creamy dressing?" said Nick.

"That's a salad *sundae*. Do you want a salad or do you want a sundae?"

"When you gonna have me over for dinner, Lance? But remind me to eat first." Nick glanced over his shoulder and gave Denny an eyebrow dance. "Isn't he a pistol?" He looked at Lance. "Tell Homer your Golden Rule."

Lance stared straight ahead.

"Come on. Tell him."

"I'm not a performing monkey."

"Sure you are. Come on." Nick kept throwing looks at Lance. "Okay, I'll tell him. It's—"

" 'Be like me,' " Lance said quickly. "That's it."

Nick looked in the mirror at Denny. "He's a loaded weapon, ain't he?"

Denny crunched on his M&M peanuts, happy to be on the fringe of the conversation.

"Laugh all you want," said Lance, "but listen to this. I was looking at my mom's high school yearbook last night—"

"Now we're talkin' fun," Nick said. "Too much fun, really."

"I saw almost no fat. Just two overweight kids in her graduating class. Almost everybody was just like me."

"Utopia!"

"You look at a yearbook now," Lance said, "and the kids barely fit on the page." He half-turned. "How about you, Homer? Were you fat as a kid?"

"Hey," Nick said. "Hey."

"I suppose I was," Denny said agreeably. "But I've never really thought of myself as fat."

Lance hooked an elbow over his seat and scoped out Denny's bulk. "Even now?"

Denny shrugged and juggled a pair of M&M peanuts in his hand like dice. "I'm comfortable. Why should I worry about it? It's not like I have to outrun wild animals to survive. All I have to do is manage the drive-through at Burger King." He popped the M&Ms into his mouth. He had actually spoken with more complacency than he felt. Lance brought it out in him—the urge to say the thing that would most irritate him. Maybe next he would lift up his shirt and invite Lance to squeeze his flesh.

Lance turned back around and faced forward. Nick had stopped at a red light, and he looked at Denny in the mirror. "What about all those diets, Homer?"

"Those were for Sarah."

"Really? I thought she never minded your weight."

Denny sighed heavily, meaningfully. "So she said."

Nick gave him a final look in the mirror, then pulled forward as the light turned green. Denny had successfully steered them back into don't-pry territory.

A few minutes later, Nick merged onto I-89. "So you gonna open up the shop now that you're back?"

Denny saw himself as a cheerful merchant behind a store counter. He extended a bag to an elderly lady. It contained her purchase. But what was in it? "I'm not sure," he said.

"Really?" Nick sounded surprised. "How come?"

Denny looked out the window. The fog pressed hard on the snow cover. "The winter commute's a drag."

Nick laughed.

"And it depends on Sarah," Denny added, jumping back into the arms of that conversation stopper.

Nick nodded.

"Who's Sarah?" Lance's question, doubtless borne of sheer irritation at repeatedly hearing her name, went to Nick. Denny leaned forward.

"She's a key player in the local music scene. Runs a big summer festival at Homer's place. A dynamo. Not to mention that she's Homer's main squeeze—at least when someone else isn't trying to put the moves on her."

Lance grunted.

Denny's loins stirred.

"Homer," said Nick, "I'm not sure if this is something you want to talk about, but you sure dropped off the face of the earth. It was a hell of a shock. There's prolly not a single person in town who knows why you went south."

"Aunt Betsy knows."

"Oh? Well, that's one then."

Denny waited for a few seconds. It was important that he seem reluctant to talk before revealing anything. That would give authenticity to other instances of reluctance up to and including complete silence. He needed to cultivate an air of mystery that never suggested obfuscation. "I had a tumor."

"A tumor?"

"On my larynx. I'd heard good things about a surgeon in Palm Springs. He and his team did a lot of work all over my voice box. For a while the prospects weren't so good. I needed a lot of time to myself."

"Jesus. Is it better now? What's the prognosis?"

"I expect a full recovery."

"That's great, man." Nick seemed a little shaken, and Denny figured the news would shut him up for a while. *Dynamo. Main squeeze.* He had never had it as easy as this. It would be like having a mail-order bride. He would just slip between the sheets in Homer's place. His goal on entering the car had been to survive. Clearly he had set the bar too low. He was on the verge of scoring!

"Palm Springs is in California," Lance said stonily.

Denny lost only a moment to panic. "Is that what I said? I meant Palm Beach."

Nick looked at Denny in the mirror. "You know Edgar's number, Homer?"

"No." Edgar?

"I want to tell him we're coming. He's been keeping an eye on your place since the break-in, right?"

"Right." Break-in? Break-in?

"Lance, look it up, will you? Edgar Grund. Horn of the Moon Road. You remember him."

Lance began to fiddle with a computer attached to the dashboard.

Nick looked in the mirror again. "I was thinking of taking you to Betsy's, but since your place is empty, we might as well drop you off there. Right?"

"Sounds good. Edgar can scoot over and turn the thermostat up."

"Well, I'm not sure how much scooting his wheelchair can do in the snow, but Rose can take care of it. Did Edgar tell you we worked that case? Chip was pretty freaked. He stumbled onto the burglar downstairs, you know."

"Yeah," said Denny. "It freaked *me* out and I was a thousand miles away."

"Don't worry. We'll nail him. Lance'll track him down." Nick looked at his partner, who had lost himself in the computer screen. He looked in the mirror at Denny. "You know, Homer, this surgery—I wasn't gonna say anything, but your voice sounds a little different to me. Is that a side effect or something?"

"Yes, that can happen. But the doctor assured me it wouldn't in my case."

"Oh? Maybe I'm wrong."

Denny leaned forward, to all appearances the picture of agitation. "How does it seem different to you?"

"Maybe it doesn't. I don't know."

"But you noticed *something*."

"I could be wrong. I haven't talked to you in a long time, I guess."

Denny slowly leaned back and pretended to brood. He was on such a roll that he felt confident toying with elements of his biography that he himself had planted. My voice different? Impossible! Also, fragments of the 1000-piece puzzle of Homer's life were coming together nicely. "Chip," who "freaked," was evidently Homer's tenant—Betsy had mentioned that Homer had rented his house—but the tenant was now gone, probably because of the "break-in," which Denny would have to learn more about, maybe from neighbors "Edgar" and "Rose." But damn that wheelchair.

And there was another problem. If Edgar and Rose had been keeping an eye on the place, they were probably in touch with the real Homer, who might very well contact them from Florida even as the fake Homer installed himself next door. Denny would have to head that off somehow. And it should have occurred to him that Nick had considered taking him to Betsy's. Denny needed to steer clear of her. As soon as she heard his voice, he would be unmasked as Denny the Marge-throwing hot-tubber, not Homer the troubled nephew.

It was bumper cars, that's what it was. Sure, sometimes he got stuck, but then he would bump free and build up speed until he was in position for a good blast. And the electricity of it! For the first time in his life, he felt challenged to a degree that matched his brainpower. He needed precisely something like this. He had needed it all along without knowing it. Ordinary life wasn't enough for him. He needed life plus something else.

Lance took a cell phone from a compartment on the dash, punched a phone number into it, and handed it to Nick, who gave him a loving smile and said in a cartoonish voice, "What a good little partner you are." On the phone, he evidently got a machine. "Hey, Edgar, Rose. Nick here. I've got Homer in the car with me. Yup, he's back, and I'm gonna drop him off at his place. I just wanted to let you know so Rose don't come after us with her twelve-gauge." He flipped the phone shut and looked in the mirror. "Want some tunes, Homer?"

"You bet."

"Stan's still at WDEV. I think he's on right now." Nick punched a radio button. Willie Nelson was singing "Blue Skies." "That's Stan, all right. Ironic programming. You get it, Lance? 'Blue Skies' in this soup. You catch the irony?"

Lance, working on the computer keyboard, ignored him.

"What the hell you doing? Downloading porn? Hey, Homer, I should call Stan at the station. He can announce that you're back. What do you think?"

"I'd like to low-key it, Nick."

"Oh." Nick reined himself in. "Gotcha." He looked at the computer screen, which was jumping with displays in response to Lance's keystrokes. "What's up?"

"I'm looking for the State Police Report from yesterday. I want to stop at the scene."

"Really? Kind of nasty outside."

Lance turned on him. "You solve a crime by looking at everything. *Everything.*" He spoke with gritted, exposed teeth.

Nick seemed a little taken aback. He called out to Denny, "He's a caution!" But this time the tone was weaker, the playfulness a little desperate, as if Lance had exposed him as a slacker. He drove in silence for a while, then said, "The fog must be from all the snow melt."

"That's a common misconception," Lance said.

Nick muttered something.

"There." Lance pointed at the computer screen. "I've got it. Just this side of the Middlesex exit, where the ledge sticks up in the median."

"Right," said Nick.

Denny, deep in enjoyment of his M&Ms, Willie Nelson, and conjured images of Sarah, was only half-listening. It wasn't until some time later, when the car slowed to a stop on the left shoulder near a tall axe head of rock, that he realized it was *his* accident scene that Lance had referred to. Lance asked Nick to pop the trunk and got out of the car. Nick told Denny they would be just a minute.

"I think I'll stretch my legs," said Denny. He joined Nick behind the car at the open trunk, where Nick pulled on a pair of winter boots. Lance was already sliding down the hill. A shaft of sunlight shot through a sudden break in the fog.

"Hey." Nick looked up. "Blue skies after all."

"What happened here?" Denny asked.

"A guy ran off the road from the other side—the same guy we were looking for at the airport." Nick slammed the trunk lid. "Do you know Marge Plongeur? Works in the Department of Education?"

"I'm not sure," said Denny.

"They hooked up last night at the Ethan Allen, and she's disappeared. It's not clear what happened between them. And we're sure not gonna find out here." Nick headed down the hill, then looked back when he realized Denny was following. "Your shoes are gonna get wet."

"I'll step in your tracks. So this guy you're looking for, do you think he did something to Marge?"

"Dunno."

"Did you talk to Aunt Betsy about him?"

Nick laughed softly. "Yeah." He said no more and hurried on down the hill. Denny followed, wondering about the laugh.

Lance stood at the indentation where Denny's car had come to a stop at the base of the rock. An oil stain darkened the snow at his feet. Lance looked up to the westbound highway, then back to the ground in front of him, then back up, as if imagining Denny's slide. He frowned and walked to a low rock in the middle of the slide path and studied the terrain from there. He came back to Nick and Denny. He pointed both index fingers up at the road shoulder.

"Creep skids off the road, going like gangbusters. He slides." Lance's two fingers tracked the slide. "He's going sideways, and he hits that low bit of ledge broadside. This rolls him twice, maybe three times." He stared hard at the ground. "You've got to imagine it. Imagination will take you to the truth."

Nick, just out of Lance's view, signaled Denny with a slow, mid-air stroke of bored masturbation.

"You know what I like, Nick?" said Lance, suddenly turning on him. "I like it when the bad guy dies. It's so clean then. It's all over. No depositions. No trial. No sentencing. No appeal. No parole. No repeat of the offense. Aren't you always glad when they turn up dead?"

Nick made a face. He wasn't going to answer that one.

Lance gestured to the highway and swept an arm down the hill. "He came close to dying. Imagine what it did to him—what kind of state it put him in." Lance made short punches of his fist as he talked. "He's all charged up. He's got a second life. He climbs out of the grave and thinks he's special now. He's ready to take on the world." Lance laughed—a single, sharp bark. "How else could a creep like that think he would have a chance with Marge? She's not a bad-lookin' gal, judging from her picture, and from all reports he's a pig. With his new power, he gets Marge into his room. But then the magic wears off. Maybe she tells him he's not so special after all. Then . . ."

"*Then* we don't know about," said Nick.

"I do." Lance shot a spurt of air through his nose. "I know this guy through and through. He's the kind of creep that makes you squirm. Walt up in Plainfield—he likes everybody, the original Mr. Nice Guy—he told me the creep made him queasy all the way from here to the Ethan Allen. His dad, too. It was a physical thing, like he gave off a chemical or something. I've had experience with people like that. He's what's known as a 'repellent personality.' "

Lance's unfocused eyes fell on Denny. "I can see him," he said, "and I hate him."

SIX

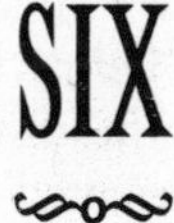

A GIANT HAND MUST HAVE REACHED DOWN FROM ABOVE and set the house and barn atop the snowy plateau. How else to explain the toy-like ensemble, highlighted by a sunbeam, so factory-fresh and shiny with promise? As he gazed up the hill from the bottom of the long driveway, Denny installed himself up there. He fancied himself at a window, wondering why that big-faced man down in the car was ogling his homestead.

"Plowed within the hour," Lance observed as the car climbed.

Nick said, "Rose must have done it."

Denny looked around for his neighbors, but not a house was within sight. For his whole life he had lived in apartments or row houses, with neighbors no more than twelve inches away.

"It's so quiet," Nick said. "This place is really jumping in the summertime."

Lance grunted.

The driveway swept to the left, taking them away from the house before it swung back toward it—an approach, Denny saw, that preserved the expanse of unblemished snow in front. They topped the hill, and Nick stopped in front of the house. A covered porch welcomed Denny, with five identical arches looping from post to post at the front edge of the roof. The house was clad in white-painted clapboard and trimmed in red at its windows and vertical corner boards. The massive barn to the right was its color complement: red with white-trimmed windows. But he suddenly worried about the barn. Its long axis, instead of being at a right angle to that of the house, was off by about ten degrees. And didn't it sit too close to the house? He wanted it about twice its present distance from the house.

Apart from that, the siting was good. The buildings sat atop ground that sloped away so gradually as to be nearly flat. But then, after a ways, the land fell sharply on all sides and yielded to woods. The pines in front were rooted well below the hilltop, and even the tallest ones did not block the view to the distant mountain ranges. The fog was blowing off, and the vista seemed to expand before their eyes. It drew the gaze of all three men. Denny found it hard to tell what was connected to what, which ridges were near, far, and very far.

"You're paying the new view tax for sure, Homer," Nick said. "Probably a Camel's Hump tax, too."

"That's next," Lance grunted.

Denny had business to take care of. Dramatic business. He needed to appear overwhelmed. After all, he was a man who had been dangerously ill, and he was returning to his beloved family farm, or whatever. He was overcome, sure, but he was also the son of a farmer, or whoever, so he was a manly man. He got out and positioned himself in front of the car. He beheld the panorama and stretched forth a hand in reverence. He also passed a large quantity of gas that had built up during the ride. He would ordinarily have let it out in the car, but he guessed Homer wouldn't do such a thing.

Everything was falling into place. What was acting but an extended lie, and what better liar was there than Dennis Braintree? Only once had he been caught in a lie, a little over a year ago. He had been at the zoo, and a small bird had flown low right at his face and then veered away at the last minute. Denny's mouth had been open at the time because he was imitating the face a chimp had just made at him, and it occurred to him that the bird could easily have flown into his mouth. That thought became the account he delivered later, at a meeting of the church mission committee: "A bird flew into my mouth at the zoo." The ladies responded with a mix of surprise and disgust. They made faces, and one made spitting sounds to eject the bird. But afterward, privately, one of them said to him, "That didn't really happen, did it?" As an experiment, he said, "No, it didn't." She said, "You're involved in the church because it's a welcoming institution, correct?" Again he agreed. "There are limits," she said.

No one would catch him in this lie, he vowed. No one. He smacked himself once on the belly and turned and walked to the house. Nick and Lance, having given the returnee his moment, got out of the car. On the porch, Denny made a show of patting his pockets and then throwing his arms out to express the frustration of a mortal who has packed his house key in a suitcase from which he is presently separated. He felt along the top of the door molding for the spare key that one might keep there.

"It's probably unlocked, Homer," Nick said as he stepped onto the porch.

Denny hid his surprise and opened the door. He entered a central hall—stairs straight ahead, living room to the left, dining room to the right.

"Chilly chilly," said Nick. "It's funny how a house that you expect to be warm can feel colder than it is outside, even when it's not." Denny noticed that Nick had kicked off his shoes and left them outside the door.

Lance called from below the porch, "Nick, we should be off."

But Nick padded across the floor in his socks and disappeared around a corner into the living room. Denny ambled the other way, moving slowly through the dining room into the kitchen. A restaurant-style booth sat under a side window. He opened the refrigerator: empty and dark. He dialed it on, and it purred back in response. A window over the sink faced the barn, and he saw another outbuilding between the house and the barn that he hadn't noticed because it was set back from the other buildings. Its roof had an odd shape, with a short front slope and a longer back slope. He strolled on through the kitchen to a room that had been a back porch but was now enclosed by windows. Through these he saw a woodshed near the house and the empty frame of a metal swing set some distance away. Snow reached to the crossbars of its legs.

The enclosed porch wrapped around to the rear of the living room, where an upright piano stood. Denny, completing the circuit, found Nick on his knees stuffing crumpled newspaper into a black stove set near a central chimney. Lance, at the front end of the room, his arms folded across his chest, watched Nick without expression—or perhaps with hatred. It was hard to tell. Lance was in his socks as well. If entering a house shoeless was the local custom, it struck Denny as a strange one.

A phone rang on a small desk behind Lance. Denny, after displaying the hesitation of a man still recovering from a close brush with death, etc., walked the length of the room to answer it. Lance was in the way and moved to the side, but not enough, and Denny brushed him lightly with his body as he passed.

Well before the receiver reached Denny's ear, a boisterous voice exploded: "Ha! So the rabble is right, for once. Homer is indeed emerged from his hibernacula. Don't pretend you don't know why I'm calling. Don't you do that."

"Um—"

"The brass isn't the same without you, Homer. It doesn't sing. I want the man who always warms up with 'Caravan.' Waaaaaaa. Wa-wa-wa-wa-wa-wa-wa waaaaaaa."

"Mmm."

"I'm prepared to offer the Dorsey hymn—that's right, 'I'm Gettin' Sentimental.' Worried about the D-flat? I can offer it topping out at a B, but if I know my Homer, and I believe I do. . . . Hang on, I've got a blasted call coming in. If it's Hutchins, I've got a serious problem with his reeds. But that will change now that my Homer's back." He hung up.

Lance was staring at Denny, as he had been through the entire conversation. Nick expressed his own curiosity by sitting back on his heels in front of the stove and raising his eyebrows.

"You don't want to know," Denny said as he hung up the phone.

Lance turned back to Nick. "We need to talk to Marge's sister."

Nick took some small logs from a metal bucket and laid them in the stove. "Ash," he said of one log. "Nice." Then, in a different tone, "You got her number?"

"No, but I've got her name. Hagenbeck." Lance turned to Denny. After a moment he said impatiently, "Phone book?"

Denny roused himself and scanned the desk, then began to rummage through the drawers. The phone, inches from him, made him jump when it rang again. He grabbed it.

"Homer?" a scratchy male voice said.

"Yeah?"

"Hap."

"Who?"

"Hap."

"Hap?"

"Is that Hap?" Nick said. He had lit the newspaper and was closing the stove door. He hurried to Denny, grinning and reaching for the phone.

"Hang on, Hap," said Denny, interrupting speech that had already begun to make no sense to him. He handed Nick the phone. Meanwhile, Lance had found a phone book in a bookcase next to the desk and was searching through it.

Nick, grinning broadly, said into the phone, "You old pelter." After a pause, he roared with laughter.

Denny went into the entry hall and up the stairs as if to reconnect with his environment but really to flee the scene. The stairs turned at a landing and issued into a long hallway that ran the length of the house from back to front. Photographs lined one wall—an astounding number, thirty or so. Denny studied them in search of Homer. He was eager for a moment of sharp recognition. But the wall of photos showed no image of anyone like himself in the embrace of a strange family—no father with a hand on his shoulder, no brother yukking it up with him, no sister straightening his tie. Their Homerlessness, he realized, lay in the age of the photos. Judging from the clothes and hairstyles, nothing on the wall had been snapped before the 1950s. He saw no facial resemblance between himself and anyone pictured. Not only that, but all of the subjects were lean, some even starved in appearance.

"Homer?" Nick called from below. "Hap wants to interview you for the *Monthly*. The prodigal son and all that."

Denny was absorbed in a photo of a waif proudly displaying a whole pie in each hand. She stood on a muddy road, balancing the pie pans on her palms, but they were tilted and seemed about to fall. If she dropped those pies, she would die of hunger, he was sure of it. "Tell him next month," Denny called down.

"Gotcha." Nick returned to the phone. Denny didn't go back downstairs until he heard him hang up.

Lance had stepped onto the porch, but now he was returning and snapping his cell phone shut. He said, "She'll meet us at the Wayside in twenty."

Nick, still standing at the front desk near the house phone, nodded, then reached into his pocket for *his* cell phone, which had begun to ring. Denny threw Lance a friendly look of surprise at all of the telephonic activity in the house. Lance stared back at him coldly. This made Denny glad about what he had done in the car after their stop at the accident scene: he had bumped Lance's seat with his knees every few minutes as he shifted position. He was *so fat*, you see, *so big and fat*, that he couldn't fit properly in the back seat. With each bump, Lance had jiggled like a bobble head.

While Nick stepped into the dining room with his call, Denny walked over to warm himself by the wood stove. A glass panel in the door exposed the leaping flames, which Denny found unsettling. It was as if Nick had lit a campfire on the living room rug. But it all seemed safely contained. The heat created a glow of warmth around the black iron box, and Denny began a slow rotation of his body. He looked at Lance.

"I feel like a big chicken turning on a spit, dripping hot fat."

Lance stared. Then he turned to Nick, who was coming back from the dining room, his phone call over. Nick shook his head and chuckled softly. "Kind of a mess at the airport. The planes started flying again, but not for long. Our guy checked a bag but didn't show for the boarding call, so they had to evacuate the plane. They've shut down everything until they look at his bag."

"That's tremendous news," Lance said. "Now we've got cause."

"To search the bag? They're doing that."

Lance shook his head. "To search for his location. Betsy said he bought a cell phone yesterday. He's hiding out in Vermont, or *thinks* he is. The oinker's too stupid to know he's walking around with a GPS chip in his phone. We'll get the specs from the phone store and pass them on to the Feds—they'll want to jump in now because of the security violation—and they can home in within a couple of meters of the chip. A slab of bacon that size shouldn't be hard to find within those parameters. I'll get Susan going on the warrant." He opened his cell phone and looked at Nick for the go-ahead.

"Doesn't the phone have to be on for that to work?" Nick said.

"Some models, not all. And he's bound to turn it on sooner or later."

Nick bounced his eyebrows a couple of times. "Let's give it a shot."

Denny's mind was more than ordinarily active. GPS chip? In his cell phone? Oinker? Slab of bacon?

The house phone rang again. Denny headed for the desk to answer it.

"We'll leave you to your many fans," Nick said. "Welcome home, guy." He clapped Denny on the shoulder. Lance was already on his way out, his own phone pressed to his ear.

When the door closed and Denny turned back to the desk, he saw for the first time that Homer's phone had a caller ID window. There he read "Ethan Allen Hotel." His hand froze on the receiver. The caller was almost certainly Betsy, searching for Homer, and she would expect to hear *his* voice, not Denny's. He pulled his hand away. When the answering machine clicked on, Denny waited eagerly for Homer's greeting—what was the pitch of his voice, how fast did he talk? But the rather tentative speaker identified himself as Chip—the tenant who had fled the premises after the break-in.

Betsy left a message: "Homer? They say you're back. Oh, I pray that you are. You're a dear boy. Someday you'll know just how dear you are. I was worried that you . . . I just worry about you. Please call me." She paused. "All right then." She hung up.

"Homer!" Denny shouted at the answering machine. "You're a dear boy!"

Encouraged by the family photographs in the upstairs hall, Denny made another sweep of the first floor and then examined the rooms upstairs. The main bedroom dominated the side near the barn, with a small computer room connecting at its front end and a bathroom at the rear. The other side of the second floor consisted of a guest bedroom, a sterile office of some kind, and a long music room along the side connecting them, full of sheet music, books, and music stands. Denny didn't find any more family photos—just cheap art prints and some pictures of ancient-looking musical instruments. He would search the house later for scrapbooks. There had to be a likeness of Homer somewhere.

First things first. He didn't want Lance the Tiger tracking down his cell phone, which presently nestled in his front pants pocket, right next to what remained of the M&M peanuts, rolled up in their shiny yellow bag. He took some out and began to munch on them. How to dispose of the phone? Could he smash it with a hammer, or was the chip indestructibly small? Better to take the phone somewhere and throw it away. Or, better still, leave it as if forgotten. Leave it somewhere where he *wasn't*, to lay down a false scent. Burlington was his last known location. Let the search for Dennis Braintree remain in Burlington.

He would need a car to get back there. He hadn't seen one outside, but one of the two outbuildings might house one. He found a down jacket in the hall closet and a pair of insulated slip-on boots in the enclosed back porch. From there he went out the back door onto a small exposed porch. His first step from there onto the snow-covered stairs was his last. His feet shot out from under him and he bumped assily down the short flight. The fall was so violent that he lay on his back in the snow for a while, enjoying the blue sky as he tongued chocolate peanuts from his molars. He raised his head and glared at the stairs that had tricked him. A snow shovel hung from a wooden peg on the porch wall. He had never shoveled snow before. Didn't the exertion kill people, especially chubby ones?

He rolled onto his stomach and groaned to his feet. He worked his way along the back of the house, sinking the full length of his legs with every step. How did people walk in this stuff? Luckily, a wire mesh fence paralleled his path from the corner of the house to the near outbuilding, and he clutched it for support all the way there.

The unlocked door at its rear led Denny not to a car but to a discovery of what Nick had meant by Homer's "shop." Homer repaired musical instruments. Denny did not know this from the hundreds of quirky, specialized tools tidily arranged above the wooden workbench. He knew it from a work in progress—a trumpet lying on a felt pad with its interior parts spread out—and from a rate chart posted on one wall. Denny found the chart fascinating. Homer charged different hourly rates for different instruments. He saw the logic: Homer was probably more experienced with certain classes of instruments than with others.

With brass instruments, for example, his labor was more efficient and therefore worth more. For work on clarinets and saxophones he charged less per hour. Under "Strings," the chart read "$ .01 / hour." This told customers that he didn't work on stringed instruments. Homer humor.

A door on the side of the workshop away from the house led to a small open area and, beyond it, the barn. Denny struggled through the short stretch of snow, this time without a fence to clutch. He more or less fell against the side door of the barn, and he braced himself for something unpleasant—moldy hay, piles of manure, dead beasts. Instead he found himself in a well-appointed recital hall. To one side, a raised stage; to the other, generous banked seating with fixed, upholstered chairs. He walked the length of one aisle to the rearmost row of seats, where he turned and took in the hall. It was splendid. The construction costs must have been staggering. Had Sarah done this? Homer? Homer's family?

Denny continued on into the foyer at the front of the building. In a corner, behind a portable partition, he found what one wouldn't ordinarily find in a recital hall: a car. Was this where Homer always parked? More likely, he had put it here for storage during his absence.

Denny made a face at the boxy sedan. Not only was the battery probably dead, but the entire *car* could be dead, along with almost all of its factory contemporaries—it was an old Rambler that dated, he guessed, from the 1960s. Its color was beige that had bleached in places to the tone of sallow flesh.

The key was in it—encouraging, that. Why have a key in a dead car? Denny slipped in behind the wheel and tried it. The engine fired to life instantly. He let out a laugh. He imagined neighbor Rose dutifully coming over to run the car and charge the battery. Good old Rose. He gunned the engine a few times, then turned the ignition off. His stomach pressed hard against the steering wheel. Was Homer smaller than he was? No—Rose must have slid the seat forward. Good old Rose. He reached down to the side of the seat to adjust it, found a lever, and pulled on it. Wrong lever: he was thrown back into a full recline. He squirmed, but the seat would not go back up with his body in it, and he had to pour himself out the door first.

The foyer floor was concrete, painted and etched with musical symbols. If he moved the partition aside, he would be able to drive the car right out the large double doors of the barn. He slid the bolts aside, but snow blocked the doors. Again snow, always snow. He sighed and headed back to the house. In his reverse trek, he took advantage of his deep footprints. He made it up the treacherous rear steps and grabbed the snow shovel and went on into the house, since he would have to approach the blocked barn doors from the front.

As he passed through the entryway, he saw the light blinking on Homer's answering machine from Betsy's message. He detoured to erase it but then saw the number "2" flashing in the message window. A second call had come in. He pressed "Play." The new message opened with a long pause, followed only by these quick words:

"I'm coming over."

A woman. No identification. An intimate. Sarah? Confidence drained from his body like blood from a corpse on the mortician's table. He wasn't ready for her. He wasn't ready *at all.* The pause at the beginning of the message seemed especially ominous. It wasn't a delay for the gathering of thoughts. It was part of the message, calculated to express strong feeling. But *what* strong feeling? What history did they have? What would he say to her? He was a fool to think they would jump right into the sack.

He looked out the window. Far below, where the driveway met the road, a silver car was beginning a slow climb to the house.

Denny yelped and ran to the back door. He more or less skied down the stairs, clawed his way along the fence to Homer's workshop, dashed through the workshop out its side door, and lurched from there to the barn's side door. He rushed across the floor along the front of the stage, leaving a trail of snow in his wake, but there was no time to bother with it. A door on the far side of the barn opened to a steep but navigable slope. At the bottom of it were dense woods.

SEVEN

HIS LAST NAME WAS DUMPLING. HE KNEW IT FROM THE family cemetery at the edge of the woods, which he could see from his refuge behind a pine tree. Two of the tombstones rose above the snow, marking the place where Oramel and Ellen Dumpling would shiver for eternity. He couldn't read their dates, but he guessed from the height of the two monuments that they had pioneered the homestead. The other markers, humble bumps, looked like snow pillows. From his spot in the woods, Denny could see that his downhill scramble had taken him right through the middle of the plot. He was lucky not to have barked a shin on a marker. The dozen or so graves sloped with the land, giving the impression that the corpses had to dig in their heels to keep from sliding.

Homer Dumpling. He tried the name a few times.

He had been hiding for about fifteen minutes. By ear, while snow melt from the pine boughs dripped on his head, he had tracked Sarah's search for him—first her distant singing out of "Homer!" from the back of the house, where she would have seen his footprints leading from the stairs to the repair shop; then he heard another call, less cheerful, probably from the passageway between the shop and the barn; then a clearly annoyed shout from within the barn. The calls made him feel like a stubborn farmer tuning out his wife. *I got chores, Maw.*

Now, through the boughs, he kept a sharp eye up the hill on the side door by which he had exited the barn. Sure enough, it flew open, and here came her face and hair and voice: *"Homer!"* She hung over the threshold, squinted in the sunshine at the path made by his lurching body, glared into the woods, and finally pulled back inside and slammed the door.

Denny hugged the pine tree. His breath came in short, delighted puffs. "You're in trouble now, Dumpling!" he said, as if Homer were the one who would face her wrath.

But because she was angry, Denny actually found her less threatening. He had his own history with her now—he had made her mad by not being available when she arrived, and they would talk about that, at least for starters. But what would he offer to explain his absence just now? That he had wanted to visit his ancestors' graves? You bet. That he had then gone into the woods to savor his native boreal forest after three years in the tropics? Who could challenge that?

He began the climb back to the barn. However, the terrain did not cooperate. In fact, there was no *terra*—only snow and more snow. The stuff looked solid on the surface, but with every step it sucked him right up to his groin. He must have been on a northern slope. That was one of the first things he looked for in a winter layout—variable depths according to sun exposure. Drifts, too. Good modelers instinctively incorporated that kind of detail. Bad ones couldn't even tell you where north was. Denny always wanted to know the layout's compass orientation within a degree, the historical date and time down to the second.

He stuck to the path he had made before, and as he passed through the family plot, he cleared the snow away from a few markers. Dumplings all. About halfway up the hill, one particularly violent extrication flopped him on his back. In this position he became aware of his heart rate. Each pulse bulged his skull and briefly blinded him. He thought it best to lie still for a while.

"Sexual intercourse," he said to the blue sky, and he began to thrust his hips up and down. Earlier, when Sarah had stuck her head out the door, after she had yelled his name he had heard a little growl of anger from her, and he gave her that sound now as he imagined her on top of him. He hadn't gotten a close look at her, but because of the way her black hair had swung out the door, he gave her a witch's face. Not an ugly face, just a sharp-featured one. She would ride him like a broomstick. It could be just ten minutes away. Ten minutes! Sooner if they didn't have to go back to the house. Was there a bed somewhere in the barn? What about the Rambler? He could tilt the front seat back. They'd fog up the windows.

He scrambled to his feet and struggled up the rest of the slope to the door. She wasn't in the barn, which surprised him. He walked up the aisle to the foyer just in case she had anticipated his idea and already crawled into the Rambler, but it was not his lucky day. He heard an engine roar in the distance and looked out a front window. Sarah's car hove into view from the far side of the house and began its descent down the driveway. He didn't know until now that a car could look angry.

"You've got yourself a bottle rocket, Homer!"

Denny turned to go, then caught sight of something. On the exposed wood wall between the window and the big double doors hung laminated newspaper reviews of performances that had been held in the building. Denny browsed them. Photos of the artists accompanied some of them. In one of these, a group of thirty or so brass musicians standing in front of the barn hoisted their horns while a small goat looked at them quizzically. Denny sensed Homer's presence in the photo before he actually saw him, and when his eyes locked on him, he laughed with relief. No wonder Nick had taken him for Homer. Denny knew for a fact that he had never held a trombone. Were it not for that, he might have been persuaded that he had posed for this picture and simply forgotten about it.

Denny leaned in close to Homer, looking for a difference, a "tell," but he saw none. He approached until his vision blurred, and he pulled back just a bit. Homer stood a little forward of the group—was he their leader? They were all caught in a shout, and Homer's mouth was the most open of all, as if he were roaring. His T-shirt had ridden up his body from raising his trombone, and a crescent moon of belly flesh smiled at the viewer. He didn't seem to be a very dapper fellow.

Denny moved on along the wall, scanning other articles. The one nearest the door told of the creation of Sarah's concert series—six years ago, judging from the date of the story. Sarah was excited, she said, about the venue, the historic barn at Little Dumpling Farm, which she was renovating with some help from her "dear, dear friend," Homer Dumpling. Denny wished she had said "main squeeze." But maybe she did, and the reporter said, "This is a family newspaper—may I write 'friend'?" And Sarah said, "In that case, please write 'dear, dear friend.' "

Denny remembered he had business to take care of. The cell phone was still in his pocket, a time bomb ready to blast his designs to Kingdom Come. He retraced his steps to the house and found the snow shovel where he had left it against the wall next to the answering machine, when Sarah's arrival had sent him scampering. The blinking number told him that two more fans had called. He pressed "Play."

"Homer?" a man's voice said. "It's Warren Boren." The rhyme made Denny laugh. "Three years, Homer. Three years. It's disgraceful. Call me at once." This was no fan. "Up yours!" Denny yelled at the machine. Next was a woman whose insincere sing-song invited Homer to serve on some town committee. It was a long message, and it became clear that her reason for inviting him was to secure his vote for her in the election for chairperson. "We're so glad you're back!" she said in conclusion, packing extra fervor into the words because she realized she should have opened with them.

"Everyone wants a piece of Homer Dumpling," Denny called to the sky as he marched to the front of the barn with the shovel over his shoulder. "And Homer Dumpling wants a piece of Sarah." He laughed hard at that. Then he looked around quickly in case someone was within earshot. Not likely on this hilltop. But from here he could see a house on a neighboring hill on the other side of the road—Rose and Edgar's place? They couldn't have heard him, but they might have seen him. Did Denny walk like Homer? How would he ever know?

He threw the shovel down and hurried back to the house and up the stairs. He had seen the TV in the second bedroom, but the thought hadn't occurred to him then. Now he pawed through Homer's collection—all the tapes and DVDs lying loose as well as those in the TV cabinet and on the bookshelves in the room. Amid the dreadful musicals and romantic comedies that Homer seemed to favor, Denny found four promising videotapes. He fussed with the machine and settled on a sagging couch to watch.

The first tape—an outdoor band concert—was shot by a fixed camera at the rear of the crowd. Homer, puffing on his trombone in the back row, was visible only when the instrumentalist in front of him bent down to pick up a water bottle. A closer view came during some hand-held candid shots of the musicians relaxing during the intermission. Homer stood with two other men, chatting. They all wore white dress shirts and khaki shorts. Homer's legs were about the size of Denny's, but they looked more solid. He wore his hair slightly longer than Denny did, and occasionally he stroked the top of his forehead with a thumb to take it out of his eyes—a gesture that Denny tried and found unnatural, but he would work on it. The tape did not pick up the conversation—closer offscreen talk and a blackbird's squawk dominated the soundtrack. As he watched the trio, Denny became momentarily disoriented and tried to *remember* what they had talked about.

That tape bore a professionally printed label, "Catamount Brass Band, Sand Bar State Park," as did the next tape, which brought to citizens who had missed it the complete public winter joint hearing of the Central Vermont Land Protection and Conservation Commission and the Green Mountain Renewability, Durability, and Sustainability Task Force—an orgy that Denny could get through only with the help of copious snacks of Homer's kitchen stash of Fritos, which he shoveled into his mouth like a fireman stoking the firebox. The committee discourse was unintelligible, consisting of mysteriously shared language that Denny had never heard before. Homer must have been confused as well, because he sat mute at the table through the entire proceedings.

Denny popped the tape out. Next up: "Softball at Dog River Field," a home movie, given the scrawl on the front label. Denny instantly recognized Homer squatting behind the plate, and he finally produced some language, though his rhetoric was far from Churchillian: he said, "Branght." He said it over and over, before every pitch. Denny began saying it to the screen along with him. One articulation by Homer was unusually clear: he was saying, "Bring it," apparently crucial words of encouragement to the pitcher.

When Homer's team was at bat, the ballplayers could be seen wandering down the first-base line to use a large sandpile near right field as a pissoir, urinating with their backs to the crowd. The camera zoomed in on one group that included Homer, and Denny had the privilege of watching him shake when he finished, though what he shook remained out of view. The woman wielding the camera giggled. Sarah? Around the dugout, Homer got little face time. Nick dominated, with pep talk and comic imitations of other players. Homer appeared from time to time, smiling mutely, occasionally clapping at a play, but his lips never parted for speech.

Denny popped the tape out and reinserted the brass band tape. He rewound it to the intermission, where he remembered Homer chatting. But his memory was wrong. Homer simply stood in inscrutable silence. When the two men he was with laughed at something, he smiled, but it was an automatic response, like the wag of a dog's tail in response to a human's happy tone. Three tapes and several hours, and all he had heard was "Branght!" Denny frowned at the dullard on-screen, angry at what he felt was a degrading of their reputation. "Speak!" Denny yelled.

The last tape: "John and Rodrigo's Mud Season Party, 2005." Three years before the present. Three years—would Homer even be in this tape? Yes, there he was in a group shot in a kitchen, listening and not talking. Later, one of the hosts had Homer down on his knees on the wooden deck in order to honor the unusual fasteners that he, the homeowner, had used in the construction of this, his perfect deck. The host: "Some people say, 'Hey, it's just a deck so why bother?' But Rodrigo and I don't feel that way. We see the deck as an extension of the house." Homer feigned interest in the home show, but poorly. He seemed uncomfortable and squirmed on his knees, and his nods looked like signals to conclude the conversation, which actually happened without his help when someone jovially grabbed the homeowner and hauled him out of the frame. That left Homer on his knees, beached on the cedar. The camera, rather than chronicle his return to vertical, moved on, but not without first capturing an inch of his butt crack.

The tape next found Homer seated on a swinging outdoor couch with a plastic or vinyl cover of a garish floral pattern. Some man was talking fast and hard, and Homer was the sole hapless listener. The man wore a bow tie, and he spoke so animatedly that it seemed to be spin like a propeller. "So the bartender says to the E-flat, 'You're looking *sharp* tonight. This could be a *major development*.'" The camera stayed with the man through several more puns, all the way to the end: "The bartender has had only *tenor* so patrons, and everything has become *alto* much *treble*, he needs a *rest*, so he closes the *bar*." Judging from the speaker's hopeful grin, the joke was over. The camera went to Homer for his reaction. Puffy-cheeked, droopily smiling, eyes at half-mast, he might as well have been orbiting Neptune.

A pan farther over showed a woman seated next to Homer, and the cameraman gave Denny a jolt when he said, in a playful, nasal tone, "Hi, Sarah." She replied with equally playful nasality: "Hi, Rodrigo." Denny scooted forward on the couch. She had witchy hair, yes, and sharp features, too, but they were intriguingly sharp. She was actually pretty. This was far more than he had hoped for. In a straight tone, the host said to her, "You're looking thoughtful. What's on your mind?" Sarah pressed her lips together and frowned. To Denny she looked like someone inventing a thought instead of recalling one. "These are my friends," she said, casting her eyes around and nodding repeatedly. "I'm thinking how good it feels to be among my friends." "I'm sorry, Sarah," Rodrigo said, "but could we do another take, and could you possibly be even *more* banal this time?" Sarah's smile, rather fixed to begin with, suddenly hardened, and a fragment of a loud laugh from Rodrigo could be heard before the tape cut to a black dog leaping for a Frisbee at the edge of a road.

Now that he knew for certain what Sarah looked like and what she was wearing at this party, Denny rewound the tape and reviewed it from the beginning. But he would not see her or Homer again until dusk, when everyone gathered in a meadow for dancing. The event was shot from a distance, showing the whole group of fifty or so dancers, and Homer and Sarah were in the picture the entire time. They started every dance as partners, even when the previous dance had distributed them away from each other. The dance caller had a microphone, and she explained the moves of each dance in advance. She described the learning curve as a sequence of "confusion, mastery, and boredom." She promised to end a dance when she sensed boredom had been achieved.

Homer, unfortunately, rarely progressed beyond confusion. He turned the wrong way, grabbed someone else's partner, advanced too far or too little. Once, at the end of whirl, he put his hand squarely on a tit, evoking an open-mouthed response from the victim—not Sarah, which was just as well, given her manifest displeasure with Homer generally. She shook her head at his stumbles, shoved him when he strayed too close, laughed outright, and looked away as if to dissociate herself from him. She made no attempt to rejoin him for what was announced as the last dance of the evening. She hid her rebuff, or tried to, by talking with demonstrative engagement to the willowy, long-haired man she had ended up with. Just before the dance began, she flirtatiously knocked her new partner's cap from his head.

The last dance consisted of comic routines that had everyone laughing, and Denny watched the action with mounting interest, finally getting on his knees in front of the TV. The song had a recurring verse:

I looked over yonder and what did I see?
A great big man from Tennessee.

Whenever these lines came up, the dancers held their arms out around an imaginary expansive belly. Homer actually had such a belly. And every time the lines were called out, he embraced his bulk with a sheepish grin.

Denny knew that grin. He knew it far too well. It was the look of concession. It made him think of the period in his life, a few years back, when he took to heart all the criticisms of his improvers and reprimanders. He did everything they demanded. He stopped calling Chicago "Chitown" and Detroit "Motown" and Boston "Beantown." He stopped amplifying his sneezes into yelps. When someone said, "You can say that again," he stopped saying it again.

And he lost weight. He sloughed off 110 pounds and came within striking distance of the top of the average range for his size. But nothing changed. His improvers just found new problems. They would always find new problems. So Denny ate fast and hard and hurried back to his former weight. If they weren't going to be nice to him, he wasn't going to be nice for them to look at. Besides, it felt *right* to be big. When he could see his cheeks again in his peripheral vision, he welcomed them back. Inside every fat person is a thin person—or so people said, and many said it to him. But it wasn't true of everyone. Inside Dennis Braintree was another fat man.

Yes, Denny knew that sheepish grin. When Homer showed it again and embraced his belly, Denny, on his knees before the TV, embraced his own.

EIGHT

CAN YOU IMAGINE ANYTHING MORE RIDICULOUS THAN A railroad? [Surprised laughter.] *Where did it come from? Most transportation ideas spring from nature. The stick floats, the bug rides on the stick, therefore* I *could ride on a stick—let's go a-boating! Logs roll—if I could ride on one I could go somewhere. Of course, I would need to be suspended free of the log's rotation or I would have a rough ride indeed.* [Much laughter.]

Denny provided both the words and the laughter. What better way to pass the time on the highway?

No lower-order creature locomotes on parallel tracks, so whence came the railroad?

He loved "whence."

Did a god deliver the idea to mankind—some stripe-capped, coal-blackened Prometheus? Or did a company inventor of unique intelligence have a brain explosion? But—poor fellow—just imagine his presentation:

CEO: I don't quite follow, Barclay. Where do these tracks come from?

BARCLAY: We lay them down, sir. In short segments that lie on wooden crossbeams.

CEO: Mmm. Wouldn't these beams be subject to loosening, rot, and sabotage?

BARCLAY: (pause) Sometimes.

CEO: There are mountains out west. Will these tracks go over them?

BARCLAY: Not directly, sir.

CEO: Oh?

BARCLAY: We're limited to a gradient of 2.2 percent. Otherwise the train slides backwards.

CEO: 2.2 percent, you say?

BARCLAY: Yes, sir.

CEO: Barclay, my 81-year-old mother sets her treadmill at 10 percent—or she would if they existed.

BARCLAY: Sir?

CEO: My point is that's no gradient at all. How do you get across the mountains without building an overpass that begins in Kansas and ends in California?

BARCLAY: Tunnels, sir.

CEO: Oh? There are natural tunnels big enough for this contraption?

BARCLAY: No, no, sir. You misunderstand me. We will make those tunnels.

CEO: We will?

BARCLAY: With shovels, dynamite, that sort of thing.

CEO: But . . . won't they collapse?

BARCLAY (after long pause): Sometimes. [Much, much laughter.]

"Sometimes," Denny said again. All he needed was a venue. In the past few years he had shopped the sketch around, and once he had been in the running for a slot at an Oak Park train show. When it fell through, he didn't mind—the material was too good to waste on local yokels. It deserved the big-time, a national convention. Keynoting wasn't out of the question.

He had a special place in his heart for the inventor, a persistent little cuss in the face of the CEO's skepticism. Their relationship was based on his and his boss's. Roscoe liked Denny's skit but said he couldn't use his regular position on the convention planning committee to land him a booking because Denny worked for his magazine and that created a conflict of interest. But Denny didn't work for him anymore, did he? So ha! to that.

Whenever Denny ran through his routine, he felt sorry for all the people who hadn't heard it. It was like his feeling about his personality. He felt pity for humanity because they were ignorant of Dennis Braintree. "I have so much to offer," he said aloud. In celebration of himself, he honked the horn several times.

The resulting bleats were as quaint as everything else about Homer's Rambler, like its "Flashomatic" transmission and its daring push-button shifting—no doubt revolutionary in its day and warmly welcomed by Denny, no friend of the clutch. Homer had upgraded the sound system, adding an AM/FM radio with CD and cassette players and a satellite radio receiver as well. Before leaving the house, Denny had grabbed his train songs CD from his carry-on bag, and he had been listening to it between takes of his skit. The only problem with the Rambler was that it did not share Denny's love of speed. Its boxy body shook every time Denny went over 70, like an old man shaking his head *no* at him.

It was dark by the time he exited the highway. He followed the signs to the airport, drove into the passenger pickup zone, and drove right out again. His goal was to retrace the route Nick had taken when he had driven him home—a lifetime ago, it seemed, and in a way it was. He knew exactly where he wanted to "lose" his cell phone. He took a right and a left. A long straight stretch, and there it was, lighting up the night in red and yellow neon: Marvin's French Fries. He had seen the restaurant from Nick's car and had whispered a promised return.

Marvin's was shaped like a flying saucer, with a bustling kitchen in the middle. "Alley-Oop" was playing on the jukebox, and Denny sang along as he sought out a booth. Only one was free, and he scooted into it despite the residue from previous diners. A young waitress passing by with a pot of coffee stopped at his table and frowned.

"Did the hostess seat you?" she said.

"I know exactly what I want," Denny said. "Three milkshakes—chocolate, strawberry, and vanilla, sort of a liquid Neapolitan"—this gave him the urge to sing "Napoli," and he succumbed to it for a few seconds, though he had to fake the Italian—"and, to go with it, a vast plate of Marvin's French fries. With mayo on the side, Dutch style."

The waitress—untraveled, unworldly—stared at him blank-faced, then looked at the table. "I'll have someone clear this."

"No rush." Denny grabbed a cold French fry from the plate in front of him and popped it in his mouth.

As she left, the waitress flashed the standard bulging eyes that her generation had learned from TV as a comment on anything outside the norm. Denny looked around. Across the aisle sat a lean man working a crossword puzzle. As if to show off his thinness, he sat crossed-legged with the ankle of his upper leg wrapped like a vine around his other leg, just above where his foot was planted on the floor.

"Let me know when you need help with that puzzle," Denny said. "Dennis Braintree is a man of many words."

The man looked up, stared at Denny, and returned to his puzzle.

Denny took out his cell phone and turned it on. He identified the phone so strongly with Lance that it was as if he had been carrying the detective in his pocket all this time. As it went through its wake-up routine, he grinned to think of the response he might be triggering in low orbit and in some earthly law enforcement office. He thought about the two phone calls he was about to make, both of them as his former self. He planned what he would say but in a relaxed way, without the severe pressure of being Homer. Denny came easily to him, like putting on old slippers. But he was certainly a noisy devil, wasn't he?

He took a slip of paper from his shirt pocket and punched the numbers on it into his phone. As he waited, he looked at four young teenaged girls chattering in the booth that he faced. The eyes of one of the girls met his. "Dennis Braintree is calling Montpelier," he said loudly to her.

"B.F.D.," she muttered, and her friends laughed.

Denny was stimulated. "A code-talker, eh? Try this. S.Y.H.I.T.T." He said it fast and he could do that because he was smart. She frowned because she wasn't, and another girl at her booth said, "Did he just spell 'shit'?" Denny called out a translation for the table: "Stick Your Head In The Toilet."

"Ah." This came over Denny's phone. "Mr. Braintree, I assume. I've been hoping to hear from you, though not exactly in those terms."

"Hello, Betsy."

"Sir, you have some explaining to do."

"Did you get my note? You're charging the room repairs to me, aren't you?"

"Of course I am. And don't think I'm not going to pad the bill. But I want the full story. Entertain me."

Denny took a deep breath and described the events of the night as he understood them: a woman's visit to his room—he confessed that she had been the one in the Jacuzzi when Betsy had knocked on his door—his errand to buy cigarettes (he omitted the condoms), the woman's probable chandelier swing and fall in his absence, her departure. In the booth in front of him, the four girls eavesdropped with mouths open enough to display their orthodonture. The two facing him looked away whenever he looked at them. Denny liked playing to the two audiences, Betsy and this gang. One audience was never enough for him.

Betsy said, "Are you aware that a certain detective has a different view of what happened? Marge—let's call the woman by her name, since I know who you mean—Marge has gone missing, and this fellow believes you pushed her from your balcony and made off with her body."

Denny would have to act as if he were hearing this for the first time. After all, it was Denny as Homer who had heard this theory from Nick and Lance, not Denny as Denny. He needed to be outraged.

"I'm outraged!"

"Yes, well, I represented you as best I could, Mr. Braintree. I told him you were harmless."

Denny banged the table with a palm. "That's exactly what I am."

"You could no more shove Marge off the balcony than I could. Not that I haven't been tempted."

"You know Marge?"

"Everyone knows Marge. She's our local Calamity Jane. She's addicted to at least three things I know of: drink, gambling, and men. I'm working on one of them—I've been trying to take away her bottle for years. She doesn't really have anybody else to help her, except for an indifferent sister and a parade of two-legged dogs in heat—and please don't bark, Mr. Braintree. My guess is that she's finally gone off to get help and that's why they can't find her."

"Did you tell that to the police?"

"I tried. This one fellow is just negative through and through. He's bent on seeing it as a murder. He's desperate for crime in our little town to justify that fancy new detective division. But why haven't they questioned you? Where are you?"

"If I told you, that would make you an accomplice."

She made some soft noises that could have been laughter. "You definitely belong in the cubby, Mr. Braintree. I just wish I had kept you there."

"Betsy, speaking of the cubby, I'm actually calling about your nephew."

"Homer? What about him?" Her tone was no longer playful.

"The strangest thing happened—I met him at the airport in Burlington. We had the nicest chat."

"So he *is* back. Where is he?"

"I was waiting for my flight to Chicago, and he was waiting for a friend flying in from Hong Kong."

"Where is he *now*?"

"At the farmhouse. He told me all about the place. He also said he has some problems that he needs to work out. He wants some quiet time there."

She said nothing for a moment. "He's got problems all right, but I don't know how he could be any quieter than he is already."

"He needs to be alone. That's the message he asked me to give you. He wants no visitors, and he won't be answering the phone."

She said, "That doesn't sound like my Homer."

"Well, it's interesting that you say that, because he said something to that effect. He said, 'Aunt Betsy will be surprised.'"

"He's never refused my help. He's always sought my counsel."

" 'She'll be surprised, but she'll understand.' That's what he said."

"He can't lick his problems alone."

"I think he's hoping that Sarah might be helpful."

Betsy fell silent again. Denny waited, his lips moving fitfully in anticipation of her words. She finally said, "He'll get no help from that quarter." There was a hardness in her voice.

"Oh?" He waited for more. "Why do you say that?"

"When can I talk to him?" The subject of Sarah was closed.

"He needs time, Betsy. Oddly enough, he seems to want to stay in touch with me. You know how you can strike up a friendship and exchange confidences when you're traveling? That's what happened to us. He'll call me again, I'm sure. If I learn anything more, I'll let you know. I'm afraid you'll just have to wait until he's ready to see you. That time will come."

She made a *hmph* noise.

"When he's ready he'll be back in that cubby just like old times." Denny said good-bye, waited to receive hers—it came slowly, with much preoccupation—and flipped his phone shut.

He was satisfied that the call would keep Betsy at bay for a while. He looked at the booth of teenagers. The two facing him were watching him and reporting to their friends. He said, " 'He'll get no help from that quarter.' What do you make of it, girls? Any thoughts? Ah."

This last was for the waitress, who had arrived with his three milkshakes and fries. He quickly gobbled half of the fries and downed the entire chocolate shake. He picked up the phone and punched the numbers. To the girls he said, "Now Dennis Braintree is calling his former boss." He attacked his vanilla shake and got half of it down before Roscoe answered the phone.

"Roscoe, I want to call in a favor."

"Oh, God." Roscoe was raising a palm to his forehead. Denny had seen it enough times in the office to know. "The police keep calling me," Roscoe said. "Why? Because thanks to yesterday's phone call, I'm your *last known contact.*" He was talking to himself more than to Denny, who was familiar with this behavior as well. "My hope was to be replaced—surely some new *last known contact* would emerge. But now the loathsome label returns to me. It is in my interest to say goodbye. Goodbye."

Denny redialed. Roscoe didn't bother with a hello. "Denny, I assume you did not actually throw a lady out your hotel window. I know you, to my regret, and I know you couldn't do this."

"Correct."

"So why haven't you gone to the police and cleared things up? That would be ideal for me. That would make *the police* your last known contact."

"It's kind of complicated. I'm calling about something else."

"*What?* Are we done with the alleged defenestration? That's the only part of this conversation that could possibly interest me."

"Do you remember my routine about the inventor and the CEO?"

"Oh, God."

"I want to deliver it at the national meeting in Las Vegas. This business will have blown over by then, and if it hasn't, I'll use an alias. I don't work for you anymore—"

"God be praised!"

"—so there's no conflict of interest. Can you recommend me? You've always liked the routine."

"I've always lied."

"What?"

"It fails on every level."

"But . . . Maybe you've missed the point of it, Roscoe. It takes something familiar and makes it strange."

"None better than you for that."

"Just recommend it to the program committee. It's a small favor, really."

"Yeah? Do *me* a favor. Go to the police."

"Roscoe? Roscoe?" Denny frowned and flipped his phone shut. To the girls he said, "I can't believe he hung up on me again." One of them said, "I can," and there was much shoulder hunching and hair shaking.

Denny left the phone on and put it in a front pocket of his pants, but shallowly. He finished his vanilla milkshake and wiggled a bit, but nothing happened. Then he began to wriggle back and forth in the booth, sliding and squirming, and he raised his hands above his head to make sure he didn't use them. One of the girls said, "Oh my God, he's ass-dancing," but they obviously didn't understand what he was doing. Eventually he was able to work the phone out of his pocket so that it plunked onto the bench beside him. He wanted to simulate an actual inadvertent loss of the phone as much as possible. He just wanted to do it that way.

He grabbed the strawberry milkshake, downed it, loudly burped the words "All done," and fished some bills out of his wallet.

As he stood up, one of the girls said, "Goodbye, Mr. Brainseizure." Denny hurried over to their table as they erupted in laughter, and he leaned down and barked his own loud laugh into their faces.

He had passed a bank on his way to the airport. He planned to return to it and, using *The Fearless Modeler's* ATM card, suck out as much cash as he could. Then he would see if he could find a cell phone store that was still open in order to buy a new one. Then he would do a big shop at the supermarket, followed by a back haul to Horn of the Moon Road. It had been a long day, and he looked forward to snuggling between Homer's sheets.

NINE

DENNY, SQUINTING AGAINST THE MORNING LIGHT, ANswered the phone beside the bed before he was fully conscious.

"Homer, you got to help me."

Denny was pleased. Back home, no one ever asked him for help. But who *was* this? "What's wrong?"

"I screwed the pooch!"

Was it someone who had already welcomed him back? It must have been, given the way he got down to business. But Denny didn't recognize the voice. "It can't be that bad."

"It's bad, big guy. You know my license is suspended, right? Sarah must of told you."

"Right." *The speaker knows Sarah.*

"June's been ferrying me around. I don't mind. Gives us a chance to talk, you know what I'm sayin'?"

"I know what you're saying." *The speaker probably cohabits with a June.*

"She's a helluva woman."

"Indeed she is." *June is a helluva woman.*

"Only thing is, the other night she couldn't drive me because of her Al-Anon meeting. Those are important to her, and I support her all the way and I don't want nobody sayin' otherwise."

"Point taken."

"Huh?"

"I agree. Yes. Right."

"So, number one is I drove to town with a suspended license. But I *had* to. The Macalester boys been lookin' over twelve acres down the hill where the ram pump was, and we been talkin' about it off and on, but I didn't hear from 'em for a long time, and I figured their interest in it went tits up. But then I get a call from Gary. They're both at the Ethan Allen bar and they're ready to deal. You only go around once, Homer. Got to grab the gusto. So I say I'll be right down. After about a hour I find the keys to the truck—June hid 'em—and off I go. Damn, it felt good to be behind the wheel again. It was Katy bar the door—I *flew* down 14. I even stopped on the way to spin donuts on the north lot. Remember that?"

"How could I forget?"

"By the time I get to the bar, the Macalesters are out in front gettin' in their truck to go home, so I leaned on the horn and skidded to a halt right behind 'em. I guess I scared Gary and kinda ticked him off even more than he was already because I was late, but I told him I ain't never been a clockwatcher, it's just the way I am. I sweet-talked 'em both back inside."

"Did you close the deal?"

"Not really." He sighed. "I was supposed to bring the survey with me—Gary wanted to see it—but thanks to June I spent so dang much time ransackin' the house for my keys that it slipped my mind."

"You could have all gone back to your place for the survey and closed the deal there."

"Actually I lost the sonofabitch." He made an angry, dismissive noise. "Surveys. Wienie with a tripod, takes an' sticks a pipe in the ground, says, 'That'll be four hundred dollars, Sparky.' I told him where he could stick his pipe. Almost did, anyway."

"I'm sorry the deal didn't happen, Sparky."

"Yeah. So, um, let's see." He had lost track of his tale. "Okay, so I've got 'em both back in the bar, and I'm hopin' they won't bring up the survey, but a course Gary does. He's sharp, you got to give the devil his due. Speakin' of devils, Buns Balestreri was in there, and she's checkin' me out, and I'm sayin' to myself, 'Sparky, think of June. Think of June. Think of June with a pair of pruning sheers comin' at ya.' You know what I'm sayin', Homer?"

"What happened then?" Denny had mastered the art of conversing with Sparky. You simply slapped him every twenty seconds.

"When Gary finds out I don't have the survey, he storms out. Jimmy was in the toilet, and when he comes back to the table, I try to close the deal with him. Gary comes back and raises a ruckus, and before you know it, Betsy throws us all out. I been given the heave-ho by the best of 'em, but never by a blind lady, and I say that to Gary, but I don't think he heard me. Buns did though. At least, I *think* she heard me . . ." Sparky, as if suddenly tiring of his own drift, snapped his next sentence out. "Long story short, we left the bar." He paused. "I drove home."

"Without incident?"

"Huh? Oh, yeah, no incidences. When I come in the house, June unloaded on me for drivin'. The whole time that she's yellin', I'm thinkin' how I didn't go near Buns Balestreri, and don't that count for nothin'? I finally said it, too, but it didn't help none." He paused again.

"I don't see how I can help you close that deal, Sparky."

"That ain't why I'm callin'. You know that shed I built outta scrap plywood?"

"How could I forget?" Sparky seemed to be triangulating to his theme.

"I keep the truck parked behind it, so it's outta view from the house. Seein' the rig just breaks my heart. So I'm out on top of the ledge above the shed tryin' to smoke a porcupine outta the brush pile up there, cocksucker got my dog the other day, almost did, anyway. I couldn't get the pile lit—it was wet, I didn't have no diesel, just gas, and I'm getting nothin' but *whoomps* from the fumes blowin' up in my face. But that was kind of fun, at least until June starts yellin' at me for the noise, and I look back to the house, and the truck is below me, sort of in my line of sight between me and the house." Sparky took a deep breath. Denny sensed the payoff was at hand.

"And then what happened?"

"Guess who I seen in the truck."

"Who?"

"Marge Plongeur."

Denny flinched. "Marge? Was she asleep? Was she drunk?"

"Hardly."

"Does she live near you? Is there a rehab center nearby that she—"

"Homer, stay focused, man. She's *dead*. She was layin' there dead in the bed of my pickup."

"Dead?"

"I'm starin' down at her from the ledge, and it's obvious from the way she's arranged that she's a goner, and I say to myself, no matter how you slice it, Sparky, this ain't no feather in your cap. Meanwhile, June's still yellin' from the house. She gets that chant goin' and it's like a wild sound. It's almost pleasant, like birds, and in wintertime you miss the birds—except for the chickadees, and I don't want to take nothin' away from them."

"Marge," Denny said softly, more to himself than to Sparky.

"Yeah. They're sayin' she fell from a balcony at the Ethan Allen. Now we know where she fell *to*. You know what's funny? I seen her at the hotel that night."

It took Denny a moment to process this. "You saw Marge?"

"She was in the lobby, headin' for the hall to the elevator when I come in the door. She looks back at me and yells, 'Hey, Sparky. I'm a winner.' Ironic, ain't it? I was probably the last person to see her alive."

Not quite, Denny thought. He thought of the way she had poked him in the chest on her way into the bathroom.

"The thing is," said Sparky, "the cops are gonna say, 'Hey, Sparky, thanks for the call and all, but did your truck take an' drive itself to town?' Yuk yuk yuk and another fine on top a the thousands I already owe. They get you comin' and goin', Homer. I can't hunt, not legally, anyways. Can't fish. Can't hardly open a can of soup. That's where you come in."

"You need me to say I drove you."

"Oh, you're quick."

"And after your negotiations with the Macalesters, I drove you back home."

"You're cookin'."

"I parked the truck at your house and left, both of us ignorant of our cargo."

"I can't hardly keep up! You're like me tearin' down 14!"

"The story is flawed."

"Huh?"

"I wasn't in the bar, so I must have sat in the pickup the whole time."

"Yeah? So?"

"Marge would have made a huge noise when she landed. It would have rocked the truck. Why didn't I notice that?"

Denny heard an intake of breath. "Dang. Good thinkin'. That could come up. Let's see. You must of got out and left the truck for a while. I know, we'll use ol' reliable—you had to take a leak."

"Where would I have done that?"

"Between the two dumpsters in the back lot of the hotel." Sparky spoke like a frequent habitué.

Denny said, "And I didn't see her body when I came back to the truck, and neither did you. That's plausible."

"Plausible? Hell, man, it happened. At least to me. I didn't see her."

Denny had to overcome momentary disorientation from hearing this intelligent, relevant remark. "Why did we take your truck and not my car? If I drove to your place to pick you up, why did we switch vehicles?"

"Because the truck needs a spin now and then to stay in shape. True fact."

The story hung together. The police would examine Marge, note the alcohol in her system, and find no evidence of foul play. Denny would cease to be a suspect, and Lance would stop looking for him.

Sparky took a deep breath and let it out. "You and me, Homer."

"That's right," said Denny. "And Marge."

Sparky fell into a long silence. Finally, he said, "Is that fuckin' Nick on the case?" Denny had expected different words—some comment on the loss dealt to the community by Marge's passing. But Sparky's orbit was a narrow one.

"Yes, he is."

"He ain't no friend of mine."

Denny said nothing.

"He's a friend of yours, Homer."

"That's right."

"There's no tellin' what I might say if he gets under my skin. I speak my mind, that's just how the good Lord made me and a tiger can't change his spots. I'm thinkin' it'd help if you was here when they give me the third degree. You'd make me legit."

Denny thought about this. He and Sparky were certainly less likely to give contradictory stories if they were together when questions were asked. "I can do that."

"Come on over. I'll call the coppers." With that Sparky was gone.

Denny let out a yelp of panic. He had no idea where Sparky lived. Even if he had thought to ask, he couldn't have because Homer wouldn't have needed to. Was there some way he could call him back and tease his address out of him? He could ask if the nearest cross street was still under repair and pretend to have forgotten its name—just inquire idly about it, as in "What's the name of that street again?" Surely such a fabrication could slip past the gatekeepers of Sparky's mind, which seemed chaotic. And once Denny was in the neighborhood, he could ask some helpful neighbor for final directions. He would call Sparky back. But when he pressed the button to show the number of the most recent caller, the ID window read only "Private Caller"—words as unhelpful as they were inaccurate in their implied primness.

Sparky. It couldn't be a first name—who names a child Sparky? Denny found a phone book in Homer's computer desk and searched it. No such surname appeared, but where it would have been, four "Sparks" listings suggested a basis for the nickname. But which Sparks? The four addresses were equally meaningless to him. Sparky had said that he "flew down 14" when he drove to the hotel. Highway 14?

Denny threw a coat over his pajamas and hurried out to the Rambler in front of the house. In the glove compartment he found a county map. He hurried back inside, spread the map on the dining room table, and located the four streets listed in the phone book. Highway 14 was a likely route to town for only one of the addresses.

The rural roads through farms and countryside were eccentrically marked. The few street signs that Denny saw *faced* him instead of paralleling his route in the normal fashion, as if some Yankee prankster had rotated them ninety degrees. But the mud was the worst part. For no apparent reason, a stretch of reasonably hard road would give way to chocolate pudding floating on frozen earth, and the car would careen wildly. Elsewhere, the road had thawed and refrozen into harsh shapes, and Denny would find his wheels drawn into ruts that looked harmless on entry but then deepened until he was up to his axle, with the rut holding the tire in place as if another pair of hands had seized his steering wheel. For one who loved speed, the mud was as bad as snow.

He kept thinking of Marge and that poke in the chest. He felt it now as an accusing finger. However she had died, Marge would almost certainly be alive if her path hadn't crossed Denny's. But one could just as easily blame Betsy for putting Denny in Mort's room. Or Mort for going home to Brandon. Or the voters of Brandon for electing Mort to the legislature. He implicated more and more people, stopping short of Ethan Allen and his Green Mountain Boys—whoever they were—only because he reached his destination.

The address was hand-lettered on a mailbox that had lost its own means of support and leaned against a tree. Next to it, at the bottom of a driveway, a big rusted car faced the road. Its hood was propped open by a piece of plywood on which was painted "BOO." Denny took the sign for a Halloween relic, but a second look showed that the "B" was an ill-drawn "8." The sign gave the asking price for the car: 800 dollars.

Sparky's driveway was steep, and gurgling snow runoff was churning its surface into canals. The approach went on for some distance, committing Denny to what lay at its conclusion. If he found an irrelevant homeowner—if the nickname derived from, say, Sparky's electrifying personality instead of from a Sparks surname—Denny would turn the car around, drive home, and make up an excuse when Sparky called to ask where he was. But then he saw Nick's unmarked police car next to the house. The driveway extended beyond the house, and farther along it stood a threesome—Nick, Lance, and a man with a hunched, furtive posture. Farther still, Denny saw a brown shed and, behind it, the back bumper of the fateful pickup.

Denny parked behind Nick's car, got out, and headed for the trio. He passed the house—rambling with add-ons, patched with planks, half painted in several colors, and decorated around one window with a trim of old hubcaps nailed to the wall. A door from the second story led to the open air—an exit for casting out mutineers, perhaps. Inside, a dog with a deep voice stopped barking only to take a breath.

Lance took in Denny's arrival with a dismissive glance. Nick looked at him more quizzically. "Homer," he said in a funny tone that expressed both greeting and surprise. Sparky was older than Denny had expected, probably in his fifties, though Denny found it hard to focus on his face because of his garb. He was clad in black leather—a cap that tightly hugged his skull, a black jacket half zipped up and exposing a bare upper chest, and chaps or leggings over his jeans, with a strange window in front that presented the bulge of his blue-jeaned crotch like a swordsman's codpiece.

Sparky said to Denny, "I'm unloadin' my inventory, bud. You see my Merc at the bottom of the driveway? I'll cut you a deal on it." He whirled fast to Nick. "Don't you be givin' me the fish eye now. My pond-dumpin' days are over. I haven't been up to Prescott in years. You know what the fine is now if they find a wreck on the ice? No sir, I've got a whole new system." He turned to Denny. "I was just explainin' it to Nick and uh . . ." Sparky looked to Lance for help, but Lance just stared at him, and Nick had to supply the name. Denny looked forward to being in a group where Lance's contempt was directed at someone other than himself.

"Like I was sayin' to these boys," Sparky went on, easily regaining momentum, "I got me a three-legged economic stool: one is commerce, like the Merc. The second is storage pending an uptick in demand." He waved an arm, and Nick and Denny, but not Lance, took advantage of the invitation to look at the surrounding castoffs emerging from the snow. Various modes of transportation were represented—automotive (four wrecks within view), nautical (a rusty pontoon boat with a caved-in canvas roof), and aeronautical (a helicopter bubble, but only the bubble). Denny wondered what else lay beneath the uneven remaining snow.

"The third is what I call *reutilization*. For starters, I'm gonna make a giant bird feeder out of that wicker in the dooryard."

"What about Marge's body?" said Nick.

"I ain't thought of a use for it right off." Whatever minimal success this witticism might have had was immediately undercut by Sparky's self-congratulation and post-joke commentary: "You walked right into that one, Detective. You shoulda seen it comin'. You got to get up early to—"

"*Show us Marge.*" Lance snarled the sentence.

With stunning flexibility, Sparky switched from backyard raconteur to undertaker. He found a solemn expression in his repertoire and, bending over in some imagined universal gesture of respect, extended his arm up the driveway. He maintained that posture and continued to face the group when they cleared the shed, as if it honored Marge in some way not to look at her.

Denny braced himself and turned to the pickup. But there was nothing to see. There was only Sparky's truck, vomit yellow in color.

"What the hell, Sparky?" said Nick.

"It's a shocker, that's for sure," Sparky said as he turned to the truck. "Imagine my surp—" He stared, mouth open. "She must of slumped down." He hurried forward and leaned over the tailgate, then looked all over the bed, as if a miniature Marge might have scurried under a scrap of lumber. The others stepped up to the truck.

"Tell us again what you saw," said Nick.

"I saw *Marge*. She was right here, I'm tellin' you. She was lyin' tits up." Sparky looked from Nick to Lance, who was studying the truck's body one square inch at a time.

"You saw Marge," Nick said. "And you're sure she was dead."

The implied alternative was a two-by-four to Sparky's skull. He staggered back a step. "There ain't no way—"

"Did you examine the body? Did you touch her?"

Sparky hung fire. Denny guessed he wanted to give the answer least likely to produce a rebuke, but he couldn't figure out what it was. Lance began to circle the truck.

"When did this happen, Sparky?" Nick said.

"Like I said—"

"Here's something," Lance said. He was standing by the driver's door and looking down at the ground. "It's blood."

"Thank you, *Je*sus," said Sparky. He hurried to Lance. Denny and Nick followed. Lance waved them all back. He was squatting over a small red patch in the snow. He rose and cast his gaze around.

"Guess I wasn't seein' things after all," Sparky said, a hint of injury in his tone.

Nick muttered something and looked up the face of the sloping rock above the pickup. "If she fell, she could have been unconscious when you saw her. Then she might have climbed out . . ." His voice trailed off as he looked back and forth between the rock face and the truck. Denny was puzzled. Did Nick believe Marge had fallen from the cliff into the truck?

"Here's a piece of fabric." Lance picked up something dark and shook the snow off it. "Gore-Tex."

"The snow's disturbed here," Nick said. He swung wide of Lance and walked a path that paralleled a groove in the snow. Sparky, hunched over, moved along behind him, then jumped forward.

"It's a bear," Sparky said with authority. "He drug her. He grabbed Marge and took an' drug her into the woods. See the paw prints?"

"A *bear*?" Lance stood upright. It wasn't his idea, so how could it be a good one?

"You betcha." Sparky, in his element, thrust his skinny chest out. "Everyone knows you never play dead with a black bear. He's likely to start chawin' on you. And Marge wasn't just playin'. Ol' Black's a carry-on eater, and that's exactly what Marge was—carry-on. This time a year, fresh outta the den, he's gonna be a Hungry Jack. And I do mean Jack—not Jacqueline. It'd take a 300-pounder to hoist Marge outta the bed of the truck. She ain't no peanut."

Lance stared at the marks in the snow. "Sonofabitch," he said softly.

"You want to find her, you follow this trail," Sparky said. With their eyes the four men followed the furrow in the snow until it disappeared into the woods. "Shouldn't be too hard to track with him makin' a big groove like that. He ain't gonna pick her up like King Kong. Gonna drag her."

"Sonofabitch," Lance said loudly, not in wonder this time, but in reference to the bear. He drew his pistol from its holster and checked its magazine.

"Whoa," said Nick. "Let's think this over."

"It's an abomination," Lance said.

"Don't be too hard on him," Sparky said. "Ol' Mr. Bear's just doin' what comes naturally to him."

"So am I," Lance said. With his jaw leading the way, he stalked off into the woods. Nick seemed unsure whether to pull rank or chase after him. He finally took out his own pistol and followed.

"Hope you know where to put that slug," Sparky called after him. "How many bear you killed, Nick?"

Nick threw his answer over his shoulder. "Fuck off, Sparky."

Grinning, Sparky turned to Denny. "Hell, we know where to shoot 'em, don't we, Homer? Pretend he's wearin' a bib—that's what

Big Timmy always said. Just like a little baby wears. You shoot him right in the bib." His head bobbed enthusiastically, then stopped. "Shit. If I'd a knowed Marge was gonna come up missin', I wouldn'ta called the cops."

Denny said, "But they would want to know what you saw. You couldn't keep that information from them."

Sparky pointed a philosophical finger skyward. "Never trouble trouble till trouble troubles you." Denny noticed that trouble must have already troubled Sparky: the little finger of his right hand was missing.

"I need to know what you've told them so far."

Sparky's face, which ordinarily belonged to the category of goofy, suddenly went tragic. "Hope that bear didn't take an' scratch my truck." He walked over and began to examine it. Denny followed. Sparky said, "Looks like he clawed it some on top. I got a little vial a touch-up." He swept his eyes over the yard jumble. "Where did I put it?"

Denny was suddenly aware of a strong tobacco smell surrounding Sparky, though he wasn't smoking. "What did you tell them about Marge?"

"I said I figured she fell from the ledge."

A dozen or so objections vied for supremacy in Denny's head. He looked at the top of the cliff. "What would she be doing up there?"

"Not my job to explain that," said Sparky. "*Their* job."

"But why did you change the story? We agreed on a story."

Sparky shook his head. "I decided to use that story as a backup. See, if my truck is sittin' here the whole time, they're not gonna suspect DLS. If they end up decidin' Marge couldn't of fell into the truck from up there, I'll have a sudden idea and say she must of fell into it the night you drove me down to the Ethan Allen. Why start off with the truck movin' if I don't have to?"

"So why am I here now?"

Sparky frowned. "Because I called you, big guy." He spoke with patience, as if Denny were dimwitted.

Denny said, "I mean why am I here *from their point of view*? My presence only makes sense if you summoned me to confirm that I drove you to town. Why would you call me if you thought she fell from up there?"

Sparky stroked his jaw. Denny could not tell if he was mulling over a repair to his obvious oversight or if he utterly failed to understand Denny's point. If the latter, as Denny began to suspect, the jaw stroking was possibly a delaying tactic while the wheels turned. What would it be like to be Sparky, Denny wondered. What would it be like to have that brain, to live life in discrete, unrelated moments?

"When *did* you see Marge anyway? You called me about an hour ago. Did the bear grab her between then and now?"

"Actually I seen her yesterday. I been wonderin' what to do about her."

A noise from the edge of the woods made them both jump. It was Nick, storming out with his cell phone in hand.

"He ain't gonna get a signal," Sparky said with a chuckle.

"It's a dead zone, Nick," Denny called out. Sparky threw him a disappointed look.

Nick forced them toward the house with outspread arms, already cordoning off the area. When he made contact with Sparky, he more or less pushed him forward. "I've got to use your land line, Sparky. Let's go."

As they hurried along, Denny said, "What happened?"

"We found her. Most of her, anyway. I left Lance guarding what's left. He's praying over her. It's the damnedest thing—he gets down on one knee to pray." Nick seemed to go somewhere in his head, then came back. "We're going to need six kinds of experts. Pathologists. Fish and Wildlife, God knows who else." His face changed again. "Marge. Jesus, I never want to see anything like that again."

TEN

When Denny stepped over Sparky's threshold, the odor of neglect swept across his face like a stale curtain. A gray film on the windows encased the house in a nicotine winter. Sparky, leading the way, jabbed a finger at the kitchen wall by way of directing Nick to the phone. As Nick reached for it, Denny turned to Sparky, hoping they could coordinate their stories while Nick was occupied, but Sparky opened a door and disappeared down some stairs, apparently kicking his dog ahead of him. The animal had declared a new level of displeasure with the visitors from behind that door as soon as they had entered the house, and after a moment he was back at it, scratching at the door and barking. Nick's response was to put a finger in one ear and shout into the phone. Denny's was to backpedal onto the front porch. There he hunched his shoulders against the cold. The house and porch, shaded by pines that lashed the roof, felt thirty degrees colder than the sunlit driveway.

A few minutes later, Nick came out, looking haggard, but he managed a fleeting smile for Denny. He said, "What in the hell are you doing here, Homer?"

"Sparky asked me to help him with his taxes."

Nick nodded. "Be sure to disclose his weed revenue." He leaned on the porch railing and looked down the driveway toward the road. "I've got people coming. We'll have Marge checked out and try to make sense of this." He shook his head. "There's something squirrelly about the whole thing."

Sparky came out of the house, his lips curled around a cigarette and pursed as if suppressing a smile over some secret accomplishment. "Found 'er," he said.

"Yeah, we know, Sparky," Nick said, still looking down the driveway. "You found her and lost her and we found her again."

"Not Marge. My touch-up." He whipped the tiny bottle of paint from his jacket pocket. "Found 'er."

Nick glared at him. "Christ, Sparky. Have pity."

"Huh?"

"Go look at Marge. Just go look at her."

Sparky threw his hands up. "Hey, I didn't ask no lady to take a swan dive into my truck." He strolled off, shaking the little bottle of paint.

Nick stared after him, then gestured to his car. "Let's go where it's warm. I've got coffee." They stepped down from the porch. "Three-legged economic stool, my ass," Nick muttered. "You know how many acres he's got left from the original three hundred? About twenty-five. Some plan—selling off your ancestral land until there's nothing left but your dooryard." When they reached the cars, Nick asked Denny to pull the Rambler around to a small parking area along the side of the house. He said he would do the same with his car to free up the driveway so that the forensics van could go all the way to the edge of the woods. Denny backed his car into the parking area, just fitting it between the house and a pine tree. Nick backed his car in close, and Denny joined him inside.

Nick poured coffee and began talking about his son Connor's youth hockey team. He abruptly stopped talking and took a deep breath and blew it out. "I feel like I should be doing something more right now. But Lance is with Marge, and I've got to wait for the troops. There's nothing more I can do, right?"

"Right."

"I hate the feeling that I should be doing more than I am." Nick stared into space for a moment, then suddenly reached both hands up and rubbed the crown of his head, mussing his hair. "Maybe Lance makes me feel that way. We have a top-dog, bottom-dog relationship, but it switches back and forth. He's on top lately—I can't say why." He sipped his coffee. "Marge. Jesus. I've seen dead bodies, but she was just meat. The bear scooped out her belly and her guts, all the soft stuff, like the rest of her body was a bowl that he was eating out of." He looked through his side window. "Now the woods creep me out." He set his cup down on the console and gripped the steering wheel. For a moment, he looked like a little boy pretending to drive. "You probably heard about me and Millie."

"Yeah," Denny said. Affirm, then catch up—this was his strategy.

"We're back together now. Things are looking better."

"That's great, man."

"The thing is . . ." Nick took another deep breath and blew it out. "Okay, I've gotta get this out. You're likely to hear some talk about me and Sarah. I dated her while you were gone." He turned to Denny. "It was at least a year after you left. I was on my own, and so was Sarah, at least from what I could tell."

"She said that?"

Nick looked pained. "Not in so many words. Whenever I asked how you were doing, she said she had no idea, and I'd say aren't you guys in touch, and she'd say no." Nick looked at Denny expectantly.

"I understand." Denny nodded solemnly.

"Nobody knew what happened to you. I mean *nobody*."

"That's the way I wanted it."

"Rumors were flying all over. One theory was that you owed people some money, that you had run up some debts."

Denny laughed.

"Anyway, I said to Sarah, 'We should do something,' and she said, 'Sure, why not?' So we went out for a while."

"How long?"

"A couple of months." Nick shifted in his seat. "It felt funny. Like there were three of us all the time—her, me, and you. I kept thinking how you and her had been together since you were kids. I couldn't get it out of my mind. The whole thing felt wrong." Nick squirmed. "I was a trespasser. So . . . forgive me my trespasses?"

"Done."

Nick stared out the windshield. "There's such a thing as loyalty, you know?"

Denny waited for elaboration. At first he understood the words to refer to Nick's loyalty to him as a friend, but then it occurred to him that Nick might have been talking about Sarah's loyalty.

"I don't know, Homer. With Millie, I go from honor roll to shit list at the drop of a hat."

A succession of thuds made them look to Sparky's house. A load of melting snow had slid from the roof and crashed onto the porch, right where they had been standing.

"Hey, we caught a break," Nick said. "Millie would make something of that. Karma or some damn thing." He grunted. "Now *I'm* being disloyal." He leaned forward over the steering wheel to look as far as possible down the driveway for the expected reinforcements.

Denny found himself wondering if Nick and Sarah had had sex. They went out for a couple of months, he had said. Was that enough time?

"I guess the last dead person I saw was Millie's mom."

Denny nodded automatically, then wondered if he should have. Did Homer know about Millie's mother dying?

"Your note meant a lot to Millie. It was great that it was a telegram—old school, you might say. Yesterday she was on the back porch—we fixed it up since you left, and that's where her mom stayed. It's where she died. Millie was mopping the floor yesterday, and she felt her mom's hand on her shoulder. So she says."

"Wow."

"It was prolly just a twinge. You get them all the time, but you have one in the room where your mother died and suddenly you're in touch with the other world. I don't buy it. It's a problem between us. Millie says my attitude keeps her mom's spirit away."

"You'd think her mother would be big and rise above it."

Nick smiled. "I miss our talks, Homer." He poured the last of the coffee, alternating their cups several times to ensure fairness. Denny watched him do this. Nick sipped from his cup and shook his head. "The way that ledge is pitched, Marge would practically have had to take a running jump to land in his truck. I don't get it."

Denny looked into Nick's face—his simple, puzzled face—and told him the truth, at least the truth that he and Sparky had created, which was closer to God's truth than the story Nick presently struggled to believe. Denny said that Marge must have fallen from the hotel balcony into Sparky's truck, parked on the street below, after he, Homer, had driven Sparky to town to meet with the Macalesters—more precisely, when he, Homer, had left the truck for a few minutes to relieve himself behind the hotel.

Nick took a long moment to absorb the news. "Well, hell, that explains a lot." He had been tense behind the wheel, but now his body seemed to relax a little. He chuckled. "Lance'll be pleased. It means his favorite suspect is still in play—the guy who stayed at the Ethan Allen. We nearly nabbed him yesterday in Burlington—came within a few minutes. Lance has some pictures of him on the way, and those should help."

Denny barely heard this. He was busy thinking about a fatal flaw in what he had just told Nick. How could he not have seen it before? The timeline was off. Marge fell from the balcony the same night Denny—as Homer—supposedly arrived at the Burlington airport, and he told Nick he had arrived there late, so he couldn't have driven Sparky to town. Nick was probably seconds away from realizing this himself.

"I actually got into town a few days before I saw you at the airport," Denny said offhandedly. "I stayed at the Econolodge to sort some things out. That's where Sparky tracked me down."

Fortunately, Nick seemed preoccupied with the idea of Marge plunging into the truck from the hotel balcony. He asked Denny several questions about the particulars—the time of his and Sparky's arrival at the Ethan Allen, the time between that and his leaving the truck to urinate behind the hotel (Nick didn't seem to find this behavior surprising), and the time of Sparky's return to the truck. He was silent for a while, and then he circled back to the new complication:

"So when we saw you at the airport and you were waiting for this friend from Hong Kong, you'd already been home?"

"Just a few days. And not home. At the Econolodge."

Nick seemed on the verge of another question when the cavalry arrived—two cars and a police van chugging up Sparky's driveway. Nick shot out the door and waved them on up the driveway to the edge of the woods near Sparky's pickup. Denny got out and slowly followed. Sparky, returning from his urgent touch-up work, stepped to one side of the driveway. He waved at each passing police car, a cigarette dancing up and down between his lips as he called out pleasantries.

"Joint's jumpin'," he said to Denny after the last car had passed.

Denny said, "I gave Nick the other explanation for why Marge was in your truck. I told him I drove you to town and that's where it happened."

Sparky's grin disappeared. "Dang, I sure didn't get much mileage out of my ledge story." He shrugged. "Oh well. Got to roll with the punches. Lord knows I been hit with 'em before."

By the time Denny neared the police cars, the investigators were on their way into the woods—all but one, who was lifting a black case out of the trunk. As he slammed the lid, he spotted Denny and waved.

"I heard you were back, Homer," the man called out. "A sight for sore eyes." He was heading toward the woods but walking backwards, facing Denny. "I expect to see you out to your camp pretty soon."

"In my mind, I'm already there," Denny said.

The man laughed hard and long. Denny had no idea what his "camp" was. It seemed strange that he could get a laugh under these circumstances. Back home, his most carefully wrought jokes never produced laughter like that.

The man suddenly turned somber. "Got to go. A grim scene up there, I expect."

Denny nodded and watched him trudge into the woods. He had no interest in joining the group and what they were dealing with. He decided to go in the opposite direction entirely—to drive back home. But a glance down the driveway showed him that his car was pinned in by Nick's.

Sparky strolled out of the house with a plastic spray bottle of blue liquid and a rag. As Denny walked to his car, he watched Sparky go to the helicopter bubble and climb in. He sprayed the inside of the bubble and cleaned it lovingly, working in sections. Then he got out, scraped a bit of snow off the outside with his glove and coat sleeve, and rubbed it clean with the rag. On his way back to the house, he sidetracked to where Denny leaned against the Rambler, and together they looked at his achievement.

"Me 'n June, when we have a toke, we like to lay down outside and look up at the snow fallin' in our faces. It gets wet and cold though. This mornin', when her snorin' woke me up, I had an idea. Me and her can crawl into the helicopter bubble, maybe cuddle up in a sleeping bag there, and watch the snowflakes come down on the Plexi." He grinned. Denny braced himself for a fresh round of self-congratulation, and here it came: they threw away the mold when they made ol' Sparky, etc. "Better check it again. June likes things perfect." He hurried back to it.

Denny got in the car and started the engine to warm it up. He watched Sparky in his idiotic enterprise. It brought to mind a moment at a staff party the year before, when Roscoe put his arm around Denny, the way someone does when they're about to say something nice, and said, "When I think of you, Denny, I think of one word: appetite. You're all appetite." Roscoe then wandered off, leaving Denny to reflect on things. Now he wanted to say the same thing to Sparky, but the appetite Denny was thinking of had nothing to do with food. It had to do with the world, which Sparky seemed to see as existing for his personal consumption. He wondered if that was what Roscoe had meant.

Denny spied Lance—his vigil concluded—striding down the driveway like a parade marshal. Both of his knees were caked with snow. Nick had said Lance prayed on one knee. Did he switch knees when one got cold? Lance stopped and called something out to Sparky. Denny rolled down his window and heard Sparky yell from the bubble, "In the kitchen." Lance then shouted something about a newspaper. Sparky hollered, "Don't believe in 'em." Lance continued striding to the house, caught sight of Denny in the Rambler, frowned, and veered over to him. Denny reached for the banana cream pie he had brought from home and went to work, digging into the pie plate with his fork.

When Lance reached Denny's window, he leaned in close, his chin pointing accusingly. "Why did it take you so long to figure out that Marge fell into the truck in town?"

"Beg pardon?" Denny shoveled a mouthful of pie into his mouth and let out a little moan of pleasure.

"You parked right in front of the hotel. You knew she fell from the hotel that same night."

Through a mouthful of creamy filling, Denny said, "You've been talking to my friend Nick, haven't you?"

"How could you not put those two things together?"

"I did. And I told Nick as soon as I did."

"How could you not put them together *immediately*?"

Denny chomped on the pie and pretended to study the question. "I guess I'm slow," he said. "Is it a crime to be slow?" He was prepared to go on in this vein, but Lance spun away and stormed off. Denny found him infinitely amazing. What, exactly, did he suspect Denny of? Not of impersonating Homer, certainly not that. But of *something*. In skinny Lance's world view, were all chubby people criminals?

A few minutes later, Sparky, having returned to the house, reemerged on a fresh mission. In one hand was a leash with the dog at the end of it, its nose scouring the snow. In his other hand was a gun—a black revolver so large that it looked unwieldy, though Sparky handled it nimbly. Denny guessed that he was going to track down the bear with his dog and shoot him in the bib to show Nick and Lance how it was done. But his agenda seemed less pressing. He and the dog wandered over to Denny. The animal—small, thin, dirty-white—had a strangely U-shaped body. The line from his tail to his head bulged outward as if someone had bent him over a knee and permanently reshaped him. It didn't look agile enough to jump through Denny's window to attack him, so he didn't roll it up.

"See my sidearm? It's for little Paul Schoomer." Sparky looked down at his dog. "He can't pee in public. Bashful kidney. Takes him an hour to work one up. I can't let him run loose or he'd tear up Considine's chicken coop, so I got to walk him, and it's *boring*. But if Paulie smells another dog's pee, he goes right away. Problem is I only got but the one dog ever since Prince Albert got caught in the splitter. I know your next question."

"You do?" Denny wasn't sure of it himself. He had so many.

"Does human pee work? The answer is *some* does. Not mine, sad to say. I'd demonstrate but I don't want to discourage you by flashin' my Jeremiah." He chuckled, an action that sent his head bobbing back and forth quickly. "Now, strange to say, June's pee does the trick. You lay some of it down and Paulie'll pee every last drop till he's drained dry, almost like it hurts. Long story short, from time to time June pees in a jug, and I fill the gun from the jug. Observe." Denny suddenly realized

Sparky was brandishing nothing more than a squirt gun. He aimed it at the ground and squeezed the trigger, but nothing came out. After several tries, he said, "With this gun you got to build up the pressure." He placed a finger over the squirt hole and squeezed several times, and when he pulled his finger away, a sparkling yellow stream shot out. The dog dashed over to it and immediately conquered it, looking up at Denny the entire time.

"Sometimes I squirt it up a tree trunk," Sparky said, "out of his reach, to see how high he can cock his back leg. He tries so hard he falls over. Damn, I shoulda done it this time. Stick around, Homer. He'll have another wad in an hour or two."

Tempting as the proposition was, Denny had had enough of life at Sparky's. "Can you see if Nick left his keys in the ignition?"

Sparky dragged the dog over to the police car and looked in the driver's window. "Bingo," he said. "You ain't gonna try to move it, are you?"

Denny swung his car door open. "Why not?"

Sparky grinned. "No reason." He lit a cigarette and waited for Denny to get out and come to Nick's car. Denny, in turn, waited for Sparky to walk away with the dog. Sparky finally wandered up the driveway, but he looked back with interest as Denny got out, opened Nick's door, and turned the key. The wail of the car siren filled the forest. Denny searched in vain for the siren switch. He turned off the ignition and removed the key, but still it wailed. He looked up. Sparky was hunched over, hands on knees, so dramatic in his laughter that he looked like a silent film actor guffawing.

Lance stormed out of the house. He opened the passenger door, leaned in, and threw a switch under the dashboard.

"Don't act mad," Denny said in the sudden silence. "Don't act mad when you're really happy."

"Happy?" Lance said. *"Happy?"*

"You're happy you have a reason to yell at me."

Lance scowled at Denny's hypothesis. "What do you think you're doing?"

Denny explained that he was trying to move the car so that he could leave. Lance began to walk around the front of it but suddenly spotted Sparky with his gun and came to a dead stop. Sparky grinned and twirled the revolver. "I got the drop on ya', Detective. I got the drop on ya'." He raised it, put his finger over the end to build up the pressure, and fired a yellow stream toward Lance, though it fell well short. Lance muttered something—Denny wasn't sure, but it might have been "fucking circus"—as he came around to the driver's door. Denny had begun to get out, and Lance yanked the door while Denny's hand was still around the handle. This created the impression of resistance, and Lance glared at him, wide-eyed with disbelief. Denny hurried to the Rambler. Lance pulled Nick's car up the driveway a short distance and got out.

Denny could now drive forward, but Lance held a hand up for him to stop. He leaned down to Denny's window. "When you were waiting for your so-called friend at the airport, how did you get by security?"

"Come again?" Denny immediately saw that he was doomed.

"You gave us the impression at the airport that you had just landed, so we didn't question your presence. But now you say you arrived a few days before that and returned to the airport. But you were in the gate area."

"That's right," Denny said. He had no explanation whatsoever. He looked at the seat to his right. The pie plate was empty.

"How did you get by airport security without a ticket?"

There it was. Without a ticket. Lance was a fool for building an escape clause into the language of his inquisition. "I spent two nights at the Econolodge," Denny said, polishing his answer with delay—polishing, polishing. "I wasn't sure if I was up to returning home. There were a lot of personal issues—I don't need to get into them right now, but I'd be happy to sometime. I finally decided I couldn't do it. I bought a ticket to go back to Florida, and that's why I was in the gate area. I was waiting for my flight. But then Nick saw me, and we talked, and I was overcome by his warm welcome. I saw I was among friends. Long story short, I decided to stay after all."

Lance was scowling long before Denny finished. "What about your bags?"

"What about them?"

"You said they were lost."

"They were. Not that day but when I landed two days before, and they were still lost, and so when Nick asked me about them, I naturally said—" Denny stopped talking because Lance was no longer listening. He had spun away and was storming up the driveway, fists clenched at his sides as he headed back into the woods.

As Denny pulled away, he waved goodbye to Sparky, who jabbed a finger at Lance and yelled, "I got the drop on him." The repetition bordered on the compulsive. If the phrase had special meaning for Sparky, Denny couldn't fathom it.

ELEVEN

THE LADY TALKING ON THE CLASSICAL MUSIC STATION FAScinated Denny. He never listened to this kind of music but did so now, on his way back home from Sparky's. He figured it was good practice to be Homer even when no one was watching. The station had just played "The Lone Ranger," and Denny, excited, had honked along with it.

But the lady doing the announcing—Jeez! She talked with a mouthful of smiles, as if her program were a funhouse of hilarity. What was hilarious here? "I can't think of a better way than that overture to jump-start our day." She said it as if she wanted to scream with laughter right there in the studio.

"Faker!" Denny yelled at her.

"There was quite a bit of horn tooting in that piece," the lady went on, "which gives me the opportunity to toot my own horn, as it were."

"Oh, haw haw haw!" hollered Denny.

"Let me tell you about a very special concert series coming up in a few months." She named some musical groups that Denny had never heard of, and he mouthed along in imitation of her, rocking his head from side to side because he was so bored. She wrapped up by saying, "I want to thank each and every one of my dear friends who have helped me in very small ways with this series. It will happen, as always, at the Little Dumpling Farm on Horn of the Moon Road. I hope to see each and every one of you there."

"Yikes!" Denny yelled. He looked at the radio, afraid that Sarah's face would shoot out of it and yell *"Homer!"* at him. She began to announce the next number, then interrupted herself in the middle of it to identify the station, adding, "We're in the heart of downtown Montpelier. Come by and check us out."

"I will!" Denny laughed crazily and admired his grin in the rearview mirror. He executed a U-turn and headed for town. He would do to Sarah what she had done to him when she had shown up at the house. He would shock her. And if things got tricky, Nick had given him some ammo that he could use to throw her off balance. He snapped his fingers to the next piece—violins and a cuckoo bird—and by the time he got to town he knew when the cuckoo was coming and chimed in.

He parked near the main intersection, figuring the station was nearby. Homer would certainly know its location, so asking for directions from the wrong person could get him in trouble. But there on the corner, in front of a bead store, was Two-Tone, the skinny, pink-and-blond-bearded mime who had directed Denny to the cell phone store two days earlier. He had not greeted Denny then or shown any surprise to see him, so it was safe to assume he did not know Homer. He could be his regular informant for directions.

Two-Tone, wearing a combination of Navy pea coat and shiny green athletic shorts, was ardently tattooing a paddleball, moving his lips as he counted the blows. He flubbed a stroke and raised his arms in a wordless rant of frustration. When he saw Denny approaching, he did a surprising thing. He gasped and ran away, streaking pell-mell down the sidewalk, his pale legs flying up behind him. Pedestrians jumped out of the way and looked after him in wonder. One of these, a brawny, square-faced man balancing a massive bag on one shoulder, was still shaking his head as he approached Denny. He grinned and jerked a thumb behind him. "He's my hero," he said. "I want to be like him in all ways." He stuck out his hand, which Denny took. "I heard you were back. What's up?"

Denny went for the truth. "I'm here to see Sarah at the station."

"Right. I just heard her." He pointed across the street. "I'm headed that way. Got to mulch the crabs at the library, and they're holding the new Lakoff for me. Let's cross." The "Walk" signal had lapsed, but the man strutted without hurry across the intersection as if confident that any cars that struck him would bounce off. Denny stuck close to him. When they reached the corner, the man said, "Enjoy," and went on down the sidewalk.

Presumably Denny was at, or near, his destination. He faintly heard someone singing and crying at the same time, and his feet took him that way, into a square courtyard serving three businesses —a flower shop to the left, an antiques store to the right, and a radio station directly ahead at the end of the courtyard. He stopped. He could already see Sarah, thanks to a large window that gave passers-by an insider's look at the studio's operation. She sat in profile and faced a big fat microphone. The crying singer shut up, and she began to announce the next piece.

Denny had a brainstorm and ducked into the antiques store to the right. Ten minutes later, he emerged with a little present—three antique sherbet glasses, frosted in lovely pastel colors. He had never bought anything for a woman before. He felt like his father, who used to grin shyly as he watched Denny's mom open a birthday present. Denny walked toward the large window but stopped short of it by about ten feet.

Sarah looked as she did in the home video: angular and sharp-boned but nonetheless attractive. She looked younger than him, somewhere in her thirties. She was reading a list of programs scheduled for the rest of the day. "Ooh, that'll be good," she said of one. She grinned mightily as she read, which seemed a little odd to Denny. He didn't think the grin was for him. In her peripheral vision she might have seen that she was being watched, but he sensed she hadn't seen more than that. After the announcements, she thanked "each and every one" of her listeners and bid them a wonderful rest of the day. She rolled her chair back. Denny braced himself, but she turned away from the large window to a smaller interior window, behind which another woman sat—the producer, Denny guessed. Sarah mopped her brow dramatically, but the other woman, though she must have seen the gesture, looked away without expression and busied herself with some equipment in a cardboard box. Sarah then spun around as if to greet her many fans watching from the courtyard, but the only one was Denny. He looked at her intently. What would she do, how would she react?

She flinched, but before she could do anything else, the door from the production room opened, and she spun away from Denny. The man standing in the doorway sported a full beard, and he held his chin pressed hard against his chest as if he were hiding a small apple under his facial hair. Sarah performed her dramatic brow mop for him, but he just signaled with an index finger that she should follow him. Whoever he was, he outranked Homer. Sarah abandoned Denny without another glance.

Denny went to the door with the station's call letters on it and entered an empty reception room. From there he looked down a hall and saw Sarah stepping into an office. She left the door ajar, and Denny could easily hear the conversation. It proved to be one-sided. The man—the station manager, apparently—reprimanded Sarah for pushing her concert series on her show. "I've never heard the word 'I' so much from an announcer," he said in a resounding baritone. "I don't want to hear 'I' from you again unless it's an emergency. 'I am having a heart attack,' for example, would be permitted." Denny heard a weak laugh from Sarah. The manager, more calm now, went on to say that perhaps he should have cautioned her in advance about pursuing a personal agenda. Then he revved up again. "But I shouldn't have *had* to caution you. It goes without saying." He calmed down again and said that she needed to be careful about commenting on other station programs. After all, to say one program will be good implies that the one mentioned before or after it might *not* be good. He said he knew it was her first day and all—Sarah interrupted and said "second day," which seemed strange to Denny; why challenge the offered extenuation?—and either because of the interruption or for reasons of his own, the man's voice got loud again. "When you say 'Mannheim school of composers,' it should be a broad 'ah.' And for God's sake the opera is *Ah-ee-da*, with three syllables, not *Ai-duh*. If you're not sure of a pronunciation, run it by Gene. Actually, run everything by him."

Denny heard a loud slap of hands on a desktop that evidently concluded the meeting, but when he saw Sarah emerge from the office, the flame in her cheeks suggested that the blow had been dealt to her face. As she approached, Denny, standing in the middle of the reception room, opened his arms slightly in case a hug was in order.

"*Jesus Christ!*" She nearly spit the words at him. "What were you doing out there? You completely threw me off."

"I'm sorry. I didn't think you saw me."

"How could I not see you? Christ." Her chin shook with fury.

"I'm sorry." Had he already said that? He thought he had, but now he wasn't sure. "I heard you on the air and just wanted to see you in action."

"You made me self-conscious. If I made any mistakes, it's thanks to you."

"Oh? I only watched you for a little while. That's a lot of mistakes in such a short time."

Sarah's surprise at his words was shading into anger when she made her face go utterly neutral, probably because the door from the courtyard opened behind Denny. He turned around.

"Ah, two of my favorite people in the world." The speaker was a bow-tied man who was vaguely familiar to Denny, both in appearance and sound, especially in his presto cadence. He pulled up close. "I've been thinking hard, Homer, very hard indeed. 'Lassus' Trombone'—bound to please. 'The Trombone King'—can't miss. But what better solo to welcome you back to the band than 'The Blue Bells of Scotland'? Or, rather"—the man hesitated, threw Sarah a nervous glance before looking back to Denny, then finally released himself from all restraint—"since no self-respecting trombonist would call it that, 'The Blue *Balls* of Scotland.' How about it, Homer? 'Blue Balls'?"

"Well," said Denny, "considering how long I've been away from Sarah, it does seem apt."

The man exploded with laughter that involved the sound of *r* a lot, a sort of "arahr arahr arahr arahr," and when Sarah joined in, clearly against her will, Denny, unless he was mistaken, heard the same noise from her. He was fascinated.

"Good good good," said the man, clapping Denny on the shoulder. He was about to move on to the station interior, but then he hesitated. "Ah, Sarah, your first day. How'd it go?"

"Second day, actually. I shared the mike last week with Gene. You weren't listening just now?"

"Mmm. No. Had a CD on in the car, I'm afraid." This sounded false to Denny. But then so was this:

"It went really, really well," Sarah said. Denny noticed with interest that the station manager had emerged from his office and stood behind Sarah, a cold twinkle in his eyes. His chin, rather than being pressed against his chest, now stood up proud, and his beard pointed at the trio. Denny imagined him quickly gobbling the hidden apple after his talk with Sarah.

"I'm sure it was a great success. Ah, the good Mr. Prescott." The bow-tied man stepped toward the station manager. "I come bearing the arts calendar, as promised. I must say, I didn't care for the *Eroica* you aired last night. More like the *Erotica*—with Bernard Hijinks conducting." Some snorts followed this speech.

"Down, boy," the station manager said rather tiredly.

Over his shoulder the other said, "Rehearsals start in two weeks, Homer."

Denny waved vaguely. How was he going to handle this gadfly?

But first and more formidably, Sarah. He looked at her. Was it time to leave the radio station? A brusque signal from her answered the question: he was nearer the door, and she waved the back of her hand at him as if shooing him out. The way he bolted in obedience surprised him. She said nothing until they were in the courtyard and the door had closed behind them. Then:

"*Jesus Christ!* What's gotten into you?"

Denny stopped and turned to her. He was surprised to see her stern face suddenly transform itself into a smiling one. Had she been joking? Was she as sweet as she looked right now? He began to smile himself, but then he saw that her focus was on something behind him.

"Nancy!" she cried. "Have you sold your Subaru yet?"

A woman approaching from the flower shop carried a cellophane-wrapped bouquet in her arms, cradled like a baby. "Not yet. I'm saving it for you."

"Such a dear friend," Sarah said, laughing brightly. She gestured to the flowers. "A spring bouquet? They're beautiful."

"Welcome back, Homer," the woman said to Denny. "How about you? Want to buy an Outback?" She raised her hand to stop his speech before he could think of any. "I know, I know. You've got your Rambler. I don't see the appeal, frankly. You must enjoy sliding off the road in winter."

"I like it for the front seats," Denny said. "Because they fold all the way back. So does Sarah, if you take my meaning." He chuckled.

The woman failed to arahr arahr arahr. She failed to smile. Nor did she frown or visibly reprove him in any way. Denny knew that her absence of expression was itself an expression, and that its meaning sat solidly on a bedrock of solemn tradition. The Pilgrims landed on Plymouth Rock just so that this woman could show him this face on this day. She tendered Sarah the flicker of a sympathetic smile and said, "Take care."

As soon as the woman was gone, Sarah surprised Denny with a stomp of her boot heel on his left instep, which was protected only by the canvas of his tennis shoe.

"*Jesus Christ!*" she said. "What are you *on*?"

Denny's eyes smarted from the blow. He suddenly felt as if he were back in high school, where bullies assaulted him without warning.

"*Are* you on something? Some medication from this surgery?"

"Yes, I am," Denny managed to say. "Did Nick tell you about the surgery?" He was encouraged by her interest in his condition, though she came at it sideways and sourly.

"Nick?" She was irritated anew. Denny kept a sharp eye on her boots. "Why would he tell me?"

Denny was at sea. It was time to play the Nick card. "Because you two are pretty tight, I understand. Didn't he get into your pants?"

Sarah threw her hands up and stormed off. Denny followed, but slowly, in order to think and regroup. To his mortification, he realized he had been pure Denny in everything he had said. He might as well have whipped out his driver's license and shown it to her. Why had he behaved like this? Because of his *appetite*—there it was. Simply knowing that she was his for the taking had made him ravenous. But "his" meant "Homer's." If he was going to feed the beast named Denny, he would have to stay in character as Homer.

And he needed to remember that his character had been away for three years, apparently without explanation. Add to that the chewing out Sarah's boss had just given her, and it was no wonder she was grumpy. He needed to be smart, to show some "social intelligence"—that was a term Ruth and Roscoe and the rest of the staff were always throwing at him. He needed to be patient and ride out the storm. Then she'd give him a ride of a different kind!

When he reached Sarah, she was still at the corner. He joined her just as the light changed. She stepped down from the curb, seeming not at all surprised to see him, and he walked beside her.

"I'm sorry," he said. He strained for the bland, sleepy countenance he knew from the videotapes, the Homeric potato face.

She nodded once, briskly. "I have to go to the bank. And I have a lot of catching up to do."

"Yes," he said hopefully, though "we" would have made more sense.

"I'm wrapping up a killer grant application, and I need some numbers from the first two seasons. They're in your computer and I can't get at them because of your goddamn password."

"Sorry."

" 'Sorry' doesn't cut it. I need to get in there *today*. It's been a complete pain in the ass." Her face had gone dark, but as they stepped up onto the other curb and she looked down the sidewalk, the storm passed, and, to his surprise, she slipped her arm through his. Denny was beginning to feel like a prop, but he also wanted to savor the moment. He had been with women, yes. He had had sex, certainly. But he had never walked down the street with a woman on his arm. "On his arm." It made him think of his father strolling with his mother and making her laugh with some little joke.

Sarah suddenly grew animated at his side. She raised an arm and waved at an approaching well-dressed couple and, as they neared, called out their names. She slowed, as did Denny, but the couple did not. They were pleasant in their greeting, and they seemed to give Denny a special look of welcome, but it was clear that there would be no stopping to chat. The clouds re-gathered over Sarah, and she yanked her arm from Denny's.

They pulled up to an ATM machine outside a bank. Sarah rummaged through her pocketbook for her card as she waited for the man ahead of her to finish. Denny looked around and noticed with alarm that the Ethan Allen Hotel stood next to the bank. What if Betsy walked out? She would not see him, of course, but Sarah might say something and force a conversation. That thought gave rise to another: Why hadn't Sarah commented on the strangeness of his voice? And why had she said nothing about his three-year absence? It was as if they had already had a reunion and this was a subsequent meeting. Could Homer have done that—sneaked back for a quickie, then returned to Florida?

Sarah touched Denny's arm and said, "We have so much catching up to do."

Ah. *Finally*. "We sure do," Denny said.

"Tom!" Sarah said, making a passer-by slow down. "Looks like spring is here. Hope to see you at the first concert. June sixteenth."

"Maybe," he said. "Hey, Homer."

"Hey, Tom."

Sarah abandoned Denny and stepped up to the machine, which was now free. He looked to where she had touched him, where her fingers had rested on his forearm. He felt dizzy with longing. It was a force pushing him forward, and he eased his body against hers. He began to wrap his limbs around her, and she leaned forward slightly in response. Was she bending over for him—to receive him, so to speak? There was another movement and a loud *crack*. He staggered backward, and it took him a long moment to understand that the noise had come from the collision of Sarah's skull with his face. She had thrown her head back violently against his mouth and nose. As he touched his lips, probing the damage, he felt an ache of sympathy for himself. It was as if someone else, with their fingers gently exploring his face, were expressing long-overdue tenderness for him.

He heard Sarah now. She was talking fast, saying that she didn't mean to do that, she was always nervous at an ATM, she had forgotten he was there, and she had felt a body suddenly pressing against her, and it had startled her. But even as she said all this, he could tell she was looking down the sidewalk, playing to the crowd again, which this time consisted of detectives Nick and Lance, walking toward them.

TWELVE

WHAT WITH ALL THE HOVERING, IT WAS LIKE HIS HIGHway accident scene all over again. While Sarah demonstratively wrung her hands, Nick came in close to check on the damage. Even Lance showed a response that went beyond repulsion, though his primary focus was on reconstruction of the incident. Sarah helped him there. "We bumped heads," she said.

Nick examined Denny's mouth. "Your teeth seem okay, Homer, but you better get some ice on that lip." As Denny wondered where he might find some, he watched Nick brush the top layer of snow off a low wall in front of the bank and scoop up a clean handful. He packed it lightly with his bare hands, then pulled a glove from his coat pocket and handed it to Denny, giving Lance the occasion to wonder out loud if Denny would be able to get his hand in it.

Denny chose to use the glove as a pad to hold the snowball as he applied it to his injury. He turned to see what Sarah might have to say, but she had stepped to the ATM machine to conclude her business. He closed his eyes and tilted his head back. He listened to the local noises—Nick and Lance conferring, the ATM machine chugging, the cars splashing by in the melting snow. He sent his thoughts back to the impact, then to the moment just before it. He had reached his arms out, leaned in . . .

"I'm Sarah." These cheery words made him open his eyes. He heard "Lance"—terse and manly in delivery—and watched the detective take Sarah's out-thrust hand. He was wearing a turtleneck again, only this one was lime green. Over it he wore a dark sport coat.

Nick still had his eye on Denny. He asked him if he wanted to sit down, and Denny shook his head. "This helps, Nick. Thanks. I'm all right."

Nick turned to Sarah. "So, it looks like you two are catching up."

"That we are," Sarah said with a big smile.

"Must be nice after all this time," Nick said.

"That it is," said Sarah. She looked at Lance. "You're Nick's new partner?"

"That I am," said Lance. His gaze was a silver band of steel running from his eyes to Sarah and wrapping around her head. "And you're Homer's old partner."

Behind his freezing snow pack, Denny thought, *Good one, Lance.*

With a sharp laugh, Sarah threw her head back—Denny stood safely off to one side—and she said, "Not that old, I hope."

"No, no," said Lance. "Not at all." Denny noticed that Lance and Sarah were similarly chiseled. If they tried to kiss each other with their heads aligned on the same plane, their protruding chins would prevent their lips from coming together. He imagined them poised in this frustration for eternity, like doomed lovers in a Greek myth.

Lance was reaching into a manila envelope, searching for something with his fingers, but he continued to look at Sarah. Was he going to pluck out a chocolate for her? The thought reminded Denny of his own gift. He looked for the bag and saw that Nick was holding it for him.

"We were just at Betsy's," Nick said. "She's anxious to see you, Homer."

Denny nodded, hoping it was understood that the snow pack against his lips prohibited a full response. Lance pulled a glossy photo from the envelope and wordlessly handed it to him. It was a picture of Dennis Braintree, person of interest in the disappearance and now death of Marge Plongeur. Roscoe must have provided the photo. It was the original for the small image that ran with Denny's features in *The Fearless Modeler*. Fortunately, it bore little resemblance to him. Like his driver's license photo, it had been taken during Denny's experimental light period three years earlier. It was a poor likeness for another reason as well. The photographer, being "creative," had positioned Denny unnaturally, angling his head downward forty-five degrees and directing him to look up with an impish smirk.

"Who's this?" Denny said.

"The guy who was with the victim," said Lance. He punched a finger at the Ethan Allen Hotel. "Right up there."

"We were showing it to the staff," Nick said. He looked at Sarah. "Did you see the paper this morning—the story about Marge Plongeur?"

"No. What happened?"

"She disappeared the night before last, and today she turned up dead."

"Dead?" said Sarah.

"Actually, Sparky's involved."

"Sparky?" She said the name with more horror than she had said "dead."

"She fell from the top floor and landed in Sparky's truck. It was parked under the balcony." Nick could have added that Homer had been the driver. Instead, he threw Denny a wink.

"Oh, God," Sarah said.

Nick turned to Lance. "Sparky's Sarah's cousin."

Lance looked hard at Sarah. "I don't see the resemblance."

"I *hope* not," Sarah said with a laugh—which, out of respect for Marge, she cut short. She turned to Nick. "How did it happen?"

"We're sorting it out. Did you know her?"

Denny awaited her answer with interest. Another dear friend, perhaps? "Not really," she said with a little frown. "Where is she now? I mean where's her body?"

"With the Medical Examiner," Nick said.

"She just . . . fell into his truck?"

"That's right."

Sarah shook her head. "That's so Sparky."

Nick turned to Lance. "You know how you sometimes see geese flying the wrong way, like going north in the fall? Sarah's side of the family calls them 'Sparkies.'"

"Actually, they're not going the wrong way," said Lance. "They're regrouping." He turned to Sarah. "But I like that. I like it a lot."

Nick shrugged off his defeat in the arena of goose ethology and looked at the photo still in Denny's hands. "Anyway, Marge's last moments were probably with this guy."

Sarah stepped over to Denny and pulled the photo toward her. He held on to one edge of it as she studied it. "What a doofus," she said.

Denny jerked it away and extended it to Lance, who was watching him closely. "I hope you find him and clear this up," Denny said.

"Look at it again," Lance said.

Denny did. "Am I supposed to see something?"

"Does he look familiar?"

Denny braced himself. "Not really."

"He should. You know him. You talked with him."

"Oh?" This made no sense, but it was good news. At least Lance was not pursuing any perceived resemblance between the photo and Denny.

"Betsy said you talked with him at the airport."

Denny nodded, buying time. "You" in this context was Homer; "him" was Denny. Ah: Denny, when he had phoned Betsy (as Denny), had told her he had chatted with her nephew at the airport; if Denny talked with Homer, it followed that Homer talked with Denny. How strange that this fabrication was circling back from this unexpected source. It was like seeing a looping train that you had forgotten about re-appear from behind a foam-board mountain.

"We *did* talk," Denny said slowly. He realized that the coincidence should have a staggering effect on him, so he staggered backward a step. "I can't believe that I talked to the very same guy you're looking for."

"Did he say where he was going?" Lance had taken out his notebook. This was now police business.

"No."

"What did you talk about?"

"I was keyed up about being back in Vermont. We talked about that."

Nick jumped in. "How did the two of you happen to start talking?"

Homer the Phlegmatic frowned. He sighed. He finally said, as torpidly as possible, "We were sitting near the baggage office. He was killing time before his flight. I was trying to track down my bags."

Lance said, "Did he say anything about his activities the night before?"

Denny took his time answering. "No."

Nick said, "Did he mention anyone he knew in Burlington?"

Long pause. "I did most of the talking."

Sarah made a tiny mirth noise that seemed to say it must have been a scintillating conversation. Lance smiled at her. Nick looked curiously back and forth between the two of them, then at Denny.

"Nick asked about Burlington," Lance said, "because *ostensibly* the creep is there. *Ostensibly.*" He seemed to like this word. He now stood with his legs slightly spread and his hands on his hips, which flared his jacket to each side and exposed his flat abdomen. "Yesterday the creep left his cell phone at Marvin's French Fries on Williston Road, and he shopped at a Shaw's there with his company credit card and made an ATM withdrawal. But Nick and I part company on the interpretation." With these words he moved toward Sarah, partly blocking Nick out. "The creep left his fingerprints all over Burlington, and that tells me that Burlington is the one place he's *not.*"

"Maybe he's just not very bright," Nick said.

"He's no dummy," Lance said. "He might be a doofus, but he's no dummy." This produced sparkling laughter from Sarah, a surprisingly delightful tinkle. "Get this," Lance went on. "We tracked his movements the day before he was with Marge. He'd been doing some work for a magazine—he writes about toy trains, for God's sake—and on his way to a meeting he stopped at the Ben and Jerry's factory. He got thrown out of the tour."

Sarah laughed. "Why?"

"He got worked up about some flavor they stopped making."

Nick said, "Wavy Gravy."

Lance said, "You familiar with it, Homer?" He might as well have called him "Lard-ass."

"No," Denny said.

"So I assume he's from away?" Sarah said.

"Chicago," Lance said. "A suburb called Downer's Grove. That's where he lives now, anyway. He grew up in a circus. His parents were clowns, of all things, and they dragged him all over. They're both in clown heaven, but I'm trying to reach an aunt of his who lives down south—a twin sister of his mom's. She was a clown, too, but with a different circus. Hell of a family."

Sarah laughed. "Sounds like he's from *way* away."

"You got that right," Lance said. "Anyway, we're hoping this aunt knows of his whereabouts." His cell phone rang and he whipped it from his jacket pocket and turned away to take the call.

How strange, Denny thought, to see this chiseled, turtlenecked monkey swing all over his family tree, fouling his loved ones with these careless, contemptuous references. Denny could not imagine a more unfair representation of his childhood.

"Is that a good likeness of him, Homer, based on your meeting?" Nick gestured to the photo, still in Denny's hands. "We were told he's large, but he doesn't look that big to me."

"It's dead-on," Denny said. "He even holds his head in this screwy way, facing down, with his eyeballs rolling up at you. That's him, all right."

"Good." Nick took the photo. "The Macalesters might have seen him at the hotel. We're going to scoot up to Hardwick and show it to them."

"No we're not," Lance announced as he snapped his cell phone shut. "The creep's right here. In Montpelier." He paused for a beat: his theory had been proven correct. "The street freak who gave us the description just saw him again, at State and Main. Actually, he didn't *just* see him. The freak ran all the way to Cumby's before he stopped to call 911." Lance favored Sarah with a goodbye smile. He jabbed a finger at Denny. "Homer, let's hope that lip doesn't fatten up any worse than it already is." He broke into a backward trot down the sidewalk, then whirled and ran with surprising speed.

Nick sighed, started to follow, then came back and handed Denny the antiques store bag. "Stop in and see Betsy."

"Right." Denny gave him his glove back and watched him hurry after Lance. He turned to Sarah. "Did I do anything wrong?"

"What do you mean?"

"I'm always doing something wrong and you're always punishing me. Let's get it over with."

She made a guttural noise. "Did you see some shrink in Florida? Or go through some flaky program?"

"You'll probably want to change your panties after that chat with Lance."

She glared at him. "That's the most disgusting thing I've ever heard. I don't know who you are or what you've become. You don't even *sound* like yourself. Right now I just need one thing from you, and that's those computer files."

Denny shrugged. "How soon do you need them?"

"*How soon?*" Sarah struggled to rein herself in. "I said I want them. That's all you need to know. How hard can it be? You enter your stupid password—the one you presumably used every day. You can't have forgotten it. I'm coming up later."

"When?"

She threw her hands up. "What does it matter?" Denny felt like a naval subordinate who had questioned the captain's order. "Just do it," she snapped.

"Okey dokey," he said. "But let me ask you one thing. Are you punishing me because I went away without any explanation?"

Sarah laughed so brightly that Denny turned around and looked for a fresh audience that might be approaching. But no one was anywhere near them. By the time he turned back to her, she was on her way down the sidewalk, a spring in her step thanks to his accidental joke. He felt a surge of pain in his mouth. He had set his palliative snow pack on the low wall in front of the bank, and he picked it up. Instead of applying it to his face, he wound up and threw it at her, but it fell well short.

He turned and walked in the other direction, past the Ethan Allen entrance, then darted into an alley beyond the hotel. He circled wide behind the building, heading for his car. Having successfully dodged Betsy, he kept an eye out for Two-Tone. Who would have figured this street person for a crime-stopper?

He remembered a saying he had read somewhere: You're not really at home in a new place until you have enemies.

Two-Tone. Lance. And Sarah?

THIRTEEN

Denny roared up Highway 12 like the Wabash Cannonball. He did his best thinking when driving, and he had arrived decisively at a theory: Homer was nothing but a pretend mate for Sarah. It took a stomped-on foot and a busted lip, but he had gotten the message—*hands off*. If he was right, what did Homer get out of the arrangement? What did she get out of it? And did other people, like Nick, know the truth about it? More immediately, what would Sarah do to Denny when he failed to produce Homer's password? He raised a hand to his mouth. His lip was so tender that it hurt to talk to himself.

He felt vulnerable on many fronts. Lance had exploded his cell phone subterfuge, and how had he learned so quickly about the Ben and Jerry's fiasco? Denny regretted the ruckus he had caused there, but he had good reason. He had known that the tours ended with free samples, and he had counted on all of the flavors being available, including discontinued ones. When he learned, mid-tour, that the tasting would be limited to flavors scheduled for future release, he protested. The resulting property damage certainly wasn't intentional. He had simply thrown an arm out to accent a point, and it had crashed into a glass display case full of packages from Ben and Jerry's first year of business—as if packaging were the important point! The next thing he knew, he was being manhandled by a local cop who thought Denny had been seized with "agitated delirium," which Denny came to understand was the superhuman strength ornery people displayed when cops came for them. The yokel must have just taken a weekend workshop on the subject because he used the term over and over to the other cops who showed up. They finally convinced him that Denny was just a big man who waved his arms a lot—an appraisal that gave Denny the rare feeling of being understood. In the end, the officers' prevailing consensus was that Denny was amusing, though not in a good way.

Wavy Gravy. Caramel, fudge, cashews, Brazil nuts, hazel nuts, and roasted almonds. He had last sampled it—through tears—from 1:15 to 1:25 A.M. on April 20, 2004. Some time in the fall before that, his mother, browsing at a general store during a seniors' bus tour of apple country in northern Wisconsin, had spotted what must have been the last pint of Wavy Gravy to be sold in North America. She snagged it, sealed its lid against leakage with packaging tape, and, when she got home, wrapped it in Christmas paper and hid it in Denny's basement freezer on her last visit with him in Downer's Grove. She died a week before that Christmas. Clowns are good hiders, and he didn't find the pint and explanatory note until four months after Christmas, when he went on a late-night snack rampage. Her last act of love! Bacteria must have contaminated it in its melted state before she could get to a freezer, but the next day's explosive diarrhea was a small price to pay.

Wavy Gravy. Mom. They were inseparable in his mind. There had been a lot at stake on that dumb-ass factory tour.

He struggled up the muddy driveway in the Rambler and slid to a stop in front of the house. Inside, he shed his coat and boots and hurried up the stairs to the computer room off the bedroom. The PC sat in an old open rolltop desk that Homer must have customized for the digital age. An upper shelf had been cut out to make room for the screen, and a sliding keyboard tray hung in place of the center drawer. Denny turned on the power and fidgeted until the screen settled down to two icons of ignorant-looking toothy animals—woodchucks, Denny guessed. Next to each animal was a name: "Homer" and "Sarah."

A click on Homer's icon opened a password box. In it he typed "music" and was immediately rebuffed. He went back and, out of curiosity, clicked on Sarah's icon. In her password box he typed "dearfriend" and was rebuffed. He typed "sharpchin" and was rebuffed. He typed "wetpanties" and was rebuffed. Back to Homer. He tried "trombone" and, rebuffed again, laughed at the ridiculousness of trying to arrive at someone's password by deduction. After all, whenever Denny forgot his own passwords, he didn't try to conjure them based on self-knowledge, and he certainly knew himself better than he knew Homer. On those occasions he either kept making stabs from memory or he tracked down his password master list—if he could remember where it was.

Homer could very well have such a list. Denny began to go through the desk drawers, pawing aside pens, paper clips, and other desk clutter. In one drawer he found a small box full of political campaign buttons promoting an Ollie Dumpling, who was "standing for" state auditor. A relative of Homer's? Under this box was a folder of concert programs with Homer's name in them. Another drawer held old letters, most in their original envelopes. Several were from Michigan; a few were from Germany.

One drawer held a folder labeled "Soc. Sec. Card, B. Cert., Passport." Denny examined all three documents and discovered that Homer was born 38 years ago in Randolph, Vermont. Thus ended the separated-at-birth theory that had been at the back of Denny's mind since his assumption of Homer's life, for he knew for a fact that he had dropped into the world in a Pullman car compartment just outside Shreveport, Louisiana, 42 years ago.

One drawer held boxes of new checks, but no working checkbook. Homer had probably taken it to Florida. A rubber band held Homer's check-writing records from past years, one register per year. Denny looked through the most recent one—no surprises, though he did notice frequent and large entries for checks made out to "Little Dumpling Farm Concert Series."

He slammed the last drawer closed. He was done with the desk—the most likely place for a password list, but he still felt confident that he would find one. Unless Homer had taken it to Florida? He didn't take the computer, but he would need the list for access to his Internet accounts. Would it have occurred to him to take it? That depended on how far in advance he had planned his departure and how long he had thought he would stay. He left other important documents here, so maybe he took off in a hurry. But why?

He heard the crunch of tires on snow. The tingling he felt was not in his loins but in his stomach. He foresaw her beating him about the head and shoulders as he hunched over the keyboard and tried to "remember" "his" password. He hurried to the front window of the computer room. It was not Sarah's car, but a brown paneled van. The driver's door opened with a creak, and a man with a floppy-eared orange cap stepped out and walked to the porch. He moved with such a pronounced stoop that his body had to hurry to catch up with his head. A gentle tapping on the door pulled Denny downstairs.

He was a shy one. After a glance at Denny, he looked to the porch floor and said by way of greeting, "Homer."

Denny said, "How's it going?"

"Can't complain. Can but won't."

Denny looked at the windowless van. *Slaughter Plumbing* was stenciled on the side. Did the house have plumbing problems that Denny was unaware of?

"Thought you'd call," the man said to the floor.

"It's been a little crazy since I got back."

"Left a message."

Denny leaned back inside and looked at the blinking light on the machine. "Yes, I see it now. I didn't check when I got in."

"Figured you'd want 'em back."

Denny hesitated. Plumbing fixtures? "You figured right."

"Got 'em in my rig."

"Good."

The man raised his eyes and looked at Denny, but only briefly. He preferred looking at the floor. "Chester's got the runs."

A noise from the van drew Denny's attention. It was a scratching sound, such as a prisoner might make on a cell wall. "The runs?"

"Ate a begonia last night. Nothin' to worry about. But you might want to pen 'im."

The prisoner's scratching transformed into claws of a dog pacing on a metal floor. Denny felt a threatening descent in his own bowels. "That's a good idea. Could you do it?" Denny pointed to his feet, clad only in socks. Throwing this request out was like throwing his body out an airplane. Would the parachute open? Did "pen 'im" mean "put the dog into the pen?" If so, did the man know where the pen was?

"Calvin too?"

God help me, Denny thought. "Yes, yes. All of them."

"All two of them. Okay then." The plumber started to turn away, then hesitated. He now stood in profile, eyes still down, hands stuffed into his pockets. "Shots're up to date." The words fell so far short of being directed at Denny that they could have been practice speech for some future occasion.

"Shots?" All Denny wanted was to be safely inside, behind the closed door.

"Got 'em last week."

"Good. Good."

"Physicals too. Both of 'em."

"Glad to hear it."

"All . . . covered." The plumber uttered these words with the pain of one rending his own flesh.

"Oh, right. What do I owe you?"

"Ninety-six dollars. If it's handy."

"I'll go get the money while you pen 'em. Okay?"

The man hesitated. "And the chicken, I guess."

"Yes, put the chicken in the pen, too."

This brought the man's face into full view. Upon it, wonder was written.

"I'm sorry," said Homer. "What did you say?"

"Chicken." The man paused.

Denny would have to wait him out. It was all he could do.

"Chicken for the boys. Maybe you already mailed the check for that."

"No, I . . . I don't think I did. How much is it?"

"Fifty-five. Like always. Dang it—I forgot to bring it." The man lightly kicked a boot heel on the porch floor—for him, a flamboyant display of unbridled emotion, though it looked more like a dance step. "I'll drop it off later."

Denny eased back inside. He peeked through the small window in the center of the door and watched the man go to the rear of the van and release two black dogs, both on leashes. As soon as they hit the ground, they ran in different directions, jerking the man's arms straight out like a scarecrow's. Then they doubled back and circled him. He untangled the leashes from around his legs and urged the dogs in the direction of the barn. They smelled every square inch of territory along the way.

As he hurried up the stairs, Denny refused to think about how he would handle the animals. He was thankful simply to have survived the moment. He counted out what he owed Orange Cap, drawing from the stash he had acquired the day before with the company ATM card. When he got back to the porch, the man was returning from the pen, walking backwards and talking to the dogs, who were around the corner of the house, out of Denny's view. The man raised a hand and waved goodbye to them.

"Gonna miss those boys," Orange Cap said when he was back to the porch. He stepped up and took the cash without looking at it and quickly stuffed it into a front pocket. The phone rang inside. Denny thanked him and reached for the door, but the man raised a finger to hold him in place. "Gonna dip tonight."

Denny nodded. Skinny-dip? Eat potato chips with dip? It would help if the man produced an occasional subject to go with his verbs.

"Bring 'em in later."

The *temperature* was going to dip. "Right. Thanks."

The machine clicked on as Denny closed the door. "Homer?" It was a man's voice. "Homer?"

"It's a machine!" Denny yelled as he walked to it. In the caller ID window he read, "Boren Electric."

"It's Warren Boren."

"Borin' Warren," Denny said.

"I called before."

"I know, Numbnuts."

"You didn't return my call."

"Oh boo hoo hoo!"

"The damage you've done me is incalculable."

Denny shut up and listened.

"I should have done what I threatened to do three years ago. If I don't hear from you, you'll hear from me. And it won't be pretty." The man hung up.

Three years ago. What "damage" had Homer done to him? And what had the man threatened to do? He opened the phone book and found "Boren Electric." The office was in East Montpelier. He looked up "Boren, Warren," found his address, and took out the county map he had used to track down Sparky's house. He was stunned to see that Borin' Warren lived on a street that intersected Horn of the Moon less than half a mile away.

Denny mulled over his options, pretending that he had several. He could take the initiative and have it out with Warren Boren—but have *what* out with him? Talking with Orange Cap had been hard enough, and that conversation had been amicable. How could he conduct an argument without knowing what the issue was?

A thump in the kitchen sent Denny hurrying in there. Next to the dishwasher, a plywood dog door connected with the dog pen. It was bolted now, but the dogs, as if aware of the imminent "dip," heaved their bodies against it. Denny watched it bulge with every blow. He felt like the next scheduled victim in a horror movie. He shrieked and fled.

Upstairs, he paced in the bedroom. He went to the front window in the computer room and looked out. All was quiet, but he saw something midway between the house and the road that he hadn't noticed before—a pond. It was still covered with ice, but he could see the banks, and all around its edge was a ring of water where the ice had begun to melt. Earlier, under the uniform snow cover, the pond had disappeared into the landscape. The brown field that gradually sloped to the pond was covered with stalks lying flat on the ground, smashed from the weight of the snow. The field was ugly and dead looking. Across the road and up the hill, some hairy, horned animals that he hadn't seen before seemed to be staring at him. They were yaks, he was sure of it. In Vermont? "Yakety yak," he said.

He wandered back into the bedroom. A double casement window next to the bed looked onto the pen. The dogs had given up on the door and were sniffing around. Chester. Calvin. He went back to Homer's computer and tried their names in the password box. Neither worked.

He heard the crunch of tires on snow again and went to the front window. A green Subaru pulled in front of the house—not Sarah's car. Nor was it a Boren Electric van. Of course, it could be Boren's personal car. The driver was taking some time to disembark. *And it won't be pretty.* But a woman stepped out—a woman with some heft to her. Denny brightened. Perhaps Homer had a girlfriend after all—a real girlfriend. She opened the back door of the car and leaned into it for something. Her ass was exactly midway in size between Sarah's and Denny's. She pulled out a cloth carrying bag—wine and cheese? Denny hurried down the stairs.

Whoever she was, they had a history. Denny could tell from her posture when he opened the door. She pursed her lips tightly and gave him a suspenseful full-body smirk, holding it for as long as possible before she burst out of it with a laugh and gave him a hug with a whispered "Homer." He was about to escalate, but she pulled back and studied his face, frowning at his injured lip.

"That *is* bad," she said. "I've brought a poultice. Two, actually." She bent down and took what looked like two cheesecloth pancakes from her bag, one slightly larger than the other. She held the larger one up. "This is a mix of comfrey and Balm of Gilead. Pull back one layer of the cloth and apply the paste right to the wound. It's moist and ready. One hour, once a day. The other one you put on once a day but just for ten minutes."

Of the three people who knew of his injury—Sarah, Lance, and Nick—only one, Nick, would have cared enough to tell someone else about it. This would be Millie. Denny felt an emotional rush in the power of pure logic. He could build an entire life out of deduction.

She hefted the smaller poultice in her left hand. "This one's agrimony. It's what I gave you when you cut your leg." She stepped close to him and gently touched his lip. "I just want to make sure it's not too deep. Comfrey can heal the outside too quickly before the interior bruise heals." She smiled. "I'm glad you're back."

"So am I," he said.

The smile left her face as suddenly as if Denny had cursed her. She looked hard at him, then shook her head slightly and stepped down from the porch. "I've got something else, too." She opened the car hatch and took out two snowshoes. Denny had seen a metal pair in Homer's mud room. These were different—long and wooden. "Remember these old guys?" she said.

"How could I forget?"

Again she stiffened. It must have been his voice. But why did she react so strongly to it? "Your telegram meant the world to me, Homer, at a very rough time. Mom would want you to have them."

"That's very nice, Millie. Are you sure you don't want to keep them?"

"She was always crazy about you." Millie stared at him. "Nick mentioned that your voice sounded different. It'll take some getting used to."

"Is it a good voice?"

"It's not yours, that's all I know. You talk faster, too." With one hand she made a big circle in the air that framed him. "Florida changed you, Homer."

"For the better, I hope."

"I'll have to see." He expected a laugh to follow, but she just pointed to the snowshoes, which she had leaned against the bottom post of the stair railing. "These old guys are great for the big dumps. They blaze the trail, and others can follow on smaller shoes. Mom blazed, we followed." She stepped forward and touched the wood. "She called them 'rackets.' " She took a deep breath. "I have another stop, and then I have to pick up the kids. I'll see you later, Homer."

"You bet." Denny watched her get in her car and drive off. He waved with an excess of cheer. She made him nervous.

He took the two poultices back inside. They felt a little creepy, like prosthetic breasts. He held them over his own breasts, then tossed them onto a chair and went back upstairs to Homer's computer.

Two hours later, he was closer to finding Homer's password only in the sense that he had eliminated a few dozen of the infinite number of candidates. The light was starting to fade. He went to the front window. The wind whipped the trees in the distance. The snowshoes had fallen over—he could see their tips just beyond the front edge of the porch roof. It looked cold out there.

The dogs resumed their banging on the little door. They must have heard his footsteps. He sighed and went down the stairs and into the kitchen. He had seen no dog food in the house—he would have noticed it immediately—but his eye fell on two sticks of smoked salami on the counter that he had bought in Burlington. He got down on his knees and examined the door. It was large for a dog door, so large that Denny wondered if it originally had had a different use. It was hinged at the top, and two sliding bolts low on each side held the bottom closed. If he set the salami down just inside the door and unbolted it and ran like the devil, would the dogs chase him or would they stop to eat? Maybe both—he imagined them eating on the fly as they chased him, working the salami like a freight-car hobo chomping on a stogie.

He had another thought. Instead of unbolting the door and feeding the dogs inside, he could feed them *outside*, as far from the door as possible, and *then* unbolt the door and flee to safety. After they ate, the dogs would try the door again, come inside, and spend the night where it was warm.

As he peeled the wrapper off the salamis, he realized he would need four servings—two for now and two for breakfast—and he cut them in half. What else did dogs need? Water. He filled a ceramic bowl and set it on the floor. He found a tray in Homer's pantry and set the four salami portions on it. Then he took a packaged submarine sandwich from the fridge, along with a liter of root beer and a bag of potato chips. After just a little hesitation, as a reward for his efforts, he added half of a coconut cream pie. He carried the tray upstairs and set it on the bed. With the computer room connecting on one side and the bathroom on the other, all of his evening needs would be met. He shut the two doors that led from these side rooms into the hall, sealing himself safely in the bedroom.

He went to the double casement window next to the bed and worked one of the cranks. The window was stuck from disuse, but it opened after a few bangs. He poked his head out. He was directly over the dog pen door. The two dogs, their heads cocked back, stared up at him. They were at his mercy. What a wretched condition, he thought—to depend utterly on someone for food.

"Poor doggies," he said.

They stared.

The configuration of the square pen was simple. The house formed one boundary, and the wall of Homer's workshop formed the one across the way. A wire fence ran along the front of the pen, anchored at the front corner of Homer's shop and at the house on the side. The fence at the rear ran from shop corner to house corner.

Denny took two salami halves from the tray. He tested his windup in the awkward conditions and settled on a backhand, as if he were throwing a Frisbee. He called to the dogs—unnecessarily, since they watched with unflagging interest. He leaned out the window and flung one of the halves at the far front corner of the pen. It banged off the shop wall into the pen close to the corner. Both dogs were already on their way to it before it had settled into the snow.

"Hey!" Denny yelled. "You!" Oddly, his words succeeded in

stopping one of them—the one who trailed in the race and was therefore open to other offers. Denny backhanded the second salami toward the rear corner of the shop, and the dog dashed for it. Denny ran out of the bedroom and down the stairs. He glanced out the kitchen window—the dogs were chowing down in their respective corners—and he dropped to the floor and unbolted the door. He sprang back to his feet and ran upstairs and closed the bedroom door behind him.

Through the casement window he watched the dogs, having made quick business of the salamis, sniff around their corners. Then, almost simultaneously, they began to trot toward each other along the shop wall. He wondered why. They passed each other, and each went to the spot where the other had dined to sniff around for leftovers. This struck Denny as funny. Then the dogs headed for the door. As soon as they disappeared from view, he heard them banging their way into the kitchen directly below. Then he heard their claws on the hardwood floor of the entryway. Would they come up and lunge against the bedroom door? If so, it would be a long night. He waited, but they remained downstairs. Perhaps they had found a warm spot, a favorite rug.

He sat on the bed and ate in silence, fearful of attracting the dogs if he made any noise. He watched the wind stir the trees through the window. He had the feeling Sarah wouldn't come by tonight; his doom would be postponed until tomorrow. What would he say to her when he couldn't get into his own computer? He was too tired to think about it. It had been a challenging day, starting with Sparky's phone call. He was anxious to get between Homer's sheets. There was something about those sheets.

He fell asleep almost instantly. At one point deep into the night, the squeak of the dog door woke him—the dogs stepping out for a pee, he guessed. A few minutes later, he heard the squeak of their return. He had seen a can of WD-40 in a utility closet. He would spray it on the hinges tomorrow. He saw himself doing it, and the image became a dream that looped over and over, so when he woke from the same noise some time later, he was surprised to hear the squeak, given all his work.

He was also surprised—and disappointed—that the dogs decided the hour was perfect for rough-housing. They scampered and banged against the kitchen cabinets. Denny imagined them practicing their attacks on him, taking turns with the roles.

You be the salami man.

No, you.

I called it first.

FOURTEEN

"DOGGIES!"

Denny, his bare belly hanging over the casement windowsill, hollered down at the dog door.

"Come on, you doggies!"

He pulled back inside and listened. He thought he heard a stirring from below, perhaps from the front hall. If they came up the stairs, all was lost—he would never get them out the dog door. The stirring stopped. He got down on his knees and leaned out the window again. He cupped his hands over his mouth and tried to shoot his words straight down the side of the house.

"Doggies!"

It wasn't working. Even if they heard him, they weren't fooled into thinking he was outside in the dog pen. He closed the window and crossed the room. Gingerly, he opened the door. No dogs. He tiptoed to the top of the stairs. At the bottom, they sat on their haunches and looked up at him—not with menace, but with soft-eyed hope. He was The Provider.

"Poor doggies," he said. One of them shifted, and Denny almost bolted for the bedroom. But they remained seated. He stared back at them. What was scary was their sheer capacity to do harm—their dental arsenal. But that didn't mean they would use it against him. He needed to remember that.

"Outside!" he said suddenly, hoping they knew this verbal cue, but they didn't move. How could he make a noise outside the dog door to attract them? What object could there be on the second floor that was long enough to reach the first?

He hurried to Homer's bedroom closet and pulled out the strange box he had seen there amidst the boots and shoes. It contained an emergency chain ladder of 1950s vintage, judging from the box-top photo of the shirtwaisted housewife happily descending it. He untangled the light chains as he dragged the ladder to the window. He hooked the curved tops over the sill and shook the chains and rungs to achieve full extension. The ladder ended just short of the top of the dog door. He tried to swing it. He had hoped to send it away from the house so that it would come crashing back, but it wasn't rigid enough for that. Then he had a different idea. By grabbing the tops of both chains and snapping them, he was able to send a wave downward that culminated in a sharp slap on the clapboard just above the door. He was getting ready to slap the house again when the dogs shot out as if some evil force had ejected them from inside. They roamed in brief confusion before they spotted him and gazed up in wonder.

Denny grabbed the two remaining salami halves from the plate on the nightstand—he had smelled them from bed through the night—and leaned out the window and gave them the Frisbee heave. The dogs ran to their two corners as if they had been doing it for years. As he hustled to the staircase, he visualized closing the bolts on the dog door and clapped his hands at his success. As a result, he was a little slow to see that at the bottom of the stairs, exactly where the dogs had been sitting, Sarah now stood.

She must have let herself in, and she was looking up at his body—his naked body, fresh from slumber—jiggling down the stairs. He shrieked and covered himself with his hands. He threw himself into reverse, but his momentum carried him a few steps closer to her before he could backtrack. Denny faced her as he stumbled back upstairs, not wanting to turn and expose his ass, but the look on her face was excruciating, so he spun around and scurried on up the rest of the way, covering his front with one hand and some of his ass with the other.

But the dogs! If he took the time to get dressed, they would come back inside, and how could he be Homer in front of Sarah if he was afraid of his own dogs? He slowed, thinking he could lock the dog door nakedly—but no, he couldn't go through with it, he just couldn't. He hurried into the bedroom, yanked on his pants, and rushed back to the stairs.

Sarah hadn't budged. He scampered down and ran past her into the kitchen. Just as he dropped and reached for the dog door, it flew open and a herd of buffalo overran him—or so it felt. He rolled himself into a ball on the linoleum and lay on his side, whimpering. After a moment, it became clear that the dogs weren't consuming him. Rather, they were licking him all over his bare upper body. He lifted an elbow to take a peek, and one of the tongues rasped his nipple, giving him a tingle. He sat up, his back to a cabinet door, and the dogs romped all over his lap. The one who had licked the nipple kept coming back to it.

"Good doggies," he said.

"*Jesus.*" Sarah stood at the end of the kitchen. At the sound of her voice, the dogs jumped away from Denny and shot out the dog door.

Denny took a moment to catch his breath. "I've missed them," he said.

"Did you print that stuff up for me?"

He rose and collected himself. "I'd like to get some breakfast first."

"It's ten o'clock." She was the chef declaring the kitchen closed. "I've been up since five. I need the first three years from the Excel files—budget, program, attendance. Print them up. Email them to me, too." Her cell phone rang and she fished it out of her vest pocket. She turned away from him and sat down in the booth with her back to him. Her end of the conversation was "No." Then "No." And "No." Then "Wait, I've got another call." After a pause, she said, "Well, hi there! What a surprise! But not really." She immediately laughed at her own joke, whatever it was. "I'll call you right back. Don't go away."

Denny eased out of the kitchen and ran up the stairs. There was nothing to do but attack Homer's computer—as in *attack*. He would pull some strategic wires, pour water into it—anything to make it act up and get him off the hook. Why hadn't he thought of that before? Sure, she'd be mad, but what did it matter since she was always mad anyway?

He pulled a T-shirt over his head and sat down at the keyboard. His jostling of the desk cleared the screen saver, and he was surprised to see an entirely new screen before him. It read, "Welcome, Homer."

Was he in? How had he gotten in? He launched Excel and saw the files Sarah presumably wanted, neatly arranged by year. He clicked on a few to make sure, and then he began to print the first three years' entries. As the printer whirred into action, he sat back in his chair and thought. Could he have stumbled on the password the night before and not known it? He remembered reading about some security software that delayed access by several seconds whenever a correct entry followed several incorrect ones, as a check against hackers making rapid guesses in sequence. Homer could have had such a program. If so, then the very last password Denny had tried must have been correct. He wouldn't have known it at the time because the screen would have changed only after he had given up and left the desk. He had no idea what his last guess had been, but it didn't matter as long as the computer stayed on. This interpretation seemed improbable even as he arrived at it, but what other explanation was there?

The printer finished its job, and Denny remembered that Sarah wanted the data electronically, too. He looked for evidence of an Internet connection and, finding none, clicked on a dial-up icon, triggering a modem squawk, a sound he hadn't heard in several years. Once connected, he opened Homer's email program. Luckily its password was saved. The screen read, "You have 421 new messages." Denny clicked on the most recent email. It had come in a few hours earlier—a welcome back from someone named Henry. Likewise for the two preceding, one from a Nguyen, the other from a Fran, both posted the previous day. But surely Homer's email account hadn't received 421 messages in the short time he had supposedly been back.

Denny jumped to the beginning of the 421 unread messages, landing at a spot almost exactly three years prior, when Homer had moved away—and had clearly abandoned this email address. The first several emails were ordinary messages from friends and customers. As Denny moved forward in time, they began to change. Some emails were resendings, with subject lines like "In case you didn't get this." A few asked where he was. Some said they missed him. One customer with a cryptic email name asked about a horn that he'd dropped off for a repair. A college development office reminded him about making an annual contribution to something called The Amelia Fund. None shed any light on why Homer left town because they all came *after* his departure. Denny scrolled back to the beginning of the unread messages. He needed to look at the last emails Homer had read just before he left.

There weren't any. The "In" box was empty of any read emails. Denny jumped to the archived mail and found that screen empty as well. Frowning, he clicked on "Sent Mail." Nothing. It was unlikely that Homer's email program failed to save all these messages. Did he actively delete them? Why? Did he do it regularly in the course of computer housekeeping, or did he do it this one time for a special reason?

"Forty-five thousand," Sarah said. She was standing in the doorway, the cell phone to her ear. Denny kept the email program open. It was a reasonable thing for Homer to be reading his email. "Forty-five thousand," Sarah said. "That's what we need. They'll match. But we need a Vermont donor for the forty-five thousand. From anywhere in Vermont." She was talking unusually loudly, Denny thought, and facing him in order to display her phone prowess. "Forty-five," she said again. "Bye." She snapped the phone shut and stood in the doorway. She seemed to want him to ask what the call was about, so he didn't.

"The data's in the printer tray," he said, his eyes on the screen. "I'll email it to you next."

She stepped to the printer. "Then get off-line so I can get on." She carried a laptop under her arm.

He turned in his chair and faced her. " 'Please'?"

She stared at him. "What?"

"Can you give me a 'please'?"

She stood very still. Then she took her laptop from under her arm and wedged it between her thighs so that it stuck out just below her crotch. "Sure," she said with strange eagerness. "I'll give you a 'please.' " She lifted her hands to her sweater until they cupped her small breasts. She lunged forward and snarled, "Can you *please* suck on these?" She moved so violently that she had to grab the laptop before it slipped from between her legs. She snatched the sheets from the printer and left the room.

Denny pondered this turn of events. He found it hard to view her behavior in a positive light, considering that he had nearly wet himself when she had lunged at him. He had felt trapped, as if he were tied to a tree in the woods and she was savagely taunting him before the kill. What she had done was not the act of a civilized person.

On the other hand, given the sexual component in the gesture, could she have been making overtures? It was an angry display, yes, but maybe she was angry because he had been slow off the mark. Maybe his pretend-mate theory was all wrong. Wasn't it possible that "suck on these" was a reminder of past shared pleasures that he, Homer, had been inexplicably slow to resume? Viewed in this light, the head-banging at the ATM in town could have been an accident after all. He imagined her fretting in the study right now, asking herself what was wrong, wondering what on earth was keeping Homer away from her.

He scooted his chair back. She had closed his door as she had left, and he quietly opened it. His expectations were clearly mixed, because he had a sudden flash of her poised outside his door, an assassin ready to spring. But she was down the hall with her office door closed. He tiptoed. As he reached for the doorknob, he stopped his hand at the sound of her voice.

"Because," she said. The tone of this single word was quite different from what he had just heard from her. Surely no normal human being could switch moods like that.

"Just because," she said.

There was a pause.

"Just be*cause*." She giggled. The girlish delight seemed genuine. But so did the Amazonian lunge. "I knew you would call because of the way you looked at me."

Denny's ears strained.

"I did not."

Pause.

"No I didn't."

Pause.

"No I never."

Very long pause. Denny heard the sound of a chair rolling and a soft bang. He readied himself to run from the door, sensing she was on her way out.

"I'm just setting up my laptop."

Pause.

"So what if I *am* multitasking? I should give you *all* of my attention? Are you going to arrest me, Mr. Policeman?"

Pause.

"And just when might I expect this brutal interrogation?"

Pause.

"Lord, no. He's just a friend."

Pause.

"Oh, you know everything, don't you? Then tell me *how* you know."

Pause.

"More than one would wish." Big laugh. Then, loudly, "Goddammit, Homer, you're still online."

Denny hurried back to the computer and disconnected the modem. It was a good thing he did because she wasn't far behind him. He innocently looked up from his desk as she stepped into the room.

"I'm off," he said.

"Here." She handed him a sheet of paper. On it were printed fourteen numbered tasks. "Do them in order. There's a backlog—for obvious reasons. These are the most pressing problems. The sander's in the car."

"Sander?"

She had started to leave the room and now stopped, clearly irritated by this delay. "For the stage? It's due back at six tonight, but you can do it. Chop chop."

She returned to her study—and to more telephonic spooning with "Mr. Policeman"? Lance, no doubt. As for who was "just a friend," Denny had thought of Nick at first, figuring Lance had asked about Nick because he knew they had dated. But then came "More than one would wish." More what? More weight/size/ pounds/bulk/fat. Homer was the one who was *just a friend*. That closed the book. There would be no instant sex in his new life.

Instead, there would be this:

1. Patch roof over stage.

2. Rewire stage subpanel and replace fuses with circuit breakers.
3. Sand stage floor.
4. Stain stage floor.
5. Apply poly to stage floor (3x).

It went on and on. Carpentry, sheetrocking, plumbing, upholstering, window glazing. Why wasn't "Build atomic bomb" on the list?

In the course of the next hour, considering that he lacked any of the required manual skills, Denny accomplished quite a lot.

First, he determined that the barn roof was way too high and steep for him even to contemplate a repair. This allowed him to check item number one from the list.

His next achievement was to find the subpanel—this after first finding an old *Reader's Digest Home Repair* book from the 1970s in the living room bookcase and looking up "subpanel." The one for the stage was in a rear corner behind a folding screen. He opened the little door and studied the six fuses in the metal box. He was supposed to "rewire" this subpanel, whatever that meant, and replace the fuses with circuit breakers. He estimated five, maybe ten minutes—not the time necessary to complete the job, but rather his life expectancy if he probed the innards of the subpanel. He closed the door and checked item number two from the list.

He knew what a "sander" was. Likewise a "car," and Sarah had said the sander was in her car. She had parked it right outside the barn doors. As he made his way to the front of the barn, he wondered if she had done this because she was thoughtful. No, fool—for speed. *Chop chop*.

The sander's long handle stuck out of the trunk of her car through a gap under the tied-down lid. He untied the rope and beheld the machine. It reminded him of the carpet sweepers he had seen porters use on the circus trains of his childhood, but he soon discovered that it had a few more pounds on it—*more than one would wish*—thanks to the motor at its base. He lugged it through the snow to the barn and wheeled it down the aisle to the bottom of the stairs at one end of the stage. He counted the stairs. He filled the music hall with the noise of six heaving groans as he hoisted the machine, one step at a time, up to the stage. He spied a dark stain on the floor and looked up above it—so far that he staggered backward a bit. The leak up there had caused the damage down here. But elsewhere the stage was also worn and scarred. He remembered reading in one of the laminated articles posted in the foyer that Sarah had found the wood from an old dance hall in New Hampshire that was about to be torn down.

The sander was a rental, and it came with copious instructions tucked into a plastic sleeve dangling from the handle. Denny studied them like a zealot with a sacred text. He plugged the ridiculously long cord into an outlet at the rear of the stage. A sanding belt was already attached to the drum, so he was "good to go," as they said in the building trade—or so he guessed, and he said it several times as he positioned himself behind the sander. He rockered the switch to "On." The sander came to life and bolted forward in a way that surprised him, so he groped for the switch and turned it off. He grasped the handle firmly this time, resolved to use the advantage of his mass to restrain it, and turned it on again. The sander started and immediately shut down—as did a bank of lights directly overhead.

Denny knew he had blown a fuse. That was why Sarah had wanted the subpanel rewired before he sanded. He had violated her task order, but he could work around it. He returned to the subpanel and opened the door. The corner where it was housed was darker now, but he was able to see that one of the six fuses showed the fog of failure. He looked around on the nearby shelves for a replacement, and, finding none, had a different idea. He unscrewed one of the remaining good fuses. This caused a bank of lights at the rear of the auditorium to go out, but he didn't need them right now.

"Clever Hans," he said as he began to screw the fuse into the slot for the circuit controlling the sander.

"*Homer!*" It was Sarah. She must have come in the side door near the stage. He couldn't quite see her. "You couldn't have done the roof already. Where in the hell are you?"

He took his time screwing in the fuse, wondering what he would say to her. Strangely, just as he finished screwing it in, the sander fired up. Had Sarah jumped onto the stage and started it? Had she decided she should pitch in? Was this the beginning of a reconciliation?

These questions were decided in the negative when, hurrying forward from the rear corner of the stage, he saw that the sander, its switch left in the "On" position (oops!), had started up when he had replaced the fuse and restored the flow of power to it. Driven by the whirring belt at its base, the sander now charged across the stage on its own. Its path was erratic, owing to the absence of a controlling intelligence, and a swerve took it toward the front of the stage. It held this course to the edge of the stage and then *off* the stage, its engine now screaming in a higher pitch as if celebrating its airborne freedom.

The leap put Denny in mind of a boy's summertime jump from a cliff. In this case, however, what lay below was not the old swimming hole, but rather an open-mouthed Sarah, standing in the path of the juggernaut.

FIFTEEN

DENNY WASN'T KEEN ON MODELING TRAIN WRECKS, BUT HE suddenly found himself assembling one. The 1891 four-train collision at East Thompson, Connecticut, seemed right for the occasion. He forced it all into a small basement with an I-beam encroaching on one corner. As an extra complication, he added a hobby-hostile wife. The modeler had to fight off the sarcasms she hurled down the stairs as he worked.

This last part was easy to imagine because Sarah was giving him some of the content and all of the volume he needed. She was like a train herself, running over him and then reversing and running over him again. He didn't understand why she was so angry. She had managed to jump out of the way, and when he had hurried down from the stage, he saw that the only damage was to a few seats in the front row and maybe to the sander.

He managed to look at her without seeing her. He used the same distant gaze he summoned whenever Roscoe and the gang went after him, though it had never been so severely tested. Sarah was pure noise, going on about all the things that were wrong with him, all the ways he had let her down. His three years' absence was mentioned—*finally*, he thought—but she focused on his indignities of the past two days: his "gross physical advances," his "sass," his "impertinence," his "spaciness." She had seen some of that spaciness just before he had gone away, she said, cycling back to that offense. She should have known something was up, that he was getting ready to let her down. She claimed everyone was disappointed in him. "But you've let people down before, haven't you? *Haven't you?*" Did he know how hard he had made things for her? Did he? She had to learn to do everything—everything! She had to learn how to use power tools. She had to take a class in how to use a block and tackle. Did he think that was fun for her? Did he?

Denny blinked and stared off to the side. One problem with modeling train wrecks was that they were static. He had an idea, though. What if the model represented three-fourths of the wreck—the moment after three of the trains had collided but not the fourth? The little Norwich Steamboat Express could be chugging along, heading for the disaster in ignorance. Of course, he wouldn't want it to crash, and he didn't want to just bring it to a boring stop. He'd have a remote-control switch, something that would surprise everyone by sending the train off onto a sidetrack, thwarting fate. A second chance.

"You've really let yourself go. What did you do for three years—lay on the beach all day? You've gotten saggy. You used to be strong. At least you had that going for you."

Setup would be complicated. He would need a hidden hatch for ongoing access to all parts of the board. Sometimes his favorite place was under a layout, just at the moment before he pushed a panel up and popped his head through. It made him feel like an underworld god. Pluto, if memory served.

"You might have heard me talking on the phone about the grant." This sentence seized Denny's full attention because its delivery was different. She was no longer driving her train over him. "There's a real opportunity here to move the series up to the next level. But I need support."

"Forty-five thousand."

Her body went rigid. "May I finish what I was saying? *May I?*" She stared fiercely at the sander as if it were a third party in the conversation. "I need seed money from a Vermont donor."

"No."

She flinched and glared at him. "What—"

"I'm not giving it to you. And don't say, 'What makes you think I was going to ask you for it?' Of course you were."

She threw her arms out from her sides. "Who *are* you? Who in the hell *are* you?"

"I'm your human tool. I'm the physical plant. The maintenance department. And the financing. Or at least I have been. Not anymore though."

"What?"

He slapped his belly. "There's a new sheriff in town."

She hurled her body forward and opened her mouth and broadcast a scream into his face so loud that initially he mistook it for a noise coming from outside the barn, like an airplane's howl just before the crash. He thought that she intended to bite his face, so the scream actually came as a relief. He held his ground, calmly sweeping his eyes over the top of her head. At this close range, her hair didn't smell very clean. When she pulled back from him, she had to reach for a breath. There was an air of unpredictability as to what would happen next. The thought occurred to Denny that it was in such uncertain moments that ordinary people suddenly committed violent crimes.

From the darkened rear of the barn came a soft voice. "Homer?" Nick stood just inside the foyer, near the last row of seats, looking like a schoolboy reporting to the principal. "Is this a bad time?"

"You can have him," Sarah said with contempt. She wasn't going to put on a show for Nick. She spun away from Denny and raged out the side door.

Nick made his way down the aisle. When he reached Denny, he glanced to the door where Sarah had exited. "Trouble?"

Denny wanted to approximate the truth. "It's not how I thought it would be."

"Nothing ever is, man. I don't know a lot, but I know that much. You've been away. Give her time." Nick hesitated. "Maybe I should come back."

Denny shook his head and pointed to the front row. He sat in a seat with a missing arm that had been clipped off by the sander. Nick sat two seats over, leaving a space between them. He studied Denny's face. "Are you using those poultices Millie brought you?"

"Not yet."

"Well, get on it or she'll blame me." Nick sighed. "I'm here about Marge. Can you tell me again—"

"Did you find that guy in town yesterday?"

"Nah. And I don't trust the sighting." Nick suddenly seemed more relaxed. "Why would he stay here? Besides, the street guy who spotted him said it was a different guy from the one in the photo we showed him. But we know that's a picture of Dennis Braintree. I hate contradictions like that. I hate the whole job. I'm not cut out for it, Homer. Lance is always complaining that I'm too slow to suspect people of bad behavior—and he's right. Even when I'm arresting someone, I'm thinking, 'I bet he didn't do it.' How can a cop think like that?"

Denny didn't know what to say to this. "Are there any other suspects?"

Nick made a strained face. "Sort of. Mainly because we haven't gotten very far with Braintree. His aunt turned up dead, which means he's got no living relatives, no friends, no job—he was just fired, apparently. He's a loner. He could be anywhere. I'm talking to all his coworkers at this magazine, past and present. Landlords too. I'm tracking down old circus chums of his parents. I want him to be the one, mainly because of where Lance is going with his latest theory." Nick reached his hands up and mussed his own hair, then patted it back down. "Exactly when did you come back to Vermont, Homer? When did you land in Burlington?"

Denny tried to remember what he had told him earlier. "Two days before I saw you there." Nick was about to speak, so Denny added, "Maybe three days. Two or three."

"We saw you at the airport on Monday. That means you came in on Friday or Saturday."

"Yeah."

"Where did you fly in from?"

"Fort Lauderdale." Denny tried to remember if he had identified an airline. Delta? "Through Atlanta."

Nick nodded. "Lance checked the records for Friday and for several days on each side of it, to be sure. Your name wasn't on any of the flights coming into Burlington."

"I flew standby from Atlanta. Could that be why?"

"Your name would still be on the manifest."

"Unless they made a mistake. They'd be more likely to do that with a standby."

"Yeah, but there's another problem. Where did you say you stayed those two nights, or three nights?"

"The Econolodge."

"That's what I thought. On Northfield?"

"Right. But I used a different name—an alias, I guess you'd call it. I was nervous about being back and didn't want the word to get out."

Nick stared at him. "That's a little strange. You're not exactly a rock star, Homer. What alias did you use?"

"I have no idea. Just some name that popped into my head. Then it popped out."

Nick screwed his face up, then made it relax. "You said your bags were lost. There's no record of lost bags in your name at the Delta baggage office in Burlington."

"Wow. That means they lost the bags and the *report* of the lost bags."

"There's also no Delta office of any kind in Barre. You said that there was."

Denny whistled. "This is getting a little Twilight Zoney. I was sure they told me that. Maybe I got it wrong."

"Did you try to go there? Did you try to call them?"

"I've been swamped. I haven't even thought about it."

Nick looked as if he wanted to jump on that, but he didn't. He drummed his fingers on the wooden armrest. "Lance is looking into all of this pretty closely."

"Oh?"

"I won't mince words, Homer. He likes you as Marge's killer."

"He *likes* me? Oh, I see what you mean." Denny tried to absorb this development. Lance now suspected *Homer*? "It's nice to be liked, I guess."

"He's really got a hard-on for you after what the Macalesters said."

Denny wondered who these people might be. Were they the father-son duo who gave him a ride to the hotel after his accident? No, now he had it: the Macalesters were the brothers Sparky had negotiated with at the Ethan Allen on the night Marge had fallen into the truck. Denny knew what was coming next.

"You said you drove Sparky to the hotel that night. But the Macalesters say they saw Sparky drive up alone. In fact he almost hit them when he pulled in. They said you weren't driving. You weren't even in his rig."

"But I was."

"They said you weren't. Just Sparky."

Denny threw his hands up. "I don't get it."

Nick looked disappointed. "Now I know you're lying, Homer. We went back to Sparky after we talked with the Macalesters. He caved. We know all about your little cover story because of his suspended license."

Denny tried to look sheepish. "Sorry." *Thanks for the heads-up, Sparky.*

"Jesus, Homer," Nick said, his voice tight. "You lied to the police."

"But not in a big way. The lie has no bearing on the Marge case."

"How can you know that? Lance certainly thinks it does."

"What are his thoughts? I mean what are the details?"

Nick looked away from Denny. "It would be highly irregular for me to share Lance's theory of the crime with you."

"I know. Go ahead."

Nick shook his head. He laughed softly and shook it again. "There's a woman who works at the Ethan Allen, a housekeeper who knows you, at least by sight. She's from Latvia or something. You know who I mean?"

"I think so."

"She insists she saw you at the hotel on the day Marge died. She saw you get into the elevator. Now, I know what you're going to say." This was good because Denny didn't. "You're going to say Betsy could confirm or deny the housekeeper's story. But Betsy knows you only from your voice, and your voice *is* different. Hell, it's unrecognizable. Lance thinks you checked in under the name of Dennis Braintree, and you ended up in Mort Shuler's room, and Marge came looking for Mort but found you instead, and if all that's true, I guess you can tell us what happened from there." He looked hard at Denny.

"I can't. Because it's not."

"And yet you and Sparky cooked up a story that's a perfect alibi for you. If you were with Sparky in the truck, you couldn't have been up in the room with Marge."

"But it was an alibi for Sparky, not for me. Besides, do you think I would fool Aunt Betsy like that—check in under a false name and not tell her it was me?"

"That seems cruel, yes. But so does not visiting her. Why haven't you gone to see her since you got back?"

"It's personal," Denny said.

Nick laughed. "Somehow I can't imagine that answer satisfying Lance. He'll say you haven't visited Betsy because she would recognize you from your voice as the guy who checked in as Dennis Braintree." He looked hard at Denny. "It *is* a weird voice, Homer. It's hard as hell to get used to. You've changed in other ways, too. I didn't really appreciate it until Millie got home after seeing you yesterday. She was freaked."

"Really? I enjoyed seeing her again."

"Freaked."

"I'm sorry to hear that." Denny tried to look wounded. "Listen, it's a crazy theory, Nick. What would possess me to travel under a false name?"

"You just said you used one at the Econolodge."

Denny hurried along. "Didn't this guy Braintree have an accident? Was that me, too?"

"According to Lance."

"But the trooper—" Denny stopped and proceeded more slowly. "Wasn't a trooper on the scene? Wouldn't he have looked at the guy's license?"

"It gets complicated, that's for sure."

"Under Lance's theory, did I just make up the name Dennis Braintree?"

"No. We know he was traveling in the area. You met him, and you borrowed his name. That's his theory."

"I did meet him, like I said before. But that was after his accident."

"You could have met him before the accident."

"And fabricated a perfect driver's license with his name on it? Lance must think I'm very resourceful."

Nick smiled. "Yeah. It pissed him off when I brought that up. One for the good guys. But it *is* weird that your paths crossed."

"It's just a series of oddities, Nick. I'll take a lie detector test. I'll be happy to do that."

Nick raised a hand, palm out. "I'm only telling you what Lance thinks."

"But not you, I hope."

"I'm looking for an explanation for what happened to Marge—not just because it's my job but also to get Lance off your ass. I'm looking at Braintree. And I'm looking at Mort Shuler. He and Marge had a history, it turns out. There's a chance he came back to the room and found her in a compromising position with Braintree."

"Or Braintree might not even have been in the room at the time," Denny said excitedly. "Maybe he was out on an errand buying condoms."

Nick raised his eyebrows. "That's a somewhat over-specified alternative, but sure, it's possible." He gave Denny a funny look. "So you're arguing that Braintree's innocent? Be careful—Lance will use that against you. He'll say it's because *you're* Braintree. He's going to come after you, Homer. I've seen him at work. If you take all his bad qualities and put them in concentrated form, that's the face he shows in the interrogation room, that's *all* he is, everything you can't stand about him."

Denny tried to imagine himself under Lance's assault. Did they let suspects eat during interrogation? A German chocolate cake would be good.

"He's high on himself right now," Nick said. "Just humming with smugness."

"Top dog?"

Nick reached up as if he were going to muss his own hair again, but then he lowered his hands. Denny imagined someone pointing out the habit to him and asking him to stop it. "People think police interrogation is some sort of Q and A. It's not that at all. It's a calculated invitation to confess. We have all sorts of tricks—we let the guy blame others besides himself, we encourage rationalization, we offer extenuation. We make this stuff up, and then we take it all away after he confesses. I hate it, Lance loves it. He's a genius at it. Think of the worst thing you've ever done, Homer, and he'd get you to confess to it in a half hour. Go ahead. Think of the—" Nick suddenly stopped. He stared at the floor and cleared his throat.

Denny waited. Why had he stopped like that?

"Anyway," Nick went on more slowly, "you can expect a call from him pretty soon. I'll do what I can to help. Probably already did too much. Sure you've changed, but three years is a long time, and everybody changes. I liked you before, and I like you this way, too." He slapped his knees and stood up. "I'll see you around. Actually, I'll see you for sure at John and Rodrigo's party. You'd better be there. I can't do artsy-fartsy without you."

SIXTEEN

After Nick left, Denny wondered what he had said in response to his comment about this party—an event he knew nothing about. He wasn't sure if he had said anything at all. He was too stunned.

I like you this way, too.

Denny knew that he had come to Nick pre-approved because he was taken for Homer. He also expected—from cruel experience—that his friend's goodwill would have an expiration date. But *I like you this way, too*. It was as if a thousand people were waving at him.

The words meant that Nick liked Denny *as Denny*, because for all his intention to adopt Homer's behavior, he was not succeeding. He was fooling people, yes, but not because of successful imitation—how could he imitate a log? With Nick he was Denny, and yet—could it be?—he was not repellent. Take that, Lance. Denny leaned back in his seat, clasped his hands behind his head, and smiled.

Some guy, Lance. His feelings were pretty clear: he couldn't stand Denny in any incarnation, neither as the unseen fugitive Dennis Braintree nor as the large entity personally known to him as Homer Dumpling. Denny tried to reinterpret his entire history in Vermont with himself as Homer pretending to be Denny instead of the reverse, but he couldn't sustain the idea. It was like trying to write by watching your hand in a mirror.

Denny had found it a struggle to invent alibis for one suspect. Now, thanks to Lance's bonehead interpretation, would he have to invent them for two? No, better to neutralize Lance, to make him irrelevant, and that meant solving Marge himself. He was actually in a better position to do that than either of the detectives because he wasn't distracted by pointless dead ends, like trying to find his sad, long-dead Aunt Norma. He also had information that they didn't have. He had met Marge, for one thing, and he knew some things about her that the police might not know.

She was a drinker for sure. Overweight and attractive. Well-known but not exactly popular. Calamity Jane, according to Betsy. Fun, according to . . . Mort? No, Mort hadn't said it. That word had come from the guy down the hall when he had asked Mort to join them for dinner. Mort would be easy to track down, and Nick and Lance had certainly done that already. The other guy was more promising. He, after all, had been with Marge earlier in the evening. She had even said she was hiding from him when she had dashed into Denny's room. Hadn't she said his name? "I like Ike." No—"I *don't* like Ike."

"Ike," Denny said aloud. There he stalled. A common Internet slave, he felt he could go no further in the Ike investigation—could not entertain another single thought about it—without going online first. But Sarah probably occupied the dial-up line now, considering that among her screams this morning was one for him to *get off*. He would have to wait until she had left.

Denny looked at the sander, lying on its side like a stricken animal. In its leap from the stage it had pulled the plug on itself, but Denny saw another outlet in front of him on the stage wall. He tried it and fiddled with the switch. The sander was a goner. He pulled Sarah's list from his pocket. Number eleven was a task he was pretty sure he could perform: "Gum under seats." He set out for the workshop. Surely he would find something suitable for gum removal among Homer's exotic instrument-repairing tools.

He did, and he also found a contraption he could roll around on as he scooted from seat to seat—a mechanic's dolly that Homer must have used to work on the underside of the Rambler. He attacked the seats and, scooting from row to row, was surprised at the quantity of gum he found. But then he remembered from an article hanging in the foyer that Sarah's series appealed to all types of people—"all classes," she had said, and that tactless word had surprised him. Now that he knew Sarah, though, it made sense. He remembered her strong reaction to hearing Sparky's name in front of the bank, as well as her "I hope not" when Lance said he saw no resemblance between her and her cousin. What kind of snob was she—a born one or a self-cultivated one who had scrambled up out of her class?

Another word of hers that surprised him was "coward." This was one of many names she had slapped him with after the sander incident. At the time, in the heat of her words, he had assigned a quick meaning to it—he was a coward for not going up on the roof to repair it—but that hadn't felt right at the time and it felt even less likely now. She hadn't known he had skipped that chore out of fear. What could she have meant?

He heard a noise that made him cease his scraping labors for a moment—yes, it was her car engine starting. She liked to race it violently to tell it who was boss. He had worked through all but the last two rows and was proud of the collected wads in his small plastic bucket—so proud that he completed the job before going back to the house. He dropped off Homer's instrument tool on his workbench and put the bucket of gum wads on Sarah's desk before going to Homer's computer.

He dialed up. "Ike," he said when he heard the modem squawk, and he said it again several times while he navigated to the roster of state legislators. He was disappointed to see no Eisenhowers in either the Vermont House or Senate, but another possibility leaped out at him: State Representative Russ Eichelberger (R.) of Killington. Contacting the man would be easy enough. Vermont was such a participatory democracy that next to each legislator's name was both a home and office phone number.

Denny stared at the wall and gathered his thoughts. Then he dialed Ike's work number. Somewhere along the line, he had picked up Lance's last name—Londo, memorable for its stupidity ("Kids, let's give a big welcome to Londo the Balloon Man!")—and he identified himself as "Detective Londo" to the woman who answered the phone. A few minutes later, a huffy voice came on.

"Is this necessary?" the man said without ceremony. "I've got three numbed mouths waiting for me."

Denny did not like Ike. "Just a few questions."

"You said you didn't want to interview me by phone again. Can't it wait until tonight?"

Tonight? "They're preliminary questions, really. Preliminary to tonight."

"You've got thirty seconds."

"Like Jimmy Doolittle!" Denny said. Then he reined himself in. He led with a question that he hoped would avoid ground already covered and also yield good information. "What kind of mood was Marge in when you had dinner with her?"

"I already told you. She was flying high."

"Like Jimmy Doolittle! Was she drunk?"

"That too. But she was flying high on her future."

"Her future." Denny said this with the deliberate air of a deep thinker.

"Quitting her job? Moving to Brandon? Being with Mort? That was her plan."

"Was it Mort's plan?"

Dr. Ike made a strange noise. "He's happily married. Married, anyway. I tried to tell her that, but she was flying. That's what happens when you win the lottery, I guess."

"The lottery. That's important."

Dr. Ike laughed. "No shit, Sherlock. Didn't you take notes?"

"I'm just thinking out loud. Like Jimmy Doolittle!" Denny didn't actually know this to be the case. He heard another voice in the background and Dr. Ike's response to it.

"I've got to go," Dr. Ike said.

"Okay," Denny said amiably. "We don't need to meet tonight after all."

"*What*? I've already made plans to drive up early. I've cancelled appointments."

"Nope. All done. Bye." Denny hung up. He wheeled the chair away from the desk and stared out the window. He allowed himself one minute to enjoy the image of Lance fidgeting while he waited for Dr. Ike to show up for the interview. Toward the end of that minute, Denny saw a virtue in the cancellation besides its vexation value: Dr. Ike's failure to appear would cast suspicion on him.

Back to the computer. He went to the web site for the Vermont State Lottery, not sure what he was looking for, exactly. He was surprised to see the names of major prize winners posted there. He looked for Marge's name, but she must not have redeemed her ticket. Possibly she had found out about the results just before she died. "I'm a winner!" she had said to Sparky—people blurted out news that way when it was fresh. Denny, still harboring a nagging suspicion of the original occupant of his room, was disappointed not to see Mort Shuler's name on the list of winners. Maybe she had given the ticket to someone else. Her sister, possibly? Denny knew her sister's last name—Hagenbeck—from newspaper stories about Marge, and he had remembered it because it reminded him of the Hagenbeck-Wallace railroad circus. Also, her house happened to be on his route into town. He constantly saw the name on a mailbox—to his discomfort, because at the end of the driveway connected to that mailbox sat Marge's car, the very car he had driven on his condom errand. He didn't know if Marge had lived with her sister or if her sister had simply come into possession of the car. It didn't matter, but he did wish that car would go away. In any case, no Hagenbeck was listed as a lottery prize winner.

Did it make sense for him to look for names besides Marge's?

Could anyone cash a lottery ticket or only the original purchaser? The web site kindly answered that for him: "A lottery ticket is a bearer instrument." The sentence seemed to invite mayhem. On the trail between drawing and redemption he saw a dozen slit throats. Marge could have drunkenly flashed her ticket in the bar, and some stranger could have followed her to Denny's room and made his move when Denny went on his condom run: Marge gets out of the Jacuzzi, hears a knock on the door, thinks it's Denny, opens it . . .

Denny had another thought. The list of winners gave the individual prize amounts, and Marge's prize would have to be substantial if it were as life-changing as she had thought it was, a sum that would allow her to quit her job and move to be near Mort. All Denny had to do was match a big award with a name. It was a good idea, but the largest prize claimed since Marge's death was $4,000—not substantial enough for a lifestyle change, even in this backward state of dirt roads and dial-ups. Clearly no one had redeemed her ticket. The web site warned that all winnings needed to be claimed within a year of the drawing. If a stranger killed her for the ticket, was he lying low? That's what Denny would do. The idea made him excited—knowing you had the ticket, taking it out to look at it, worrying. What if you lost it? What if you fell into a coma and didn't wake up until it was one day too late?

Over dinner, he thought of calling Mort as he had called Dr. Ike, but Nick was already on Mort's trail. If there was strong evidence against him, Denny would learn of it, either from Nick or from the newspaper. Besides, he had already meddled with Dr. Ike, even cancelled his appointment with Lance—an indulgence he now regretted, since Lance, once he heard Dr. Ike's side of the story, might suspect Denny of the Londo imposture. No, better not to call Mort, at least for now.

Later, as he tried to fall asleep, he kept seeing Sarah's face lunging at him. He heard her denunciations, one after another. The shots she fired, though larger in bore, were otherwise like the "suggestions" for changes in his behavior that he regularly got from Roscoe and the gang. What gave people the right to declare that they didn't like you, whether civilly (Roscoe) or homicidally (Sarah)? If this was adulthood, he didn't want any part of it.

He would take life in the circus any day—full of fawning and petting and praise. Everyone loved him, not just his mom and dad but all the performers and musicians and roustabouts who came and went. When they traveled, his mom used to tell him that every little boy dreamed of running away with the circus. "And look at you, Denny. That's exactly what you're doing." He would get so excited that he'd run the full length of the train.

There was that one spell, though, when his world was less than blissful. It was just a few days, but they were the worst of his life. He was seven years old. He was playing with his train set in the dressing room during a show at the Salt Palace in Salt Lake City, half-listening to the crowd's *oohs* and *ahs* and incorporating them into his play, when he heard an *oh* that wasn't right. He ran out, heading for the ring, but he couldn't get past the crowd, all legs and bodies. His dad suddenly scooped him up and explained what had happened. Some trapeze rigging had fallen and hit his mom. She was being taken to the hospital.

Denny's memory of the days following was blurry. But he certainly remembered his mother walking into their coach compartment, leaning unsteadily on his father and wearing a huge bandage around her head. And he remembered her saying to him, "There's my dumpling." He suddenly had her back after losing her. She was different—she had trouble with her memory, and sometimes she would burst out crying for no reason—but his dad said that could happen when people got conked on the head. And Denny really liked one of the new things: the way she always called him her "dumpling." Now, here in Vermont, the joy of having a loving mother flooded him every time he heard Homer's last name.

Denny clasped his hands behind his head. He remembered Nick's friendly words and let them ring in his head until he fell asleep.

SEVENTEEN

Denny often wondered what it would be like to be married. Now he knew. Over the course of the next week, he got a taste of it with Sarah.

Sex, for example. There was sex in Denny's "marriage"—just not with him. Two days after the sander mishap, from overheard phone chat ("My nipples are *still* sore"), Denny shrewdly guessed that Sarah was getting her share. And when Lance showed up at the farm for a lunch-hour quickie the next day, Denny knew for sure who had usurped his conjugal privilege. Denny was in Homer's workshop at the time, taking apart a clarinet to see if he could put it back together again, when he heard Lance's car drive up. He went to the window and watched the skinny detective head for the front steps, beating his fists against his tight abdomen as he walked. Denny hurried to the house, not just to listen to the lovemaking outside the spare bedroom (she: noisy, exaggerated; he: silent, driven), but also to deep-fry a big batch of Twinkies so that he could give one to Lance after his exertions. The offer was declined.

Nagging. This minor fault line of most marriages was the bedrock of Denny's. Incapable as he was of doing almost all of the chores dictated by Sarah, he was a consummate slouch. "Fell dead birch by barn." Easier said than done, m'lady. Denny wasn't even sure how to conjugate the verb. "Trim barn doors." "Mud bathroom drywall." "Re-laminate refreshment counter." He stalled. He complained of pulled muscles and missing tools. And the nags rained down. One order gave him special pause. She had added it to the original fourteen she had given him. "Kill the fuckers." Whatever it meant, Denny wished she had drawn a mitigating smiley face next to it. But far from it—her pen had gouged the paper.

Conversation. None to report. Sarah's speech consisted of commands and criticisms. Denny, a born word man, forgot himself from time to time and tried to chat. One attempt happened after he listened to another nasty phone message from Warren Boren. Fishing for information, he told Sarah over dinner that the pest kept calling and making threats. "If I didn't know better," Denny mused, "I'd say he was threatening bodily harm." Sarah looked up from her haddock, eyes wide, chin at attention. For a moment, Denny felt his fears about Warren Boren were confirmed. But then he got the point. Her expression said, "What does any of this have to do with me?"

Cooking. One day she declared, "I want number six tonight." Denny's hopes soared, even though he wasn't able to fashion a union of two bodies from the contours of the number. "With Italian dressing," she added. Ah—she was requesting a meal, number six. A take-out order, probably. But from where? "It's funny," he said, "but it's been so long, I've forgotten what number six is." Sarah went to a drawer in the kitchen. "Funny?" she said. "*Funny?*" She pulled out a manila folder, slapped it on the counter, and huffed out of the room.

The folder contained twelve meals, one page per meal, with main courses of fish, skinless chicken breast, or tofu, along with a vegetable and salad. Photocopies of recipes from different cookbooks were taped to each meal sheet, front and back sides. Notes had been added, in a small, crabbed hand, entering substitute ingredients (she seemed not to like mushrooms) or issuing special alerts to the chef. All the information he needed was right there, and he could manage the cuisine, though no doubt there would be complaints until he exactly duplicated Homer's preparation. The real question was could he eat it? Denny was a casserole man. Noodles, beef, rice, cheese, sausage: these were the foundation blocks of his food pyramid—and its apex, too, for that matter. He knew how to get just the right browning of cheese topping and the hard-baked crispy noodle. A mouthful of food should contain the soft and the crunchy—soft and hard cheese, or soft and hard noodle (or soft ice cream and four kinds of nuts—but adieu, Wavy Gravy!). Food wasn't food unless it contained the soft and the hard, and not just side by side, like a floppy fish next to crunchy escarole—ugh.

Once, while poaching a piece of cod for Sarah, he decided to taste it. Just a taste was all he wanted, but he couldn't stop himself, and it was suddenly gone, as if the whole fish had jumped from the pan into his mouth. It only made him hungrier, and he had to scoop a little bowl of Coronado Casserole out of the oven for himself, even though it was ten minutes away from perfection. He quickly poached another piece of fish, and it was all he could do not to wolf that one down, too. How could anyone consider such meager fare an entrée? A proper entrée should leave you hurting afterward.

But he cooked number six—and number eight, and number three, all by request. She would let him know in advance when she wanted dinner at the house. She was thoughtful that way. Meanwhile, he cooked casseroles for himself. His apparent departure from custom raised an eyebrow when they sat down to eat, but she said nothing. She was likewise silent on the subject of dessert. Denny capped off every meal with cookies, pie, cake, or some combination. One night he had three scoops of different ice cream flavors, lined up in the three lovely pastel sherbet glasses he had bought for her and given to himself. For that he got a raised eyebrow *and* a thrust of her chin.

About the chin. Daily exposure rendered Sarah progressively less attractive. Her face sometimes seemed stretched tight from behind, as if elastic bands anchored at the base of her ears retracted the corners of her mouth. Her at-rest expression was therefore a grimacing half-smile. She looked her best when, as was often the case, unhappiness beset her and she transitioned into a scowl—but it was only on the way to the scowl that she looked good, and you had to be quick to catch it. He preferred not to dwell on the scowl itself, involving as it did a bunching of her features in the area of her nose.

Sarah had an apartment near town, and her comings and goings were unpredictable and unmarked by ceremony—the dogs gave Denny better greetings than she did. She would go right to her office and close the door, and he might not see her again until she left, if then. He eavesdropped on her phone conversations, which were almost entirely about the concert series, both this coming summer's and next summer's. When she talked about music, she liked to say "roots" and "funk" and "fusion." She always said "top-drawer" and "world-class" to describe performers. And "killer," as in "a killer floutist." Mrs. Malaprop dropped by from time to time: "intensive" for "intense" was a favorite, and after ridiculing a male vocalist for being "too syrupy," Sarah restated her view by calling him "syruptitious." When she wasn't praising or condemning others, she lauded herself: for the quality of her bookings, her ability to economize by paying musicians as little as possible, and her fund-raising ability. Evidently she was closing in on a Vermont donor for the 45,000 dollars of matching funds to fulfill the terms of the grant, which Denny reluctantly found impressive. But such a symphony of self-congratulation! "I amaze myself," he heard her say more than once. The self-regard reminded him of another Vermonter of his acquaintance, Sparky; Denny saw the likeness an instant before remembering that the two eminences were cousins. He wondered about the exact connection—his last name was Sparks, hers was Notch, so someone's mother was involved. Once, probing, at dinner he said, "I wonder what ol' Sparky's up to right about now." The perfect absence of response made him wonder if he had said the words out loud or merely thought them.

She objected to pretty much all noise in the house. The dogs got the message and fled into the cold whenever she arrived. (Denny guessed she was the one behind the no-dogs-upstairs rule.) If he walked around too much, she hollered a quick *shut up* from her office. Once, when he plunked a single note on the piano in the living room, she sang out from her office, "*No!*" It was a melodic "*No!*" that a stranger—and a fool—might have interpreted as playful. Since then, whenever she was in her office, the piano called to him like a Mars bar with a peeled-back wrapper. Play just one note again, the keyboard said, just one. If, when she arrived at the house, his train songs were roaring from Homer's elaborate sound system, she derailed the engine with a flick of the switch. But she never put on a CD of her own choosing, nor did she turn on the radio. Perhaps she heard all the music she wanted to at the radio station. He heard her on the air from time to time, and she made no mistakes, as far as he could tell. She must have persuaded her boss with the apple under his beard to let her tout her summer series after all, because she continued to do it. Denny found her broadcast style hard to imitate until he did it with the biggest smile he could muster. Then he nailed it and filled the empty house with it.

One of Denny's improvers once called him "oppositional." He immediately understood but pretended not to, which was actually kind of oppositional right there. He was willing to admit that he carried the trait further than most. Yes, he *opposed* people's preferences and positions, but he also became the *opposite* of whoever he was with. If you were energetic, Denny would yawn. If you were relaxed, he would agitate. Want to discuss world affairs? Denny would recite a limerick. He knew why he positioned himself contrariwise. It made life interesting. Agreement was boring. This had always seemed perfectly reasonable to him. The Homer in him had gentled this beast, but Sarah stirred him up again. She was an oppositionalist's soul mate. Her steady state at Little Dumpling Farm was a businesslike grimness, as if she were the commandant of a death camp. That attitude, combined with her contempt for every molecule of space Denny occupied, turned him into a big punch toy, a bottom-heavy bouncy man who sprang back happily after every shot in the face. He wasn't just putting on happiness—he felt it deeply. "She has made me the happiest of men," he would say someday on a TV talk show, though he wasn't sure why he would be invited.

Sarah berated him for real slights, to be sure. Yes, he shouldn't have sneaked the broken sander into the hardware store and left it just inside the door and fled. The store was bound to call her when they found it didn't work. Was he *trying* to embarrass her? And, yes, it was too bad that his car got stuck sideways in his driveway and blocked her from leaving for a crucial meeting. (Lance saved the day, roaring up in a police car and whisking her off.) Yes, it was annoying that he locked the door when he left the house, stranding her out in the cold twice. He explained that his Florida neighborhood was plagued by burglaries. "This is *Vermont*," she said, not in the spirit of a proud booster but in the spirit of you're a moron. Her hatred flared high at such moments, but how to explain the constant low burn of antipathy? Denny didn't think it was because of Homer's still-unexplained three-year absence, for there was something seasoned and practiced in her treatment of him.

Despite Denny's ignorance and incompetence, Sarah never seemed to doubt that he was Homer. He could honestly claim only part of the credit. The rest went to her peculiar vision. She never looked directly at him, and she seemed generally blind to entities other than herself. In this, again, she was like Sparky. Denny's errors, because they provoked hostility, actually reinforced his identity as the man she treated with contempt. Denny talked to himself, Homer evidently did not. When Sarah heard him, she said, "Christ, will you shut up? Where'd you get that stupid habit?" Denny picked his nose, as did all mortal men, or so he assumed. Denny perhaps strayed from the norm in that he rolled the extraction between his fingers and tossed it across the room at a suitable hard object, thrilling to the impact. When Sarah caught him in the act, she rebuked him with a hoarse "*Homer!*" But she did not declare him a fraud.

Another blunder, a terrible one: at their first meal together, he sat on the wrong booth bench in the kitchen alcove. He had failed to notice that the other side of the table had a gently curved indentation carved out of its edge. This was where Homer's stomach went—a cracker-jack idea, especially since the booth did cramp Denny terribly. (Prior to Sarah's arrival, he had simply pulled a chair up to the end of it.) When he sat down on the wrong side, Sarah just stood there, plate in hand, until he realized his mistake. After relocating, he made the further mistake of relishing the indentation, fitting his stomach into it like a man happily slipping into tailored trousers.

To reduce the chance of a career-ending error, Denny conducted research. Every closet, cabinet, and drawer was an archive labeled "Who Is Homer?" The bookcases in the spare bedroom showed not just what

Homer had read but where he had gone to college, for some still contained store receipts from Ann Arbor, Michigan. Homer seemed fond of history, American especially, with an emphasis on slavery. One book on the shelf, a transportation history, was familiar to Denny. He took it down, went to the railroad chapter, quickly tracked down the page he wanted, and entered a correction of an erroneous date.

On the top closet shelf were board games to enliven the farmhouse on winter evenings—Monopoly, Sorry, Clue, Scrabble, Boggle. A Yahtzee box filled with used scorecards showed names Denny didn't recognize, along with Homer's. The closet also housed boxed sets of ancient television series. Denny watched segments of *The Mitch Miller Show*, *Your Hit Parade*, and Leonard Bernstein's *Young People's Concerts*. He danced to Lawrence Welk's music—his mother had been known as "The Dancing Clown," especially after her injury, when she took her act in a new direction, and she had taught him all her moves. He enjoyed *The Glenn Miller Story* and *The Benny Goodman Story*, but he stared in disbelief at love stories like *David and Lisa, Dr. Zhivago, Roman Holiday, A Man and a Woman,* and *Love Story* itself. The overriding emotion he felt was embarrassment that Homer was such a sap.

On the closet doorjamb of the spare bedroom he learned Homer's probable adult height—the last pencilled line of a series plotting his growth, birthday by birthday. The record ended at age seventeen, when Homer was 5'11", an inch shorter than Denny's present height. In the medicine cabinet of the bathroom off Homer's current bedroom, he discovered something that gave him a jolt: a half-full box of Accu-Chek lancets and a warranty sheet for a blood glucose monitor. Homer was a diabetic! Denny wished he had known this earlier. What diabetic would eat sweets the way he did? But even this blunder had not betrayed him. The chin that Sarah had thrust at him in reaction didn't mean, "You're not Homer." It meant, "Go ahead and kill yourself—see if I care."

Homer's workshop was all tools and gun racks and business files. The files helped in an initiative Denny undertook after a former customer left a phone message about a possible repair. Denny culled email addresses from Homer's records and created a group list, adding to it addresses from customers who had sent Homer business-related emails early in his three-year absence, thinking he was still home. To this group of nearly 150 recipients, using Homer's email account, Denny sent warm thanks for their business in the past and an announcement that owing to "personal problems" he had no immediate plans to re-open his repair shop. He included Sarah in the mailing, having gotten her address from some terse messages she had sent Homer in those first days after he disappeared. Consistent with her policy to date, after the email went out, she expressed no curiosity whatsoever about his "personal problems." Somewhat to his surprise, neither did anyone else.

There was Betsy to deal with too, who had been a model of patience. Denny finally called her at the hotel to give her the first of his promised updates on her nephew's status. He said that Homer was doing well, he was getting his house organized, and he had taken up model railroading. Denny was surprised to hear himself add this last spontaneous fabrication to his otherwise bland, prepared summary. "Hmph," she said. "He's playing with little trains instead of visiting me?" Denny protested that the avocation had a strong historical base, but she interrupted him and asked if he, Denny, had been in touch with the police yet.

"No," he said guardedly. "I'm still on the road."

"Then I have some sad news that you might not have heard." She told him about the discovery of Marge's body and the likelihood that she had fallen from the balcony after all. Denny made appropriate noises. Betsy said, "It's very sad. I shall always think of you as Marge's last fling, Mr. Braintree. She didn't have much happiness in her life. I hope she had some with you."

"I think she enjoyed the Jacuzzi."

Betsy chuckled, though Denny had intended no humor. After a pause, she said, "Mr. Braintree, about my Homer—did he ever tell you what has weighed on him all these years?"

Denny went on alert. "No, he didn't." Did she know, or was she hoping to learn it from him?

After another pause, she said, "Tell him I'll give him a few more days, and if he doesn't come down here, I'm going up there, Sarah or no Sarah. Tell him that."

"Will do, Betsy." She had spoken with a force that made argument pointless.

Shortly after noon that same day, a mild Sunday, Denny was perusing Homer's old tax returns when he heard Sarah shout an order for him to meet her at John and Rodrigo's at 3 o'clock. This was followed by a slam of the front door. He waited for the familiar punishing roar of her car engine, but instead he heard a shriek and a curse. By the time he reached the front window, she was emerging from the workshop with a skimming net attached to a long aluminum pole. She stomped down to the pond, which was now completely clear of ice, and began to scoop out chunks of something and heave them backwards over her shoulder. She catapulted whatever it was—unwanted vegetation?—into the field, but then, apparently having a better idea, she aimed for the road below the pond and managed to reach it with most of her throws. When she was done, she tossed the pole aside, walked to her car, spit once on the ground, and drove off.

Denny put on a sweater and walked down to the pond. Well before he reached it, as he picked his way through the muddy field, he saw what she had done. She had *killed the fuckers*. They were frogs—mating frogs, some still connected even in death. The ones that had been following their urges at the center of the pond, out of her reach, had been spared, and several of these had since drifted shoreward, and not just in pairs. Groups of three and four were linked in thrashing watery orgies. They were all doing what they were meant to do, and they were happy. Denny knew this as certainly as if he had grown up a member of their colony. He also guessed it from their upbeat chirping noises. He spent the next half-hour combing the field, still soft from snow melt, scooping up stunned survivors with his hands, and returning them to the pond. The ones who had hit the hard road surface were goners. When he had saved all that he could, he picked up the net—Sarah had left it by the pond, doubtless for a follow-up massacre—and he carried it down the hill into the woods, where he tossed it out of view. She would think it had been stolen. It could happen, even in Vermont.

Back inside, Denny went right to Sarah's office. He stood in the doorway and surveyed it. A fake-wood corner station housed Sarah's desktop computer, printer, and fax machine. Long, folding tables covered with forms, brochures, and CDs stood against adjoining walls. A metal filing cabinet was next to the closet door. The walls were bare. He had come to the room with the intention of getting to the bottom of Sarah, of solving her once and for all, but he realized he was already there. He understood her as well as he would ever want to.

Something about the room was strange. It was joyless in every respect but its color—a pastel blue on the walls and an even softer blue on the ceiling. It was the room of a girl. Denny had an idea and went to the closet door. There on the jamb were the same kinds of markings that plotted Homer's growth on the closet door of *his* childhood bedroom, horizontal lines identified by date and age. These pairings trailed well behind Homer's, and the last age entered was an "8." Denny had another thought and went to the closet in the spare bedroom, the one containing the old board games. The Yahtzee scorecards showed several names, but only two with consistency. "Homer"—in a child's print—regularly defeated "Amelia." The girl did win a few games, and those scorecards were decorated with light blue stars. Across one card giving Homer the victory was scrawled, "Homer cheated!!!"

Denny pulled down the other boxes but found no other scorecards. One, a faded game box labeled "Hurry Home," contained not a game but handwritten letters, all signed, "Hanno." A few postmarked envelopes were in the box as well, addressed to Erlangen, Germany. Denny ran his eye down a few of the letters, observed the diary-like nature of the record, and saw what they were—letters home, written by an exchange student who lived at Little Dumpling Farm for the 1987-88 school year. A quick calculation told Denny that that would have been Homer's senior year of high school. The letters were in English, perhaps so that Hanno could show off to his German family.

Denny set the box on the bed and began to sort the letters. When he had them in chronological order, he read them from beginning to end. They told of school sports—Hanno was not modest about his role in the school's soccer victories—Homer's musical skill, and little Amelia's antics on the backyard trampoline ("So komisch!" he wrote, opting for German at unpredictable intervals). The letters compared Vermont and Bavarian farm economies and animal husbandry in more detail than Denny would have wished. They marched through the seasons in the rural northeast, describing the leaves of fall, small-town trick-or-treating, Thanksgiving ("turkey and pumpkin pie—das schmeckt!"), Christmas caroling, skiing, maple sugaring, mud season, the Washington County Fair held on the farm grounds, and the approach of a sad summer farewell. His last letter home concluded, "I shall never forget these genuine, sympathetic people of the land!" Hanno was an exclaimer!

When Denny reached the last letter he realized it was of a different order. Dated April of the year following Hanno's stay with the family, it showed an Erlangen, Germany, address as its point of origin, whereas all of the other letters originated from Little Dumpling Farm. This one was an expression of condolence to Homer's family. Hanno thanked Homer's father for taking the time to telephone him with "the tragic news." The letter did not identify the news, but Denny knew what it was—knew it as certainly as if he had received the phone call. Hanno went on to say that he was sending them all of the letters he had written home as an exchange student. "These letters are a treasure to me," he wrote, "for they tell of a golden age of contentment as I dwelt in a family of perfect love." Hanno seemed to need to sacrifice something of his own that was precious to him to show that he shared in the family's grief.

Denny got up and again examined the dates next to the lines charting Homer's growth. Then he went back to Amelia's marks and dates. Homer would have been eighteen years old at the time of her death, in his first year of college. Denny imagined him, away from home, receiving the phone call too.

He wandered the house. It felt different now that he knew the family had lost a young child. He felt different as well—ill-prepared, unqualified to fake this side of Homer. Luckily, it hadn't come up so far. Nor did it seem likely that it would, not just because it had happened some twenty years ago, but because the house contained no trace of Amelia. Just some marks on a doorjamb in a pastel blue room.

EIGHTEEN

THE STREET CLIMBED STEEPLY FROM THE HEART OF TOWN, and Denny had the feeling that the Rambler might flip over on its back. One switchback was so severe that if he had been driving a very flexible train, the passengers could have high-fived out their coach windows. The road finally leveled, and, working from the invitation he had filched from Sarah's desk that morning, he followed the street numbers to John and Rodrigo's—a yellow clapboard house perched on the hillside.

Sarah stood near the front door and stared at him without expression. He drove by, looking for a place to pull over, and suddenly found a two-car gap in the long line of parked cars. As he eased into it, he heard a "No" loud enough to reach him through his closed window. The speaker, a woman standing on her front porch, shook her head at him with a frown. A sign above her garage read "Take Back Vermont," and she evidently meant to take back this parcel in front of her house. He drove on to the end of the line. As he walked past the woman's house, he found her delivering the same loud message to two women who had pulled their Subaru into the forbidden spot. One of the two—the passenger—was rolling down her window to engage the homeowner, but the driver restrained her, presumably acting in the spirit of her bumper sticker, "Vermont: Keep It Civil."

When Denny reached John and Rodrigo's, Sarah turned and went in ahead of him. She walked briskly between two tall men in the living room, interrupting their conversation and making them stagger back and look at each other with surprise. One said to the other, "Ai-*duh*," and they laughed. But when they spotted Denny, they sobered up.

Denny spoke first. "How's it going?"

"It's going well, Homer," one of them said guardedly.

Denny kept moving. Where had Sarah gone? As he navigated through handshakes, claps on the back, and punches on the arm, he used his quest for her as an excuse to avoid conversation. More than one old friend expressed a desire to "catch up," but without sufficient urgency to slow him. Denny worked his way to the kitchen at the back of the house, opened a sliding screen door, and stepped out onto a large wooden deck that boomed with conversation. Seventy or eighty people seemed to be talking all at once. Denny's eyes went from group to group. It was a vast social complex, staggering to contemplate. If he could get through this party, he could get through anything. He could be Homer forever.

A man to the right was talking about color balancing. A woman to the left was excited about her new kiln. Someone said "open studio weekend." The words "artisanal cheese" floated his way. In the middle of the deck, looking bored in a group of four people, stood Nick. He brightened and gave Denny a wave, which made Millie turn and half-smile in greeting. Denny took a step toward them, but a golden-skinned man with a round, shaved head bore down on him, his arms stretched wide for a special Homer hug. At the last instant, however, the man opted for a handshake. "Good old Homer," he said. "If I had known you were going to disappear for so long, I would have been nicer to you last time." The man's skin was a lovely tone that Denny had never seen on flesh before. His rounded head looked like a honey-flavored Tootsie Roll Pop. "I was a poor host. I barely talked to you at all, and then—shazam! You disappeared. I'll make it up to you today, promise. Actually, when we heard you were back, we decided to give this year's party two themes—'Goodbye, Winter,' and 'Hello, Homer.' John even got a banner."

Denny looked around, overhead, into the trees. "Where is it?"

The host—Rodrigo, certainly—pressed his lips together. "It got kiboshed. Sarah said you wouldn't want a fuss to be made over you. I told her she was just jealous. She didn't like that, I could tell." Rodrigo gave Denny a wild-eyed look, which seemed to make his dome shine more brightly. A group of people emerged from the kitchen, and he called out, "If you're looking for John, he's over on the Manchurian Candidate couch." Denny's eyes followed the direction he had indicated. One of the men on the swinging couch, wearing wire-rimmed glasses and a black ponytail, looked familiar. So did the couch. "I've got to pull something from the oven. We'll catch up later, Homer. I insist on it."

Denny watched him go, then looked around. He had been here before—not in the flesh, but as a viewer, when he had watched the videotapes at Homer's. This was the same cedar deck that Homer, on all fours, had been forced to admire by the other homeowner, John, who was now seated on the ugly floral couch. Honey-domed Rodrigo had been behind the camera at the time—he remembered Sarah, on that very same couch, using Rodrigo's name when he had filmed her. He also remembered that there had been dancing in a meadow at the end of the party. Where did that happen? He walked across the deck. What he saw over the railing was more like the opposite of a meadow. A sheer cliff dropped almost vertically to the town below.

From this perspective, two or three hundred feet above the rooftops, Montpelier looked more than ever like a toy town. Denny gazed down one street, then another, assessing its realism. He admired the accuracy of positioning, the triumph of forced perspective, the surprising elements like the empty lot with an old concrete foundation in it—what a good idea! He liked it that the people on the sidewalks were moving.

"Tempted to jump?"

Denny turned to his lipophobic nemesis. Lance's body-hugging black turtleneck flowed so seamlessly into his ski pants that it might have been a one-piece outfit. He joined Denny at the railing.

Lance said, "I guess falling bodies are on my mind." He pointed along the face of the cliff. "You can see your aunt's hotel from here." Denny leaned over the railing and saw the Ethan Allen, about three blocks distant and partly obscured by foliage. "You have a special room there, I understand."

"My cubby."

Lance flickered a sneer, as fleeting as an eye blink. "Betsy showed me. It seems strange that you would ever want to sleep there. You've got that big farm. All that land."

Denny said nothing.

"Do you think you don't deserve what you have, Homer? Do you have a low opinion of yourself? I would understand if you do."

As Denny pretended to ponder the question, he spotted Sarah working her way toward them without looking at them. She touched and greeted several people as she passed them. One of them tried to return her greeting, but she had breezed on by.

"I ask," Lance went on, "because I can't see any other reason why you would want to sleep in that little room."

Where was he going with this? What did it have to do with Marge?

"Hey, Homer," a man in a cap and overalls yelled from a group farther down the railing. His hands were oversized. He seemed out of place in this crowd. An artist's spouse, Denny guessed. "Edgar and Rose still runnin' those Scottish Highlanders?"

"Kilts and all!" Denny answered. The man guffawed and returned his attention to his group.

"The old Homer humor," Lance said wearily. "Actually, I think it's pretty lame."

"So do I."

Lance's surprise was cut short by the arrival of Nick and Millie. "Damn, Lance," Nick said, "Millie says I never go to a party unless I know a cop is going to be there. Tell her I didn't know your sorry ass was invited." Instead of waiting for a response, Nick reached an arm behind Denny. "Homer, I don't like the way you're standing so close to that railing—just take a step or two this way, will you?"

Denny obliged. Nick's request had not included Lance, who was in equal danger if any existed. Lance's cell phone rang. Denny wondered where he kept it, given his skin-tight garb. Lance quick-drew it from a little Velcro holder on the outside of his left biceps and stepped away to take the call. The farther away he went, the more absorbed he became in the call.

Millie was about to speak to Denny, but Sarah arrived and interrupted her with a "Greetings, all!" The return greetings lacked her brightness.

Millie leaned toward Denny. "How's your lip, Homer?"

"The swelling's gone down. The poultices really helped."

"But your skin looks irritated. I wonder if you're having an allergic reaction." She reached up. Denny hoped she would touch his lip, and she did. "I gave you the same herbs when you cut your leg that time. You didn't react to them then. I don't get it."

Nick beamed and said, "I have an idea." He left the group. Millie turned and watched him cross the deck to a group of three women, and when she turned back to Denny, her eyes were suddenly hard. Without a word, she spun away and walked to a metal circular staircase that led to a patio below the deck.

Nick returned with a woman whose gray hair was braided in two coarse ropes hanging to her waist. She scared Denny, so he welcomed her with extra cheer. "Hello there!" he said.

She stiffened. "Have we met?"

Nick said to her, "I don't think you have. Angela, this is my friend Homer. And this is Sarah." He looked around for Millie. Denny said that she had gone downstairs. Nick looked puzzled, and then he winced and reached up and tousled his hair. But he forged ahead. "What do you think?" he said to Angela. "Is that an allergic reaction?"

The woman peered at Denny's face and seemed not to like what she saw there. "Yep."

"Angela's a dermatologist," Nick explained.

"Very resourceful, Nick," Sarah said with a laugh.

"Nick told me you've been using a poultice," Angela said to Denny. "Obviously you should stop using it." She looked at the cut on his Adam's apple. "There's no irritation on your neck. I take it you haven't applied it there."

"No." Denny didn't want to risk elaboration.

"That's from Homer's surgery," Nick said. "To remove a tumor."

Angela snorted. "I don't think so." When they looked at her, she said, "That's not a surgery incision. The scar is too short, and it's ugly."

"I had it done in Florida," Denny said, as if this would explain everything. "By a Floridian." He was conscious of Sarah at his side.

The doctor squared herself, bracing for battle. "Let me get this straight. You had a laryngeal tumor?"

"That's right."

"Glottic or supraglottic?"

The second sounded more complicated than the first. "Glottic."

"What stage?"

"Pardon?"

"What stage cancer?"

Denny wished he could use her braids to lower himself down the cliff for a getaway. "I'm not sure." He worked up a smile, but it felt feeble. "My attitude was just fix it."

"Right on," said Nick.

Angela turned to Sarah, astutely identifying her as one who would enjoy the mockery scheduled for delivery. "Obviously not a champion of 'informed consent.' " To Denny she said, "A hemilaryngectomy scar doesn't look like that at all. It would wrap around your neck like a necklace. Besides, your voice is perfectly normal."

"But it's not," said Nick. "It's really different. Right, Sarah?"

If Sarah meant to respond, the doctor beat her to it. "Obviously by 'normal' I don't mean the same as it was before. How could I know that? I just met him." She threw her hand out at Denny on the *him*, effectively changing its meaning to *the asshole*. "With a hemilaryngectomy, you always get hoarseness." She pointed at Denny. "His voice is clear as a bell."

"His voice?" said a newcomer coming up from the patio. Denny was so used to pretending to know strangers that he was surprised to see a familiar face. It was the visitor to the radio station, Blue Balls, who said in passing, "If you want clear as a bell, you should hear him on the trombone!"

Angela let out a bored sigh. "I believe my work here is finished." She walked off.

Nick looked after her. "That was pleasant." He took a deep breath. "I have to see what's up with Millie." He headed for the circular staircase. Without a word, Sarah left as well.

Denny was suddenly alone again. Thanks to Dr. Obviously, he felt in real danger of exposure for the first time since becoming Homer. His best hope was that Sarah hadn't gone right to the idea that Denny was an imposter but instead had settled on a less drastic theory—perhaps Homer had *pretended* to have had cancer, possibly as an excuse for his three-year absence. Maybe she was dancing between this interpretation and the imposter interpretation. But even if she was dancing, Denny was doomed, because it would take little reflection on her part to see that his recent behavior had been riddled with anomalies. How could he bring her back fully to the belief that he was Homer, albeit a changed Homer with a funny voice?

He faced the crowd. A few minutes passed. No one approached, which struck him as a little odd. Wasn't the party practically given in his honor? Finally, he walked across the deck to the hors d'oeuvres table. On his way, he heard a white-bearded man say to a gray-bearded man, "Twice? That's nothing. I was tear-gassed *three* times, once in '69 and twice in '70."

On the other side of the hors d'oeuvres table, a woman was going on about some bird she had seen, and a man's voice made listening noises. Denny loaded up his plate with chips and a spread made of refried beans, guacamole, sour cream, and tomato. He turned to watch the crowd and began to scoop big portions of the dip into his mouth with one chip after another, holding the plate close to his mouth for speed. Behind him, the topic shifted from birds. The woman said, "How long were you off the air the other day?"

The man said, "Two hours and forty minutes. A real John Cage moment."

"Wow. Goodbye, listeners."

"Not to mention ad dollars. Plus there's an FCC fine. Prescott was fuming."

Denny knew that name. Prescott was the man who hid apples in his beard—Sarah's boss. He turned around and recognized the speaker as one of the two tall men he had seen when he had first arrived—the one who had said "Ai-*duh*" after Sarah had passed by. Denny circled the table, joined the duo, and asked them point-blank what they were talking about. The woman took his arrival as an excuse to go somewhere else. Did Homer have a bad history with her? Maybe it was just time for her to move on.

The man said, "I was telling Mary about a problem at a relay station. We had almost three hours of dead air."

"What happened?" Denny said.

"An odd bit of sabotage. Some switches were thrown, nothing that couldn't be easily fixed. But whoever did it added some time-consuming obstacles. The saboteur—that's what we've come to call him—broke all the light bulbs and chained and padlocked the access door. Unsophisticated but effective. Sort of a guerilla action."

"Any suspects?"

The man laughed. "He did leave a trace of himself behind." He leaned forward to share the confidence: "He pissed on the wall."

"DNA," said Denny.

"Exactly. If only there were a national registry." The man quickly raised a palm and looked around nervously. "Not that I'm proposing such a thing. It was pretty high up on the wall, from what I understand. A tall saboteur, it would follow." He chuckled, then stopped. "It's not funny, actually. This morning Prescott discovered a wavy line cut all along the studio window facing the courtyard. Someone took a glass cutter and etched it from one end to the other. We're wondering what's next—a brick through the window?"

"Could that happen?" Denny said. "While someone's announcing?"

"Who knows?"

Denny realized he should express more particular concern: "I'm worried about Sarah."

The man raised his eyebrows.

"It could happen when she's in the studio," Denny said.

"But . . . she's not with us anymore. Didn't she tell you?"

"She's not announcing? Since when?"

"Friday was her last day."

Two days ago, Denny thought. He wanted to ask precisely when the sabotage had occurred, but he didn't dare put the topics side-by-side. Good God, he thought. If she was this bad, she was even worse than he had thought. She was bad to the bone.

"So she announced three or four times? That's it?"

"Something like that. Cutbacks. And maybe the fit wasn't quite right."

"What do you mean?"

The man looked uncomfortable.

"Speak freely," Denny said, and the man laughed.

"There was a kind of . . ."

"Agenda?" Denny said. "Pushing her concert series?"

"Oh, there was that, certainly. But something more. A certain indefinable . . ."

"Egomania?"

"No, but now that you mention it—"

"Philistinism?"

"No, but there, too—"

"Testiness? Peevishness? Truculence?"

"I was going to say 'insincerity.' "

"Interesting," Denny said.

The man smiled and frowned at the same time. "Are you two still together?"

"We are as we have always been."

The man chose Denny's word. "Interesting." His eyes roamed the crowd. Lance was approaching, raking his fingertips over his tight abdomen as he walked. "Who's this curious fellow?"

As Denny considered an answer, Lance pulled up to the other side of the hors d'oeuvres table, whipped his cell phone from his biceps holster, and took a picture of Denny. He studied the result, took another one, and went on his way.

"You have an admirer," said Denny's companion.

Denny's eyes followed Lance into the house and through the kitchen.

"So. How was Florida?"

Denny gasped and grabbed the man by the upper arm. "Thank you for asking. You're the only one who's asked. *The only one!* But I've got to find Nick." As he eased away from his puzzled companion, he added, "I hope you don't have any more problems at the station. When did this vandalism happen, by the way?"

"The studio window was damaged late last night. The relay station was messed with earlier in the day, in the morning. Exactly when Sarah would have been on if she were still . . . you know."

"Right." Denny went on his way. The man's face had given away nothing. Earlier he had even referred to the saboteur with a "he." And Denny knew why: pee on the wall. How had she done that? Had she hung from something overhead, like a spider monkey urinating from a treetop? She could have pissed into a jar and splashed it against the wall. The notion reminded him of Sparky and his water pistol full of his wife's urine. Had Sarah borrowed Sparky's idea? Maybe the pistol itself?

Just as Denny reached the circular staircase, Nick emerged from it, looking more careworn than usual. He took a long drink from his beer bottle. "Millie wants to go home. Here's a rule to live by, Homer. Don't second-guess an herbalist by calling in a dermatologist for a second opinion. What kind of idiot wouldn't see that coming?" He made a fist and knocked himself on the head and then belched softly. "I gotta find Lance. He's all hopped up about something." He raised a hand to shake in soul-brother style, and Denny stumbled through it. Nick wandered off, sucking down the rest of his bottle and setting the empty on a table.

Denny scanned the crowd, his mind on the many fires he felt in need of putting out. The Lance fire seemed beyond his control at the moment. What about the Sarah fire? Rodrigo wheeled a gong out of the house and positioned it behind Dr. Obviously, who, having found fresh meat for contradiction, was lecturing to a group. Rodrigo took a mallet from a hook on the gong frame, wound up, and banged the gong hard. The dermatologist jumped and glared at him.

"Time for contra-dancing, everyone," Rodrigo yelled. "A storm's on the way, so we're going to start early. If you want to join us, head for the park. If you don't want to join us, the hell with you." He laughed fiendishly and, for the fun of it, banged the gong again.

People began milling toward a short staircase leading to the driveway. But many of the guests made no effort to move. Among the latter was Blue Balls, whom Denny spied swinging on the couch and holding forth. Was he telling a joke? Sarah stepped up from the patio below, and Denny, inspired, grabbed her by the arm.

"I want to say goodbye to someone," he said to her. "He may be gone by the time we come back from the meadow." He steered Sarah toward the swinging couch. At first she resisted and huffed, but she was no match for him. Rather than make a scene by ripping her arm from his grasp, she succumbed.

Blue Balls interrupted himself to welcome Denny to his group. Denny said, "Down in Florida I tried to tell someone a joke of yours, but I couldn't remember the line about the tenor and the alto—"

"Oh, Lord," Blue Balls said excitedly. "The climax! 'The bartender—' "

"You told it the last time I was here, three years ago, right here on this couch."

"Yes, yes. Here it is. 'The bartender has had only *tenor* so patrons, and the *soprano* out in the bathroom, and everything has become *alto* much *treble*, he needs a *rest*, and so he closes the *bar*.' "

Denny threw his head back. "Oh, that's prime." He turned to Sarah. "Isn't it prime?" She ripped her arm from Denny's grasp and stormed off after the others going to the park.

Denny, hoping he had done his cause some good, followed her and the group she had joined, but he made no effort to catch them. After a few turns in the road, they reached an open field where dancers were organizing themselves. While the musicians tuned up, the caller directed the crowd to form two circles. Denny joined Sarah in the inner circle.

He had a decision to make. When it came to footwork, Homer was a manatee on land. Denny had watched him stumble and grope in the videotape. He had seen Sarah's scornful stares. He knew what he had to do to be Homer on the field of dance. But instead, inspired by his little victory with Blue Balls' joke, when the music began, he chose to be Denny. He had never performed these dances before, but the caller gave good instructions, and they came naturally to him. For all his supposed faults, Denny was a graceful man. He knew how to work with what he had. There would be no handstands or cartwheels. But there could still be delicacy, fleetness afoot, a balloon-like floating on pixie legs. He imagined everyone saying, "Look at Homer go!"

Later, as he drove home, he saw the possibilities. He had already tried to modify Denny toward Homer, tempering him with Homer's bovine passivity. Now it was time to modify Homer in a Denny direction, judiciously injecting him with *life*. The golden mean between the two would produce a perfect social being.

He was still charting his destiny when he stepped into the dark house, so it took him a moment to notice how toasty the downstairs was. A glow from the living room told him that the fire had been stoked. Sarah had left the party before him, he assumed to drive to her apartment. Had she come here instead? But he hadn't seen her car, and it certainly wasn't like her to tend the fire. He heard the jangle of a dog collar from the darkness of the living room.

And then he knew. He knew an instant before he heard the voice from the easy chair in the far corner of the room.

And what everyone said was true: his voice wasn't anything like Denny's.

NINETEEN

He sat enthroned in the corner armchair, his subjects at his feet—one lying on the floor, the other resting a chin on his knee. The light from the entry hall reached him just enough to show a walking stick or cane resting like a scepter across his lap. Was he an invalid? Did he have a bad foot from his diabetes? Denny noted the possible attributes for future exploitation even as he recognized that the game was up.

Denny felt scrutinized when he took off his jacket and tossed it on the desk. Was he taking liberties tossing it like that? It was Homer's living room, after all. For that matter, it was Homer's jacket. He didn't like having these thoughts. He wanted him to go away.

"No," Homer said when Denny stepped to the other armchair that faced the stove. "Move it back first. Sit away from me." He raised the cane from his lap, which turned out to be not a cane at all but a long-barreled gun. Denny grew excited. He didn't want to get shot—he certainly didn't want that. But the gun was definitely exciting. He pulled the chair away and sat down.

Homer turned on the nearby floor lamp, and Denny got his first full look at him. He looked like a worried version of himself. He opened a hand with his palm facing upward—an invitation to Denny to speak. He said, "What were you thinking?"

Denny shrugged and opened one of his own hands. He intended a different message from Homer's, but the gesture must have looked like an imitation. "I saw an opportunity."

"An opportunity?" Homer's voice was deep, but it cracked on the question. "You haven't taken any of my money, so that's not it."

"Oh, no. That doesn't interest me."

Homer shifted in his chair and disturbed the dog resting its head on his knee. It resettled on the floor. "Were you unhappy with your own life, so you took mine? I could have come back at any moment. I *have* come back. What was your plan then?"

"I didn't think about it."

Homer made a deep-throated noise. "You're not serious."

"I've just been taking it a day at a time."

Homer stared at him. "You must be confusing every single person I know. I have a lifetime of history here. How could you possibly fake that?"

"It's working out fine."

Homer stared some more. Denny wished he would stop doing that. Couldn't he say something right after Denny said it? Denny felt like a fleet track runner lapping a lumbering farmer.

"You don't know anything that I know," Homer said. "As soon as you open your mouth, it should be obvious you're not me."

"It's going smashingly."

Homer frowned—again the pause before speech. Denny reached out a hand and made a spinning wheel motion that only deepened Homer's frown. He said, "I take it you stay in the house all the time."

"Oh, no. I just got back from John and Rodrigo's mud season party. I fooled 'em. Rodrigo, anyway. I didn't talk with John."

Homer seemed thrown by the way Denny tossed out these names. "What about other people there? Larry? Anne? Tully? Fran?" His words came out too slowly to constitute a rapid-fire challenge. The man was clueless about confrontation.

"Can't say. I don't remember those names."

"Nick?"

"Oh, Nick for sure. He was the first one I fooled. We're great friends."

"You fooled Nick." Homer seemed crestfallen, but it was hard to tell for sure. Denny couldn't read the emotions on his face. He didn't show a lot of range.

"Millie's got me worried, though," Denny added.

Homer blinked. "Millie."

"She's a tough nut to crack. But she gave us her dead mom's snowshoes. They used to call them rackets. Isn't that odd? Your condolence telegram was a big hit, by the way."

Homer couldn't keep up. He shifted in his chair. "You talk like this is an ongoing operation. You talk like I'm not here."

"I know you're here. I'm not crazy or anything. I meant it as a warning. Millie seemed suspicious from the moment I met her. She's *really* going to be suspicious when she hears your voice. So is everyone else. I told them we had an operation, a hemilaryngectomy. You'll just have to tell them your voice spontaneously changed back. There's a certain dermatologist you should avoid, though. Hey—she's someone I know that you don't. You'll have to catch up with *my* history." Denny grinned.

Homer brought both hands to his face in a slow wipe from top to bottom, then looked at Denny. "Who *are* you? Did you spring up from the ground? Where did you come from?"

Denny could appreciate Homer's confusion on this point. He delivered a brief chronicle of the events that landed him on Horn of the Moon Road—his I-89 accident, his stay at the Ethan Allen, Marge, the detectives at the airport. "Nick thought I was you," he said. "One thing led to another."

Homer was leaning forward. He seemed to struggle to understand something. Then his face cleared and he sat back. "I've been following the Marge case online." He pointed at Denny. "You're the guy who was in the hotel room with her."

"Dennis Braintree." It felt funny to say the name. Like a surrender.

"You're a suspect in her death." Homer adjusted the rifle in his lap.

"Among others." Denny decided not to tell Homer that he, too, numbered among the suspects.

"You're hiding behind my name." Homer fell silent. Denny sensed he was plugging him into the Marge story. "You must have met Sparky."

"Yep. Fooled him, too."

"Big surprise."

Denny laughed and was surprised when Homer didn't. Then something occurred to him. "Do you read the *Times-Argus* regularly?"

"I lived here for thirty-five years," Homer said. "It's hard not to."

"So you saw the story about you being back home. That's what brought you here from Florida."

"Why this talk about Florida? It was in the newspaper."

"Because you've been living there."

Homer shook his head. "I've been in Texas the whole time. Austin."

Denny was so used to the idea that he—Denny—had spent the past three years in Florida that he found it hard to make the adjustment. "Why did everyone think you'd gone to Florida?"

"I have no idea."

"You know, almost no one at the party asked me anything about those years."

Homer's face was more difficult than ever to read. "It's Vermont."

"I know it's Vermont."

"People respect privacy."

"It felt more like indifference. Three years!"

Homer shrugged.

Denny looked at him. "What do you weigh?"

"Three forty. You?"

"Three thirty. You do look a little heavier than me." Before Homer could respond, Denny said, "I know why you went away."

"I doubt that."

"You left because of Warren Boren."

Homer's rich, booming laugh surprised Denny.

"He keeps calling and threatening us," Denny said. "He says he's going to do what he should have done three years ago. I expect him to step up to the porch and blast me with a blunderbuss. Did he chase you out of town?"

Homer's face became lined with confusion. Then it suddenly cleared and his shoulders slumped. He stirred with unhappiness. "This is awful. He's calling about his French horn. It's completely my fault. I feel terrible."

"French horn? What the hell are you talking about?"

"I sent it to a shop in St. Johnsbury before I left. It was a complicated repair. I gave instructions to return it directly to Warren. That must not have happened. The poor guy. He's been without his favorite horn all this time."

"He's stalking us!"

"It's important to him. But I certainly didn't leave because of him."

"So why did you?"

Homer slowly shook his head. Then he threw a hand out toward Denny. "Look at the way you're sitting. I never cross my legs like that." He set the butt of the gun on the floor so that the barrel pointed to the ceiling. He lifted a foot and crossed his legs in the open male fashion, with an ankle resting atop a knee.

Denny held his closed position and, to irritate Homer, bounced his airborne foot in a delicate manner. "I can't sit like that. It hurts my knee."

"Not a very supple fellow, are you?"

"I've got you beat on the dance floor, anyway. You're going to have to take lessons before John and Rodrigo's next party."

Homer stared at the fire. "I don't think that'll happen."

"Why the rifle?" Denny said.

Homer laughed lightly. "You're quite the Vermonter, aren't you? It's a shotgun. I brought it from the workshop—and loaded it—because I didn't know what kind of person you are. I *still* don't."

"Why did you leave?"

Homer stood up, leaned the gun in a rear corner of the living room, and knelt before the stove. He took the poker from its rack and opened the glass door. "I've replaced the logs you brought in with a different stack. You've been burning pine. You wouldn't do that if you'd ever seen a chimney fire. The pine outside is for bonfires. Use the hardwoods for fires in the stove. They're to the left of the back door." The big man labored with the poker and logs. It required little effort, but his breathing was noisy. "Your snow clearance is a disgrace. I almost broke my neck coming up the front stairs."

"It's boring, all this shoveling. How can you stand to live here?"

Homer laughed lightly again. He closed the stove door, hung the poker back on its rack, and eased into his chair with a grunt.

"I left Vermont," he said, "for a song."

TWENTY

"A SONG?" DENNY SAID.

Homer stared into the fire.

"A song?" Denny made the spinning wheel motion again with one hand.

"Stop that," Homer said calmly. "It begins sixteen years ago."

Denny suppressed a groan.

"In college. My senior year at Michigan. I was in the marching band, and it was football season—a crazy time of constant rehearsal and travel. We were on the bus going to Columbus when the word went out." He paused.

Denny almost said, "The word?" But Homer was picking up speed.

"I was sitting next to Woody Schneithorst, a percussionist. He opened his backpack to get something, and he said, 'What's this? A flyer?' Woody was a talker, always verbalizing everything. But he was quiet as he read the flyer. That got my attention. He handed it to me with his eyebrows dancing all over the place.

"The flyer announced a contest in musical composition. Nothing unusual there. We learned about contests all the time. The prize would go to whoever wrote 'the most beautiful piece of music'—kind of a bald statement. There were some guidelines, but nothing about form or instrumentation. Just 'the most beautiful piece of music.' All entries were due by the end of the semester—about three weeks away. Kind of short notice. And there was no identification of a sponsor or a foundation behind it. That was one of the first things you looked for. The field, too—you always wanted to know who you were up against. This one was open only to members of the University of Michigan Marching Band. An odd bunch for a composing contest.

"So all those things were strange. But it was the prize that really set the competition apart. 'The winner will be rewarded with the favors of a member of the April Quartet.' That's what it said. It's the kind of sentence you read twice, and even then you don't think you read it right. 'Favors'? Sexual favors? No, it must mean everyday favors, like doing your laundry or something, but that's ridiculous, so you go back to sexual favors. And your mind runs wild."

"Was it four women?" Denny said.

Homer didn't take his eyes from the fire. "The April Quartet was a graduate student group. They were pretty good, but they weren't destined for greatness or anything. They were actually most famous for their looks—two knockout women, two striking men." He glanced at Denny: all would be revealed in the fullness of time. "When they played, their looks made their music better than it was. They were more than good-looking. They radiated sex. Everyone felt that way about them. It was a perfect group for fantasy because it had something for everyone. One of the women was straight, the other was a lesbian. The same for the two men—one straight, one gay. Four human desires were embodied right there on the stage. When you watched them perform, if it was dull—Brahms, whatever—you would picture each of them with a suitable partner. You just couldn't help doing that. This variety meant the contest would appeal to everyone. In the flyer, 'the favors of a member' presumably meant the member of your choice. It *had* to mean that. It wouldn't be much of a prize if the fit wasn't right."

Denny squirmed with agitation. He wanted to be in a contest like that. Not writing music—it would take him too long to learn enough about music to win—but a railroad modeling competition, with sex as the prize. Why didn't he have that kind of luck?

"The talk on the bus was pretty lively. Flyers had been stuck in everyone's backpack or instrument case—I checked later and found one rolled up in the bell of my trombone. At first the buzz was kind of restrained because a sentence at the bottom of the flyer said the contest would be cancelled if word of it reached anyone outside the marching band. Sometimes we sneaked other people onto the bus, but after a check we saw that there weren't any on this trip, and speculation ran wild. At least for a while. Then people began to stare out the windows. Some had staff paper with them, and they took it out, looking kind of sheepish. By the end of the trip, music was being created, no doubt about it.

"Lots of people thought the contest was a hoax, of course. Most of the time I thought that myself. But in the weeks that followed, people kept plugging away, just in case. Or just for the sake of the music. The whole band was thinking about musical construction. My theory prof complained that students were suddenly changing their term paper topics. They wanted to write about *beauty*, of all things.

"Naturally it would have been nice to know what the players in the quartet had to say about it. All it would have taken to kill the contest was for one of them to say, 'Never heard of it!' But they weren't available. All four of them were in a chamber group in residence in Malaysia for a month. The mastermind behind the contest had timed it for a period when they would be gone. The timing supported the idea that it was bogus, but it could have been a coincidence. Everyone *wanted* it to be a coincidence. If someone had really tried, they could have tracked them down. This was before cell phones and even before most people had email, but there were contact numbers, and they could have been reached. Instead, everyone preferred to believe this bizarre thing was real, that the quartet was willing to use their bodies to commission a piece of music. They were certainly vain enough for it to be plausible. They liked to be looked at—you could tell. In their publicity photos, they were always draped all over each other.

"The winner of the contest was to be announced at the end of the fall semester, on the day after the last final exam. It would happen in the music auditorium. The marching band gathered there—almost everyone put off going home for the holidays to get the results. We waited for someone to come onto the stage and make the announcement. Instead, the room got dark, the number '1' appeared on a screen, and a piece began to play over the loudspeaker. It wasn't a particularly good piece, and people muttered to each other that *their* composition was much more beautiful than that one. But that wasn't the winner. After sixty seconds—that was the limit, the submission couldn't be any longer than sixty seconds —another piece began, with the number '2' on the screen. Then a '3' and another one. We finally figured out this wasn't a ranking from top to bottom. All of the entries were going to be played, and this was just the play order.

"I should explain the format for submission. Entries were anonymous, and there was no paperwork. Just a tape. You could tape it alone on the keyboard, but not everyone played keyboard well enough to do their piece justice. A few used guitars. If you could assemble a group, all the better, for color, but then you had to depend on people playing as well as they could, and since their piece was up against yours, you couldn't count on that. I played trombone for a few recordings, so I knew the temptation. Some people went outside the band. We heard all sorts of ensembles. But most people did it alone on their own instruments, and if they had a recognizable tone, you'd hear their name being muttered all over. About halfway through one piece—a tenor sax disaster—someone yelled, 'No nookie for you, Wamser!'

"We listened to the entries, we wisecracked. At the beginning of every piece, there was complete silence, because you were wondering if yours was up but also to see if you would be moved by the beauty. That didn't happen—being moved—until number eighteen. On the keyboard. Not a peep from the audience until it was over, and then someone shouted, 'Play it again,' and others joined in. By then number nineteen had begun, but the crowd booed it down, and number nineteen came to a stop and number eighteen began all over. The crowd called for it again and again. They would buzz after each playing and then shut up when it started again. Finally after five or six run-throughs they stopped clamoring—they knew the whole program had to be gotten through—and nineteen cranked up again. There were sixty-five entries, and none of the others had a chance. One nice piece caught my ear, a catchy flute ditty. But, really, it was number eighteen all the way."

Homer fell silent. Denny heard raindrops drumming on the porch roof in front. The rain seemed to have come from nowhere, so the storm was a quick mover. Homer glanced at the front window, then turned his gaze back to the fire.

"When it was over, there was a lull. What now? We kept looking to the back of the auditorium, way up high, to the control room. It was dark, and we couldn't see a thing. We could have stormed it and found out who was behind it all, but people seemed more curious about who the winner was, so everyone sat tight.

"Then a female voice came over the loudspeaker: 'Would the composer of number eighteen please step up to the stage?' That's when we realized what was going on. We were not just the contestants—we were the judges, too. The mastermind had trusted us, even in our cutthroat little world, to respond uncontrollably to beauty. There was kind of a stunned moment as we all realized that. But no one went up to the stage. People started chanting, 'Eighteen, eighteen, eighteen.' It didn't happen. The winner didn't want to identify himself."

"It was you." Denny's words rushed out ahead of the thought.

Homer sat. His big face was unreadable. "It was the right decision. It would have been awful."

"Why?"

"You know perfectly well why. You know what they would have thought. *Homer?* With *Juliet?* She was the second violinist in the quartet, and she would have been my prize. I didn't claim her, but I did get to sit there knowing that my sixty seconds of music had conquered this rowdy group. Things kind of wound down from there. Someone jumped up and said, 'It's mine! I wrote it!' and then everyone else did, too. I joined in, and it felt good to shout and claim it. We finally all shuffled out of the auditorium. Some people ran upstairs to the control booth, but it was empty when they got there. In a way, it was a fitting conclusion. It was as if the composer picked the music out of the air and then cast it back. I almost felt that way about it myself, as if I was barely responsible. It was something that came to me, a little flowing line in three-four time. A waltz. I love three-four." Homer closed his eyes. " 'Ashokan Farewell.' 'Scarlet Ribbons.' 'Cavatina' by Stanley Myers. 'Are You Lonesome Tonight?' 'I Dreamt I Dwelt in Marble—' "

A gust of wind threw a bucket of rain at the porch window, making Homer flinch and open his eyes wide. Almost immediately, another gust pelted the window. When he resumed speaking, he picked up the pace.

"The waltz had a little second life after that. Someone had recorded the whole judging event—a guy who always carried a tape recorder with him, looking for 'found music,' and he found a lot that day. People made different mixes from his cassettes. A clarinet player took the waltz and wrote out parts for the entire band and distributed them. She was a whiz at instrumentation, and I liked what she did with it. I would have done a few things differently, but it came out well, overall. Michigan went to the Rose Bowl that year—we lost—and at the end of the game, the band played it for the first and only time. We hadn't even rehearsed it. It was a farewell to the season. The crowd probably wondered why we were playing a waltz. They were filing out, but lots of them stopped and listened. The director was baffled. He just stared at us, and when we finished, he said, 'What was *that*?'

"After I graduated, I came back home and worked the farm with my mom and dad, and then just with Mom after Dad died, and the margins got tougher, and everything kind of slowed down until it was almost just a hobby farm, and when Mom died so did the last of the farming—I'd had enough. I'd opened the repair shop long before then and knew that was what I wanted to do. Then came the barn renovation and the concert series. That was it. That was my life. And it would have been my life to the end." He turned away from the fire and looked at Denny.

"And?"

"Three years ago, I got an email from the mastermind—the woman who ran the contest. She was a graduate student back then—I didn't know her at all—and she explained the contest to me. She said that she hated her composition class because it was so technical, and everyone was writing out of fear of failing. She wanted to create a positive environment, with 'wooing' as the motivation. That word was in the title of her MA thesis, or was going to be: 'The Woo Factor in Composing.' She wanted to recreate the environment that produced great pieces inspired by love and longing—you know, in the spirit of Schumann, Berlioz, and practically everyone, at least in her view. Her plan was to take the best pieces from the marching band contest and the best pieces from her awful composing class, and test them on different listeners. But she never got that far. She had some family problems right after the contest and took a leave from school, and when she came back she wrote a completely different thesis. But my waltz stuck with her."

"And so the April Quartet didn't know about it?"

"Of course not. They're not important."

"This Juliet, she never knew that you—"

"No. Stop thinking about them."

"I can't!"

"Yeah, well, you would have fit right in with the band." Homer began to smile, but another pelting of rain startled him.

"How did the mastermind figure out you were the composer?"

Homer stood up and went to the window. The dogs raised their heads and watched him. He shielded his eyes and leaned close to the glass so that he could see out. He came back to his chair, resuming his tale before he sat down. "She found me with a tune-searching program. You type in a few notes of a melody—you can use the letter keys to do it—and it'll pull up all the web pages that contain that melody. She still had one of the mixes from school with my tune on it, and she worked from that as she typed the notes in. Only one web site in the whole world came up—the one I created for the Little Dumpling Farm series. My waltz greets you on the opening page. She got my email address from the web site."

The lights suddenly went out. Homer stood up again. In the firelight Denny could see him go to the corner of the room and grab the shotgun. He carried it to the front window, set its butt on the floor so that it pointed straight up, and grasped it by the barrel. He looked like an early settler on the lookout for some expected attack. After a moment, Denny joined him at the window.

Homer continued, "She's a filmmaker now—the mastermind—she and her husband. She asked about the rights to my waltz—the rights! She said they wanted to use it as the main title theme for a film, and she wanted to show me some footage that they needed other music for. They asked if I could come to Austin. I hadn't been out of New England since college." He squinted, struggling to see through the blur of raindrops running down the window. "The lights are out down in that draw. See how dark it is? When they go out up here, it means they're out down there. That's where Sarah lives. She's afraid to stay in her apartment when the power goes out."

Denny looked from the dark valley to Homer's face. This was the first mention of Sarah. Still looking out the window, Homer swung the barrel of the shotgun back and forth, though its butt remained planted on the floor. Denny said, "I'd better get out of here." He started to turn from the window, but Homer grabbed his arm and squeezed it hard. He put his face close to Denny's.

"I took my trombone." The sentence sounded ridiculous under the circumstances, coming from the suddenly terrified face of a big man with a shotgun at his side. "I took just one suitcase and nothing else except my trombone. I took it because I knew I was going to stay. It was either that or . . ." He released Denny's arm, lifted the shotgun by the barrel, and banged its wooden butt against the floor—once, hard. Then, calmly, he pulled it up and cradled it in the nook of his left arm. He seemed out of words.

Denny said, "If she's coming, I need to go."

"No." Homer stepped to the entryway, grabbed his coat from a hook, and hurried to the rear of the house. The dogs sprang to their feet and ran after him. Denny heard the rear door open and slam shut, followed by footsteps on the back stairs and soft whines from the dogs, still inside. Denny looked out the kitchen window and watched Homer enter the pool of light under the workshop door and step into the shop, but he did not turn the lights on. Denny guessed that he wanted to get the shotgun out of the house—to put it in its rack in the shop—but felt there was not enough time to do that and make it back to the house for Sarah's arrival.

And Homer was right. Within seconds a car pulled to a stop in front of the house. Denny followed Homer's example and took flight himself, hurrying up the stairs to the bedroom. He would get to be Homer for one more night.

TWENTY-ONE

IT ALWAYS BEGAN WITH THE INSIDE OF HIS THIGH RECEIVING a furtive caress under a banquet table at a model railroad convention. The touch came from the woman seated beside him—a big-boned, full-figured gal famous for being the only serious female modeler in the Chicagoland area. He would be telling a good railroad yarn, commanding the full attention of the table, when the hand would suddenly begin stroking his shiny black pants under the linen tablecloth. He always wore a tuxedo to the banquet.

The hand would cause a hitch in Denny's tale, but he would soldier on, his musket rising, as it were, and he would periodically favor his secret admirer with exactly the same warm gaze that he distributed to the general company. The hand would wander from his thigh up to the command center, where it would try to encompass the entire tightly packed nexus—try *and fail*, for only by touring its magnificence could it survey the whole. Denny's story, and only his story, would climax. As the laughter erupted, the hand would withdraw, the tide recede, the encounter end.

On this occasion, though, the plot took a strange turn. The hand touched his thigh, yes, but it touched the bare skin of his thigh. Where had his pants gone? Had she yanked them off? Denny was delighted, but was this initiative consistent with banquet-table discretion? And his formal wear puzzled him. What about the cummerbund?

Now this: many fingers touched his flesh. His storytelling skills had never been so challenged. He would make it to the end of the line as long as she didn't overstoke his firebox, but before he knew it, he was roaring like the Big Boy highballing down the west side of the Wasatch. He covered his mouth with his napkin, but he roared and roared.

And now he was bellowing not across a linen tablecloth but into his downy pillow, which he had pressed over his mouth as if he meant to eat it. He shook himself fully awake, examined his environment, and eased his body away from where his little party had taken place. He sat up, dizzy with disorientation. It was still dark. The front door closed with a thud. Was it Homer, returning to the house? Leaving? Or Sarah? As Denny hurried to the window, something occurred to him—something that fell into the category of *unfortunate*. He looked down and saw a flashlight beam dancing across the ground. It was Sarah, running to her car.

He watched her drive off. His groans must have awakened her and driven her out in disgust. She would say nothing about it though. This was the advantage to having a relationship with no communication. He staggered back to bed and, spent by what he ruefully recognized as the best sex he had had in years, immediately fell back asleep.

But in the light of day, certain incongruities hit him full in the face. Why would he suddenly have a wet dream, his first since he was an adolescent? Why had Sarah carried a flashlight when her car had been parked right in front? And why, now, as he lay on his back staring at the ceiling, were his toes exposed to the air?

He sat up and looked at the foot of the bed. The bedclothes had been pulled up at that end of the mattress. Could his thrashing have done that? He had a sudden image—as real as a memory, though not a memory—of Sarah lifting his blankets and top sheet and stealthily entering his bed from the footboard, crawling along the length of his legs. He saw her carrying the flashlight in her hand—no, in her mouth, commando-like—her little salt-shaker of a body working its way up his tree-trunk legs. But what was the purpose of her raid? Was this, at long last, her overture to him?

No, fool. He knew the reason, and it fell into the category of *dire*. He groaned with dismay and got dressed.

The power was back on, and a large pot of coffee was waiting for him in the kitchen. Homer must have returned from wherever he had spent the night and brewed it, but he was nowhere to be seen. Denny clutched a load of laundry, including the sheets, and he took it on down to the basement to start the washer. When he came back to the kitchen, he became aware of the tapping of a hammer from the barn. From the end of the front porch he could see Homer straddling the barn's roof ridge. Homer hammered, scooted back, and hammered again. He worked briskly and confidently. He did this several more times, then sat fully upright and looked around. The rain had freshened the air, and Homer seemed to sniff it. He spotted Denny on the porch and gave him a big wave. Then he lifted a trap door of some kind and disappeared from view. It hadn't occurred to Denny that one could get to the roof from inside. It would be a good feature to put in a layout—the roof door propped open, the farmer just emerging to perform a repair. He would wave to the train.

Denny went back inside and poured himself a cup of coffee. Next to the toaster was the chore list that Sarah had thrust at Denny some time ago. Homer seemed to be making good on it. But why? Did he intend to move back here and become her serf again? The face that he had shown Denny the night before, in anticipation of Sarah's return—wasn't that the face of fear?

As Denny fried his bacon, he heard the roar of a chain saw from the area of the barn. Through the window over the sink he saw the tall, dead birch on the far side of the barn fall away from it in a slow, dreamlike way. The thud gave Denny a small thrill. He went back to the stove. The chainsaw went on for a while, but by the time Denny's breakfast was ready, Homer was tapping away at something else. From the sound of it, he was now working at the front of the barn.

After breakfast, Denny went upstairs and put on his own clothes for the first time since his arrival at the house. He felt like a stage trouper at the end of a long run. A soft rain had begun to fall. From the bedroom window Denny spied two sawhorses near the door and some boards leaning against the barn, just out of the rain. The light was on in the workshop. Denny had never seen the light on in there before.

He went down to the basement and put the wash in the dryer. All of the clothes he had borrowed would be clean for Homer. He poured himself another cup of coffee, then filled a second one and carried both cups out the back door. He hurried through the rain along the dog pen fence. The dogs watched him from the shelter of their small, roofed den next to the house. If they were confused by all the Homers, they didn't show it.

When Denny entered the workshop, Homer turned to see who it was, but he didn't seem startled. How could he be so calm? What if Sarah showed up again and found both of them there? Homer was packing the odd tools he used for repairing instruments into wooden crates with layers of sheets protecting them. He raised his eyebrows at the cup of coffee Denny set before him.

"I need to alert you to something," Denny said.

"Oh?"

Denny watched him examine a tool and set it into the wooden crate. He tossed the next one into a metal drum—a reject, evidently—and it clanged when it hit the bottom. "I've bought a shop in Austin," Homer said by way of explanation. "I'm taking my tools with me." He reached for his coffee.

"You're going back?"

Homer looked over his cup at Denny. "I thought that was understood."

"What does that mean for me?"

"You stay here—at least long enough to pack some things for me. I made a list last night at my camp." Homer plucked a folded sheet of yellow paper from his pocket and gave it to Denny. "Actually, you can stay until I sell the place."

"This place? You're selling the house?"

"The house, the barn, the shop, the 180 acres. All of it. After the sale you can still stay in the area, if you like. My camp's on Woodbury Lake. It's nearly winterized. It wouldn't take much to finish it."

"But what about Sarah? What's it mean for her?"

Homer shrugged. "A new owner might not like the idea of music lovers clomping all over the land in the summer. It's possible she'll have to take her concerts elsewhere. At a minimum she'll have to find a new office."

"She won't be happy."

"Isn't that the status quo?"

Denny pulled a stool up to the workbench. "When you say I can stay in the area—"

"As me." Homer smiled. "You probably think it's odd that I would let you go on being me. Then again, maybe you don't. Maybe you don't think anything's odd. The point is, I don't care how well you represent me, because you're not me. You're a body wearing my name. What everyone thinks of you—that's not me either. That's just a bunch of ideas. How could a bunch of ideas be me? The only me is the person walking around wherever I'm walking around."

Denny reached for his own coffee cup. He wanted to slow things down. The man before him seemed altogether different from the quaking soul of the night before. "Where's Sarah now?"

"She's in Bennington at a barbershop quartet festival, scouting to fill a hole in her schedule."

"How do you know that?"

Homer was frowning at a tool—the one Denny had used to clean gum from under the seats. Homer pointed it at Denny, but only to emphasize what he was going to say. "Leonard Bernstein once said to someone, 'You're just like me. You want everyone in the world to love you personally. But that's impossible. You just can't *meet* everyone in the world.'" He laughed and tossed the tool into the discard barrel. "That's confidence. It'd be nice to be like that. They say a real Vermonter doesn't care what anyone thinks of him. That's my goal, and this is the maximum test: I'm me in Austin and I let you be me here, even if you ruin my reputation."

"Why would I ruin your reputation?"

Homer smiled as if at some private joke. Then he tossed another tool into the discard drum. "I don't mind throwing these away because they've been used. But I can't stand it when something fails to find its proper use. If I'm building and it's the end of the day and I find a nail in my pocket, just a single nail, I never throw it away. That nail was meant to be used. Everything needs to realize its desired use." His eyes roamed the workbench as if in search of stray nails with thwarted potential. He looked at his watch. "We've got business to attend to. You'll be the one to sell the house—you as me. I'll give you a five percent commission for doing that. You'll earn it. After all, you'll have to tell her." Homer's eyes widened. "I could never do that. I couldn't do any of this without you. I don't have time to pack everything today, and I can't stick around." He paused. "It's important that I not see her." He looked at his hands. "I can feel myself getting weak right now just thinking about it." He looked up at Denny. "You said you wanted to alert me to something."

"Well, now it's an alert to me. Are you circumcised?"

Homer made an uh-oh face.

"I'm not," Denny said.

"Uh oh."

"Yeah. I think she saw me. I was kind of bounding down the stairs. I'm not sure where her eyes went, but . . . and then last night . . . in any case, it's a problem."

Homer seemed to fall deep into thought. Denny would not ask how Sarah knew what Homer's penis looked like. To do so would declare to Homer that Denny was aware of the asexual nature of their relationship, and if he were Homer, he wouldn't want that declared. She could easily have stumbled on him in the bathroom. Or she might have seen him naked when they were children. *Hey, Homer, I see your wee-wee.* Or *Hey, Homer, you're getting so fat I can hardly see your wee-wee.*

To Denny's surprise, Homer clapped his hands and looked around with the air of one moving on. "I've got several hours of house fix-up ahead of me. I've also got to scoot up to St. Johnsbury to get Warren's horn. I called the shop. It's ready, needless to say. I'll walk it up to his place—his driveway's a mess in mud season. He lives about a quarter of the way up Little Dumpling. On Sundays, in good weather, he climbs to the top and plays 'Till Eulenspiegel.' She hates that. Actually, she hates barbershop quartets, too. It's hard to say what she *likes*. Anyway, tonight I'll give Warren his horn and settle his hash, and then I'll be out of here for good. I'm taking the Rambler. I've missed it. You can tell her you sold it."

"Won't that be out of character?"

Homer's laughter was rich. "Aren't you *always* out of character? My rental car needs to be returned. I want you to do that. I flew into Bradley because Burlington would have been too risky. I'm always running into people there—the way you ran into Nick. You'll drop the car off at the airport and take the train to Montpelier. 'The Vermonter.' You'll like it. It blows a B-flat all the way from D.C. to St. Alban's."

"But how am I going to get around?"

Homer laughed again. "Good one. You steal my identity, and then you complain when I reclaim my own car."

Denny said nothing.

"I didn't answer your question—about how I know where she is right now. I read her email. Not regularly—why would I do that?—but just when I need to. I know her password." He looked at Denny. "That's how I learned you moved in here. She wrote to someone about Homer being back in town, and I thought, '*What?*' Then I saw an email to her from someone who said they spotted me driving in Williston. I figured it was time to come see what was going on." He smiled. "I admire your work. I even helped you out. I typed my password into the computer for you. Did you figure that out? I had to squeeze in from the dog pen because the doors were locked. Why do you lock them? This is Vermont."

Denny struggled to stay with Homer's flow. "I lock them because someone could break in. Someone *did* break in, before—"

"Me again. I came back for some music I'd written and left in the piano bench. I didn't mean to scare my tenant off though." Homer had completed a row in the crate. He folded the sheet over and began a new row. "The realtor will be here at 10:00 tomorrow for the walk-through. The land is protected, so the sale's going to be a little complicated. I'll leave the documents out for you."

"Protected?"

"From development. I financed the remodeling of the barn by selling the development rights to a land trust—just the development rights, so the property itself can still change hands." He looked around at his workshop. "I've got a lot to do. She gets back late tonight. She'll probably be worn out and won't come up here. Still, I should be gone by 9:00 to be safe. After you drop the rental off, you'll have to catch a cab from the airport to the Windsor Locks station. The train leaves there at 3:30, so you'll need to get out of here within the hour unless you want to spend the night in Connecticut. I parked the rental where the road loops around below the family plot. A path from the barn will get you there. It's overgrown after three years, so be careful not to get side-tracked." He took the car keys from his pocket and gave them to Denny. "I might be gone before you get back. Come through here and say goodbye before you go."

The rain had lightened to a mist. Denny had much on his mind as he walked back to the house. He could go on being Homer, but not in this house. Instead, he would be at a lake somewhere. How did one winterize a cabin? And after last night's exploration, could he even go on being Homer? Only if he got circumcised and re-flashed Sarah. But he liked himself too much to part with even those few precious ounces.

On his way upstairs he stopped by the phone machine to listen to the single message that had come in. It was Nick, reporting that Millie had made up a new poultice for him. Denny felt a surge of impatience with Nick and Millie and Vermont and its tiresome ways. He never wanted to hear the word "poultice" again. Nick concluded by saying he was about to leave the house and would drop it off sometime today. When would be a good time? Denny called him back in a hurry.

"Homer," Nick said. "I'm glad you called." He spoke with an urgency that hadn't been evident in the message. "Things have taken a strange turn. I need to prepare you for the worst."

Denny closed his eyes. Was this a new worst or a familiar one? Yesterday, in the dance meadow, his world was without limit. He wanted that expansive feeling back.

"Lance took your picture yesterday. You must know that since you were looking right at the camera. He sent it to Braintree's old boss, the editor of that model train magazine. The boss said it was definitely Braintree. He was so sure of it that he asked Lance to give Braintree a message—something about calling him about his old job. Which means you must look exactly like him. Lance's theory—sorry I'm talking so fast, but Lance is on the other line. He was giving me the skinny when you called, and I've got to get back to him. His theory is that you've got some sort of Jekyll and Hyde thing going. He figures you met Braintree at the airport or somewhere, you were struck by how much you look like him, and you had the idea of pretending to be him whenever you got the urge to do something that you would never do as Homer. Like get it on with Marge Plongeur. You can ponder that while I get back to him. Stay on the line."

Denny was free to laugh, and he did. There was something deeply wrong with Lance. In possession of all the elements he needed to arrive at the truth, instead he burrowed more deeply into a muck of error.

"I'm back," Nick said. "And now I'm really confused. I—"

"What prompted Lance to take my picture?"

"Right, I didn't explain that. Did I tell you we had someone searching Braintree's storage locker in Illinois? His mom's old storage locker, actually. They found a good photo of Braintree and sent it to Lance. He got it yesterday at the party on his phone. That's when he saw the similarity, but there was some confusion about the age of that photo, and that's when he had the idea of taking your picture and sending it to Braintree's boss. But something brand-new is in the works. While I was talking to you just now, Lance got a call that somehow changed everything. He said I shouldn't take any action against you. Get that—against you! I don't know what the hell's going on. He said he would call me back. Anyway, I'm here, so I'll drop this thing off."

"Where's 'here'?"

"Step out on the porch and you'll find out. Oh, never mind. I see you. Ha, that pesky barn door again."

Denny eased over to the living room window and saw Nick's car pull to a stop in front of the house. At the barn, one of Homer's arms was wrapped around an open door, holding it steady while he did something out of view on the other side of it. At the approach of Nick's car, he stepped out into full view—from habit, Denny guessed. Homer seemed to flinch, glanced at the house, and began walking quickly toward the car.

Nick got out to meet him. He extended the poultice for Homer, and Homer responded by grabbing him in a bear hug and lifting him off the ground. Then they talked, mainly Nick, but Homer, too. Denny, watching, squirmed. What about his voice? The conversation seemed to go on forever. Nick finally headed back to his car. Homer stood in place until the car had descended and gone out of view. Then he walked slowly to the house. Denny met him at the front door.

"This is for you." Homer handed him the poultice. His face was unreadable.

"How did you pull that off?"

"I whispered. I told him I'd strained my voice at the party yesterday."

"But I was just on the phone with him, talking normally."

"So he said. Nice heads-up."

"I didn't know he was coming, for God's sake."

Homer's face went weak and rubbery, then straightened out. "He was worried about my larynx. Worried that the loss of my voice meant something was wrong again. God, he's so innocent." Homer burst into tears—a terrific bawling—but then he shut it off immediately. "He said my lip seemed completely cured. I said yeah, it was doing a lot better, and he was so happy. He's just so good." He looked at Denny, then at his watch. "You'd better go."

"But I've got a million questions."

"I'll leave all the information you need on the desk."

"But—"

"Go."

TWENTY-TWO

DENNY HAD TO REIN HIMSELF IN SEVERAL TIMES AS HE tooled south on the interstate. When his mind raced, so did he. A pullover for speeding and a check of his license could lead to a background check on his name, which would certainly land him in the back seat of some square-jawed, tilted-hat state trooper's car.

Before leaving Little Dumpling Farm, Denny had brought Homer up to date on the shaky condition of his impersonation. He had told him of Lance's Jekyll and Hyde theory. ("I like that!" Homer said. "I should have embarked on such a career ages ago.") But this theory, Denny explained, had probably been dumped for a new one, and here he had to tell Homer of Sarah's flashlight-assisted exploration and her likely report to Lance. Homer's eyes twinkled at the tale. The Jekyll and Hyde Hypothesis, Denny said, had doubtless given way to the Hypothesis of the Two Johnsons. Under Jekyll and Hyde, Denny was still taken for Homer; under the Two Johnsons, Denny was exposed as Denny.

Homer quickly but calmly voiced the next likely developments: Nick's partner would brief Nick, if he hadn't already. After Nick recovered from the shock, the two detectives would drive to the farm to expose Denny as a fraud. Homer would welcome them. If they wanted to see him naked, they could see him naked. If Nick tried to stump him with questions about a shared past that only the real Homer could answer, who better to prove that Homer was Homer than Homer? Denny liked the plan. Nick would be relieved, and wienie Lance would be thrown into his deepest confusion yet. Denny gave Homer his cell phone number with instructions to call if anything went awry, and Homer gave Denny his own cell number. He also gave him a special going-away present: the password to Sarah's email account. "You'll want to stay a step ahead of her," Homer said in farewell.

Now, impatient for information, Denny pulled into a rest stop in southern Vermont and called Homer, who immediately answered with "Nervous fellow, aren't you?" He had nothing to report and said he was about to leave for St. Johnsbury to pick up the French horn. Denny then called Nick. When he didn't answer, Denny left a message—a *whispered* message—asking him to call his cell number back to let him know what Lance had told him, if anything. Denny doubted that Nick would return the call. It occurred to him that he might have blundered by calling in the first place. What if Homer's prediction of Nick's next move was correct? Denny could have left this message precisely when Nick was at the farm, and Homer couldn't be in two places at once.

Weary of the churning in his head, Denny turned on the radio. He was surprised by what he heard—the murmuring of a crowd, as in an auditorium, and then a female voice saying, "Number seven." The crowd fell silent when a guitar began to play a slow melody. A pause, more murmuring, then "Number eight." He realized he was listening to a CD, and he popped it out and read the label: "April Quartet Favors." Homer had been listening to it in the rental car, for old times' sake, perhaps, and he must have forgotten it. Denny slid it back in. He resisted the urge to skip from the beginning to number 18. He wanted to experience the event as Homer had experienced it in college.

It was as if Denny were there. The muttering, the wisecracking, and, finally, number 18. After one hearing, Denny was about to hit the reverse button to hear it again, but cries from the crowd stopped his hand. It was Homer's competition demanding a replay of number 18. It played, and they called for it again and again. It was pretty, Denny would give him that. Beautiful? Denny hummed it. *Now* it was beautiful.

From the beginning, Denny had assumed that Homer had left Vermont for a bad reason—because someone was coming after him, if not Warren Boren then someone else, or because he had done something regrettable, even criminal. But Homer had left Vermont for a *good* reason. "For a song," as he had said.

Later, Denny's cell phone rang. It was not a live call but rather a voicemail alert to a call that must have come in when he was driving through a dead zone. He listened to the message. It was Nick, calling from town and saying that he hadn't heard back from Lance. In fact, Lance was nowhere to be found and wasn't picking up his calls. Nick had no idea what was going on but would keep him posted.

Denny breathed a little more easily. Good old Nick.

* * *

It had been thoughtful of Homer to imagine Denny enjoying the train ride back to Montpelier. But trains are no fun when you're in a hurry. Denny wanted only to be at Little Dumpling Farm. He wanted to be sure the whole plan hadn't gone to smash. Vermont's uneven roadbed threw him from side to side, creating general agitation all the way home.

He disembarked at the Montpelier station with a handful of other passengers. It was almost midnight, and a ticket agent standing under the single light on the platform greeted them one by one. She seemed to give Denny, the last to exit, an especially warm welcome before hurrying to the parking lot, her job done. The other passengers stepped with similar purpose as they met loved ones or evoked beeps from their waiting cars. Denny felt a wave of loneliness—something he hadn't felt in a while—which gave way to the more manageable specific regret that he hadn't arranged for a taxi in advance. What was the chance of one waiting at this hour in this remote spot?

But he was in luck. A solitary cab stood at the end of the platform. The dim light of the station reached just far enough to outline its driver sitting on the middle of the hood, his legs crossed beneath him. A cigarette end flashed with his draw on it. The other travelers shook their heads at his repeated "Taxi? Taxi?"—a marketing message that struck Denny as inane since the taxi was obviously a taxi. The cabbie slid off the hood and flicked his cigarette away. Denny suddenly recognized the furtive, coyote-like posture.

"Sparky!"

The cabbie cringed as if fearing the long arm of the law. But when he saw Denny approaching, he grinned and stood nearly upright. "Bet you didn't expect to see me here, Homer. That's me through and through. The original bad penny. Yes, sir." He seemed prepared to extend the self-tributes, but Denny interrupted him:

"You're driving a cab? You shouldn't be driving at all."

"Au contrary. I'm legit. Who woulda thunk it, huh?"

"Is this your cab?"

"Wrong again. Abe Goodlow's. I'm subbin' while he gets a new hip from some overchargin' sawbones down to Hanover."

"Well, I need a ride."

Sparky's head bobbed in furious agreement. "I done it again. I *knew* I'd get a fare if I come here. Enterprise is my middle name." His face suddenly went somber. "I got to charge you, Homer. I got to."

"No problem."

"No freebies. Abe said."

"Fine. Let's go." As Denny got into the front seat, it occurred to him that he had no story to explain his arrival from the south by train. But then he realized he wouldn't need one. After all, he was back in Sparky World, which contained only one organism of real value and interest, and that organism could presently be heard emptying its bladder behind the cab.

As they drove out of the lot, Denny asked Sparky how he happened to get his license back. Sparky said nothing, so after a moment Denny repeated the question.

"Dang it, I can't tell you, Homer. I was hopin' you'd get the hint when I didn't answer, but you sure didn't."

"Oh, sorry," said Denny.

After a long silence, Sparky said, "Dang it all, I just can't."

"*Fine*," Denny said.

Sparky made an impatient noise, as if Denny had been hounding him all night for a full accounting. "All right then. Long story short, I got friends in high places."

Denny was silent. He was mainly thinking about how this actually *was* a long story short.

"That's right. Friends."

Denny looked out his window.

"Not so much *friends* as *a* friend. And not really a *friend*. Just a certain personage I got over a barrel. Someone I got the drop on. Yep. I got the drop on him. You got to get up early in the mornin' to beat ol' Sparky. They don't make 'em— "

"Is it Lance?"

The name produced a one-man-band effect of sundry noises from Sparky, which finally issued into a series of snorts. "Don't you pump me no more. I mean it, big guy. I'm drained. The well is empty."

Ordinarily, Denny would have never put these two men together, but Sparky's language had made Lance pop into Denny's head. He remembered the phrase "got the drop on" from when they had all been at Sparky's house—when Sparky had waved his urine-filled water pistol at Lance and joked that he "got the drop on" him. But Lance would not pull strings to get Sparky's license reinstated just because he had been threatened by a water pistol. What could Sparky possibly have on him that would make him subject to his influence?

Sparky turned onto a main road. Ahead and to Denny's left, the golden Statehouse dome, lit by floodlights, rose like a local sun. Sparky cruised through a red light and then turned left through another one. Denny looked at him.

"Coppers are bustin' up a high school party on Murray Hill. We can make our own law." Sparky raced through downtown, which had retired for the night some time earlier, at about 40 miles per hour. When they reached Highway 12, he was limited by its engineering to a speed of 70 in the 40 zone.

"Hey, Homer. Remember this?" Sparky turned off his car lights.

"Not really," Denny said, shifting in his seat.

"How about this then?" Sparky eased the car into the lane for oncoming traffic. He looked at Denny. "Bring back memories?"

A distant glimmer of headlights made Denny shout, and Sparky moved back into the right lane. But he kept his lights off. The other car shot by, and its driver honked to alert Sparky that his lights were off.

"A two-pointer!" Sparky said. "Made you shout and made him honk!"

Denny gritted his teeth. He couldn't imagine Homer at any age participating willingly in this game. Soon they reached Horn of the Moon Road, and its mud and ruts made Sparky turn on his lights and slowed him down. He had satisfied the impulse that had seized him, and for the rest of the drive he seemed almost depressed, like a drug user coming down from a high. At the foot of the driveway, he stopped and peered up the hill.

"Looks kinda gooey, Homer. I'll drop you off here. The fare is twenty even. That's just the fare."

"What's the customary tip, Sparky?"

"Hmm. Lemme think. Rural drop of a solitary fare from a public transportation venue? I'd be lyin' if I said it was less than forty percent."

"You'd be lying if you said anything."

"Huh?"

Denny handed him a crumpled twenty-dollar bill. "I just wanted to be able to assign a dollar value to my punishment."

"Huh?"

Denny got out of the car, but he leaned back in. "Homer's an old friend. Why would you do that to an old friend?"

"You're right, you're right. Sorry, big fella. Thirty-five percent tops. I said forty because it'd be easier for you to figure. Lemme give you some back." Sparky unfolded the bill. Denny slammed the door and began walking up the hill. He heard a high-pitched voice, rendered puny by the closed windows of the car: "You only give me a twenty!" More words flowed, but they grew fainter with every step Denny took, and Sparky finally drove off to his next rendezvous with destiny.

Up ahead, all was dark, save for the porch light that Homer had left on for him. The main thing on Denny's mind right now was how

Sparky had gotten the drop on Lance. As he slopped up the driveway, he went through the events of that morning at Sparky's—the elusive Marge, Nick and Lance searching for her in the woods, Lance's solitary vigil by Marge's body while Nick phoned for help, the arrival of reinforcements, Lance's emergence from the woods. Lance had then gone into the house to use the phone, and Sparky had followed him in. Denny knew this because Sparky had fetched the pistol and the dog and had come out ahead of Lance. What could have happened in the house?

He remembered that Lance, when he had emerged from the woods, had asked Sparky for a newspaper. He remembered it because it was odd. What could be in the daily paper that would have bearing on the body he had been sitting beside—and praying beside? He prayed on one knee, so said Nick. But both of his knees had been smudged with snow. Did he switch knees because one got tired? Or did he do something else that required him to kneel on both knees? Did he examine Marge's body? He wasn't a forensics expert—Nick said he had *summoned* forensics experts. Did Lance search her? Did he go through her pockets?

Feeling something like a hard smack against his forehead, Denny hurried the rest of the way to the house. Once inside, he was at Homer's computer within seconds, dialing up. He clicked his way to the state lottery web site, which he had last visited after his phone call with Dr. Ike. He now found that there was indeed a toll-free number that one could call to learn the winning numbers of recent drawings. Lance would have known about Marge's winning lottery ticket from his interviews with people like Dr. Ike. With Marge's ticket in his hand, Lance could have called the toll-free number, and Sparky could have overheard the call. Sparky knew that Marge had won *something*. On that fateful night, when she had seen him at the hotel, she had said to him, "I'm a winner!" Sparky, whose middle name was Enterprise, put the two together, and he got the drop on Lance.

Denny would know for sure that Lance had purloined Marge's ticket if Lance's name appeared on any of the lists of lottery winners. Denny searched through the various contests. One award leaped out for its size—a little over 67,000 dollars. Next to it was not the name of Lance Londo, but rather the name of a useful stand-in for him—a woman with a body-mass index similar to the detective's, on whom no suspicion would have fallen when she claimed the winnings. No doubt about it: she knew how to enter into liaisons of direct benefit to her.

TWENTY-THREE

WHEAT TOAST, COTTAGE CHEESE, AND TWO SOFT-BOILED eggs. These were mere props on his plate in case Sarah waltzed in. He had already downed his greasy breakfast in private. All of his real dining would be secretive now, in light of Sarah's suspicion and Homer's diabetes, which he could no longer ignore. He couldn't be as brash as he wanted to be. He couldn't be Denny, not even a little bit.

On his figurative plate were so many bubbling casseroles that it was hard to keep track of them. Pencilled on the realtor's card on his desk was "10:00 A.M."—Homer's reminder of the scheduled walk-through. Denny hoped Sarah showed up by then. He would inform her of the plan to sell the farm in the presence of the agent, who would serve as a human heat shield. The flames were likely to be especially hot since she now had funds to take her concerts "to the next level," as she said far too often. Considering where she had gotten the 45K, she wasn't quite the grant-writing genius he had taken her for, was she? He would have liked to think that Lance had bought his way into Sarah's bed, but the seed money was probably an aphrodisiac for both of them.

Lance's initiative—that crucial moment on his knees in the snow, when he had lifted the lottery ticket from Marge—had shifted Denny's classification of him from *wienie* to *criminal*. Lance had certainly committed a crime of some kind—theft, if not from Marge then from her estate, and tampering with evidence. Denny could imagine the rationalizations Lance produced, perhaps whispering them into Sarah's ear between nibbles: the ticket would have been buried with Marge or thrown away if he hadn't found it, Marge would have just spent it on booze, we're spending it on culture, you're very bony—is this what it means to "jump someone's bones"? The last was out of character, Denny knew. It was hard to keep himself from intruding.

Filling his plate to overflowing was the question of what Sarah did after her flashlight excursion. Denny's reconstruction, based on his last phone call with Nick: (1) Sarah takes the news to Lance that she is certain Denny is an imposter; (2) Lance, poised to brief Nick and to bring his prime suspect, Homer, in for questioning, is stunned, for Sarah's news means that Lance's Jekyll and Hyde theory is a stinker; (3) Lance cancels his meeting with Nick to digest this development. But what then?

Meanwhile, Denny had not been idle. He knew that he needed to remove the cornerstone of Sarah's theory, namely that he had a foreskin and Homer didn't. Working under the assumption that if a notion can be conceived of by the human imagination then it will exist on the Internet, he searched for one that had struck him, and he found it immediately, along with an associated product. He then opened a new email account under a fictitious name, and, after logging in to it, sent an email to Sarah promoting the product and linking to its purveyor. Then, using the password that Homer had brilliantly given him, he went to Sarah's email, discovered his just-sent message in her Spam box, where he knew it would land, and moved it into her In box, where it sat right on top, its subject line bound to grab her attention: "Foreskin Restorer." If she opened the email—how could she not, that morsel of flesh looming so large in her life right now?—she would find a picture of a small silver cup attached to a stem, rather like a tiny toilet plunger. With it a circumcised man with time on his hands could coax excess penile skin forward over the head of his penis. Denny could see her jaw drop. He could read her thought: was this yet another bizarre path Homer had taken over the past three years? In addition to becoming an obnoxious, groping, lazy, flabby, incompetent, fast-talking, nose-picking glutton, had Homer reversed his circumcision? She would rush to Lance for an urgent and ridiculous tête-à-tête.

The sound of boots stomping on the front porch floor made Denny jump in his seat. He hadn't heard a car drive up. He looked around for anything that might incriminate him as not-Homer: breakfast, check; clothes, check; reading material—agh! He stuffed the O-gauge equipment catalogue under his ass. The front door opened without a knock. In the kitchen booth, well out of view, he leaned forward and listened. Lance was speaking.

". . . the place to ourselves."

"Yeah," said Sarah.

Denny almost called out a zany, high-pitched *Hewwo!* just to annoy them, but that was not-Homer. He scooped up a spoonful of cottage cheese as the front door closed.

Sarah said, "I'm going to take a shower. God, I hope I never have to do that again."

"I doubt that you will." A grim chuckle.

"Maybe once more. I'd like to put Prescott in Prescott."

"I could use some coffee," said Lance.

"Let me show you where the good stuff is." Footsteps came through the dining room toward the kitchen. "It's going to be hard to find. The dipshit never—" Sarah's speech and body came to an abrupt halt when she saw the dipshit sitting in the kitchen booth. She stopped walking so suddenly that Lance banged into her from behind. She gasped and a hand went to her mouth. She stared at Denny, eyes wide. "Oh, my God," she said softly.

Denny, though puzzled, opted for silence. He would let them lead. He plopped another dollop of cottage cheese into his mouth and tongued the curds around as he looked at the duo. Lance stared over Sarah's shoulder with his head cocked slightly, his eyes not wide like hers, but narrow. He stood so close to her that they formed a two-headed beast.

"When—" Sarah said. She cleared her throat. "When did you get back?"

Denny, frowning, thought and pretended to think at the same time. Did she know he had been away yesterday? Even if she did, was it odd that he was back? Why was she so surprised, or dismayed, or whatever she was?

Lance suddenly and strangely took charge. He stepped past Sarah, actually shoving her aside, and thrust a hand out to Denny. "Sarah's told me a lot about you, Homer. Glad to meet you. Lance Londo."

What bizarre kind of game was this? Was it called "Let's Start All Over"? Denny swallowed his mouthful of cottage cheese and took Lance's hand, giving him a dead fish just because he knew it would irritate him. That was Denny, too, he realized. He could not *not* be Denny. And it was the Denny in him that made him scrunch up his face and say, "What the hell kind of name is Londo anyway?"

Sarah was screaming before Denny reached the end of his sentence. She quickly backpedaled all the way into the dining room and banged into a chair. She turned and ran off. Denny heard the front door open, then her footsteps on the porch. He and Lance were engaged in an indifferent stare-off as they monitored Sarah's movements. Her car door closed. Then came another scream, muffled by distance and closed windows. The car started and drove off.

This left Lance in charge of the social niceties. "Fuck!" he said.

"Fuck!" Then, with a glare at Denny, "You fuck!" He spun away and hurried out the front door.

Denny went to the window. Sarah had stopped her car at the bottom of the driveway as if she knew Lance would follow, which he did, and fast. He got in on the passenger side, but the car didn't move. Denny saw a wild hand gesture from Sarah, then another. Lance got out, walked around the car, and tried to enter on the driver's side, but he seemed to have to force Sarah to scoot over. He finally got in and closed the door. The car sped down the road.

Denny had never had such a dramatic impact. Repellent personality indeed—one sentence had sent them fleeing. His first thought—and his last thought, his only thought—was that because that sentence contained Lance's full name, it must be crucial to some shenanigan, probably the lottery, even though they had used Sarah's name to claim the prize. Denny could not stop thinking about the lottery—about Lance on his knees, filching that ticket from Marge's half-chewed body. He had actually caught Lance in a crime! But he couldn't complete the connection between that act and their behavior just now.

He cleaned up from breakfast, went upstairs, and took a shower. When he came back downstairs, a phone message was waiting for him. Lance or Sarah, apologizing for their rude exit? He pressed *Play*.

"Homer." Pause. "You know who this is. You said you would deliver the horn by 10:00 last night. That is now exactly twelve hours ago. I've counted every one of the hours as they've passed. I demand satisfaction. I am prepared to take action. And soon!"

Warren Boren cut such a pathetic figure, with his three years of impotent ultimatums. It was laughable, but Denny didn't laugh. Instead, he wondered why Homer hadn't gotten the horn to him, especially since Homer had been so mortified by what he had felt was a professional lapse on his part.

Denny called Homer's cell phone. He was glad to have an excuse to talk to him again, but he just got Homer's greeting. He left a message for him to call back. He thought a moment, then went to Homer's computer and searched for musical repair shops in St. Johnsbury. He found two. He called the first one, posing as Warren Boren, and when he asked if Homer Dumpling had come by for his French horn, the owner said yes he had and what a horn it was and the French horn posed a peculiar challenge for the "musical tinker," which he liked to call himself, because after all, when you stopped and thought about it, that was what he was, and Denny hung up on him.

Denny frowned and gazed out the window for a bit, then called the

Vermont State Police to ask if any accidents had occurred yesterday between St. Johnsbury and Montpelier. He identified the car he was concerned about—a beige 1961 Rambler Classic.

The woman at the other end was silent for a moment. "Is that Homer Dumpling's car?"

Denny inhaled sharply. "Was Homer in an accident? Is he all right?"

"No, no. There was no accident. I just recognized the car. Why are you asking about it?"

Denny hung up on her. He wondered if Homer had decided to spend one more night in the area and then return Warren's horn to him in the morning. Could he be at his camp on that lake? He went upstairs to see if Homer had left a note of explanation. He found nothing, which didn't surprise him. After all, Sarah might see it, and why would Homer write a note to Homer? All Denny found on the desk was the thick file of documents related to the sale of the house. The agent's card was stapled to the front of the folder.

Out of ideas, Denny phoned the agent to see where he was, since he was past due. The agent—excited, all but panting at the size of the prospective commission—said the appointment was for 2 o'clock. Yesterday evening he had left a message rescheduling it on Homer's machine at home. Hadn't he gotten it? Denny said that Sarah must have picked it up and deleted it—an improvised lie that, as he thought about it, could actually be true if Sarah had come back early from her barbershop quartet affair. The agent said he would be happy to discuss any questions he might have about the listing over the phone right now, and Denny hung up on him.

If Sarah heard that message, how would she have taken it? As he thought about this, he heard the roar of a car coming up the driveway. He hurried to the front window at the end of the upstairs hall. It was Sarah and Lance, with Sarah back behind the wheel. She must have mastered whatever feelings she had.

Her return caused Denny to review the events of the morning in rapid sequence—her scream when he had spoken, Lance's greeting him as if for the first time, Warren Boren's phone call, the agent's report of the phone message.

"Homer," he said softly. He cried out in anguish.

Then he cried out in fear.

He bolted down the stairs and ran to the back door. He made for the workshop, running along the rear fence of the dog pen. The two dogs, having been drawn to the front fence by the approach of Sarah's car, now turned and seemed to rejoice at the sight of The Provider moving with such unwonted speed, and they dashed to the back fence. Lance must have noticed the dogs' shift of attention, because he was suddenly at the front fence, yelling for Denny to stop. Denny kept running.

"Stop or I'll shoot," Lance called out.

No one had ever said that to Denny before. He was stimulated, but not in a good way. Lance indeed had a pistol trained on him. He stopped.

Sarah clambered down the rear steps of the house. "Kill the fucker!" she yelled to Lance. She hurried to the woodpile and grabbed a split log. She ran toward Denny, wound up, and threw the log at his head, but he dodged it. He wanted to run from her, but he was compromised by Lance's order. He looked back across the dog pen to Lance, almost for sympathy. Lance was no longer there.

Denny took off, running away from the pen and deep into the rear of the property. He would have to cross a long field before the land dipped protectively into the woods. Sarah had gone to the woodpile for another log, and she was coming after him. She tossed the log aside and began to close the distance. Now Lance yelled from the back porch, and Denny slowed and looked back. The gun was aimed at him again, so he stopped. Lance yelled at the charging Sarah to stay out of the way.

"He made me do it!" she screamed, and then she was upon him.

Denny had a vague expectation, unsupported by experience, that he would be able to hold her at bay with his sheer bulk, so he was surprised to find himself on the ground. She poked one of his eyes and raked his flesh. Denny covered his head with his arms, and then he heard Lance's voice as he pulled Sarah off him.

Sarah stomped around Denny's huddled body and waved her arms, almost dancing. "Kill him!" she yelled. "Kill him!"

"I *can't* kill him," Lance yelled.

"What do you mean you can't kill him?"

"We'd have to move him for one thing," Lance said. "Look at him. Do you want to move him? You want to dig a hole for him right here?"

Denny rolled onto his hands and knees and struggled to his feet. With his good eye he saw Sarah lunge at him, but she stopped short of attacking him. "He made me kill my Homer!" She spit at his feet and staggered back to the house.

"Don't move," Lance said to Denny. He hurried after Sarah and caught up with her near the back porch, making her stop. They talked. All the while, Lance kept glancing at Denny, who was busy taking stock of his condition. Blurry vision was returning to the eye she had poked, though it watered freely, almost gushing down his face. As he watched them talk, all he could think of was her question, "What do you mean you can't kill him?" She had asked it as if it were perfectly reasonable. He was clearly outmatched. His Foreskin Restorer ploy was looking pretty feeble right now.

Sarah hurried into the house. With his gun, Lance signaled to Denny to come closer. When he did, Lance waved him ahead and followed. "Upstairs," Lance said. As the two of them passed through the kitchen, Denny could hear Sarah opening and closing drawers in Homer's bedroom overhead. They climbed the stairs.

"You brought this on yourself," Lance said. "You shouldn't have run. All you had to do was pretend to be ignorant. If you had acted like you didn't know something had happened, everything would be fine." Denny thought he was done with the subject, but then, as they reached the second floor, he said, "I can't believe you ran. The same with her in the kitchen. She shouldn't have screamed. I'm surrounded by stupidity." Lance swallowed the end of the last sentence because Sarah was storming out of the bedroom. She huffed by them to the guest room.

"Look in the closet," she said.

Lance hesitated. "Which—"

"The *bedroom* closet," she snapped. "Up high. I couldn't reach up there. They'd be in a cigar box. We used to play with them when we were little. We'd lock Homer in."

Lance pushed Denny into Homer's bedroom. "Get on the bed and stay there." Denny complied. Lance began to rummage through boxes on the two shelves at the top of the closet. He pulled several down and set them on the floor. Denny's view was blocked by the open door, but he heard the jingle of metal: keys. Lance leaned out of the closet, a cigar box in his hand, and shouted, "I've got it."

"Hang on," Sarah yelled. She seemed to be in her office now. "Goddammit," she said, but it was a mutter, not directed at them.

Then Lance—a tidy fellow—picked up every box he had set on the floor and returned them to the two top shelves. When he was done, he paused—to admire his work? The open closet door blocked Denny's view of him. He finally closed it and looked at his captive.

"You've got to see it from Sarah's point of view."

"I do?"

"She thought you killed Homer in Florida. You can see why she did. You show up here at his farm, you know all about his life . . ."

"I didn't know anything about his life."

"How did you fool everybody then? Even Sarah. She figured you must have met him. I can see her train of thought—you meet him, you're both astonished at the resemblance, you pretend to become his friend, you pump him for information, and you eliminate him. You had to eliminate him. Otherwise he could show up here and ruin everything."

Sarah went down the stairs. Lance listened to her movements. Then he resumed:

"Then she finds out you're trying to sell the house. There's the motive. You didn't want to *be* Homer—you wanted to pose as him for the money. She thought she was next on your list because you would realize she was on to you. Of course she didn't mean to do what she did to Homer. She was defending herself against *you*—or so she thought. She was like an abused person striking back. It's easy to see it that way."

"Especially if you want to go on screwing her with a clear conscience."

Lance pointed at Denny. "By my count, if you didn't exist, there are two people who would."

It is hard to argue against a guilty thought you've already had about yourself. Denny looked away. Another drawer slammed below, and Sarah ran up the stairs. When she came into the room, she looked capable of anything. "Here." She handed Lance a roll of picture wire. "I couldn't find rope. This is better anyway." She pointed to the nightstand as she headed for the door. "Get that phone out of here. And get his cell phone."

Denny said, "It's in the kitchen."

"You shut up," she snapped. "You're a dead pig." She stomped out of the room.

Lance unplugged the nightstand phone from the wall, slowly wrapped the cord around it, and tucked it under his arm. He moved slowly, like a philosopher deep in thought. He took the cigar box to the door connecting to the computer room, closed it, and tried different keys until he threw the lock. He tested the door, pushing on it hard. He crossed the room and did the same with the lock on the far bathroom door. This meant that Denny would be confined to the bedroom and adjacent bathroom. The inclusion of the bathroom heartened him. It suggested he was meant to live for at least as long as one toilet-requirement cycle.

Lance stepped back into the bedroom with a hand towel, which he gave to Denny. He pointed to the side of his face where Sarah had raked her claws. Denny pressed the towel there and looked at it—it was streaked with blood, which he now saw had run down to his shoulder. He held the towel against his cheek and neck. Lance went to the one window in the bedroom—the double casement window overlooking the dog pen—and gauged the distance to the ground. He tossed the roll of wire onto the dresser. "Fat chance of you going anywhere."

Something in that gesture—refusing to bind him with wire—filled Denny with the urge to plead his case, to appeal to the *better* Lance, since there did seem to be one. But Denny feared it could backfire. "What are you going to do with me?" he said.

Lance paused at the door to the hall. "When did Homer come back? How long was he here?"

Denny's mind raced. How could he use the question—and Lance's interest—to save his life? "He was here just long enough to meet me and arrange for me to box some things up and ship them to him. He put me in charge of that. He seemed to trust me."

"So you didn't meet him before?"

"Never."

"Wasn't he mad about what you had done—about pretending to be him?"

"He was a little suspicious at first. Then he was fine with it."

Lance shook his head. "*Two* oddballs." He stepped out and started to close the door.

"How did she kill him?" Denny said.

"*Lance!*" Sarah yelled from below.

"Coming," he called out. He released the doorknob, and, without looking at Denny, made a driving gesture with two hands on a pretend steering wheel. Then he closed the door and locked it behind him.

All through the rest of the day, Denny heard them talking, usually in the kitchen but sometimes in the living room and backyard. His fate was a river of words, and he couldn't make out a single one—just the rises and falls, or a sudden foot stomp or hand slap on a table, and, once, a loud laugh. He kept thinking about Homer—how he would have spent the day yesterday, when his path would have crossed theirs. If Sarah had run him over, where had it happened? Had she done it with her car? When had Lance signed on? Had he helped her from the beginning or only with the mop-up?

Near dark, Denny heard a car drive up. Its door opened with a creak. He had no access to a window facing the front of the house. He was tempted to shout for help, but he didn't want to get another innocent person killed. There was talk outside between Sarah and a man. Denny heard a whine from one of the dogs, and he went to the casement window over the pen. At the front fence, the dogs began to dance with excitement, and the plumber in the orange cap appeared at the gate, leashed them, and took them away. He had probably been told that Homer had gone back to Florida. Homer was being phased out.

Denny tried not to move too much. He figured the less noise he made, the longer he would live. But he did get off the bed to check one thing, and he did it just as soon as Lance left the room. He went to the closet, opened the door, and looked down at the floor. The happy housewife descending the chain ladder smiled up at him from the top of the box. Denny bent down and checked to make sure the ladder was still inside it, then shoved it aside with his foot to a dark corner of the closet. He tiptoed back to the bed.

He was surprised Lance hadn't seen the box. But he *must* have seen it. The *better* Lance must have seen it and decided to give him a fighting chance to escape. But, if he had, he had doubtless also seen the words "250 lbs. max. capacity" on the front of the box.

TWENTY-FOUR

THE BACK DOOR TO THE ETHAN ALLEN HOTEL WAS LOCKED, momentarily foiling Denny's plan to seek refuge in the cubby. He would have to enter by the front door—if it was unlocked, and if Betsy wasn't at the counter. He certainly didn't want to see her now that he knew what had happened to Homer. As he worked his way around the hotel, he scanned the building in search of an alternative stealth-route—a pipe he could shinny up, gaps in the wall face enabling a free climb. But he was getting carried away. A successful descent via chain ladder from a second-story window, even in defiance of a weight limit, didn't exactly make him a Navy Seal.

Fortunately, Lance and Sarah had cooperated. He hadn't dared try his escape while they were downstairs because they would have heard the ladder banging against the kitchen wall. They had come upstairs about 11:00, talking as they had been all day. They paused at Denny's door. Lance opened it and looked at Denny, lying on his back and contemplating his fate, and then he closed the door without a word. In appearance, the act was tender, like a parental check on a sleeping youngster. They then accommodated him further by having monumental sex. Their noises were like cheers rooting him on as he made preparations—tiptoeing to the closet, untangling the ladder, sliding its bottom end out the window, and easing it down along the wall until he could hook the top ends over the windowsill.

At that point, he paused and gazed down at the dog pen, wondering if this was where Dennis Braintree would cease to be. He took a deep breath and straddled the sill. He set one foot on the rung he could most comfortably reach. As he eased his full weight onto it, a link popped, and the rung and his foot banged onto the rung below before he could catch himself by seizing the sides of the window frame. He pulled back into the room and took stock. It had been a mistake to put all 330 of his pounds—80 *more than one would wish*—on one end of the rung. He needed to distribute his weight. But to place his feet simultaneously on a rung, he couldn't straddle the sill for his first step—he would have to back out, feet and ass leading the way.

With that in mind, he slowly slid the bed around, moving it by silent increments until its side was against the wall under the window. The top of the bed was at the same height as the sill. He climbed onto the bed and backed out the window, making sure his feet were separated when they reached the rung below the one he had broken. With his belly lying across the sill and his hands holding each side of the window frame, he settled his full weight on the rung, his feet as far apart as possible. It held. Still belly-down on the sill, he rocked his body up from the rung and eased down to the next one.

After two such operations, he had to leave the safety of the window frame, which meant that to set both feet simultaneously on the next rung down, he would have to lift himself by grasping the rung in front of his face and doing a chin-up. He wasn't strong enough—he didn't have to try it to know. In a panic, he saw himself suspended there until dawn, too weak to go up or down without breaking rungs. A sudden move could send him cascading through the entire ladder to the ground. After moaning into the clapboards for a while, he tried different maneuvers and found one that at least held some promise: he fit his elbows through the space between the rungs until his armpits hung on the rung and his arms clasped it tightly against his chest, and at the same time, his hands were free to grab the rung above the one clutched under his armpits. This enabled him to use two muscle groups to hoist his bulk. In this fashion, he made it down to the next rung. Groaning and whimpering, rung by rung he descended.

When he reached the ground, he wanted to run for his life, but there was one thing he knew he would need. Did he dare? From above he heard, "Yes, yes, yes," which he chose to interpret as an answer from on high instead of banal sex talk. He squeezed through the dog door into the kitchen and grabbed his cell phone from where he had left it on the counter. As he backed out the dog door, the sex talk again reached him, this time audible through the floor, but now it was "No, no, no!" Lance must have made a bad move.

Denny scuttled across the dog pen and through its open front gate. He hurried past Sarah's car, which was partly illuminated by the front porch light. Again, every molecule of his body wanted to hurtle on down the driveway, but he made himself backtrack and inspect her car, feeling its sides and front end. Then he got out of there. It was a long way to town, five miles or more, and he ducked down the bank into the bushes whenever a car approached from behind. It was after 1:00 A.M. when he reached the hotel.

Now, at the front door, he saw Betsy at the counter, feeling along it and tidying as if marking the end of the day. He would wait until she left the desk. But what if the door was locked? He tested it, making no sound at all—or so he thought until Betsy sharply turned his way. He froze. Behind him, two boisterous couples appeared, heading for the door. As he stepped aside, he had the idea of using them the way besieged cowboys use horses in Western movies, as a protective shield in a getaway. One of the men swiped his hotel key in the door lock, and Denny swept inside with them, mingling like a fellow reveler.

"Have a good outing?" Betsy called.

The gang assured her that they had and then peeled away from Denny toward the bar for more good times. This left Denny stranded in the middle of the lobby, where he had foolishly stopped. If he had just kept walking to the stairs, Betsy would have taken him for one of the guests going to bed. He took a silent step forward, his eyes on her. Then another. She stood still, then turned her face fully toward him.

"Mr. Braintree? It certainly must be Mr. Braintree."

Denny sagged. "Hello, Betsy." He walked to the counter.

"My strange night owl returns," she said. "Are you still 'on the lam'?" She jiggled her torso from side to side in a jaunty accompaniment to her words.

"No, no." She was sadly behind the curve. "Just back in town on business. I need a room for the night. I'm exhausted."

"The hotel is chock-a-block. Let me straighten up the cubby for you. I'll just need to smooth out the bed a bit." She smiled as she walked around the counter: she had a secret. "My Homer took a little nap there." She gestured to the hall leading to the elevator.

"Homer? When?" Denny found his hopes rising—foolishly, he realized.

"Yesterday afternoon. His visit was a real surprise. We talked for some time. Then he napped, and then he was off."

"Do you know where to?"

"St. Johnsbury. An errand of some sort. Then back to Austin, Texas. And we thought he was in Florida all this time." They stepped into the elevator. "I don't know when I'll see him again. My mind has been on him all day. I'll miss him, but that's not the most important thing." She took a deep breath and let it out. "He's a changed man. I believe he's put all his troubles behind him." She fell silent.

The elevator opened on the top floor and they walked down the hall and turned into the rear wing. In the cubby, she ran her hands over the bed, smoothing the spread. She stepped back toward the door, but then she turned and walked around the bed and knelt down in the corner, feeling for the purple vinyl jewel box. There was uncertainty in her reach, as if she was checking to be sure it was there. On making contact with it, she squared it into the corner.

"That was Amelia's," Denny said.

Betsy pushed on the bed to raise herself from the floor. "He told you about her?"

"I just know that she died." Denny didn't want to lie to her.

"He said nothing more about it?"

"No." Technically true, Denny thought.

She hesitated, then sat down on the edge of the bed. "Have you ever ridden a snowmobile, Mr. Braintree?"

"No."

"Are you familiar with snowmobile 'skimming'?"

"No."

"Let's say you're going across a lake that's frozen and covered with snow. You're going at a fast clip, fifty miles per hour. Let's say you're very far from shore, and the ice suddenly thins out and you find yourself heading for open water. What do you do?"

"Turn around?"

"There's not enough ice left for that. You'd be on the water before you completed your turn. Here's what you do: you speed up. You go as fast as you can, you speed up to 60, 70, 80 miles per hour. It doesn't work very often, but if you're lucky, you will skim across the water. You must not stop under any circumstances, or you will immediately sink. And in water that cold, that far from shore, of course you will die." Betsy took a deep breath. "What if your young sister is with you on your snowmobile? What if, at the moment you hit the water, something happens to her grip on you? Maybe there was a bump as you left the ice. Maybe fear seized her and cramped her arms. What if you find that she is no longer holding on to you? What do you do? You can't turn around when you're skimming or you will sink. The choice is clear. You can try to go back to her, or you can go on at full speed. In other words, you can die, or you can live. That's your choice."

Denny saw it immediately. He saw the moment of decision, and he saw the rest of Homer's life.

"Homer made a choice, and he's lived with it ever since. He invented a story about it when he got home—that she fell through a thin patch when she was walking on the lake, and that he wasn't able to get to her.

That's what he told his mom and dad, not for himself but to spare them from knowing everything, because knowing what really happened makes it even more horrible. He had to tell someone, though."

Betsy slowly stood up. Denny, not knowing what to do, rose as well. "This was Amelia's playroom when she came to visit me," she said. "Sometimes she would bring a little friend from school. They all liked my johnnycake. She kept some toys here." Betsy smoothed the bed where she had sat down and stepped toward the door. She paused. "Homer told me that she got on the snowmobile with him earlier in the day, at a different lake, because friends were jeering them, saying she should ride with them, not with Homer, because he was more likely to sink. They weren't talking about any real added danger. They were just being unkind because of his size. Amelia rode with her brother. She defied them. They were far away from the others when the accident happened." She reached for the doorknob. "He's come to terms with it by taking steps, one after another. The last step was leaving here altogether. If he needs to be away to be happy, I'm all for it. He's going to write me this time. He promised."

After Betsy left, Denny sat on the cubby bed for some time. He didn't know which angered him more—that Sarah had killed Homer precisely when he had found peace, or that she had exploited his guilt over the years in some sort of sick mock romance. Denny was sure that was what she had done. If she didn't do it outright, with words of malice, then she did it cunningly, with the knowledge that Homer was a helpless soul. She might not have known the full story, but she didn't need to. All she needed to know was that Homer suffered from guilt, and to look at his face was to know that.

One phone call was all it would take, and the wheels of justice would grind her to a pulp—and her skinny mate with her. Denny pulled out his cell phone and turned it on. He looked at Nick's number on his contacts list. He would explain that he was a fake Homer, and then he would have to say that the real one was dead.

He snapped the phone shut. There was justice, yes, but there was mercy, too—for Nick, for Betsy. Mercy required that they never learn of Homer's death—that they go on thinking he was alive. *Altruistic impersonation.* This odd pairing of words leaped into Denny's head as if deeply rooted there, like some remembered moral guideline from childhood. Denny had fooled people into thinking he was Homer in person, face to face. Certainly he could fool them from a distance. Only two people besides him knew the truth, and they weren't likely to go public with it. Homer lives!

But a sudden thought struck him. If Homer's body were found and identified, it would undo everything. Denny could prevent that from happening if *he* found it and removed all of Homer's identification. But no—the body would still be recognizable as Homer's. Denny felt a push, an almost physical sensation, to the logical remedy: he could plant his own ID on the body so that it would be taken for the corpse of Dennis Braintree. That way there would be no grief. Who cared about Dennis Braintree? Just as Denny had been Homer in life, Homer could be him in death.

Only two people knew where Homer's body was. Denny opened his cell phone. It would be an enjoyable phone call on many levels—waking them up, surprising them with the news that he was no longer in the house, extorting the location of the body with the threat of exposure. But it wouldn't work. All they had to do was wait for him at the site and pounce, and this time Better Lance would not prevail. He snapped the phone shut.

What had the golden couple said when they returned to the house? "I hope I never have to do that again." Do what? Bury him? Burn his body? There had been other words. Sarah had called Denny a "dipshit," but that wasn't helpful. She had mentioned her ex-boss at the radio station with a laugh. "I'd like to put Prescott in Prescott." What could that mean? Was Prescott a town? A forest?

Denny backtracked a bit. What car had she used? Certainly not hers—he hadn't found a trace of damage when he had inspected it. Probably not Lance's either, since, according to Lance, she had been the driver. If she had somehow used the Rambler, she and Lance would have wanted to dispose of the car as well. How would they have done it? If they stuck it somewhere in the woods, eventually it would be found. A "pond dump"? What kind of term was that, and how did it even occur to him? Sparky hunkered into view, protesting his innocence from disposing of wrecks by parking them on pond ice. "My pond-dumpin' days are over," he had said to Nick. In many ways, Sarah had Sparky's brain. She had borrowed his pistol-of-urine idea. She could just as easily have borrowed this idea, too.

Denny opened his cell phone again, this time to set the alarm. He chose 3:30 A.M. Surely the front desk would be empty at that hour. If Betsy left her computer on, he could go online and call up a map of Vermont. And if she didn't, surely he would find a map of the state in the lobby brochure display. And surely—yes, he felt for his keys in his pocket—surely, Marge's car was still at her sister's house. Before dawn, he expected to be driving that car north to an ice-covered lake that was surely named Prescott.

TWENTY-FIVE

LAKE PRESCOTT WAS A TEARDROP BELOW THE HIGHWAY, with its bulbous end in Vermont and its northern reach tapering into Canada. When it came into view in the early light, the dull, metallic sheen on its surface certainly *looked* like ice, but how thick was it? Working in his favor was a mountain to his right as he approached the lake. It would block the sun's rays from reaching much of the southern shore until well into the spring. That area, he guessed, would be the slowest to thaw.

All the way from Marge's sister's driveway he had visualized the identity switch. He would remove Homer's wallet from his pocket and stuff his own in its place, he would grab any other papers he saw that Homer would be likely to have on his person, and he would get out of there. Whatever else of Homer's remained in the car would be seen as stolen property. If the body was found, the interpretation would be that this unpredictable Braintree character had made off with Homer's car and possessions and had been killed and left here.

Not just killed, but *killed by Sarah*. This crucial addition had struck Denny mightily on the highway. It changed his mission from a preventive one to forestall grief in case Homer's body was found to a bold initiative with discovery of the body as a key element. If Nick could find the body not by chance but because Denny had directed him to it with a letter mailed or left somewhere before he died, a letter confessing to his imposture and expressing his fear *that Sarah intended him harm*, there was a chance of justice after all. Denny could say he suspected Sarah had tried to run him over and he feared she might try again. He could also say he had heard her making phone calls inquiring about the ice thickness on Lake Prescott.

This plan unfortunately gave Lance a free pass, but Denny worried that introducing another level of complication at this stage could put Nick off the whole idea. There were some loose ends, of course, but Nick could deal with those. How had Sparky put it about a problem that would puzzle the police? *Their job* to explain it, not his job. His job was to present them with a pair of unassailable givens: Dennis Braintree was the name of the hapless fool in the car on the ice—or at the lake bottom if Nick didn't get to it in time—and Sarah was the party who had turned the living fool into a dead one.

The highway, still well above the lake, curved to the east. Denny knew from the map that a Camp Road would deliver him to the lake. It finally appeared, and soon he was angling downward. The road was well maintained for some distance, with shuttered cabins sprinkled along it, but it gradually lost respectability, and he weaved to avoid holes, fallen limbs, and small banks of snow. Much gear shifting was required, and he filled the woods with grinds and engine whines. The cabins thinned, then disappeared entirely as he drove more deeply into the mountain's shadow. Pines below blocked a clear view of the lake, but then the road dropped steeply, and an opening revealed a beach and a large, round cove.

Denny stopped the car and stared at the lake through the windshield. There was no car on the ice and no obvious hole where a car might have sunk. He got out and put on the winter boots he had grabbed from under Betsy's front desk before leaving—Homer's fringed "pussy boots." He slogged through the mud and slush on the beach, looking for tire tracks, but he saw nothing. At the edge of the lake, he took stock. It certainly was a hidden cove. A car deposited not far from shore would be visible just from this beach and from the opposite shore only with binoculars. The ice that stretched out before him was actually water on ice, and that was the source of the dull sheen he had seen from above. How deep was that surface water, and how thick was the ice below it? He had no idea. At his feet, cold, dark water rhythmically lapped through a gap between the ice edge and the shore.

He slumped with disappointment. There was no body here, and without a body there could be no justice. But there could still be mercy—he could be Homer from a distance and hope that Homer's body was never found.

He heard a strange sound. It was so unexpected that his mind achieved recognition in stages, like a steam engine chugging up to full motive power. The sound was a horn—not a car horn, but a musical instrument, a solo horn playing in the wilderness. It was Homer, and he was playing his waltz.

Denny threw his arms out with excitement. Then he became still. He turned his head, trying to pinpoint the origin of the sound, but it had stopped. It had come to him so faintly that he began to fear that, like so much else in his world, it had existed only in his head. Then it returned, the same tune. Was Homer on the mountaintop? Was he on the road? Denny turned his head. The sound wasn't coming from above. It came from farther down the lake.

Denny hurried along the shore in that direction. The cleared beach gave way to thick, impassable woods. He couldn't possibly reach Homer on foot. He had another idea, hurried to the car, and drove back up the hill. When he reached the spot where he had begun to drop down to the lake, he saw what he had hoped for—another road, one he hadn't seen before, that followed the shore but from high up. He took it, and when he cleared a ridge, he saw a second cove, a larger one. In the middle of it sat Homer's beige Rambler.

Denny's thought, as the road took him down, was that Homer was playing on the shore in some kind of celebration. Then he realized that Homer could still be *in* the car, trapped, playing as an alarm. But why wasn't he blasting? Why play beautifully?

When Denny reached the lake, he got out and ran to its edge. He saw two sets of tire tracks. One stopped short of the shore—Lance's or Sarah's car—and the other went all the way to the edge of the lake—the Rambler. Denny cupped his hands and hollered at the car, some two hundred feet away. Homer couldn't hear him over his playing, so Denny waited for a lull. When it came, he yelled Homer's name.

There was a pause, then two toots of the horn, as if he was repeating the syllables of his name.

"It's Denny!" Denny shouted.

After another pause, Homer resumed playing his waltz.

Denny looked down, and a problem that had only half-registered now hit him with full force. The land was separated from the ice by a border of water that was at least a foot wide. Not only that, but where the ice began, it looked dangerously thin. He could bridge the gap with a step to the ice, yes, but wouldn't he immediately crash through it? How to get out where it was thicker? Sarah and Lance had driven the Rambler out there, and that would have been just a little over 24 hours ago. The ice could not have melted that much already. How had they solved the problem?

He examined the tire tracks approaching the edge of the lake and saw that they stopped a few feet short of it. From there to the water, instead of tire tracks, two big grooves pressed deeply into the mud. Denny could see the objects that had made them as vividly as if they were still in place: boards to traverse this watery patch and the thin ice. Sarah and Lance had anticipated this thawing at the shore, and they had brought their own boards. The quality of their preparation gave him a chill.

They would have been long boards, needing to be tied to the top of Sarah's car—one more exertion that he hoped they weren't up to at the end of their labors. He looked around wildly but saw nothing. He ran along the edge of the lake to the woods, and he spotted the two boards, chucked into a snow patch in the forest. He grabbed the end of one of them and began to drag it through the mud. The lumber was strangely thick—some ancient part of the barn, he guessed. When he reached the water, he laid the board on the beach at the water's edge, pointing to the lake. He planted a foot on each side of it, bent down, grasped it, and heaved it forward. It landed on the ice, splashing the surface water aside. Still straddling it, he slid it a few feet at a time until only a foot of its length rested on land and most of it lay on the ice.

Homer tooted again—the same two-note sequence as before, but really saying, "Where are you?" Denny cupped his hands over his mouth and sang in response, "Coming!" He tried to sing it, but his voice quavered terribly.

He took one step onto the board, his eye fixed on its other end. A second step. It held. He hurried to the end of the board, where he tested the depth of the surface water with his boot. It was about two inches deep. He took another step and put his full weight directly on the ice. He looked back at shore. If he broke through here, he could scramble to safety. He looked at the Rambler. If he broke through there . . .

Homer played his waltz, and Denny found himself sloshing forward. He could feel the cold through Homer's boots, but they kept the water out. He walked a straight line, hoping that since the ice had supported the car, it would support his mere one-sixth-of-a-ton of weight. With each step, he punctuated Homer's melody with his own small moans of fear. These grew quite loud when he reached the car and saw that a semi-circle of open water lay just beyond it. Why had the ice thawed there? He had no idea, but it was clear that Sarah and Lance had brought the car out as close to it as they dared.

Denny knocked on the trunk.

Calmly, Homer said, "Get the stuff out of the back seat." Denny went around to the side of the car, and from this perspective he could see that it was tilted forward, sitting unevenly on the ice. He opened the back door and immediately saw the situation. Homer, locked in the truck, had kicked the seat loose, but he had freed it only a few inches because it pressed hard against boxes and crates that in turn pressed against the front seats. It was a logjam, and Homer hadn't been able to dislodge any of it. Still, those few inches had created a gap big enough for the horn to be heard, because the windows were rolled down. Why? To speed up the car's sinking. They had planned that, too.

Now powered by rage, Denny began hurling stuff onto the ice. When he slid a small metal file cabinet out, the car shifted a few inches. He visualized the car dropping before his eyes and taking him and Homer into the hole with it. Homer, impatient now, made the job harder by kicking the back seat and pinning the remaining objects against the front seat. Denny snapped at him to stop doing that, and he heard a muffled "Sorry" from the trunk.

A minute later, Denny gave Homer permission to have at it. The seat flew forward and Homer began to emerge, clumsily inching out feet first. Denny helped by pulling on his ankles, and Homer finally tumbled out the door and onto the ice, the French horn still in his grasp. From his knees, he surveyed his surroundings, blinking against the light.

"Jesus Christ!" he yelled. He struggled to his feet. "Go! Go!"

Denny went. Homer followed, stiffly at first, but then he picked up speed. Neither said a word all the way to shore. When they reached land, Homer dropped the horn in the mud and stumbled halfway to the woods. He fell to his knees, then onto his hands, and screamed several times—inarticulate cries, finally issuing into the repeated cry of "Oh God. Oh God. Oh God."

It was clear that Homer had had no idea where he was. There was much else that he didn't know. Denny drove and simply listened as Homer spoke. He had pulled off Homer's wet shoes and socks after helping him into the car, and Homer slowly rubbed his bare feet under the heater fan as he narrated his incomplete version of events:

He remembered parking the Rambler, all packed for his trip to Austin, at the bottom of Warren Boren's muddy driveway on his way out of town. This was about 9 o'clock at night. He entered Warren Boren's driveway on foot, carrying the horn in its case. He thought he remembered a car driving up the road as he stepped into the driveway, but he paid no attention to it. Before he had gotten very far up the hill, he heard the roar of an engine behind him, and he turned and saw the approaching car in time to jump away. He definitely remembered jumping, horn case in hand, but he remembered nothing else until he came to in the trunk of the Rambler. He didn't know right away that it was the Rambler, and he certainly didn't know it was sitting on thawing lake ice. The engine was running, but the car didn't move—a situation that persisted for hours, he thought, but he couldn't be sure because he kept falling asleep. Even now, he said, he felt woozy. With those words he stared ahead through the windshield.

Denny waited. Finally, he said, "What then?"

Homer resumed his tale as if Denny had thrown a switch to turn him back on. He said he tried kicking in the back seat, and when that didn't work, he didn't panic, thanks to meditation techniques that Millie had taught him. At some point the car engine stopped—out of gas, Homer guessed. He fished around to see what else was in the trunk and tried prying his way out with a tire-changing tool. Warren Boren's horn, in its case, was in there as well, making the space even more confined and getting in his way with every move he made. Then, instead of cursing it, he took it out and blasted notes in the hopes that someone would hear him. When no one came, he settled into playing it.

"I dabble in just about every kind of instrument," he said in a dull, disconnected tone. "There were some things I never quite worked out in 'Amelia's Waltz,' and I absorbed myself in trying to solve them."

Denny wanted to scream. How could it not occur to Homer that Sarah had tried to kill him? On her return to the farm—earlier than Homer had predicted—she must have seen the Rambler pull out of Homer's driveway and go up the road. She would have seen Homer as he got out and carried the horn up Warren Boren's driveway, and, certain that it was Denny, she had commandeered the Rambler and tried to run him down with it. Homer must have struck his head on something when he jumped. Somehow Sarah had gotten his unconscious body into the trunk. Denny again wondered when Lance had come into the picture. Had he been in Sarah's car with her and witnessed the attack? Denny's guess was that Sarah had called him after the fact.

"Homer," Denny said, "someone tried to kill you." He would introduce the idea by stages. "They tried to run you down."

"No, no," Homer said almost good-naturedly. "I think it was a car theft gone bad. I left my keys in the car, and when they stole it they must have thought Warren's driveway was the main road. The curve in the road there fools people all the time. They ran into me and thought they killed me, and they decided to cover it all up."

Denny looked at him in disbelief. "Why didn't they just take off after the accident? What's the point of dumping the car?"

"Fingerprints?"

Denny suddenly realized something else. "All that stuff I took out of the back seat—when you packed the car, you must have put it in the trunk originally."

"Right. They took it out of the trunk to make room for me."

Denny didn't speak his next thought. The back seat was packed solidly and tightly for the clear purpose of pinning the seat closed so that the captive in the trunk could not kick his way out. This meant that Sarah knew he was alive when she had stuffed him into the trunk. He thought of Sarah's grief—her *ostensible* grief—when she discovered Denny at the kitchen table and realized she had killed the wrong man. She had seemed stricken, overwhelmed. And yet she had shown no interest in returning to the lake to try to save Homer.

Denny wondered what to say when Homer asked him how he happened to come to the lake. But Homer seemed content to sit and stare out the windshield—not content, exactly. Stunned into silence. He did ask whose car he was riding in. Denny said it was Marge's, and that threw him into silence again.

Finally, Denny spoke the words: "It was Sarah who ran you down, Homer. She thought you were me."

"Why would she do that?" Homer showed a lopsided smile. Denny couldn't assign an emotion to it, but he was pleased that Homer had questioned only Sarah's motive, not her ability to kill.

"She found me out and thought I did away with you as part of a plan to take over your life. She thought she was next." Denny didn't like drawing from Lance's Sarah-justifying summary, but this part of it could actually have been true.

"That would have been an unpleasant way to go." Homer cast his gaze back toward the lake, though it was now well out of view.

"She needs to be brought to justice," Denny said.

After a long silence, Homer said, "I wish you well with that."

Denny looked at him. "You're not going to help me?"

"What I'm going to do is return to Austin and sell the farm from there."

"But—"

"I'm wet and cold and tired, and all I want right now is some dry clothes. A few miles ahead is a town with an old department store. It's at the traffic light. I guess I don't have to tell you what sizes to buy." With that, Homer leaned his head against the window and fell asleep almost immediately.

Denny swallowed his protest. What about Sarah and Lance? Would they just go on with their lives after what they had done? What would happen when Homer tried to sell the house from Austin? Sarah would think it was Denny orchestrating it, up to his old tricks as Homer, only this time in Texas. She might even track him down and attempt the same mistaken murder again. He looked at Homer, who had collapsed against the door and window. He wanted to kick him awake and insist on his help.

Instead, he went shopping—a surreal interlude under the circumstances—and tracked down clothing that he hoped would satisfy Homer, who was hardly a clothes horse in any case. Denny found him still deep in sleep when he returned to the car, and he didn't wake him until he had pulled into a gas station. Homer changed in the restroom and fell asleep again as soon as he was back in the car.

As they approached the Burlington exit, Denny woke Homer again and suggested they go to the hospital.

"Why would I want to do that?" Homer said.

"So that you can be examined for a concussion and carbon monoxide poisoning."

"I'm fine," he said. "I want to go home."

Denny tensed. "By 'home' you mean . . ."

"Austin." Homer looked at him. "What's wrong with you? Take me to the airport."

Denny drove him there. When he passed Marvin's French Fries, he could almost see himself, back when this all began, agitating at the booth next to the window. Who *was* that man? Meanwhile, Homer had sprung to life. He had pulled a pencil and a blank sheet of paper from Marge's glove compartment and had quickly drawn several parallel lines across the sheet, and now he was writing musical notes and humming to himself. Denny guessed he was recording the changes in the waltz that had occurred to him on the ice. Lance was right about one thing: *two* oddballs.

Denny pulled into the drop-off lane and stopped at the curb. After a pause, Homer said, "I'm certainly traveling light." He said it in a dimwitted way. He took out his wallet, checked his credit cards, and riffled his bills. This, at least, was a sign of lucidity.

Homer got out of the car. Before closing the door, he leaned down and thanked Denny. He glanced into the back seat and grimaced with guilt at what he saw there. "Be sure to return Warren's horn to him, will you?"

TWENTY-SIX

Although Homer wasn't all that clear in the head, Denny envied him the clarity of his destination. As long as Denny was a suspect in Marge's death, he couldn't go back to his apartment in Downer's Grove. Nor, for the same reason, could he report for work. He didn't even have a workplace to report to. Not wanting to be a dead pig, he had ruled out a return to Little Dumpling Farm.

Sarah and Lance. How could he prove they were killers without a body? There could be no justice without a body. He remembered Lance telling him that there were two people who had died because their paths had crossed Denny's. Homer was one, and luckily Lance had been wrong about that. Denny thought about the other one as he pulled away from the airport curb and grinded into second gear. He had an idea. By the time he had covered the short distance from the airport to Marvin's French Fries, he had a plan. He pulled into the lot, took out his cell phone, and punched the numbers.

"Sparky," he said, "it's Homer. I need you to do something for me."

"You name it."

"That night at the hotel, when you saw Marge—"

"Yeah?"

"—and she told you she was a winner—"

"Yep."

"—and she headed for the elevator—"

"Yes sir."

"I need you to say that someone else was there in the lobby."

"Well, let's see. Betsy was behind the counter. She's no fan of yours truly, so I creeped in on the QT, but then when Marge belted out,

'Hey, Sparky, I'm a winner,' Betsy yanked her head around and give me the fish eye. Sort of."

"Besides Betsy, I mean. I need you to say someone else was in the lobby. I need you to say that Sarah was there, and that she heard Marge tell you she was a winner, and that she followed Marge to the elevator."

Sparky breathed noisily for some time.

"I need you to say all that."

"Sarah come out of the bar with Marge."

"Well, you could say that if you want to, yes. That's consistent."

"They were talkin' as they come down the hall from the bar."

"Yes, that's fine." Denny was struck by Sparky's eagerness to please. But a born liar was born to lie.

"Then Sarah shut up quick when she reached the lobby because her and Betsy ain't too chummy neither. We got that in common, you might say."

"That's perfect. So Betsy wouldn't have known Sarah was there. That would explain why she never reported it."

"Sure, I can say all that. Sarah give you the go-ahead?"

"The go-ahead?"

"You know, did she give you the okay for me to say it? She told me she never wants Betsy to know when she's in the hotel."

Denny was puzzled, but he figured it was safe to affirm whatever Sparky was saying. "Yes, that's what she did. She gave me the go-ahead."

"Huh. Maybe her and Betsy patched things up. Hard to see that though. Do I say I saw her later, too? When I was leavin'?"

Denny hesitated. "I'm not sure what you mean."

"She come out of the alley from the back of the hotel, and she run across the street. I was next to my rig—still sweet-talkin' the Macalesters, tryin' to close the deal, and they were gettin' into their truck. I hollered to Sarah but she kept goin'. Didn't hear me, I guess."

Denny was more puzzled than ever. Sparky seemed to be leaving out some necessary verbs or something. Why was he talking about these hypothetical events as if they were real?

Because they were.

"Oh, my God," Denny said. "She *was* there."

"Do I include that part or not? And who am I supposed to say all this to, exactly?"

"She was there. And she told you not to tell anyone."

"Homer, focus, man. Who do I say it to?"

"The police."

"Nick? No fuckin' way."

"You've got to. Listen to me. When Sarah told you not to tell anyone that she was in the hotel, it wasn't because of Betsy. It was because she went up with Marge. She wanted that lottery ticket. She watched her go into that room, and she waited and went after her when she had the chance. There was probably a struggle on the balcony. That's how Marge ended up in your truck."

All Denny heard, for an excruciatingly long period, was the sound of Sparky's breathing. Then: "Huh."

"And when you saw her later, coming out of the alley—"

"Yeah, she kind of rounded the corner like she was beelinin' for the front of the hotel."

"But she saw you and the Macalesters, and she took off."

Sparky was silent.

"Sarah killed Marge for the lottery ticket." Denny would say no more. Justice came down to an unmappable network of Sparky's neurons. Denny held his breath.

"That ain't right."

Denny exhaled. "And that's why you've got to tell Nick."

Sparky grunted. "Hell, Nick ain't so bad. It's that other pencilneck. I hope he ain't gonna be there."

"He's been neutralized."

Sparky fell silent again. Denny, hearing only his breathing, feared he might be having second thoughts.

"Sarah," Sparky said. "Hmph. June always did say that side of the family was trash."

After his call to Sparky, Denny sat for a time in his car, drumming his fingers on the steering wheel. Then he dialed Nick's number. He owed him a goodbye, but, more important, he didn't want to leave the initiative to Sparky. Before pressing "Send," he worked to overcome the sudden dizzying, godlike feeling his latest discovery had given him. He had fabricated a story implicating Sarah, but it wasn't a fabrication at all. It was as if he had created reality by having an idea. It was like setting a plastic figure on the balcony of a miniature hotel, with her arms stretched straight out in a pushing posture. Hey, what's she doing up there? Did she just shove somebody?

As for plastic Lance, Denny hadn't put him anywhere. He would let fate deal with him, just as Lance had let fate determine what would happen with Denny on the chain ladder. Sarah would probably prove to be a surprise agent of justice, taking Lance down with her, claiming *she* didn't steal Marge's lottery ticket, *he* did. Sparky could confirm that. The trial would be interesting. Denny would follow it online. Homer would, too, he was sure.

Nick was home, nursing a cold from the sound of it. Denny asked him to call Sparky in the next day or two if he didn't hear from him, because Sparky had just called *him* saying there was something he needed to get off his chest.

"Did he say what it was?" Nick said. The cold made him sound grumpy. Maybe he *was* grumpy.

"No, he didn't. Listen, Nick, I've got something to tell you. I'm leaving. I'm going back to Austin."

"Yeah, I . . . what do you mean Austin? Austin, Texas?"

"That's where I was all this time. Not Florida."

Nick laughed. "I'm glad you finally got around to telling me."

"I'm going back."

"Hell, I know that. I knew it when you gave me that hug the other day. Nearly broke my back. I understand, Homer."

"You do?"

"This place isn't really your home." Nick made a strange noise. "I can't believe I'm saying that. You of all people. The original woodchuck, eighth-generation and all. But it's true. You're not happy here, and I know why. I watched you at the party, when you were standing at the railing. I couldn't believe it. Here you'd been away three years, and you were there all by yourself. People don't treat you right." Nick cleared his throat. "I hope I treat you right—"

"You treat me fine, Nick."

"—and I hope I'm not out of line saying all this. I just want you to know I understand. But, man, stay in touch this time, will you?"

"You bet."

"Listen, I just learned something interesting." Nick's tone was different, suddenly enthusiastic. "You'll like it. I know you'll like it."

"Yeah?"

"It's got, like, human interest."

"Fire away."

"Braintree."

Denny flinched to hear his name.

"The train buff. Marge's killer. Or not. Whatever. Remember him?"

Denny said, "How could I forget?"

"A coupla hours ago I got a call back from some old-timer in Georgia who was in the circus with Braintree's parents. Remember, the kid grew up in the circus. The old-timer remembered him well. We had quite a chat."

"Yeah?"

"The guy doesn't know where Braintree is or anything. But he gave me some background. Prolly has no bearing on the case, but it's got, you know, human interest."

"Right."

"Between the death records I've been looking at and what this old trouper told me, I've pieced it together. Now, listen up. Little Braintree—his parents were clowns, remember—when he was just a tyke, a trapeze artist fell on his mother in the middle of a show in Salt Lake City."

Denny jerked with surprise. Nick was certainly making progress. But it was actually equipment that fell on her—trapeze rigging. "Yeah?"

"She went to the hospital."

"Yeah?"

"Two days later, she died in the hospital."

No she didn't, Denny thought. "Yeah?" he said uncertainly.

"You remember we were looking for Braintree's aunt to get a lead on him? We never found her. The reason is she dropped off the face of the earth—exactly at the time this accident happened. The boss of her old circus—remember, she was a clown, too, but in a different circus—her old boss said she disappeared and he never heard from her again. We got the same story from an old roommate, a flight attendant she shared a place with in Memphis. The aunt just disappeared. Now, I have the death record for the woman who died in the circus accident that night. It gives the aunt's name, not the mother's name."

Denny relaxed a bit. "So . . . the aunt was the one who performed that night." This made little sense to him even as he said it. "She substituted for the mother, and she died."

"No, no. The aunt did perform that night, but in Oklahoma City. These two women were identical twins, Homer. I think Lance mentioned that, but I forgot. Who listens when he talks anyway? The mother definitely died, and someone—her husband, must have been, Braintree's father—lied about her identity. He gave the aunt's name instead. He must have gotten in touch with the aunt during those two days when his wife was in the hospital in Salt Lake City—maybe he knew she was a goner—and he must have convinced the aunt to move in with him and his son and take the place of the mother. The aunt's old roommate told me the aunt never married and always wanted to have kids, so she would have been game for it. A hell of a thing. When I told Lance about it, his first reaction was that the father and the aunt were having an affair all along, and the father was only too glad—"

"They did it for the boy!" Denny cried out. "Oh, God, they did it for the boy!"

"That's what I figured," Nick said. "I knew you'd see it the way I did."

"What an act of love!"

"It gets you, doesn't it? Of course, they might have had a regular-type marriage from that point on. Maybe Lance was partly right. Maybe they—"

"No," Denny said softly. "They did it for the boy."

"I knew you'd be interested, Homer. Hell, anybody with any humanity in them would be, and you've got tons. Millie had an interesting take on it. She says there's no way the kid didn't know the woman wasn't his mother. At some level, she said he'd have to know. What do you think?"

Denny pretended to consider the question abstractly while his entire brain seized it. "It's hard to say, Nick."

"Yeah. But it's something, isn't it? Listen, when are you going back?"

"Right now."

"Wow. No time for a goodbye visit, I guess. But me and Millie are gonna come see you, okay? Next mud season."

"You bet." As an afterthought, Denny added, "I'm hoping to have my old voice back by then."

"You think so? Well, either way."

Denny said goodbye and clicked his phone shut. For an instant, he was a seven-year-old boy again—a boy who had lost his mother. He expected to feel a wave of sudden grief, but he didn't. He could not do what was required to feel grief. He could not remove his mother from his young life because he had continuously had a mother until she died two years ago—after buying him a pint of Wavy Gravy. He could not feel otherwise. What he felt sweeping over him now, replacing the attempt to feel sad, was gratitude. His father and his aunt had spared him from the pain that no child should ever have. Yes, she had seemed different afterward, but he had blamed it on the accident, and better different than *dead*. He had had a mother for all those years, from age zero to age seven, and then again from age seven to just two years ago—no, not *again*, but *still*.

With these thoughts Denny drove back to Montpelier. At one point on the interstate, he sensed a friendly presence far to his right, and he turned to look. It was the Vermonter, heading south, rolling along at a speed slightly faster than his. He watched it overtake him, car by car. He loved watching trains because he wanted to be inside them. It wasn't true of any other kind of transportation. He wanted to be there instead of here. But it was a pleasant wish, not an itchy one.

The Vermonter was a "Train Going South." He loved reading old schedules, with their headings "Trains Going East" and "Trains Going West." He needed a "Train Going West." He could go back home now that the finger of accusation pointed at Sarah. But what was home? It was a place where everyone gathered around in order to tell him what was wrong with him. It always puzzled him why people didn't like him more. He liked himself just fine. Evidently the Denny that others saw from without had nothing to do with the Denny he saw from within. What did they see? He fixed his imagination on the arm-waving buffoon in Marvin's French Fries. "God, what's to like?" he said aloud.

But how could he be any different? How to un-Denny Denny? As Homer, he had kept himself in control because every conversation had been a challenge. That was all he asked from life—that it be *interesting*. When he got home, how could he make his Chicago conversations interesting? By filling up his mind with something in addition to the conversation? Should he think about square roots? No, he should think about the immediate situation, the environment. . . . No, he should think about the people he was with. Their hair, their clothes, their eyes. . . . No, he needed to see *inside* them.

No. He needed to see *from* inside them. He needed to see the world according to, say, Roscoe. That would be hard, and because it would be hard, it would be interesting.

He reached for his cell phone and made the call.

"Denny. I thought you might be dead."

"Hoped, you mean."

"Not at all," said Roscoe. "Why do you say that?"

"Because you can't stand me."

"Denny, Denny, Denny."

Think, he said to himself. *Think like Roscoe.* "You're waiting for me to say 'Roscoe, Roscoe, Roscoe.' "

"No, I—"

"I'll say it if you like, Roscoe. I won't, if not."

"Well, no, Denny, it's not necessary. Listen, I'm sure you've seen the latest from our noble competition, *Model Railroader*."

"I haven't seen it, Roscoe. You'll be surprised that I haven't seen it."

"Well, yes, I *am* surprised. I'm afraid they beat us to it. They profiled Rod Stewart's layout."

"Ah. You're telling me this because I've suggested this celebrity profile for years. I understand. You're also couching the news as if your magazine was on the verge of doing it—as if your competitor beat you by just an issue or two. I understand why you're doing that, so as not to appear completely flat-footed. You want to minimize both your error and my foresight. I have no problem with any of that, Roscoe."

"Well, I don't know if I'd put it in such a one-sided way, but . . . well, I guess you're right, Denny. Listen, it's funny that you called because I was just thinking about you this morning—"

"You're saying that even though you've been thinking about me for some time."

"Well—"

"You don't want to admit it because you don't want to be taken for someone who depends on others. I understand that, Roscoe. It's a normal kind of overcompensation rooted in your generalized fear. The very name of the magazine you founded, *The Fearless Modeler*, refers not to possible embarrassment grown men might feel for playing with toys, but rather to your own desire to be *free* of fear—fear of intimacy, of the future, of the unknown, and, ultimately, of death."

"My *goodness*, Denny. I . . . I'm certainly not prepared to get into all that right now, but I'll concede that you've been on my mind for quite a few days. I thought of you when I read the freelance write-up I commissioned of Tom Blunt's Super Chief. I saw Tom's layout for myself when I was in Rochester. The idiot put the dining car in backwards! He actually had the first-class passengers walking through the kitchen!"

"I understand. Because you had seen that horror show, when the write-up did not address it, you immediately thought, 'Denny, for all his many faults, would never overlook such an error.' "

"We seem to be in tune today, Denny. I won't beat around the—"

"You want to hire me back."

"Well, you certainly are on top of—"

"But you don't want to lose face, and how can you hire me back after firing me without losing face? You certainly don't want to apologize, because you believe apologizing is a sign of weakness, and from what you've said about your father and your childhood I can see why you cling to such a ridiculous precept to project strength. I understand, Roscoe, and I accept."

Roscoe fell silent. "You've rather taken my breath away this morning, Denny. But I'm delighted you're coming back. Go ahead. I know you want to crow. Feel free."

Denny imagined someone throwing his head back and cawing like a crow. It was a repulsive display. "I'll report to work Monday," he said quickly. He shut his phone, floored the accelerator, honked his horn, threw his head back, and cawed like a crow.

* * *

Denny pulled into the Montpelier train station lot, killing Marge's engine for the last time a few feet short of where he meant to park, but it was close enough. He wrote Warren Boren's name on a piece of paper and wedged it between the valves of the French horn. Nick, the likely investigator, would certainly wonder how Marge's car had gotten here and how Warren's horn had ended up in it.

As Denny walked to the depot, he heard a distant whistle. A B-flat, he was once told by a better. Inside, two women were talking over the ticket counter—the agent and a customer. He would have enough time to buy his ticket, though the women seemed determined to catch up on every piece of local news before that happened. They finally finished, and Denny stepped forward.

"Hello again," the ticket agent said. Denny recognized her as the woman who had greeted him and the other arriving passengers at the station when he had taken the train back from Connecticut. He was surprised she remembered him. "And where might you be off to this time?" she said.

"Chicago."

"My, my. That'll be different. Round trip?"

"One way."

The woman raised her eyebrows. She seemed to want to say more, but she just quoted him the price. Denny paid in cash. As she handed him his change, she said, "Chicago." It was a question.

"That's right."

She slid the ticket across the counter to him.

"Big city."

"Yes, it is."

"You couldn't pick a place *less* like Vermont."

"I suppose not."

"To each his own." Her tone implied he had lost his marbles. Sensing that the woman might perish on the spot unless she received an explanation, Denny gave her one:

"I just want to get away from all the crime."

The woman laughed and laughed at that. She shook her finger at him and said, "The old Homer humor."